INFUSED RALLY

THE METIER APOCALYPSE
BOOK 4

FRANK G. ALBELO

MOUNTAINDALE
PRESS

ACKNOWLEDGMENTS

The fact that we've made it to the second arc of Metier feels like an amazing dream come true. It was thanks to you all.

I want to especially thank my wife and my family for all the support they gave me through this process. When life gives you lemons, you write a book... or something like that anyways.

Now, go forth! I hope you enjoy more of those magical shenanigans with Ron and co!

PROLOGUE

"Marcus, you can't keep doing this to yourself," Dale said, frowning as Alexia wrapped a bandage around his fists. It didn't take long for the blood to soak through, but thankfully the bulk of the blood had already stopped flowing.

"This isn't the early days, Dale. We can't just bend over when they trivialize us. Even Tripsen has turned coat on the very people who are the life of this place." Marcus had to resist the urge to clench his fists as he considered that private from years before. He'd been the one last decent military guy in the Bunker, the only one that tried to respect the young professionals and survivors who shared his situation, but even he had been corrupted by the sleazy power Starden commanded.

"You may be right, Marc, but that doesn't mean you can lash out. The rationing—" Alexia tried to inject an argument, but Marcus wasn't having it.

Without waiting for her to finish, he stood and cracked his back. The many bruises from the fight blared like poorly concealed alarms, but Marcus just used them as a reminder that he was alive. That he was fighting for what he thought was right. He hesitated with his hand on the door, thanked the pair, then strode up to the greenhouse floor. He *needed* to see his wife.

The doors of the hydroponics wing slid open silently as he crossed the threshold. The gentle hum of the pumps and the occasional splash of the fish tanks did wonders for his frayed nerves, but he could still feel the strain of the last few years pushing him toward action. Toward… something more.

"I don't think the plants appreciate the increase in temperature, you know," a voice chided gently. Marcus spun, surprised that he'd been so caught up in his thoughts that he'd missed his wife tending to some of the growing beds. She rounded the corner, smiling up at him until she spotted the black eye and the bloody bandages. Her dazzling smile lost watts by the second until she was frowning. "What is this?"

"Tripsen… I caught him fiddling with the food report. The rest of his team were close by and things… escalated," Marcus said, meekly. His eyes couldn't help but drift down to Clara's belly. To the first child of the Bunker. To his son.

"Does your mother know?" Clara said, frown still firmly in place, but she moved with practiced motions to adjust the bandages he hadn't let Alexia tend to properly. The Velcro bits at the end pulled on his wounds, but Clara wasn't particularly concerned with his pain at the moment.

"Not yet. Alan has been doing really well and I didn't—"

"When will they get up?" Clara said, straightening his shirt and spotting a bit of blood on his sleeve.

"There were six of them, so I couldn't put them down quite as hard. Maybe twenty more minutes?" Marcus said. The adrenaline rush of the fight left his perception of time as something less than desirable.

"Elias won't be able to protect you from this, Marc. They will put you in the brig," Clara said, gripping his shirt with a surprising amount of force.

"I-I know. But maybe now they won't be able to hide their hoarding quite so easily. Ben and Clementine have been working hard to project our usage, and if we can get a good estimate then the Bunker—"

"Marcus Metier. Again." The familiar flat voice grated immediately on Marcus' ears.

"Starden. To what does the hardest working floor of the Bunker owe the pleasure?" Marcus snapped back. Clara tried to hold him back, but he removed her hands with a gentleness he never knew he could produce.

"You know damn well what I am doing here, boy. Now move along unless you want things to get… messier than you made them already."

Marcus turned to look behind himself as the stomp of boots echoed in the small room. He watched as one of the soldiers knocked over one of the pails of algae, spilling its contents all over that corner of the wing. The hour it was going to take Clara to clean that mess up and feed it to the fish tanks almost made him dip into the growing pool of rage in his gut. But he didn't. He strode forward as four guns trained on his chest. He recognized the black and blue form of Tripsen as he glared down his iron sights, but he ignored it. *Starden* was the colloquial rotten apple that spoiled the bunch.

"Marcus—"

"It's alright, Clara. I'm sure these gentlemen just want to have a nice, friendly chat to justify their inflated food requirements," Marcus said without missing a beat. He turned his back to them when he was less than five feet away, offering his wrists in an exaggerated gesture as he met the eyes of the other Bunker survivors working the greenhouse floor that had come to check on the commotion. He could practically hear Starden hissing under his breath, but unfortunately the man didn't rise to the bait.

A pair of cuffs were slapped on his wrists and he was led up the stairway to the trio of rooms that served as the 'brig' of the Bunker. On the way up, the group ran into Elias, his mother, and young Alan. Elias immediately tried to intercept Starden, but Ingrid held him back. Her eyes had met with Marcus' and the slightest shake of his head was all the sign she needed. Getting entangled with the strong-arming soldiers while they worked to help Clara and poor morning-sick Agatha Fallon would serve no one. Marcus couldn't recall a time when the wrinkles on his mother's face had been so pronounced.

"Keep moving," Tripsen huffed, wedging the butt of his gun into Marcus' side right where one of the soldier's wild punches had connected. He gritted his teeth against the pain, keeping his expression neutral. However, the pool of rage within him roiled and bucked against the shores of his self-control. All the talks with his father and the pleas from his mother since they awoke in the Bunker that had reigned in his anger fractured in the face of a cruelty he'd never experienced before.

You will all pay.

CHAPTER ONE

New Limits

"I'm trying to figure out where to go from here, you know?" I said, gesturing from Blobby to the palm tree towering over the two of us.

Of course, the slime didn't have a comprehensive response other than to jiggle. Through the time we'd spent together, I'd come to understand that the traitor of the Dreg was intelligent but not particularly philosophical. *It's certainly smart enough to sneak in and steal food from the kitchens in Wildwood.* I couldn't help but wish that Blobby could actually speak, even if I knew that was a difficult prospect. *But what will happen when he gets to the size of a Category 2 Metier Crystal?*

The slime had been one of the few to actually come out *better* from the assaults on the Dreg two weeks prior. The once hip-tall gelatinous creature was probably more akin to a bear after acquiring two Metier Crystal shards in the Death Territory. With the time between then and now, it had acquired the bulk to use those crystals and mitose four ways. It was impressive, and slightly concerning, to see multiple Blobbies ambling about Wildwood.

However, I was almost sure that the creature was doing it on purpose. For all that I knew Blobby was strong in direct combat, it was inherently stealthy. Even the gradient change from a solid lime green to an emerald-jade shade as it grew stronger hadn't affected its ability to hide in plain sight. Only its larger, joined form struggled to be hidden. Somehow, Blobby knew that the people of Wildwood needed a reminder that their struggles and losses hadn't been for naught. I was almost certain it was why the creature had followed me from Wildwood all the way to the strongest threat we first encountered since arriving at the surface. A reminder. Or that was what I wanted to think, at least. With how turbulent my thoughts had been, it was entirely possible I was attributing things to happenstance.

"You don't need to baby me, Blobby. I'm not the green fighter you helped out that day," I said, glancing sidelong at the slime. I could have sworn I watched it form an appendage just to shake its 'head' at me. "Just because I'm a little stiff doesn't mean I'm weak."

That I was certain about. While before, the creatures I encountered on the road watched the passage of me and my friends through the woods with wariness, they now actively scrambled the moment my perception landed on them. It was as if their own senses were warning them I was a danger.

My vibrosense tickled almost constantly with the passage of spiders, deer, coyotes, and a half dozen other creatures in the woods, but all their ripples moved away. I could hardly blame them. It was difficult for *me* to believe I was Quotient 6 now. With a mental flick, my status jumped to the corner of my vision.

Subject: Ronan Terrigan
Health: 100% (Unafflicted)
Mana: 100%
Metier Quotient: 6 (18.75%)
Dreg Accumulation: 0%
LPS: Wildwood Bunker, FL
Communications

Party
Skills - *(2) Selections Available*
Traits - *(0% Banked)*
Attributes - *Growth Quantified*
Skills:
Offensive
- <Stone Spike> / **Imbue** / <Mineral Strike>
Defensive
- <Mudpit> / <Earth Shell> / <Earthen Barrier>
- <Freeform>
Misc
- <Pith Mana Lock>
- <Infusion>
- <Memory Canal>
Traits:
Limestone Skin (12%)
Quake Osseum (24%)
Slurry Ichor (8%)
Harmonic Sinew (31%)
Attributes:
Strength: 1.79 > 1.93
Mobility: 1.63 > 1.68
Perception: 2.09 > 2.20
Refinement: 1.42 > 1.54
Containment: 2.28 > 2.41

My face scrunched as I stared at the strangest change in my traits. It wasn't the first time I'd seen it, and I doubted it would be the last time I stared at them as if it would spit out an answer.

"Progression... to my traits," I drawled, scratching my thickening beard as I tried to think of how that would manifest.

My traits were a large part of why I'd even survived the fight against Galloway. Between the warnings from Harmonic Sinew's vibrosense, the coagulation from Slurry Ichor, and the force dispersal and reinforcement of my Limestone Skin and

Quake Osseum, it was *still* a wonder I'd pulled one over on the Appendage. Unfortunately, neither Tec nor Wec nor Bec had answers for that. They could only speculate that Gec, the Gigantic Entity Cluster we'd freed from the Aberrant Entity, had interceded on my behalf after I overdrew my mana and then took a Pith shower.

As for asking Gec, it had remained silent despite all probing. There had been no lack of trying on part of the scouting crews or my friends, but the Entity remained silent. Even with the threat of the Aberrant out of the way, the towns were still fighting back against nature.

"So, here we are. You got any answers for me, bud?" I said, focusing on the palm twenty feet away from me.

<Coconut Palm>

<Attunement: Earth>

<Refinement: Geodes>

<Perceived Metier Quotient: 6>

When I'd first seen it, I'd barely registered what a Quotient that high meant, other than bad news. Now I knew it meant this tree had somehow managed to kill an exorbitant number of creatures to get to this point, or a select number of really strong ones. Samuel's research into attuned plants was still in its infancy, but there was something heavier about the palm than any of those experiments. Its trunk swayed, lighting up the ground in ripples of motion even in the absence of wind. A coconut fell inconspicuously from its crown.

I almost wanted to call it out on its bullcrap. Sending a silent prayer to the bird that had died to teach me of the Geode Palm's attack, I triggered <Stone Spike>. A thrum of discomfort reverberated through my body as mana flowed into the spell chain. Even with my focus set on minimizing it to less than five percent of my mana pool, the attack equaled that first yard-long spear of rock I'd coalesced months ago.

Like a homerun hit, the <Stone Spike> struck the coconut and sent it flying high into the trees on the edge of US 301. My eyes watched as the coconut cracked midair and spread its deadly payload of mineral shards to cleave the canopy off some trees like they were paper. The sound of snapping echoed down the empty road as the palm and I glared at each other. Then it did something surprising.

One of the palm fronds manually plucked one of the coconuts. Like a strange, many-fingered hand, the geode palm grasped the coconut and released it. Its whole trunk bowed, letting the coconut roll down its body instead of impacting the ground. It repeated the process another time, two coconuts waiting patiently at the foot of its trunk. As if to make a demonstration, another of the coconut bombs thunked on the far side of the tree, exploding into a glimmering mess of crystals a few seconds after impacting the ground. The two plucked coconuts remained perfectly still.

"Some kind of bait?" I asked, quirking my eyebrow at the tree.

All I got in response was a sway of its body, but it was worth considering. Thinking back on the unfortunate result of the plant infusions with Samuel, it was entirely possible the Geode Palm was sentient to a certain degree. I wasn't some kind of Turing test expert to evaluate the borderline of sapience, but if the palm was trying to resolve my visit peacefully, it brought yet another ethical complication to the problem of fighting creatures on the surface. Pith, and even Dreg, were all about evolution, after all.

"You think you can snag that for me?" I asked Blobby.

As hardened as I was by my traits, I had no illusion that getting an exploding coconut to the face would leave me shredded. Probably not dead, but definitely hanging sullenly by its door. While some might call my visit idiocy of the highest degree, it was the safest high-level creature I could approach in the hopes of gleaming some answers.

Blobby gave me a 'look' before one of the cores in its body rolled out of the larger bulk. The slime shrunk considerably, its gelatinous body pulling tight around its three remaining crystals. Not waiting for further instructions, the smaller Blobby rolled forward. The Geode Palm shivered, rustling its leaves, but didn't move as Blobby sucked the two coconuts into its body. Less than a minute later, I sat holding the two fruit-seed-geode things. I was tempted to try to open it, but opted against it without at least having a healer handy.

Not feeling any closer to the answer of my original question, I took leave of the palm with a sigh. It swayed gently as I turned, but I wasn't sure if it was the wind or it was waving of its own power. At the very least, the two 'offerings' would cause a stir in town.

It wasn't long after leaving the palm that I entered the range of other implanted. Blips of the Dreg Warriors appeared in the minimap at the corner of my vision as I strode toward the forward base Wildwood had set up to deal with the spider dungeon. It had gotten the very *original* name of Base Arachne, but the people there didn't seem to mind. With the constant presence of at least one squad at the fortification, they'd even gone so far as to make a little patch to fasten below their Wild Guard emblems to signify they were part of the squads that rotated there regularly.

As they saw me approach boldly down the road, the watchman hailed me and they started to open the gate to let me in. The other two squad members hidden inside the fortified walls were excited and surprised to see me arriving. An older human with some turquoise ridges flaring out from his triceps that went by Creek was the first to actually form some words.

"Mr. Vanguard! We didn't know you were planning to head this way," he said.

"Just out for a walk. I've been too stiff… the last few weeks," I said, losing some of my social cheer as I recalled what had led me out of town. *Dai would be proud of my loner moves.*

The slight shift wasn't missed by Creek, and he nodded gravely. "Yah. It's a bit unnerving how quiet things have been since the raids."

"Thank you so much, sir!" the guard that had been up on

the wall blurted. He was practically twitching as he wrung his slender elvish hands.

Based on the fact that I didn't actually recognize him, he had to be part of one of the trainees being given experience before being assigned to a squad. With the impetus of the Tendrils scattered, the Wild Guard had pulled back on their push to form squads. Instead of having four newbies to a veteran, they had flipped the ratio while rotating out those suffering from Ava and Sarah's training.

Almost simultaneously, Creek and the other woman guard, also an elf, smacked him on the back of the head. "Learn to read the room, Larry!"

Despite the hazy cloud in my thoughts, I couldn't help but chuckle at the youth's enthusiasm. *Youth, huh? I'm not that much older than he is.* "It's alright. There really isn't anything for you to thank me for. What we did…There was no chance I could have done that alone."

"Oh, I agree, sir, but it doesn't make it any less awesome! From your status, you made it to Q6! Everyone knows what you, The Torch, and The Whisper did," Larry said, enthusiasm not at all diminished by the reprimand from his superiors.

"Well, that may be the case, but I wouldn't call 'The Torch' that unless you want to smell like smoke for the rest of the day," I said, shaking my head at just exactly what had happened when Daniela had finally discovered her nickname. "Plus, you forgot about The Flower."

The youth looked more aghast at the fact that he'd forgotten to mention Ophelia than the possibility of Daniela lighting his trousers on fire. You had to respect his commitment to the image of the 'named' Wild Guards.

"Mr. Vanguard—"

"Ronan, please," I insisted.

"Ronan," Creek continued. "Since you are here, I was wondering if you could help with something…"

"Out with it, man! I'm just another guy; if I can lend a hand, I am more than willing. What did you need? Particular critter making your lives difficult?" I asked, giving the status of the three a cursory glance. Other than the Q2 of Larry, both the woman and Creek were Q4s. Not the top of the Wild Guard by any stretch, but if they were struggling with a creature, it had to be a tough Q4 or even a Q5—

"We were hoping to expand Arachne. Sarah wants to send more of the fresh recruits here, but the space is… cramped as is," Creek finished lamely.

"Oh. Ah, yeah, that's not an issue," I said, surprised. A strange buzz flowed through me as I realized I wasn't going to fight. They wanted me to *build*. Suddenly the fog that clung around me wasn't quite as oppressive, and I started to ask a flurry of questions about the basics of the improvements they wanted. Creek was reserved, the woman—who I learned was named Mav—got way too detailed, and Larry went absolutely bananas with the idea that I was going to be working on the base.

At the end of almost an hour of discussion and of walking the fairly barebones base, I had a very good idea for what I wanted to build. Just because it sounded hard, I even opted to take one of Larry's harebrained ideas. It wasn't the fight I'd been jonesing for when I took an escapade into the woods, but it was just as good.

Ever since arriving at Q6, I'd been holding back testing the extent of my power. The qualitative change was hard to gauge, despite all my attempts to quantify it. Prodding at the new limits of my mana and skills was the best way I'd found to test it. Now I had an excuse.

For the sake of showmanship, I moved to the other side of the road from the old world building that had been turned into Base Arachne. I eyed the short stumps of ankle breakers I was sure Timothy the fae had made around the base, and I eyed the rough wooden wall that had been erected around the whole building. It was flanked by both the road leading to Wildwood and the wide, cracked blacktop of US 301.

With a deliberate motion, I planted my hands on the

ground. My antler helm thrummed as I fed it enough mana to trigger the first step of <Earthen Barrier>. Instead of releasing my grip on the mental 'button' of the skill to feed it the mana required to augment to <Earth Wall>, I visualized how I wanted the wall to form. The dimensions were hard to specify since I didn't know the baseline for my Q6 <Earth Wall>, but I focused on the concept of a square. It was more akin to a pillar than a wall proper, but thanks to gaining access to defensive freeform, my control over my skills had extended beyond just fractionally decreasing their power and empowering them. Now I had a hand in how the spell chains shaped mana in reality.

As soon as that visual was there, and I noticed that the guard trio was giving me weird looks, I sheepishly released the hold on another twenty percent of my mana.

For a breath, nothing happened. Then the ground rumbled, dipped, and *heaved*.

A square column of stone roughly three feet wide sprouted from the ground at a not insignificant rate. Five, ten, fifteen, 'til just shy of twenty feet. The dull ache in my body from expending almost half of my mana pool was completely forgotten as I looked at the unnaturally smooth structure. Striation patterns of various soils that had been compacted together marred the surface of the column, but it didn't detract from that fact I'd created the two-story tall column in less than five seconds.

The guards were equally speechless, until Larry broke into wild cheers and hurrays. "That is freaking awesome! Am I going to be able to blow over something like that when I get to Q6? Can I get faster? Will I...?"

The overeager youth's voice drifted into the background as my eyes took in the whole of the stone column. It had been costly, mana-wise, and the ache in my body wasn't insignificant after forcing my visualization on the skill to form it, but it was damn worth it. *And it gives me a direction.*

Even if the Dreg were scattered to the wind, it didn't mean Earth was safe. There was more out there... I just knew it! The sacrifices and struggles up to this point weren't over, because kids like Larry still needed to learn to use their powers to survive the next critter or corrupt thing that went bump in the night. There was still a future to build, and I had just the right power to start laying the foundations.

CHAPTER TWO

Build and Rebuild

After the first bit of flashiness and self-reflection, I paced myself mana-wise while also making quick progress on my devious plans for Base Arachne. The design I had in my head was so ridiculous that I found myself chuckling even as I used my steps to mark out the distances of seven other columns identical to the first.

The squad assigned to the base looked at me funny as I continued to raise pillar after pillar. Once I was done, I took a good hour break to let the soreness in my body pass. Even if the time between casting the skill let my mana regenerate, the side effects weren't so quick to dissipate. With the early success in reshaping my skill to make ramps, and now columns, I was confident I could make my plan happen. *It's just going to take a day or two...*

A glance at my status and then at the line that marked Communication told me that Daniela was out of range, but Samuel, Ava, and Alan were not. The thought of Alan sent a jagged spike of guilt into my gut but I pushed past it. They would be okay while I worked on Base Arachne. It was a productive way of helping Wildwood while figuring out where I stood.

Feeling the urge to distract myself from my thoughts, I once again threw myself at the construction. The looks from the posted squad continued to grow as the day turned to night. They offered me a hasty dinner from their supplies, but all three were mute through the meal. There was an intense glimmer in Larry's eyes, but he also didn't say anything.

After that profoundly awkward experience, time went by in a blur of mana soreness and dirt. While building, I didn't try to think overly much, just letting myself get lost in the process. The smooth grain of compacted sand on my fingers, the earthy scent that clung to me as I cleared away sections of overgrown old-world ruins and the strange satisfaction of using their remains to construct something new. The chains of responsibility that I carried close were hung up for a minute, allowing me to really experience what all that pressure had allowed to grow within me.

Very quickly, the general shape of the structure started to materialize. After reinforcing the wall around the old building, I improved the ramparts by adding a layer of stone to the wood. The front, where the gate was, I raised higher and left four large gaps. To the upper pair above where the ramparts actually reached, I added two small platforms using <Earthen Barrier> on the inside. Once those reinforcements were complete, I stretched slats of stone from the wall toward the eightpillars around the base's sides. That process took a day in and of itself, but I hardly felt it. Despite the soreness in my body, and a budding headache the more I tried to manipulate <Earthen Barrier> and <Earth Wall>, I threw myself even harder into the project.

The following day, walls sprung up to form small 'watch-boxes' at the top of each of the eight pillars. Even without the utility of my crystal pickaxe, I found that targeted <Mudpits> with a little shaped nudge from my freeform skill worked just as well to create features for my structures. Even if my hands ended up covered in mud, and the windows, doors, and crenellations I created were by no stretch of the word *aesthetic*, they were done entirely under my own power. There was something humbling and distinctly invigorating about that prospect.

With the rough extension of the watchtowers, I turned my attention to the main building. Liberally using <Mineral Strike>, after checking that the guards weren't within the building and supplies were cleared out, I proceeded to demolish entire sections of it. In their place, I raised mana-created stone that seamlessly blended with the walls that remained. When I wasn't satisfied with the first floor as enough of a square footage expansion, I spread the footing with the passive form of my skills. On those reinforced pads, I raised a pair of towers on either side of the new building. Thanks to my improvements in control, I was able to use short spurts of <Earth Wall> to create a pair of winding staircases that led up the side of the main building.

As I considered how I needed to implement the new access design for the fort in the Bunker Camp, I had a sudden epiphany while staring at the dead end of my staircase. All my efforts in using <Mudpit> to create openings had been a concerted effort of punching circular holes of various sizes so I could push the mud-like state of the rock and create the actual gap. Each of those had been based around using the absolute minimum amount of mana to get a controllable amount of mud. *What if, instead, I try to spend what I need to fulfill my objective? It's not a stretch from what I did when I made those columns using <Earthen Wall>.*

"<Mudpit>!" I shouted, not using a percentage to control the skill, instead letting my visualization guide the skill into reality. A semi-circle at the top, and a tall rectangle for the main portion of the opening. It was a simple shape, and nothing in the description of the skill said it had to be circular. However, the new application sent a sharp jab of pain right to the back of my mind, even as the normally circular band of umber glyphs shifted in the air. The glyphs stretched, creating the outline I had imagined, before my mana winked into the spell chain. It wasn't even ten percent of my mana pool, but the strain was much more acute.

My hand gripped the wall as everything spun. I wasn't sure how long I stood there panting, but it was enough for the liquifying effect of my skill to run out. However, the skill didn't disengage before proving my hunch. The semi-circular portion at the top of the wall and the upper portion of the 'rectangle' that I'd marked for the window had slumped to the ground. The resulting section was the smoothest I'd been able to produce. I didn't bother to look at the knee-high mound of hardened mud at the foot of the opening, because I knew that was more an effect of not removing the stone rather than my skill experiment failing.

While I was racking my brain on why the spell chain had changed relative to the other modifications I'd done to <Earthen Barrier> and <Earth Wall>, vibrosense blared around me as the entire structure I was on lit up with ripples. <Mineral Strike> formed in my hand on instinct. None of the stationed guards wanted to come close when I was working, instead opting to call out if they needed anything or to let me know it was meal time. They were hoping to avoid taking a wall to the chest like Larry did when he was over eager on day one. I'd felt extremely bad for the young elf and apologized profusely, but he just seemed *thrilled* to have survived collateral damage from the Vanguard. *He needs some help with his degree of fascination.*

I shook my head of my ambling thoughts and focused. The ripples were light and bipedal as they approached the building, but they were moving too fast to have good intentions. The only thing that could have bypassed the guards and matched that description was a humanoid Tendril. Fully intending to catch it by surprise, I leapt out of the opening <Mudpit> had created and released the shard of cinnabar that had formed on my palm.

"Ronan, what the——"

My eyes flew wide open as I saw Daniela around the corner. They then snapped down to the explosive crystal I'd just released. Horrible things flashed in my mind as to what might happen if it took the slight brunette in the chest, so I dumped as much of my mana as I could into <Rock Cocoon> in the blink of an eye. My mana flowed into my helm and then shot right into my friend before the cinnabar struck. As the covering of rock started to crawl over her skin, twin blasts of flame bloomed out of her hands and propelled her further away from the attack. This gave her more than enough time to be encased in stone all the way to the small of her back, even as the crystal fragmented and peppered the cocoon.

The impact with the ground one story down did more damage to her than the mitigated explosion did, but Daniela still shrugged it off and burst out of the <Rock Cocoon> positively fuming. Literally. Burning chunks of the armor I'd conjured for her peppered the muddy grass between Base Arachne and the wall, retaining the flame for much longer than simple sandstone had any right to.

"You ignore us for weeks and then the first thing you do is try to blow me up!" she howled, flames escaping out of the fire gills on her throat. "If you wanted to be left alone, all you had to do was say so, you jerkwad!"

"I-I——" Words failed me in the face of Daniela's bluntness.

"Cat got your tongue, rock brain? Answer me! Why have you been avoiding me, Ron? Why!" Danny howled.

My brain ground to a halt. I'd been finding a little semblance of peace while building, but my friend's sudden appearance had thrown that Zen right in the toilet. Honestly, I just let the first that came to mind slip out of my mouth. It didn't come out quite as disarming as I'd been hoping.

"I don't know what I'm doing, Daniela!" I snapped, feeling some heat of my own rising. "Can you just understand that I need time to process all that happened? All the things that I am responsible for, I-I…"

"So you talk about it!" Daniela said, shoving me in the chest with enough force to remind me I wasn't the only Q6 in town. Almost unexpectedly, her information jumped at me as if she'd willed it to me.

<Daniela Vega (Human)>

<Attunement: Fire>

<Refinement: Flame>

<Perceived Metier Quotient: 6>

"Danny, you didn't tell a bunch of people to charge to their deaths!" I yelled.

"That decision wasn't made final by you. Maybe you supported it, but you aren't the only one grieving, and they understood the risks. Did you even remember that the memorial is tomorrow? You've been a ghost ever since you talked with Tec, and now I find you out here? Doing what? Living out your life doing extreme home makeovers?" she snapped.

"Daniela—"

"Mr. Vanguard? Is everything okay?" Larry called. The young elf didn't wait for a response as he used a gust of wind to propel himself onto the roof. At least, that was what he intended. His angle was too sharp and the burst of wind sent him careening into the side of the building a beat too quickly.

His fingers managed to grip the ledge even as I winced inwardly. My thoughts floundered a bit at the youth's interruption, but before I was able to get my thoughts back on track, he clambered up only to be struck by the fact that there was a fiery Latina beside me.

"What's his deal?" she snapped.

"The T-T-T-Torch…" Larry stammered.

"What did he just call me?" Danny's eyes narrowed on Larry.

"He doesn't know what he's talking about. He's not even part of this conversation," I said, stepping between the elf and Daniela. She was already running hot, and it wasn't directed at

Larry. The kid didn't deserve the ire that was rightfully mine. *Not that I want it!*

"You and I aren't done, Ronan. There's been more than enough dung piled up on top of our relationship, and I think it's high time we clear it away," Daniela said, stabbing her finger into my chest. "I better see you in Wildwood tomorrow, because I'm not going to blow smoke up your ass like everyone in town. Those deaths we lay at the feet of the Dreg, *not* you."

Danny kept her eyes locked on me. Thin veins of red permeated her iris and they almost seemed to glow with the intensity of her stare. They almost demanded that I challenge her, so that they could release the beast lurking under the immaculate curls. When I couldn't muster up a response, she huffed smoke in my face. Without missing a step, she back-flipped off the building. Twin spurts of flame let her spin in the air and she landed on the ground silent as a gust of wind. If vibrosense wasn't lighting up her steps in progressively smaller ripples, I might not have heard her at all despite all the growth to my perception.

"M-Mr. T-Terrigan?" Larry asked after Daniela left our line of sight. Releasing the breath I hadn't realized I was holding through my teeth, I turned to the elf.

"Are you alright, Larry?"

"Oh, ah, yeah," he said. For good measure, he patted himself down as if he'd somehow missed an injury from his brief interaction with Daniela. "I did have a question."

I'm seriously not in the mood for this. Why do I—"Go ahead."

"Am I going to be that intense when I reach Quotient 6?"

I couldn't help the harsh laugh that escaped me at that. Thankfully, Larry didn't seem offended, just confused as his gaze shifted from me to where Daniela's silhouette had last been.

"Not necessarily. Daniela and I have a… confrontational connection. The surface, I think, has made those confrontations sort of escalate," I said. *Why am I telling you this?* Not that I didn't *want* to talk about it, but Larry was a stranger. He couldn't understand.

"I totally understand, sir. Most of the time, I just want to strangle my little brother. Somehow, he really knows how to get under my skin," Larry replied, nodding sagely.

The youth's response was not what I expected, but it made a sort of sense. I viewed both Daniela and Samuel, as well as most of the people of the Bunker, as family. Being age-contemporaries certainly made me feel like they were my siblings. The context in which this connection was revealed, however, still left me with a frown intense enough to drive the energetic youth away all by himself.

Both happy and sad that the relationship between Daniela and I was recognized as so close, I finished the broad changes to Base Arachne while my thoughts drifted. The second staircase opening, I formed with my primitive <Mudpits> technique, but I didn't forget that there was still plenty for me to learn about my skills. With a flourish, I created four rooms on the second floor and one additional staircase in the center that led to the roof. These areas were much rougher in spacing than the rest of my work, but I doubted the posted guards would mind the new sources of personal space.

As much as I wanted to keep sinking time into building, it wasn't appropriate. There was a time and place for everything. My place, as much as I wanted to avoid the ache it caused, was with Wildwood's leadership at the memorial.

So, it was when I was putting the final crenellations on the much taller roof space that Creek found me.

"Thank you for all your help, sir." The older man nodded respectfully.

"Really, there's no need for all that formality." I sighed, my arms dropping to my sides as I leaned back against the mana-created stone and really paid attention to the sun starting its descent into night.

"Ronan, sir, I can understand your worries. I will take a little responsibility in deceiving you," Creek said.

"Huh?"

"Your guilt has not gone unnoticed. Neither has your presence. As part of my daily report, I informed Councilwoman Sarah that you were here and she urged me to speak with you. However, not only am I not a very verbose man, but I also know when what someone needs is an outlet. You performed well and above on the one I sought to give you," Creek replied sheepishly. His ridges twitched, visibly marking his nerves.

"You didn't really need an upgrade to Base Arachne, did you?" I said, the dots connecting. Creek nodded. "Wow. So much for my double-human-potential-perception."

"Ronan… The reason Councilwoman Sarah urged me to talk to you is because she noticed how much you are laying on yourself. As much as I didn't want to overhear your discussion with The Torch, she isn't what I would call quiet." Creek paused, wringing his hands as he worked through his own thoughts. "Those people we lost in the fight against the Dreg… They aren't the first we have lost. They won't be the last, if this blasted planet has its way. I was young when the Fall came, but I still remember the constant fear and helplessness.

"What those people that died and those that survived experienced was not helplessness. It was fear, true, but tempered by the fact that it was their choice. For once in many of our lives, we'd opted to charge at the problem and make it submit to the full extent of our power. Such a thing was only possible because you and the other Bunkerites lifted the blinders we've been holding on to so tightly. That, somehow, the world was going to go back to the way it was. By all intents and purposes, you are all fresher to this carnage, and yet it was your group that acted with the conviction necessary.

"Those deaths are not on you. They gave their lives so that we might all live ours. It is a burden we must carry, even as we continue to defend the rest of us unable to by putting our lives at risk."

Creek didn't stick around for long after revealing his well-meant deception. He squeezed my shoulder and walked down the central staircase I built. My eyes lingered on the purple and orange majesty of the sunset even as my mind spun a million different ways. Of all the things I dreamed I would deal with while on the surface, living with the consequences of my actions and how people viewed me were *not* some of them.

CHAPTER THREE

Solemn Walk

The following morning, I left Base Arachne together with the squad assigned to it. For the first time since I arrived, I actually saw the other two members. A surprisingly wrinkled yellow fae that acted as their healer joined up with the group during breakfast, followed close behind by a very young magenta fae. The girl smiled meekly, but she hid behind the wrinkled fae when I returned the gesture.

"Where have you guys been hiding?" I asked, surprised that none of them had even registered in my vibrosense.

"We are responsible for feeding the group here. Thanks to The Druid's direction and the implants, growing food for a small contingent of people has been mighty easy," the yellow fae replied. "I'm Pierre, by the way. This is Xi."

Shaking the man's hand, I nodded. It was true that Samuel had basically revolutionized the food industry for Wildwood, but it was curious to see it already being implemented so widely. "Good to know we've been able to help with that. Food was always... tight, in the Bunker. Nothing quite as deadly as the situation up here, but working with limited resources can be stressful."

"Of cour—"

"Did you turn our base into a spider?" Xi asked quickly. She peeked her head out for just a second, enough to get the words out, before hiding back behind Pierre.

"Obviously, Xi! Don't you see the magnanimous design the Vanguard has graced us with! It could use some refinement, but I'll have you know he only took three days to do all of this. Alone! Why, it might be possible for you two to just build a farm within the walls to make us even more impervious!" Larry announced loudly.

Creek was ready to swat the youth in the head, but I waved him away. Xi's eyes were glimmering as she looked at the *rough* spider I'd created. It was the building stick figure equivalent of one, but there wasn't much more I could do about it. Daniela was right. I couldn't skirt my responsibilities just because they made me uncomfortable. My chest still felt like it was being crushed by guilt, but I wasn't called the Vanguard because weight and pain held me back.

The two youths spoke animatedly for a few minutes while Mav and Creek finished a sweep of the base. There wasn't anything particularly important in Arachne, but they wanted to make sure it wouldn't be *too* easy to use it against the town while they weren't guarding it. Of course, their usual foes would have little issue climbing the walls, but it was the thought that counted. There weren't really doors to lock, but you always had to do a walk around the house before leaving for any length of time.

As soon as they returned, we left at a steady clip to Wildwood. The quiet conversation between the squad faded to the background as I focused on my vibrosense. It was still not seamless to manage, as evidenced by my blunder with Daniela, but I wanted to keep improving it. Blobby rolled along just out of sight in the trees, carrying the two geode coconuts. While rolling, I could feel the slime shifting across the undergrowth more due to the disturbances that it caused than by its actual ripple signature. The five people walking behind me all had slightly different ripples, but just focusing on them to try to separate them gave me a headache. *Good to know there is always something to get better with.*

"Why are his eyes closed?" Xi asked, her small steps passing close to my left on the cracked asphalt road.

"They say he has a trait to help him sense people from miles away!" Larry whispered back.

"People tend to exaggerate things," I replied, cracking an eye to pin the magenta-skinned girl to the spot. "But it's good to expect people's actual abilities to be higher. It helps to grow, when you think you are the underdog."

My memory of fighting Devon was clear as the words left my mouth. I hadn't had to fight any other lightning-based creatures or Tendrils since then, but it had gone a long way to remind me that even my prodigious defense had weaknesses. Thinking about the speed that Devon and Daniela displayed, backed by their Q6 skills, sent a shiver down my spine.

Thankfully, my words seemed to have a profound effect on the two youths. Larry's excitement dwindled, but I could see something more serious lurking there. Xi frowned like she'd eaten something sour, but actually closed her own eyes and tried to imitate me. To my utter surprise, she didn't stumble too much for almost thirty seconds before they fluttered back open. The frown was plastered there, but the glimmer of her eye was back.

"Train up, little Xi. We'll have you scouting the marsh before you know it," Pierre said, patting the girl gently on the head.

"Marsh?" I asked, drawn by the word. "There wasn't a whole lot to scout around Gec, unless I missed something."

"Oh, no," Creek said. "Pierre is talking about the marsh to the west. Past the Ashlands, there is nothing but cypress trees and muck up to your knees."

"Not to mention the snakes," Larry added, shivering with the first real hint of fear I'd seen in the youth. "I haven't been able to look at another vine the same way since my first mission that way."

"Huh," I said, frowning. It was true that we hadn't really explored much further west than the Fire Ant's territory, but such a change from the forest was surprising. Though, considering how drastic the environments around the dungeons were, I couldn't be surprised. I still had a sneaking suspicion that there was something more to that process.

The veteran guards added a few more comments about their own experiences exploring the edges of the unknown before the conversation petered out. There were plenty of things vying for everyone's attention, so I opted to gather my thoughts instead of prodding further as we passed the western field of Wildwood.

Knee high spinach and other leafy greens I couldn't recognize off hand rose up in neat rows. Closer to the wooden palisade of the town were rows and rows of cabbage, the lower profile of the plant giving a clear view of the hundred or so feet to the wall. Even if they were double the size of pre-Fall cabbages, the view was still better than the taller greens. Atop the wall were evenly spaced guards, the farthest two just at the edge of my vision.

Upon seeing us, the guard closest to the gate sounded a whistle. Someone within the wall opened the gates and let our group enter into the town. Compared to when Daniela, Samuel, and I had first arrived, it was hard to imagine we were in the same town.

The road had been reworked within the walls to give it a smooth finish, thanks to a number of earth-attuned Fallen using their passive Gifts while training. Swirls of black and white gave the road a strange visual effect as the asphalt and limerock base of the road mixed to fill in potholes and heaves the almost three decades since the Fall had produced, despite the lack of traffic.

Not only was the road changed, but the homes had too. As an unfortunate side effect of the regular attacks by the bile crows, many of the homes had been turned into the real estate equivalent of Swiss cheese. The few surviving homes had been quickly reinforced with the help of mana-created stone or mana-grown plants. The result was an odd fantasy-setting feel to the town, where stone block houses, bark-lined huts and tall vine-canopy tents replaced the cookie cutter American suburb that had once stood in Wildwood. Several had even been emboldened by the creation of the crafting hall and were trying their hand at building apartments of a sort on one of the empty lots.

A handful of people waved at our approach, but there wasn't the usual jovial energy spread throughout the town. Even the smattering of children in the town found the somber mood clung to them and their play was subdued. The handful of salesmen that usually pandered the goods of the crafters in town were instead passing out white roses free of charge for all the people slowly making their way east. Creek and company were immediately subdued when they saw that, and I opted to split from the group.

"The memorial is going to be outside the wall to the east, Mr. Terrigan," Creek said, bowing his head as he led his squad down the main road of the town. I watched them for a few seconds before setting my stride. The memorial was scheduled for midday, so I knew there was still a bit of time. Even if I wasn't much for formalities, I wanted to at least get a proper shower for the event.

My feet took me through the motions mechanically. More polite waves and a handful of excited children made their presence known, but none engaged me directly. I found myself just outside the training fields, seeing the changes that had been wrought even in the few months we'd been on the surface. Gone was the plain sandy area used for Gift practice. Far in the corner there was still such a location, more for general assembly than anything, but now the training space had taken on some truly fantasy features.

Towering spires rose three stories into the air, formed by who I speculated was one of the Stoneshapers with some Wildwoodian help. Several platforms were lashed tightly to the spires with vines that looked fairly familiar, but didn't necessarily have to come from Samuel's <Vine Whip>. A number of ropes and hanging bridges spanned the distances between the spires. At the base of the spires was a recently dug pond that probably kept the trainees from breaking something *too* often. It was hard to gauge with Danny's mom, Ava, and Sarah cooking up the training regimens.

At the edge of the pond was an obstacle track that would have given the old show *Wipeout* a run for its money. Considering how long I'd been avoiding actually coming to the training area and the dojo where me and the other Bunkerites were staying, it was a much more impressive product than Base Arachne.

"You going to gawk all day, or are you going to actually show up to the ceremony?" a gruff voice said behind me. I'd felt the approach; it wasn't particularly hard to pick out the heavy stomps of an orc. However, I'd opted to let them approach me. I was still wary of being too jumpy and being able to tell where people were around me, even through walls, felt a tad invasive the more I thought about it. *Something else to work on.*

"Hey Sarah. Yes, I was going to take a shower. Just… admiring the sights." I gestured out toward the upgraded training area. "I might need to give it a run."

"You should. The newly Gifted loved seeing Danny demolish the original course. Seeing your lumbering behind crack the earth might dissuade them from worshiping the Bunker Busters so much. It's making us *'mundane'* squads look bad," the woman said, stepping up beside me. She wore what I could only imagine was Sunday's best after the Fall. The emblem for the Wild Guard was firmly pinned to her chest and a patch beside it read 'Council of Wildwood.'

"Nice tag," I said, leading the way back to the dojo's apartment. After the extraction of the Aberrant by the giant death-death crow Appendage, Sam and I went full tilt on reinforcing the building. It was not *pretty* but there was definitely something manly about all the layers of stone built around it and the vines and bushes that almost camouflaged it. Ablative armor, the blonde had called it, before disappearing to one of his many food growth experiments.

"With Kirby gone and the Dreg routed, giving some proper structure to things is important. People are tired of fighting but not knowing where they stand," Sarah said.

We lapsed into silence as we clambered up the stairs to the apartment above. Sarah didn't need to ask for permission, having received an open invitation from Daniela and Ava to hang out whenever, as she set herself up to wait in the dining area. Plus, we were technically the ones squatting in their town.

I entered the bathroom and scrubbed the grime of almost two weeks of work off of my body. I'd taken dunks in ponds and rinsed off more than once while working or traveling, but the homemade soap and brush left me a new man as I left my faded body armor to hang by the window. The light Kevlar was more noodles than bullet-stopping materials and my usual cargos were fifty shades of burnt from the fights we'd encountered. When I finally stepped out, I noticed a new simple rough-spun shirt and a new pair of cargos had been laid out beside my dirt-caked boots.

The shirt already had the Wild Guard emblem pinned to it, along with a patch depicting a pointy triangle wrapped in an emerald vine while the whole thing caught fire.

I put the clothes on without comment, taking a deep breath and feeling the weight sitting firmly on my shoulders. When I went to get Sarah, she raised an appreciative eyebrow in my direction. "You know, if Jolene wasn't hissing at everyone that talked about how good looking and rugged you are, I'm sure someone else would have already tried to snag some Terrigan for themselves. I'm almost tempted myself. You certainly have the constitution to survive some fire-attuned... interactions. Have you even—"

"Is it really the time to talk about the magical birds and bees?" I snapped, feeling a muscle on my face twitch.

"Yes and no. What do you think this memorial is for, Ronan?" she asked, veering the conversation.

"What? To remember those who died," I said, taken aback.

"Obviously. I am talking about what it *means* to us. To you."

"I…"

"Creek told me about your talk. Just for the record, I agree completely with him. I wanted to talk to you before we head over because I know how hard-headed you are, if it wasn't already subtly reinforced by your friends. This memorial is not for those that are gone, but for those that remain," Sarah said.

"I get it. Don't feel guilt. Yes, this isn't the first time I've been told that. You don't need to baby—"

"I'm not babying anything, Ron. You don't get it. It may be a bit callous of me, but I know you haven't lost anyone, not really. I don't need your life's story to know that I'm sure there are gaps in your family. But you didn't see your mother eaten or your brother taken by the wilderness."

I stammered as I tried to keep up with Sarah's words. "See, you didn't even know I had a brother. And you know what that is? It's fine, that's what. Because that is my burden. I lost things that I love, so I opted to love more things. Everyone inside the walls of this town are people I love, your friends included.

"But for so long, that was all I had. And I was forced to watch as those I loved were lost to the unknown and even to a threat right under our noses. For heaven's sake, Kirby was at my birth, Ronan. I've been hurt more than you could possibly understand." Sarah wiped her eyes before leveling them, and a finger, at me. "But you three made a path. Now I have things I can love beyond the boundaries of the wall. Beyond even Summerfield and all those lost in that first attack. Because now all those losses we mourned have a meaning and they give us strength."

"Sarah, I never meant to offend," I said, finding my voice catching, even as I thought about losing the people that had been part of my whole life. That impotent rage when Daniela was taken was a pang I couldn't ignore, and I'd managed to get her back. All my mind had been able to picture since the battle of Summerfield was Samuel amidst the other dead, gone because of something I'd agreed to. Then that thought itself cycled into guilt for caring more about my friend than the others that had been lost.

No winners in that flashback.

Sarah's voice softened, drawing me back from my thoughts. "I know. What I need you to do is remember that you don't carry the weight of those deaths alone. We are the pillars that hold ideas and dreams larger than ourselves against the weight of a world that wants to crush us. Before it was the Dreg, it was hunger, or the creatures of the wild, or even other humans if the stories from Irwin and my dad are anything to believe. Loss is an unavoidable part of this equation, but you must balance it before it consumes you. You *must*. If you and the others hadn't stopped the Aberrant, how many more would have died? How many children like Larry or Xi? Orphans of this world that you've opened a door for because you dared to hope for a future. I'm not saying avoid the emotions and forget your part in it. I'm saying take it, and turn living into the gift they gave with their lives. Surviving is hard, especially as more people… As more people fall around you!"

Sarah was practically yelling at the end as her emotions surged. The power of her voice caused ripples through my vibrosense, driving her words even deeper into me. The orc woman saw my strained expression before turning away and drying her face on a rag on the counter. "Just think about how much more value those lives you carry would have if you saved another."

Sarah left, heavy steps echoing down the stairs and I found myself following.

CHAPTER FOUR

How the Magic Changed Us

I wasn't really prepared for the blunt honesty. The walk from Base Arachne had settled my thoughts a bit, only for them to be stirred up again thanks to Sarah's comments. Perhaps the clear-cut rationale was some schism in the way of thinking for those who survived on the surface versus those in Bunkers.

Whatever it was, it left my thoughts tumbling into each other so hard that I would have probably sat trying to put them in order for the rest of the day had the orc woman not pulled me along with her determined stride. Blobby followed silently behind as we headed north, then cut east to a part of the wall I couldn't ever remember visiting.

The gentle thrum of restless feet reached me first; the intensity of the sensation through vibrosense was strong enough to distract me from my thoughts. As we drew closer, I had to actively suppress vibro and focus on my sight, lest the sensory overload leave me stunned and disoriented.

When we arrived, and Sarah finally led me out of the eastern gate, I discovered the source of the ripples. Most of the town of Wildwood had gathered and now stood at the edges of the road leading out. Squads and their families clung together, speaking in hushed tones even in the wide-open space beyond the wall. Not only that, I spotted a handful of people from the two other towns, as well as the Summerfield refugees. The leaders of the other towns were quick to spot us approaching and a wave of silence, followed by murmurs, rippled out as the general population turned our way.

"Good thing you weren't the last to arrive," Irwin said, pulling us two forward and essentially pressing the 'play' button on the whole gathering. Groups of friends and family mingled and spoke, a quiet roar taking over once again.

"I didn't know the whole town was coming," I whispered, somewhat hesitant to head deeper into the press of bodies. It was the single largest gathering of humanity I'd seen, even compared to when the squads were marching on the Dreg-occupied Summerfield.

"Well, the other towns finally had a safe path here. We thought it would be good for us to remember together. We all lost people," Rachael interjected. The leader of Stonecrest reached her hand out to shake mine and I nodded in greeting.

Maurice and Ian followed close behind, as well as a lady that introduced herself as Teresa, ex-leader of Summerfield.

"I'm sorry that things escalated to this level," Teresa said, glancing over to where her people were gathered. "I think we all thought that the status quo could be maintained…somehow. Maybe if we hadn't been so trusting of the Tendris, things wouldn't have ended as badly."

"There was never a balance," Sarah said plainly, and the Weirdians nodded in agreement. Perhaps more than Stonecrest and Summerfield, they were aware of the struggle as they fought to keep even a fraction of their space against the alligator territory that was contained in their namesake, Lake Weir.

"Yes. Perhaps you are right," Teresa said, drifting off and dropping the conversation thread with a mollified expression.

The group did some small talk, and I did my best to stay far away from it. My eyes roved through the crowd in search of the mop of blonde and head of brunette curls that would mark my friends. Samuel was the first I spotted, sitting far from the group with a morose Marie at his side. The young girl was turning a wayward twig into a pretzel with ease, her expression distant even as she worked.

"Good to see you, Ron," Sam said, jumping to his feet as soon as he saw me approach. Without waiting for me to say anything, he pulled me into a half-hug, which I returned partly in surprise and partly realizing it had been a good while since I *had* hugged anyone at all. Marie smiled, but returned to her work as it slipped from her face.

"She doesn't like funeral stuff," Sam whispered, turning away from the girl slightly to speak with me. "But I'm glad Danny was able to shake you out of your funk."

"It was more of an intervention than I anticipated," I said, wincing. Samuel could tell there was more there, but he didn't press. "But suffice it to say, I'm sorry for drifting. The last few days…"

"They were hard. I get it. We can talk later. I'm just glad you are here. There is only so much placid plant growing I can do before I need some nonsense in my life."

That got a chuckle out of me, and even a half-snicker from Marie. The young girl had somehow managed to shift position from the road rubble to a quivering, unhappy Blobby. How she cornered the slime and sat on it like a mount, I had no idea.

Both Sam and I caught up on the last few days to pass time while the sun rose higher and *more* people coalesced outside the wall. Most of mine were summed up with my visit to the Geode Palm and then working on Base Arachne, not mentioning the general wandering and fire-putting-out the aftermath of Kirby's death had brought. He, on the other hand, did his best to remain mysterious. He promised we would exchange pointers as soon as everything settled down, and he was particularly excited to check out the coconut geodes.

Not long before the sun reached its zenith, a simmering brunette and her mother joined the gathering. Daniela joined our little group, but refused to look me in the eye, so Ava was the one to address me. "Thank you for coming, Ronan."

"I wouldn't have missed it," I replied gently. A lot of my frustration and guilt had been spent between Daniela, Creek, and Sarah. I felt somewhat empty, in all honesty, but I was sure I wasn't the only one feeling that way at the memorial Another part of me was thankful that I had blown through the most excitable bits of frustration I had accumulated, because I wouldn't have wanted it to resurface during the memorial. It wasn't even my place to hurt as much as the people that had known the lost for longer than me.

"Thank you, everyone," Dylan said, ringing a bell three times to get everyone's attention. The crowd and assembled defenders had grown to such a size that I was almost worried the towns were *too* vulnerable. "The joint towns all appreciate your presence. We know that losing so many of our family has not been easy, but I urge everyone to remember how they enriched our lives.

"The last few months have been a dark time. From the revelation that there was a group betraying us from within, to the losses we incurred with our youths and Summerfield, to the battle against the threat of the Dreg." Dylan walked down to the middle of the road and gestured to the various leaders of Wildwood and the other towns. "However, it has brought us together to a degree that hasn't been seen since the Fall of our society. It was through the sacrifices of people like them and those before, that your children and mine were able to begin taking the mantle from our shoulders. The mantle that was necessary to build their own future. Along with the mantle came tools, and answers, at the hands of wonderful friends. The Bunker has been the largest boon any of us could have expected. If all they provided was their knowledge, that would have been plenty, yet their connection to the entities we long thought against us brought clarity of purpose."

Something clenched within me as I listened to Dylan. His

fiery hair flickered and pulsed with his words, magnifying the impact of the speech by underlining them.

"We will now do the walk in silence, in memory of those who have been lost and in hope that the rest of us that remain are only taken when our lives have burned the brightest." The man turned smoothly, striding down the road further to the east.

The Wildwoodians fell in step instantly, the other folks stuttering but falling in behind them. The Bunker group, and Marie who seemed intent on clinging to Samuel, pulled up the rear of the group.

The large group remained incredibly silent and none of the creatures of the wild even attempted to engage. More than likely, it had something to do with the sheer presence of so many high Quotient guards, but there was also something else; my vibrosense reacted to the air around me in a way I couldn't recall other than from mana-infused stone. Some of the other higher Quotient individuals flinched and looked around as the walk continued.

No one spoke, since it was part of the whole point of the memorial's gesture, but I felt my thoughts come crisp and the crunch of earth beneath me flow clearly to my ears as if they were pressed to the ground. Then we started to see the graves.

Some in the shadows of ruined buildings and others out just by the road. A handful, then some more, then *dozens*. Grave markers of all shapes, sizes, and degradation signaled the last remembrance of those gone. As we walked past what had to be hundreds of graves marked amidst the remains of some collapsed building, wisps of black and gray seemed to curl out of the ground. Like soot given life, the wisps danced through the air and suffused everything nearby.

The brushstroke nature of the wisp immediately struck me as familiar and I realized what I was seeing: natural mana. The same energy that segregated and became visible within the Blessing of Magic, Tec's area of influence, was manifesting here. It wasn't a big jump to recognize the wisps as death-attuned bits of energy, but the fact that the effect was manifesting without an Entity pulled me up short. My friends were equally stunned as we passed more graves and entered a small park. A stone had been grown using magic, names etched into it, even as fresh graves were set into the ground at the foot of it.

My throat caught as I saw the death energy curling so tightly around the monument. It drew it in like a slow-moving vortex, and I watched more than one wisp of mana emanate directly from the people around me. As we stopped closer, that feeling of clarity grew sharper. As I focused on the two dozen names, many unknown, the ones that I recognized brought vivid memories to the fore. It wasn't like <Memory Canal>, where I plunged into the perspective of the person I connected with. This was more like my own memories were being polished, raised up to be put on a mantle for others to see.

Thick shreds of the dark mana flowed out of my chest and I watched them join the growing vortex. I had no words, or strength, to comment on the phenomena. Those around me seemed just as locked in place as wisps of their own were joisted into the current. Some people released torrents of them, while most only fragments and thin curls. No one spoke, but I didn't think it was just because of the purpose of the walk of silence.

As the last of the mana joined the vortex, it swirled inward, growing denser as the force of the mana was drawn tight against the monument. The etched rock was lost from sight, but we didn't need to wait long before the mana vanished almost completely. Where before there had only been a magically hardened slab of limestone, there now stood an opaque shard of black quartz. A gentle purple light highlighted the names that had been carved on the monument, even as flakes of dark mana radiated from the transformed rock.

"This..." Dylan, for once, was at a loss for words. The councilman of Wildwood glanced in the direction of me and my friends, but a soft shake of my head informed him of the confusion present in us also.

"A miracle," someone in the crowd whispered.

"It's a testament to their memory!" another called.

Similar, but wildly variable, explanations were given for the phenomena. Regardless of it all, it had marked something significant for the groups gathered. A common loss, now marked by the magic of the surface in a way they couldn't comprehend even with the growth Quotients had given them.

CHAPTER FIVE

The Price Paid

The actual ceremony was sped up by the transformation everyone witnessed. Dylan said some additional words, reading out the names of all the lost and detailing some of their exploits in life. A handful of the fighters—survivors of the attack on Summerfield—walked to the front and told of the last moments. The wisps of mana curled and twisted as they spoke, the strange shard of crystal throbbing like a monolith of death.

I recognized several of the people that went up to speak as the ones that had the death-attuned wisps circling more vividly around them. There was definitely a connection there, but I wasn't in the headspace to draw it. Instead, I let the flow of the crowd take me back to Wildwood and to the edge of a bonfire that burned for most of the night. More stories, not only of the lost but also those who'd gone before, passed around the fire and I let myself be submerged in the identity of the town. Becoming part of the flow was easy when someone broke out the kegs to help grief.

Our little group of Bunkerites stayed somber through the ordeal. As the ones least invested in the lives of the people that died, it felt somewhat disrespectful to dig in, but we made sure to act as the responsible adults when a few of the people got a bit too out of hand. And so, the day and night blended together.

The next morning, by the time I woke up, everyone had left the dojo apartment. I could hear quiet explosions and groans from outside. When I peeked out the window, I saw that Sarah and the Wild Guard were already up and at it. A more subdued group was lined up to the side with Ava. They looked younger, and I could only guess they were those who'd awakened a Gift but were not old, or able, enough to join the more... rigorous portion of the training the guard had started using.

Somewhat at a loss for purpose, I stood, ate a quick breakfast, and started for the crafting hall.

Many of the regular people in town were still recovering from the previous night's rager, but a handful of crafters were still up and at it regardless. A small group of demon Fallen were flattening the dirt that had been turned over by all the people lingering on the dirt roads. One of them was even pulling a wagon with a water barrel to clean off where some people hadn't been able to keep their drinking to themselves.

Moving through town, I spotted a caravan with a squad of Wild Guard making its way north toward the bridge and the car wall. None of the people on it were the people from the other towns, so they had either left already or were still lingering in Wildwood. With the Dreg scattered and the teams of the respective towns now supplied enough to have climbed in Quotient, Stonecrest and Lake Weir were the safest they'd ever been. That was how much of a difference the MetierTech Implants made.

"So he *hasn't* died, has he?" Arnold the dwarf quipped from the top of the crafting hall.

More specifically, from the addition that had been made to my original crafting hall in order to accommodate all the people seeking to contribute to the fighting indirectly. Vibrosense told me he was working to densify the walls, expanding on the strong wall concept that I'd made with his help. I was fairly certain that if I kept training, I would be able to match the density he was achieving with his <Stone Anvil>skill. For now, I could at least compensate with thicker walls and being able to repair them.

"Needed some space," I said, focusing on the ground below me. I didn't have my antler helm to amplify <Earthen Barrier> to <Earth Wall>, but my efforts manipulating the amplified skill still let me direct an empowered cast to lift me the ten feet to be level with Arnold. That it cost me half my mana pool and a slight twitch in my abdomen was a factoid I kept to myself.

"Heh. Well, it's good to have someone with half a brain for building. While I was busy putting<Infusion> through its paces, someone decided it would be a good idea to jump on the urban planning train."

I pressed my hand against the stone he was working and rapped on it with my knuckles. Constant ripples traveled down the whole structure, giving me a detailed view of where the construction had slacked. It wasn't terrible, but it could definitely use work if the expansion to the crafting hall was meant to be permanent. Eager to test my ability to shape <Mudpit>, I agreed to do a small correction of the structure. Arnold snickered as if he'd tricked me into free labor, but I just took it as training. Two weeks of only putting out fires and ambling like a zombie was enough time for me to realize that I was the only one falling behind. At least with Base Arachne and the crafter's hall, I was working with *intent*.

Even in infusion crafting, which was the thing I'd contributed the most to Wildwood outside of combat, people were pushing ahead with their knowledge. I wasn't resentful of that, but it just served to highlight how much of a funk I'd let myself fall into.

When I followed Arnold into the building, I watched as my silent tagalong started to act strange. Blobby started to poke and prod at the walls, quivering and sniffing as if looking for something before deflating. The two of us shared a confused look as the slime entered the testing room and promptly disappeared from sight. Despite that odd behavior being worth some investigation, it was pushed out of my mind by what I laid eyes on: what had once been Samuel's stroke of engineering genius. The magic, ox-powered tank was a shadow of its former self.

As I'd been told, it was the only reason the group had been able to upset the balance when the death crow Appendage joined the fight. Samuel and the young operator he'd commandeered for the vehicle had struggled together to deflect the sheer death aura around the creature. Further, many of the range-proficient fighters had been tangled up with the bile bombardment that followed in the Appendage's wake. *That*, as told by everyone, was the moment that decided the fight. It was that moment when the biggest losses had come, as the bodies of the Wild Guards and other town fighters were melted from their very bones.

It was the moment that had left me freeing a half-dozen people from the prison of Dreg Afflictions. There was still no easy solution to that I could think of, and my daily visits had only left me bitter as I watched the Afflicted work to reacclimate to their changed bodies. The Wild Guard trainees were heading up this effort by adapting an area of their training course for them, but they *themselves* were still coming to grips with the price that they paid.

"Ronan, you don't have to do this, you know," Arnold said gently, placing his hand on my arm and breaking me from my spiraling thoughts.

"Thanks, Arnold, but I do. And I don't mean just help with the building. People keep telling me I need to move on and accept, but I think I'm realizing that I'm not okay with that."

I turned to him and slapped my hand down on the tank, hard. The rotted wood buckled and the pitted metal groaned under my increased strength. It wasn't impossible for humanity before the Fall to reach my level of strength, but it required a lifetime dedication. Surviving long enough had been all I needed to do to gain it. Just like that, pieces started to fall into place in my mind. It was such a simple contrast, and it was also something that the implants and the Entities had highlighted. Growth, and freedom to grow. To have infinite possibilities for the future, instead of being trapped by circumstance. The people of Wild-wood had grasped for that, and it was the reason they were still alive today despite the price they had to pay, knowingly or not. If we hadn't reached outside of our comfort zone, the other towns would have been lost a metaphorical stone throw away.

"I've come to realize that I am going to stay *not* okay until I can put some tracks on the crazy train that is our current world. So I will move on. I will move on to the next fight, the next person in need and the next God-damned thing that tries to take good and twist it for its benefit. They better hope they are prepared, because they are not going to be able to foot the bill. The price we've paid is too much already," I growled. I ground my teeth to keep from snapping at the dwarf. It wasn't his fault, and he'd been the one trying to comfort me.

"Good then!" Arnold called out, slapping me on the arm with *his* own prodigious strength. "I was thinking loss had turned you into one of the numb folks. Good to know it just took some time to get your bellows going!"

My earlier thoughts were derailed by the sudden agreement from the man. That, coupled with the force behind the slap, was surprise enough for me to focus on him. His information manifested in the corner of my vision.

<Arnold (Human)>
<Attunement: Earth>
<Refinement: Compression>
<Perceived Metier Quotient: 4>

"When did you get to Q4?" I asked, surprised.

"You can't infuse worth a damn if you don't have the mana for it. Plus, everyone and their auntie wants one of my <Stone Anvils>. You think we only need people that can knock out a person with a flick of their finger?" he shot back, gesturing with his hand at the tank. "Some sorry bastard had to make the shield you tote around."

"I'll have you know, the sorry bastard that made my shield was Rommel," I added, smirking.

"Oh, bloody hell. You know what I mean!" He sighed loudly, throwing his hands up in the air and walking back toward the garage-sized entrance to the room with the broken tank. He paused before glancing back. "It's good to have you back, Vanguard."

The man left without another word. His footsteps sent ripples that quickly blended with the busy hive of ripples that was the main building of the crafting hall. It was somewhat cathartic to watch his single set of ripples add themselves to the one of the masses, marginally augmenting the imprint the building had on my vibrosense. It was a good representation of what Wildwood had accomplished and what it was seeking to continue. Despite my moping around, the town continued to struggle and it was time for me to add my own ripples to their efforts. My friends were way ahead of me; it was a shame it had taken me as long as it did to figure it out.

— + —

The rest of the week was a blur. It was an exercise in discipline I hadn't had since living in the Bunker. Each morning, I would do a round of general exercises, like I would have done as part of our health training in the Bunker. Except, the 'general' part of the exercise consisted of the max push of anything I could have done before the implants. A look at my attributes put just where I stood in perspective.

Attributes:
Strength: 1.93
Mobility: 1.68
Perception: 2.20
Refinement: 1.54
Containment: 2.41

The Entities never specified which 'average' they pulled the reference point from for the attributes, but my six Quotients and the exertions of magic had pushed them almost a whole humanity's worth higher than when I stepped on the surface. As it were, my mana pool—thanks to my Containment—and vibrosense—due to Perception—were my most outstanding, and I tried to work those to the fullest. Apart from mile-long sprints and full body workouts involving hunks of my <Stone Spikes>, I worked to fine tune my vibrosense to avoid it being a hindrance during a fight by quickly switching between my first five senses and then only vibro. As for my mana, the work of revamping the expansion to the crafting hall proved taxing enough. If one considered that manipulating the shape of the spell chain for <Mudpit> felt like turning my intestines into pretzels to be taxing. Which I did.

Seeing the training Ava and Sarah set up for the trainees each morning showed me that while I could overwhelm most creatures we'd encountered with my magic, that wouldn't always be the case. Bad match ups with more intelligent creatures or similar Quotient creatures, or both in the case of Appendages, would still leave me unprepared. Unfortunately, the world didn't wait for me to be fully prepared or for my abilities to be perfectly in my grasp.

On the fifth day after the memorial, while I was working out how to add crenellations using <Earth Wall> instead of a bunch of <Stone Spikes>, Alan arrived at the crafting hall.

CHAPTER SIX

The Attention of an Entity

"Ronan. The Town Entity Cluster would like to speak with you," the synthetic voice read out from the tablet in Alan's hand. The man wasn't in sight from where I was working, but the machine voice was unmistakable.

I climbed down from the roof of the building using the series of steps I'd created by minimizing <Earth Wall> to as much as my body could tolerate. By the time I made it to the figure of Alan, he was striking a tuning fork against the mana-created stone and taking readings on the same tablet that let him speak. My chest clenched as I looked at Alan, and not for the first time.

In his bid to save us, the non-Fallen had pushed his traits to their limits. Quite literally, the man had burned himself out to reach the death territory in time to stop the Aberrant and Galloway. The price had been his voice and a disconcerting number of scars that seemed to trace either nerves or veins. Much like healing dismemberment and other more serious ailments, the life-attuned had not been able to help Alan completely. Ophelia and Diana had been able to purge and stabilize the man enough not to drown in his own blood, but that had only aggravated the injuries when they attempted to do a more precise job.

Regardless, the wheezing husk that was the brightest mind on MetierTech, spell chains, and mana in general didn't seem bothered by his injuries in the least, at least when it didn't concern struggling with communications.

"Hello Alan. I'm glad to see you are doing well," I said by way of greeting.

"Platitudes, Ronan. My health is stable, and my work is unimpeded. The Entity has requested your presence in exchange for further data collected in the core influenced region of its energy field," the tablet read out as Alan typed madly away. "Haste, if possible."

"You know you could have used the comm-plant, Alan," I said. For my own benefit, I added softly, "The mental communication works just as well as the verbal ones, per your design."

"Multifaceted trip," Alan replied. "Ava has suggested that my research topside has affected my level of physical activity. My body seems to agree, so I conglomerated the tasks."

"Sure, don't let me stop you," I said, shaking my head at the man's oddities. Nevertheless, if he was here, it had to be something important. 'Conglomerating' of tasks aside, Alan was a master at prioritization.He completed the implants in less than two years with minimal testing, and created the Aberrant purging device in roughly a month. Said device had not survived the task, and it had required more than a little elbow grease on my and Devon's part, but it was the only reason any of us were still alive on the surface. Of course, he had decades worth of research to ground the projects in, but he was the only one with the mind capable of implementing it.

"Magnificent. As for your development in the usage of your active genetic modification…"

For the short walk from the crafter's hall to the Metier Crystal in the center of town, Alan pestered me about how my Harmonic Sinew was developing. Other than updating him on my improved control of my vibrosense, nothing had changed with the trait. The appearance of the progression percentages for Devon, Olivia, Danny, and I was something that still seemed to stump the quirky researcher. To the joy of my budding headache, the moment I arrived within the Blessing of Magic, a tentacle of crystal reached down from the bulk of Tec's body to pluck me into the whitespace.

"You know, he was mid-sentence," I called out into the white void. Three glowing orbs of pulsing light materialized in the air above me. The orbs shifted, taking on different geometric shapes in an attempt to make themselves more identifiable in their unifying iridescence. The only time the three Entity Clusters had been on a magical conference call at once had been in the aftermath of the fight with the Aberrant, where there had been more questions than answers even for the artificial crystalline minds.

—Authority above our own has called this gathering.—

---Affirmative. Expediency was key.---

<He really doesn't even know what is going on. Plus, he isn't an Entity and is not subject to our authority; how would you expect him to know the urgency?>

"Hey, Bec. Good to hear a sensible voice amidst those two," I said, nodding toward the pulsing light that had opted to remain an orb instead of some weird prism. It was hard to match the way the light shifted, but the sensible tone and equally sensible shape spoke for itself.

Before the Bunker Entity Cluster could respond, the whitespace vibrated around me. What looked like stress fractures spiderwebbed all around, letting in a gray-tinged darkness not dissimilar to what I saw when I freed Afflicted from the Dreg. As the fractures covered more and more of the space, a pyramid of pulsing light on a different magnitude of intensity manifested above the three smaller Entities.

[-] Perceptive. Should facilitate our discussion. Human, contact the representatives of your group and seek an audience at my physical manifestation.[-]

Just as quickly as they'd appeared, the cracks vanished,

sealing themselves in reverse order of their appearance. The pyramid popped like a soap bubble and the whitespace was restored. I blinked to clear my eyes from the strange visual effects and mind-numbing contrast of dark and light before I was able to formulate a response.

"What the hell was that?" I asked, turning to Bec in the hopes of getting a coherent response.

<That, my dear Dreg Warrior, was Gec.>

"You want us to do what?" Sarah asked.

"I need to put together a group of people to represent all of our interests," I said. "There is something inherently different about Gec. I'm not sure what, and the other Entities haven't told me anything they didn't already. The only explanation lies in the fact that Gec is a category above either Tec or Wec."

"Can we trust this Entity?" Dylan asked, leaning back and steepling his fingers. The man had been surprisingly quiet since the transformation of the memorial and the death of Kirby. Everything he did took an extra moment of deliberation and this seemed to be no different.

"No idea. While I trust the Entities we've dealt with so far, I don't think our relationship with Gec is going to be a simple thing. If someone charges into your pleasantly relaxed meeting, guns blazing, you certainly get an opinion about them," I said.

"Ironic," Irwin said, gesturing vaguely at me and my friends. "I seem to recall something quite familiar happening not too long ago."

"Irwin, it's not the time for us to lecture them on their lack of political soft touch," Dylan said, wagging his finger all the while. *He clearly wants to do just that.* "I just want to make sure we aren't sending people to get swallowed up by this rock. Is it completely free of that… Aberrant thing?"

"After Devon and Ronan killed Galloway, the corrupted crystal melted into sludge before dissociating like all the other stuff. I can only hope that the assurances from our Entities are enough," Clara said, speaking for the first time in the meeting.

"If it gets frisky, then we get frisky right back," Daniela added with a flat expression. The council, other than Sarah, still didn't look convinced. "What? Not the first magical rock we've…well, rocked."

"Daniela," Samuel groaned, holding the bridge of his nose.

"What about Alan? Can your researcher tell us anything?" Irwin asked, turning to me.

"Alan isn't looking into that right now. He's working to figure out the percentages that some of our traits have acquired. He's particularly interested in why they show up at Q6 and in a handful of Q5 individuals. Until he reaches a comprehensive stopping point… it would be difficult to redirect him," I replied, thinking of Alan. The moment I'd left Tec with the message from Gec, the man practically dove into the large crystal. At least him and Tec didn't like to mince words, otherwise the two would never leave the whitespace. Less of a problem for Tec, but Alan still needed to eat.

"So what? We chance going into its home turf?" asked the fishermen's councilman, Trey.

"I don't see many options. As much as this fight was a win, there is a whole world out there," I said, thinking of my words to Arnold. Wildwood was important, but there were likely others that could use help. They didn't even have to be far from the town, just outside of where their power had been able to reach.

"I am inclined to agree with the Vanguard," old man William said. "Isolationism was what led to our current predicament. Perhaps if we'd reached out earlier after the Fall, our struggles would have been lessened. If we'd *cooperated*? Ha!"

The farming councilman made it no secret that he wasn't a fan of the Bunkerites, and even Samuel only got the occasional nod of approval thanks to what he'd done for Wildwood's farming industry. That he verbally agreed with me showed that

Clara's message to interconnect the towns had finally gotten through some of the most stubborn heads.

"I still don't like it," Trey said.

"Good thing this is a council and not a dictatorship," Irwin said. "Anything else to add before we let the Bunker Busters move forward on this?"

"Do we still pretend that we tell these three and their family what to do?" Sarah asked, leaning back in her chair. That got a round of chuckles out of the scattered Wild Guard in the room and a grimace from the older councilmembers.

"Point made, Sarah," Dylan said, giving his daughter a 'we'll talk about this later' look that the orc woman poignantly ignored. "All in favor?"

Every hand, even the ones from non-council spectators, went up. Trey sighed deeply before joining the others.

"I'll send a squad to relay a message to Stonecrest. We have close to a wagon's worth of goods for Lake Weir, and you can do double duty escorting it," Irwin said, holding a clipboard gingerly in his clawed hands.

"They should have some of the things I requested available to ship south too," Samuel added, which put decidedly positive expressions on Irwin and William's faces.

"Good! Maybe we can finally get a proper economy going," Irwin said. I could almost see the dollar signs replacing his pupils.

"Who's gonna ride our coattails?" Daniela asked, leaning back in her chair further than Sarah. The chair balanced perfectly on two of the legs. The orc woman glared at Daniela, but all she got in reply was a mischievous grin.

"'Ride your coattails'?" Irwin asked.

"We can't speak for Wildwood. We speak for the Dreg Warrior effort and for the Bunker. You should speak for yourselves," I said. I waved my hand vaguely at the people sitting around the large meeting room. "Gec asked for representatives. I want to make sure everyone has a seat. I have a sneaking suspicion that this is going to be a...*weightier* discussion than we expect."

"What makes you say that?" Dylan asked, his fire hair simmering low on his head.

"I've never heard the Entities talk about an authority that affects them," I said. The room fell silent as everyone contemplated my words.

CHAPTER SEVEN

A New Metric

Thanks to the number of times that Wildwood had needed to mobilize since we arrived on the surface, the efforts for a caravan north were completed by nighttime. There was a brief discussion about leaving immediately, but considering that nighttime was when the creatures in the predator territory ranged farther out, it was quickly vetoed. Even if Daniela and I were now Q6, the prospect of fighting something at a matching level was still dubious. My vibrosense would give me a small warning if anything approached, but I wasn't willing to risk the whole trip just to hurry along.

The next morning, right before the crack of dawn, Sarah, Dylan, and Clara met up with our group at the foot of Tec's Blessing of Magic. Sarah was in the regular set of clothes she wore every day for training, plus the Wild Guard emblem. As for Clara and Dylan, they were dressed for trouble. For the first time that I could remember, Dylan looked ready to tango. One of the armor blueprints I'd created, the lighter segmented cowl, was draped on his form along with a short frost step spider sword. It had been discovered early that non-Fallen could use infused items at the cost of their physical stamina instead of the mana they seemed to lack. It was nowhere near the efficiency that the Fallen could achieve with the Items, but when your life was on the line, it made it an easy trade.

Plus, the infused armor was just stronger than anything humans could muster from before. I still wore my armored vest, but without the Kevlar plates. While I hadn't tested my <Earth Shell> against bullets, much less the large caliber beast that Ava carried, the stone armor was much more versatile; it also overlaid my clothes, which made it extremely convenient. As I waited for Dylan to finish talking with Sarah, I glanced at the two pieces of equipment that had survived the fight with Galloway.

<Quotient 4 Chitin Scutum>
<Attribute: Strength>
<Trait: Force Dispersal>

<Quotient 2 Antler Helm>
<Attribute: Strength>
<Trait: Accretion Amplitude>

Without them, I would have been dead much earlier. Without the spider naginata, it would have been a struggle to even get close to the Appendage, and I sent its charred remains a silent thank you. Lacking a weapon was somewhat unnerving, and the pistol Ava had forced on me felt next to useless, but I hadn't had time to create something to sustain the rigor of my fighting style. It was part of the reason armor lacked appeal. As strong as infused materials were, there was only so much abuse they could take; replacing my stone armor just took mana.

My mind drifted off as I tried to think of what weapon to make with what Wildwood had been able to gather. It was somewhat ludicrous how many low Quotient infusions and creature materials they'd been able to accumulate even as they burned through them for the effort of equipping the other towns.

"Oy, rock brain. We're ready," Daniela said, smacking me on the back of the head before taking the lead on the group.

I blinked as I realized Sarah and Clara were chuckling while Dylan and Sam shook their heads. Ava was messing with some of the supplies stacked up in the wagon. An awkward look around told me that no oxen had been brought for Sam to guide, which also left me confused. When I voiced as much, the life mage smirked. "You are the ox for today, Ron. The town is working on a new field for me to work, so the oxen are all accounted for. The ones we lost in Summerfield cut the available animals by almost half. Cows don't really grow on trees, now do they?"

"What about Anthony? I don't see our resident giant ant. I'm sure he could manage now that he's about my size," I replied smartly.

"He's staying to keep an eye out for Alan," Ava said, not even bothering to look over her shoulder.

"I think it's time you pay Raymond a visit," I said, crossing my arms. "That bull is probably nice and fat off your vegetables and here I am pulling a wagon."

"Fair enough. Should have brought it up *before* the not-so-friendly neighborhood rock told us to visit," Sam replied, lifting an eyebrow.

"Can we get this rolling?" Ava called. "I thought I was leaving the babysitting to Sarah."

"Mama, they gotta get the quips out now, otherwise we will hear them all through the trip," Danny said, smirking from where she stood tapping her foot impatiently.

"I concur with Ava. I expressed urgency in the message to Ms. Barron in Stonecrest. We should make it our priority to arrive post haste," Dylan said, straightening his cowl as he stepped into the middle of the group. Everyone, Ava included, gave him a look that told him just what everyone thought about his bantering skills before the group got into motion.

Sam provided me with a handy vine harness that was easy to slip in and out of and I started to trundle forward. I channeled a trickle of mana into my tower shield and the boost to my strength helped me pull the wagon with only a bit of strain. As soon as I was able to build some momentum, I released the channeled mana and really felt my muscles engage with the wagon. It wasn't comfortable, per se, but I much preferred to keep the use of my mana low.

"Look at that, all those muscles *are* useful for something," Daniela said, making a mock expression of surprise before settling into her lengthened strides.

"Party up before you vanish, hothead!" I called, matching words to action as I sent the group a party request. The Latina grumbled, but accepted the invitation.

She was still not thrilled about how I'd been the past few days, but her mood was positively cheery as we headed out into the wilderness between towns. After the knockout that had come from getting to Q6, Ava had been keeping her close to town. As far as I knew, the trip to talk to me at Base Arachne had been the furthest she'd been since the battle.

Crossing the bridge across Lake Sumter was a simple endeavor. Since the pathway north had been used so often after the AE-1 road had been established, the car wall had even been modified into a proper rolling gate. It was still three feet of crushed car metal, but now I didn't have to summon a wall up and over it just to get the wagon beyond it. The squad leader posted up on the wall greeted us and reported that the night had been quiet.

The wind rustled gently as the sun finally poked all the way over the treeline just as we plunged into the shaded path. At some point, Blobby had uncamouflaged to roll beside the wagon. When I tried to ask the slime where it had been all along, it actually shaped itself into a rough rectangle before squishing itself up and down. Somehow, I was able to read the frustration in its jiggling and draw the connection. The slime had still been kidnapped by Marie and the young girl had used him as either a bed or some kind of trampoline. I couldn't help but chuckle, which only caused my slime companion to jiggle with more agitation, before it slunk off into the woods and out of sight.

Thanks to the efforts of the Stoneshapers, there was actually very little difference in smoothness between the old world's roads and their magical reproduction. My back was grateful for that as we settled into the longest stretch of the trip to Lake Weir, the wild gap to Stonecrest.

As I got into a rhythm with pulling the wagon, the quiet conversation between the others dissolving into the background, I actually closed my eyes and focused on vibrosense. The steady grinding of the wagon wheels on the road sent constant ripples that illuminated everything around me.Small clashes occurred where those waves met the smaller ones generated by our walking group, but being able to see those interactions actually helped me acclimate to using my newest sense.

It wasn't as clear as my eyes, but there were plenty of those to go around in the party. Danny was ranging along at the northeastern edge of the implant range, and would ping anything that entered her perception. Since I had something to contribute, I set to work on training my senses.

It was easy to get a broad scope of everything around me. Objects were obstructions for the ripples I made. A tree here, a person there, the edge of a building or some dilapidated sign structure overgrown by vegetation. The minutiae of my trait came in being able to differentiate what those things were without having to look at them directly. Not to mention the fact that vibrosense worked for things all around me, and I certainly didn't have the peripheral view for processing that information. Interpreting the interactions of the vibration ripples was the only way to make proper use of the ability.

As I got more proficient at filtering out my traveling companions, the dense road under our feet, and the many trees flanking us, vibrosense was able to reach further. The ripples were quickly swallowed up by the vegetation, but I could almost follow the surface curves, bushes, and undergrowth as the ripples spread across their surface.

It was because of this weakened extended range that I stopped us from being ambushed. When a bush flared with more ripples than it had any business having, I knew something new was in range. I'd observed a handful of spiders and two deer explode through the bush in a panicked dash away from our caravan. This was similar, except the creature remained almost perfectly still. If it hadn't been for the active monitoring at the edges of my vibrosense, I was almost guaranteed to have missed it.

"Eyes up," I said, still keeping a steady pace while pulling the wagon.

"Ron?" Sam asked, matching my pace and cutting his conversation with Clara short.

"There is something watching us beyond the trees."

"It didn't do a runner?" Clara asked, still walking, but I sensed her adjust her posture through vibro. Each of her steps became lighter, as if she was ready to jump at the closest shadow.

"No, they are over toward our left. We will be passing in front of them in less than five minutes," I said, watching as more of the bush lit up in vibro. "Seems like it might be more than one thing."

"Councilman, climb the wagon. Ms. Ava, if you would?" Clara said, snapping orders in a no-nonsense tone. Ava quickly followed, causing me to strain my muscles as the load increased. I heard Dylan start to protest until a chill ran down my back.

I actually opened my eyes to see Clara using her strange <Fear>skill on the councilman in order to get him to acquiesce. The next second, he clambered on and I was forced to feed a trickle of mana into my shield to pull the wagon forward under the new weight.

"They are directly to our left," I whispered through the comm-plants. My minimap at the edge of my vision showed Daniela making her way back at double speed, but she was still at the far reaches of our range. If we were attacked, she would have to be the reinforcements.

The bush quivered and six significantly bulky masses prowled out of the cover the bush gave them.

"Some kind of quadruped. Get ready!" I called out, squatting to drop the wagon's harness and hefting my shield. *<Earth Shell>*. My armor crawled down my body, focusing first on my limbs as the stone flowed out of my skin and hardened. A huge ripple marked the pounce. "Incoming! <Earth Wall>!"

Half my mana was gone in one fell swoop as a wall twice as tall as me rose out of the ground. With it being a freestanding wall, its abilities to counter lateral forces left something to be desired. A moment later, it toppled, but the momentum of the charge was arrested and our enemies revealed.

A family of cats, two the size of Sam's first tank and four that easily reached up to my chest were yowling and snarling as they gathered themselves from the dust. Wildly colorful waves patterned their fur, like a kaleidoscopic rainbow that almost left me with a headache just from looking at them. Their information bloomed at the edge of my vision even as Ava started lighting them up with gunfire.

<Bioluminescent Panther>
<Attunement: Life>
<Refinement: Brilliance>
<Perceived Metier Quotient: 4>

<Bioluminescent Panther>
<Attunement: Life>
<Refinement: N/A>
<Perceived Metier Quotient: 3>

A simmering cloud of caustic gas formed between us and the panthers with perfect timing. Their namesakes came into play as a halo of light managed to penetrate the fire-augmented skill Clara used. Like sitting too close to a fire, I felt the portions of my skin not covered by armor flinch at the sudden burn. The effect was muted by the caustic cloud and then muted once again by my Limestone Skin. The others did not have the same advantage.

Clara in particular was doubled over as the light burned out her eyes, forcing her to her knees as I watched smoke curl from her gray skin. Ava and Dylan were forced to duck over the side of the wagon in an attempt to cover themselves. Sam was shaken, but at least he didn't seem as affected by the light-based attack.

"Hold them still, Sam!" I called out, taking a deep breath as I plunged through the caustic cloud shield first. Wisps of the skill clung to me, leaving my skin sizzling more than the light, but I had a target and our number equality was taken right from the start.

<Mineral Strike>.

The skill formed in the palm of my right hand just as I body-checked one of the Q4 panthers. Standing inches from the creature felt like looking at the surface of the sun. Thankfully, I didn't need my eyeballs to release my skill. The crystal shard flew up over my head like a laid-up basketball. A few seconds later, the shard exploded and fragged the whole family of predators. Their fluorescent light dimmed as patches of their fur were covered in bloody gashes, but the beasts were much too large to be taken out by just that attack.

The panther I'd tackled growled and tried to take a bite out of the top of my tower shield. Feeling particularly clever, I used my free, rock-encased fist to punch it in the nose ever-so-roughly. Instantly, the panther released its hold on my shield, caterwauling as it tried to scamper away. Its body was outlined perfectly by vibro and I made it pay for its withdrawal. <Stone Spike>.

The skill manifested at half power right in the path of the large cat. Being a feline augmented by its Quotient, it almost managed to dodge, but not before carving a large wound across its ribs. I even spotted bone throughout the injury, so I knew that cat would take a moment to rejoin the others.

As I focused on the other beasts, I could see they were

attempting to come to their companion's aid. Unfortunately, they were contending with the fact that the forest had come alive around them. One of the nearby trees acted like a verdant octopus as it gripped the other Q4 panther, blocking the light and preventing it from mauling the rest of the group. A veritable carpet of vines rose out of the ground to grasp the ankles of the four lower Quotient creatures. I couldn't help a grin from splitting my face as I watched Samuel completely dominate in the crowd control department.

"<Simmering Infection Wasps>!" Clara yelled, her staff flaring with a roiling maroon light.

Zipping blurs of that same maroon light rocketed through the air away from the staff, finger thin trails the only way of marking their passage. The blurs acted like seeking missiles as they curved through the air, dodging the living carpet Samuel controlled, until they collided with the hides of the panthers all around me. The individual impact of the attack was somewhat lackluster, but I watched as the pelts of the creatures grew angry orange, glowing blisters. Their defiant growls quickly turn into miserable whimpers as they tried to disengage.

Unfortunately for me, my attention had drifted too much when I saw our overwhelming opening. The injured Q4 panther pounced, leveraging its car-sized bulk to press me to the ground. I felt my <Earth Shell> protest the pressure, cracks lighting up in vibrosense like warning signals of the crushing weight.

Crossed <Stone Spike>!

The thought brought my skill to the fore. With a franticness I hadn't felt since the fight with Galloway, I slammed my mental hand on the trigger for the offensive skill. It was a simple application of my reduction control of the skill, but thanks to my Quotient, even a quarter-powered <Stone Spike> was bigger than the first time I'd cast the skill at full power.

I dipped down, panther paw trailing and raking a jagged series of lines on my armor with its claws, as the earth on either side of me was pinched by my spell chain. I'd never been at eye level with the strange glyphs as they flared into crisp detail, but their stark complexity had an inherent beauty that struck me for that moment. Unfortunately, that was all the time I had. When the spell chain triggered, two <Stone Spikes> stabbed into the panther's chest. The compressed earth struggled for a second against the weight of the creature, but stone was stronger than flesh and the panther was hoisted six inches off my chest.

A faucet's worth of blood showered me as one of the spikes nicked something important. The caterwauling from the creature set my ears ringing, and I even noticed as the creature's last gasp vibrated through my spikes, sending ripples notable for my vibrosense. If I hadn't been training with the sense, the sheer force of the creature dying would have left me dry heaving and disoriented.

To make doubly sure the creature was dealt with, I cast a tenth-powered <Stone Spike> with the last of my mana. The X of spikes grew an extra spoke, pushing up into the panther's throat and into its mouth.

CHAPTER EIGHT

Dreg but No Pith

As the panther above me sagged completely, bled and battered by my skills, I struggled to extract myself from beneath it. Just because it didn't crush me didn't mean that the rest of my body wasn't pinned by its bulk. In the end, I spent the precious last five percent of my mana channeling into my tower shield. With the attribute boost, I was able to squirm out from under the creature and survey the battle. While I was out of mana, that was hardly going to stop me from taking a blow meant for my friends.

My concerns were unnecessary. As I watched, one of the Q3 panthers got a broadside of gunfire. With the target more or less static thanks to Sam's vines, Ava put the creature down efficiently. Clara was locked in a closed-eye staring contest with the Q4 panther while strange black wisps curled around her eyes. Dylan took that opening to dart in with his sword, leaving the large panther fileted and partly frosted over as he triggered the trait of his sword.

The last three panthers probably received the most brutal part of the fight. Blobby had one of the Q3 panthers sunk entirely in its body; the slime twisted its cores around its bulk to dodge the cat's weakening attacks as it suffocated. The other two got a face full of Latina. Daniela crashed out of the treetop like a meteor. <Heat Touch> and the Desiccating Haze trait of her fang daggers shone in the few moments she *wasn't* eviscerating the lower Quotient creatures.

Within three more breaths, the fight was over.

Daniela panted, steam curling out of the fire gills on her neck like a bellowing engine as she regarded the blood that coated her. She didn't seem bothered, more like inconvenienced. The others were more or less the same. I called up my status for the sake of confirming something.

Subject: Ronan Terrigan
Health: 87% (Caustic Fog / Radiation Burn)
Mana: 3%
Metier Quotient: 6 (18.75%)
Dreg Accumulation: 0%
LPS: Wildwood Bunker, FL
Communications
Party
Skills - *(2) Selections Available*
Traits - *(0% Banked)*
Attributes

I am... tapped on mana, but pretty much whole.

The two afflictions, <Caustic Fog> and <Radiation Burn>, were obviously from Clara's skill and the panther's attack. As I watched, a percent of my health ticked down and both afflictions cleared. Other than that, however, the damage I'd taken was almost negligible. On a strange level, I could feel that the damage, that missing fourteen percent, was related to the extent my skin was damaged. The light had gone through everything but my stone armor, leaving what I could only describe as a serious sunburn on a lot of my body. That was even after being exposed to it more directly than all the others.

Traits make an astounding difference. Not only that, but Quotients...

How much would I have been squashed flat at Q3 or even Q4, shield or not? I couldn't shake the image of Galloway playing around with us. It took constant healing from Ophelia for me and Devon doing his 'leaf in the wind' routine to even be able to maneuver around the outnumbered Appendage; we weren't even able to force him to budge unless we committed our full power. The memory threw some cold water on the sense of strength our overwhelming victory had given me, but it still put the path forward into perspective. *I need to figure out how to progress.*

"*Ugh!*" The groan snapped me out of my reverie. I turned from the dead panthers, dismissing my status, and watched as Samuel used his <Health Bump> on Clara. The demoness had been propped against the wagon at some point during my daydreaming, and my friend was tending to her wounds. Ava and Dylan also looked a shade tanner, but the death-attuned woman looked the worst for wear.

"Is she alright?" I asked, walking closer.

"I'm not worried about her skin, but that stuff seems to have burned at her eyes," Sam said, brow creased in concentration. His hands held Clara's temples gingerly as golden green energy unspooled from Samuel's hands. "Clara, can you open your eyes for me?"

The demoness flinched, but eventually complied. The gray-tinged sclera of her demon eyes was bloodshot and her pupil was nothing more than a pinprick as our whole group leaned forward to look at her.

"I can see a bunch of rubberneckers," the demoness said, blinking her eyes shut. "But stuff is a little blurry and it hurts to keep them open."

"I'll give you another bump and then we'll load you on the wagon. Try to keep them closed. When we get to Lake Weir, I'll heal you again and hopefully that will help," Sam said, matching words to actions as he channeled more healing magic right into her face. She visibly relaxed as I watched the burns, visible even on her dark skin as sporadic blisters, scabbed and healed better than with the freshest of Alexia's medicinal balms down in the Bunker. "Who's still injured?"

Sam stood and swayed, but I gripped his arm to keep him steady. I didn't know the specific costs of his skills, but it didn't take that information to know that using his augmented <Vine Grasp> on the Q4 and the other panthers had sapped him. He'd then selfishly followed up with healing for the others and Clara. Truly a man only out for himself…

"Let's give you a rest, huh? Let your mana come back and we'll get patched up after. I don't think anyone else is in danger," I said, gesturing to the others. There were nods all around, Danny even going so far as to pick him up and carry him onto the wagon. "I'll dissociate the panthers. Can you keep an eye out, Danny?"

"<Flame Wisp>," she whispered. Her orb of flying fire rose up over us, casting shadows out of the trees but illuminating anything close. "Hurry up, Ron."

I gave her a nod and shuffled out toward the bodies. It had been a few minutes and the bodies were certainly free to loot. There always seemed to be a variable time between killing the creatures and being able to dissociate them. The Entities weren't clear on that, and Alan was still working on it, so it just became a known fact for those that ventured toward the spider dungeon and fought in the post-Fall wilderness in general.

Nudging each of the bodies without activating my miscellaneous <Pith Mana Lock> initiated the crystallization dissociation earth-attuned triggered. As I made my way back around to the panther I'd killed, strung up on my <Stone Spikes>, I thought about those few days before we found and dragged Bec to the Bunker. It was entirely possible one of these creatures had been the ones I'd warded off one of those nights. With it slowly turning into smoky quartz, the whole thing felt like it was coming full circle.

As the Pith gathered above it, and the other bodies, it coalesced into a glittering cloud of energy. Six tendrils of energy extended out from the cloud to rush toward our party.

Unlike usual, the energy that entered my body left only the stomach-coiling aftereffects of my mana. The sensation was so sharp and sudden that I actually dropped to a knee. Another strangled cry sounded behind me and vibrosense told me someone had dropped to the ground hard. My insides felt like they were twisting into knots, but I managed to turn around enough to see Daniela twitching on the ground.

"Danny!" Ava cried, rushing forward with Sam on her tail. Dylan actually moved up to me, trying to help me to my feet, but struggling with my trait-enhanced body. Having slurry for blood, stone as part of your skin and probably your bones tended to up your number on the scale.

"I-I'm fine," I got out through my teeth. "These are mana side effects."

"Why are you fine?"the councilman asked, eyes widening as he looked between me and Daniela who was slowly settling down.

"Unfortunate instances of practice," I said, forcing myself to take deep breaths to clear the waves of nausea that followed the pain. It wasn't anywhere on the scale of the death-attuned, but having your insides twist didn't do wonders for the contents of your stomach. "Is everyone else okay?"

Dylan looked to himself, Ava, Clara, and Sam. They almost looked *better* than before the Pith cloud had been dispersed. "Just fine. A bit jittery, but that comes with the magic stuff."

"It must have something to do with your Quotient," Sam said, still a tad unsteady, but he was checking Daniela. His hand was pressed to her forehead until she smacked it away.

"You think? I'm burning up. Get me up so I can breathe properly!" Danny said, hoisting herself up. Just like me, she took a deep breath, except her gills flared as she did. The exhale was a cloud of steam out of her nose and gills. Immediately, her posture straightened and her weakness vanished. Ava fussed over her nonetheless.

As Dylan helped me back to the group, I called up my status again.

Subject: Ronan Terrigan
Health: 91% (Unafflicted)
Mana: 47%
Metier Quotient: 6 (18.75%)
Dreg Accumulation: 2%
LPS: Wildwood Bunker, FL
Communications
Party
Skills - *(2) Selections Available*
Traits - *(0% Banked)*
Attributes

My health and mana had ticked up, which wasn't surprising, but my Quotient progress was exactly the same. The Dreg accumulation, on the other hand...

"We only got Dreg from those kills," I whispered.

"Same here," Daniela said, her eyes unfocusing as she stared at her implant prompts.

"This is highly concerning," Ava said. "Neither of you have dissociated anything until now?"

"I have been working with the afflicted and building," I replied.

"You've been having me run the trainees. I punched a spider once, but I didn't get any Pith for that," Danny said.

"I think we need to go see this Entity as soon as possible," Dylan said. He turned to me. "There are a dozen people on the cusp of Q6 in the town. If they breach the line while we are gone without knowing the dangers..."

"Blobby!" I called out into the woods. The large form of my slime companion slid into view. He was slower than before, but the partially digested panther within him was the likely answer for that. "Gather what dropped from the cats. We're going to pick up the pace."

I didn't wait to see if the slime followed the directions. I'd long accepted that, for whatever reason, the slime was intelligent enough to understand what was going on in its surroundings. The creature hadn't betrayed us and it had saved me more than once. It had earned its autonomy.

Daniela eyed me when I walked by. Some of the frustration she'd been holding toward me was there, but there was a shade of concern visible on her face too. "Can you walk?"

"I'm alright," she said. "I think I'll hold on scouting for a minute."

"Stay with the wagon. I'll use the shield to get us to Stonecrest. We'll take a break there. If anything even looks at us wrong, roast it," I said, meeting her eyes.

"With pleasure."

Clara and Sam loaded up onto the wagon, while Ava and the councilman walked to our flanks. Daniela took up the rear while Blobby slinked in the shadows. Probably. With a deep breath, I slipped into the harness and channeled mana into the shield. Four Quotient's worth of strength flowed into my body and I took off down the road at double our previous pace.

— + —

"Hail!"one of the guards at Stonecrest called out. Their car wall was barely visible, but the man easily recognized us. He ducked out of view while we pulled up on the wagon.

"You lot are early!" Rachael the dwarf shuffled through the zig zag entrance into her town before approaching our group. I was sweating like it was going out of style, but the others looked none the worse for wear. Sam had improved quickly and dismounted the wagon, but he'd forced Clara to remain. At a light jog, we'd arrived before midday at the allied town.

"Some slight complications," Dylan explained. The councilman, regularly interrupted by a cranky Daniela, explained the information our group had encountered. Rachael locked even more sour than usual as she asked the guard that had greeted us to get Angel, her second, and a woman named Jasmine.

"Angel and I just broke Q5, but Jasmine, our chief healer, is much closer to Quotient 6. I'll have this passed along and I'll have her come with me. I was going to run solo, but if there is a chance we learn more about this Dreg and Pith situation then I want her there," Rachael said firmly. None of us had anything against it and before long Jasmine the Satyr and Angel arrived. She gave them the breakdown, making sure to tell Angel to have the hunters focus on getting to Q5 and no further until she returned with news. The usually cheery man looked grim as he returned, pulling the guard along.

"No pack animal?" Rachel asked, raising an eyebrow.

"You are looking at it," I said. "The benefits of the one with the highest strength in the group, plus a shield that gives him more."

"Good to see those muscles being used for something," Rachael huffed, walking past me as I slipped the harness back on.

"Hey!"

"I think I'm going to like this new travel companion of ours," Daniela said, smirking as she sauntered over to Rachael to continue making fun of me. I let out a quiet groan as I channeled my mana to get the wagon moving. *At least Clara is nicer to me, and she's the one I have to carry.*

"Don't mind her too much," Jasmine said as she matched pace with the wagon. "She only pokes people she respects. I think your little Gift Wrestle and everything after that really put you in perspective for her."

"Seems there are a lot of shifts of mentality going around," I said between pants. The wagon pull had started easy, but it definitely took a toll on me. Thankfully, the stretch to Lake Weir was much shorter.

"Yes. Perhaps that is for the best," Jasmine said, her ears perking up as she gave me a soft smile. The harness bloomed with flowers which let out a soft lavender smell. My soreness immediately abated as some healing skill or Gift pulsed through my body. I thanked the woman for her help, but she just returned a smile before moving to the front of the group to speak with Samuel.

Left with my own thoughts, I returned to my practice with vibrosense. Its usefulness at stemming an ambush proved just how useful the trait and my perception were when I wasn't overwhelmed. It had been a close thing during the fight with the panthers, so I didn't let my effort flag. Unfortunately, just as I was entering that meditative trance with vibrosense, the ripple profile of Lake Weir came into view.

It was strange to 'see' a place with vibrations. There was a level of depth my eyes couldn't pick up, but vibrosense filled in the gaps with glee. Metal-studded, mana-formed stone rose ten feet up in a smooth curve around the town. The walls were practically humming with the mana incorporated into them. Trailing like spokes on a wheel were the covered pathways the people in town had built to protect against the bile bombings of the crows. With that particular threat gone, I could feel the signature of living vegetation growing on those same pathways.

As a very excited guard, who was flanked by one of the Wild Guard squads assigned to help the Weirdians, opened a stone gate, the rise from the muck the town had experienced truly showed.

Coming to the surface had always been something of a fantasy for us Bunkerborn. We'd often joked about how the world would have infinite marvels to explore or ancient cities to discover. Walking back into Lake Weir proved to be the first such situation that left me speechless. And I wasn't the only one.

The Lake Weirdians had turned their misfortune into a blessing somehow; their entire town was transformed into a hanging garden of magical proportions. The vegetation I'd sensed on top of the walkways was just the beginning. Chest high planters were draped with vines and colorful flowers while rows upon rows of vegetables lined the spaces between the walkway. Thick brambles with grapes hung heavy from the roof, and strawberries as big as my fist drooped under their own weight as teams of Weirdians harvested them by the basketfuls.

Even the cleared training area where I could see people

working on their Gifts and skills looked more like a tropical jungle than an actual field.

"Seems our verdant developments have caught you off guard," Ian said, materializing in front of our collective group. I almost jumped out of my boots. The man's approach had been deathly silent; I wasn't sure if that was a factor of me being distracted or the man's skeletal feet trait.

"What happened?" Samuel managed, walking forward and running his hands through a nearby bush that looked just shy of emerald green. "There is so much life to pull from here…"

"I believe that will be the soil finally coming to terms with the garbage those birds threw our way," Ian said, gesturing around them. "Our farmers have found much success growing stuff now that the acid has leveled out. With some magical elbow grease, of course."

"Aren't you worried about what's in the soil?" Ava asked, grasping at a nearby berry.

"Our strongest healers ate them to test it. The only anomaly we were able to find was that the plants grown in the disposal ponds are actually attuned to death. Everything else grows magnitudes higher," Ian explained. "It's how we were able to meet Samuel's demands for these strawberries. Why did you want so many, son?"

"Let me run some tests and then I'll tell you if it pans out," the blond replied from where he was running his hands through the soil and gently caressing one of the hanging plants. He added in a whisper, "These grapes might work even better."

Instead of trying to pull him from his concentration, I drew the group back to the original point of our visit. Ian told us that Maurice would be their representative. His son was out with a hunting group, trying to eke up his Quotient, and was meant to turn back after midday. Our group settled into one of the nearby storage rooms, resting from the tense trip over. Ava and Dylan spent some time explaining the information on Q6 we'd encountered, Sam was neck deep in a bush, Blobby was nowhere in sight, and the other girls were off speaking with each other.

As I contemplated what an odd gathering of people we had arranged, I couldn't help but chuckle. It wasn't too long ago that I only knew less than three dozen people. That number had now ballooned. Despite all the pain and struggle of the surface, I couldn't imagine anything else for myself. The memory of my time wallowing soured further, but I tried not to beat myself up too much. Everyone had to process things differently, it was just a matter of not letting the past control the future.

The determination I'd gripped while talking with Arnold firmed. The meeting with Gec worried me, but it was just another hurdle. Humanity would rally around hope, and I planned to carry that as far as my body let me.

CHAPTER NINE

The Not-So-Dead Territory

In short order, Maurice reentered implant range. The thorn-haired human hustled back and the group finished passing the goods on to the Weirdians. Ian and his son parted, and before long, I was straining under the mental weight of a nine-person party. We considered minimizing and splitting the parties, but after the last trip to the death territory, I wasn't ready to leave anyone exposed. So, with a mild persistent headache, we plunged into the wilds.

Freed from the strain of the wagon and no longer stuck with traveling AE-1, we cut a straight line toward the death territory.

While the oldest members of our group shouldn't have been able to keep pace, the gains from growing Quotients let them stay on pace. Dylan and Ava refused to hold the group back, and I watched as their own advantages, in the form of curious traits, made themselves known. Dylan's steps seemed to take him just an inch further as a cushion of flame caught his feet, flame hair receding with each step taken that way. As far as Ava, she took deep breaths that caused her weight to vanish as she stepped lightly over gnarled roots and under low branches.

As for the youngest non-Fallen, Maurice, he used his vine

hair like a very strange system of grapples. It didn't speed him up, but it gave him a frightening amount of mobility as he navigated the woods. He even swung himself on occasion to clear an obstacle entirely.

The rest of our group used a different variety of means to enhance our speed. Unfortunately for me, I was locked into making huge tower-shield-powered lunges while everyone else had a tad more finesse. Simplest was Sam with his <Adrenal Surge>, but the others weren't to be outdone. The person I'd expected to be the slowest due to her stature had pulled out an unforgivably awesome Gift.

"Soil Surfing!" I panted from my position firmly in the middle of the party.

"Some of us have spent the proper amount of time Gift Wrestling to acquire better control over our abilities. You have only yourself to blame for your bullish way of traveling," Rachael said as she bent her knees, causing the soil beneath her to heave just enough to pull her stone surfboard over a thick root.

"Just you wait until we get to the plains," Jasmine gasped, using something similar to <Adrenal Surge> to boost her stamina to keep up with the rest of the group.

Daniela just cackled from the front of the party as she used flame bursts from her legs to propel her from branch to branch. It didn't take a genius to notice she was purposely being loud and boisterous with her speed advantage. What others might not have read was the tightness at the corner of her smirk and the heaviness of her steps whenever she was forced to move on the ground. The strain of not being there for the ambush that hurt Clara, now lagging at the back with Sam, lingered on her. She longed for the true speed scouting let her have, but she wouldn't risk it with the group so close to their goal.

The rest of the trip went by smoothly. Due to the speed of travel, the level of detail I received from my vibrosense was nowhere near what I'd been able to process while pulling the wagon. Nevertheless, I was able to work a little on fine-tuning the broadstroke aspects of sensing the ripples of vibration around me. It was how I was able to detect the handful of creatures that circumvented our group entirely as we got closer. The only evidence of their presence was the unnatural rustle of a bush or the trailing waves of something moving away quickly.

By the time we arrived at the water-attuned cypress we'd used before charging the Aberrant, many changes could already be seen in the area. The vegetation, for one, had undergone a ridiculous amount of growth; it wasn't dissimilar to what we'd seen from Lake Weir, except there were no magic users to tend to the area. *Or were there?* More wary than ever, we crept to the edge of the death territory.

"Guess we're going to have to change the name," Daniela said, letting out a long whistle.

Lake Weir and the region approaching the death territory had only been a precursor. What had once been a gray, black, and beige marsh was now a localized tropical rainforest. Trees poked high into the sky with trunks easily as wide as me at the shoulders. A gentle buzz tickled my vibrosense and I knew that there had also been an explosion of smaller wildlife within the strange self-contained biome. The group hesitated as we contemplated the thick vegetation and undergrowth that laid between us and the entrance to the cave where we'd found Gec.

"Any ideas?" Rachael asked, crossing her arms.

"Plow through. The cave is marked on the map. Trying to do anything fancy will just delay us further," I said, gesturing at the small space between the old treeline and the new. There were only a meager number of signs that there had ever been a marsh in front of us, but the trio of flooded, bushy islands between our group and the towering trees were proof enough.

Before we headed forward, I stomped my foot onto the ground as hard as I could manage. Ripples tore out from it and into the muddy water, instantly slowing down like molasses. Another two stomps later and I was able to piece together a modest profile of the marsh between us and the trees. There were two gators lurking out of sight in the water.

"Point them out, Vanguard," Rachael said, cracking her fingers.

Unsure of what she planned to do, I gestured to the spot on the left where the beasts were lurking. Rachael took a deep breath, inhaling more air than I thought she had lungs for before starting to weave together the burnt umber light that was earth-attuned mana.

Her hands drew sharp lines in the air before she punched her hand forward at each corner. When there was a hovering spell chain unlike any I'd ever seen, she released the Gift. The light sunk into the ground and the earth *roiled*. A moment later, the two crocs were thrown up in the air along with their muddy surroundings before they hardened into stone. It immediately started to crack as the reptiles growled their displeasure and tried to engage their patterned death-enhanced death roll as a means of freeing themselves. Their heads twisted left and right as purple energy curled out of their scales.

"I'm not making art here!" Rachael yelled. "Hit them!"

Bullets, crystal fragments, fireballs, and a caustic cloud fell upon the two gators, putting them out of the fight within seconds. I almost felt bad for the creatures until I remembered how one nearly took one of my legs on our flight through the original territory. With the combat out of the way, and the creatures Pith Locked for the sake of Daniela and I, we picked our way into the ex-death territory.

Somehow, either through raising the soil level or some other magic shenanigans, the rainforest had solid ground. A light layer of dead brush lined the forest floor, but our steps were sure. I had my vibrosense running on full blast and my eyes locked on the treetops almost ten feet above me. With as many perceptions above the human average as our group had, I would not have liked to fight the thing that managed to sneak up on us.

Other than the occasional rustle and swaying tree, nothing happened on the walk. The trip felt both longer and shorter than the last time I'd walked into the territory; I figured it was a factor of the level of adrenaline in me. Before long, we arrived at the yawning maw that led to Gec. Our group hesitated, sharing several uncertain looks, until *Blobby*, of all things, rolled forward out of nowhere. *I seriously hope there aren't more slimes as stealth capable as this one…*

With the ice broken, we all followed after the green slime.

As we moved deeper underground, my vibrosense started going haywire. Deafening ripples forced me to shut the sense down and rely on a fire spell chain Daniela formed to guide us. There was an astounding concentration of magic in the rock around us that simply wasn't there the first time we'd gone down it. The structure of a cave near the surface of a marsh was odd enough, but that was easily explained with magic. It felt like the very magic that had shaped the cave entrance was now back in play. Its objective was still unclear.

Before too long, we encountered a curious issue. A strange, bubble-like membrane had arrested Blobby in his tracks. The rest of the group went forward and prodded it like true scientists while I rubbed my brow in consternation. I finally had to say something when I saw Daniela ready to poke at the membrane with her dagger.

"What are you doing? You don't even know what that is!" I said, gesturing at the membrane.

"Well, do you?" she countered.

"You know that I don't, but *stabbing* it is not the answer!"

"It's served me well 'til now. How about—"

"ENTER." Daniela's words were drowned out as a voice loud enough to shake the ground around us spoke. The others looked momentarily stunned, but I was fighting for consciousness. Like the worst raving strobe light I'd ever seen, vibrosense flared with an intensity I'd never encountered. It actually took Samuel shaking me to bring me back into the moment.

"Ronan? Are you okay?" the blond asked, concern etched on his face.

"I-I'm fine. The voice and my senses… they don't much like each other," I said, blinking as I tried to focus my mind solely on sight. If the voice, who I was almost completely certain came from Gec, spoke again, I didn't want to be blindsided.

"Should I stab it then? I'm not a fan of being given commands," Daniela said, dagger once again poised to strike.

"Darling, we all know that," Ava said evenly, getting a pout from her daughter. "Perhaps it would do you well to remember that the Entities get *louder* the bigger they get? If Gec is larger still than Tec and Wec, then it isn't hard to imagine that was just its… inside voice."

Not willing to risk the Entity giving vocalization another shot, I strode forward and pressed my hand against the membrane. It was almost like a soft plastic and it had some give as I pushed. However, when I kept pushing, I felt the *give* continue instead of 'popping' the membrane. Straining against some invisible wall of magic gelatin, I pushed my way through the membrane. Just in case, I held my breath as my head went through the barrier.

Little good that did, because the moment I was through, my jaw dropped and my breath trickled out of me.

If the Blessing of Magic field that Tec, and now Wec, generated was filled with wisps of the different elements in the atmosphere, then this was a nebulous cloud. Like a drunk rainbow, colors swirled through the air, casting shadows that then themselves came alive with purple light before swirling into gold and green. Red coiled around blue, spawning gray that tumbled through brown before it intermingled with the purple-black and green-gold.

Identifying the corresponding Attunements didn't take a genius, but as I stood stock-still in the presence of the magic in the air, I could hardly tear my eyes away. There was something… primal and fundamental about the way the cloud moved. As one of the coiling rainbows approached, I traced it all the way until it hit my body and it percolated through my limbs and body. My eyes widened as I watched all but the brown mana in the air exit as it passed through my arm.

"I'm glad we didn't bring Alan," Ava whispered as she stood

next to me. The woman was equally as shocked as I was, but she had at least been able to verbalize her thoughts. The rest of the group—sans Blobby, who seemed stuck on the other side of the membrane—was in various degrees of mute astonishment.

"APPROACH."

The voice reverberated through the air. Thankfully I had prepared, and the voice only elicited a light headache. Most interesting was the effect on the nebula of mana around us as it quivered for a moment before it resumed its chaotic swirling. *Gec's voice even affects the mana around us. That's not intimidating at all...*

We all shared a look before I took the lead to head deeper. The cavern where we'd purged the Aberrant and killed Galloway appeared after only another minute of walking. None of the grooves, scorch marks, or even the <Earth Walls> I'd conjured remained in the room. Instead, there was a smooth walkway flanked by pools of water that had a strange inherent glow. The iridescent light of the back wall, however, still stole the show. Just the visible segment of Gec matched Wec in size, and the crystal pushed smoothly into the ground above *and* below.

As the Entities had the tendency to do, the moment we were all in range, crystal limbs extended out to reel us into the main crystal body. The difference between Gec and Tec, however, was that Wildwood's Entity Cluster didn't radiate a physical wave of energy that left my hairs standing on end. My instincts screamed at me to run even as I was hoisted into the air and I found myself being pulled into a *very* crystalline surface. The world went black for a second before the whitespace came into focus.

It took a few seconds for me to get my heartrate under control, but I quickly noticed that there were three notable things about the whitespace. The first was the presence of Bec, Tec, and Wec hovering in the air in their geometric glowing forms. The second was the physical table with a perfect number of chairs for the party. The last was the distinct absence of Gec.

"Uhh, where is Gec? Didn't it call us all the way here to talk to us?" I asked, turning to look at the Entities.

—The Higher Entity has informed us that it will not manifest itself until an accord of future cooperation has been struck between those within its domain,— Tec provided, flatly.

"Can I get a translation on that?" I asked, tilting my head to look at Bec's sphere.

<Gec says that it won't come out to talk until you guys hash out the details of how you will work together in the future. As you are affiliated with us, and it is the higher Category Entity in this region, we are in its domain.> The Entity didn't sigh, but I could practically hear it concealed in its voice.

"Oh, this has started on the best of feet," Daniela complained, huffing and plopping onto one of the chairs at the rounded wood table projected into the whitespace.

---We do not have feet--- Wec countered.

<That's not… You know what? Never mind. Please, representatives of Attuned Earth, take a seat. The parameters of cooperation outlined by our Authority are… exhaustive.>

CHAPTER TEN

The Allied Wild Towns

It turned out that when the Entities said that Gec wanted us to outline our cooperation, it meant *thoroughly*. It was a good thing that each location had sent a representative to the meeting with some level of pull in the structure of their respective towns, because that was what the meeting aimed to solidify. Bec explained that Gec did not want to interact with isolated neighboring groups but one proper, holistic front. It had perceived the potential after the extensive cooperation in the struggle against the Dreg, and the call for this meeting was some kind of 'official' summons to make sure everyone was on board.

Thankfully, everyone present understood that messing with the Entities was a nonstarter. Even if they disagreed with the heavy-handed and pseudo false pretenses they'd been given to gather to Gec, the cooperation of the strongest Entity they'd encountered wasn't something they could just brush off.

The initial points of the meeting went by fairly easily as they related to the sanctity of life and the overall goals the allied front Gec would interact with would adhere to. Chief amongst those things was that the Entity Clusters were not things of inherent evil, even if they cooperated with beasts to form what

I'd colloquially called the dungeons. The higher purpose of the Entities, eradicating Dreg, would be the ruling metric for how the Entities would act should there be a conflict with humanity. None of the representatives were happy about that point, especially when they brought up the fact that the dungeons had claimed lives before, but none of the Entities were able to provide a concession. Even Bec agreed that the dungeons were free of their intervention so long as they didn't turn to the path of the Dreg. It didn't help that none of the three Entities were sure *what* that represented or how they would know ahead of time; they all deferred to Gec on those points, causing the frustration in the group of humans to climb even higher.

That last point confused the whole group, and Bec was forced to translate for Tec as the Entity tried to explain how fighting the Dreg and Aberrant could cause conflicts of interest in the humans. It was something I'd never considered, and hoped never to experience. The fact that there were conscious humans under the thumb of the Dreg was a scary enough thought; having someone complacent to their efforts just made things much worse. My mind had drifted to Galloway, and the other handful of Tendrils that had been capable of communication. There was more at play with the Dreg than we knew, and I couldn't help but feel helpless.

Despite all the power I'd gained, it was clear I was just a fool with a hammer trying to lead humanity through a series of ever-growing doorways that required finesse more than my set of skills. I'd even let myself become withdrawn the first time I'd experienced loss and a grander responsibility. I'd let the guilt swallow me, yet the world still turned; that world was now much bigger with no plans on stopping its growth.

"I have a proposition for the future of our cooperation," Ava said, cutting off yet another argument between Dylan and Rachael that Clara struggled to mediate.

"Do enlighten us," Maurice said, leaning back in his chair and rubbing his temples.

The man had expressed the desire to swap out with his

father on multiple occasions, but the Entities had told them that Gec had considered their choices 'locked' as far as who represented who. Lake Weir, for better or worse, was in Maurice's hands. Thankfully, the man wasn't inept, just more of a meathead than a politician. This had, of course, led to conflict with Dylan's perceptions, but they'd made it work over the last few hours.

"I would like to propose turning our Bunker into a sort of boarding school for the children in our towns," Ava said, evenly. Protests were already rising out of Dylan and Rachael, but Ava was used to dealing with hard-headed children, and now the trainees, so she plowed forward. "The facilities we have there have kept our people whole for almost three decades without the benefits they are receiving now. Beyond that, other than a handful of potential fighters, the population of our Bunker are all decidedly non-combatants. Doctors, engineers, researchers, mechanics.

"We taught Daniela, Samuel, and Ronan all they know about the world today, including the one that came before. There are lessons to be had, if only we listen to the preserved knowledge of humanity. We must think not about us or the now, but to my child's children. Or yours." Ava's words elicited a furious blush from Danny, but the other members of the group had thoughtful expressions. No one mentioned how they had had quickfire arguments prepared.

"How would this help solidify our cooperation?" Rachael asked. Her hand waved lazily in the direction of me and my friends. "Those three have already done more than anyone that came before."

"I don't disagree, but the children are not the only thing to come from the Bunker. Neither should they be held to such standards. And yes, Daniela, I know you are not children," Ava said, cutting off her daughter's argument before she could even voice it. "My point is that, if not this, teaching and passing on our knowledge, what was the purpose of our survival? Three people can't run a world all by themselves, and if I know

Ronan, he plans to follow through on his high-minded idea to secure the world."

It was my turn to blush since I could hardly argue her point; she'd nailed the goal I'd come to after talking with Arnold.

"If your Bunker becomes so specialized, then where does that leave us?" Maurice asked. "Lake Weir doesn't have the construction skill of Stonecrest, nor the combat force of Wildwood."

"You all do seem to possess quite the green thumb," Sam said, joining the conversation.

"To my understanding, that was mostly happenstance," Maurice countered.

"Make it *not*," Sam said. "From the experiments I've run on the trip here, the strawberries should work wonders on my project. Leverage your current advantage and entrench yourself into becoming the breadbasket of our area."

"That...Hmmm. We do have a fairly versatile workforce. That leaves a problem. If we commit to doubling down on growing, how will we manage the gator threat? Those reptiles are a constant concern and until we were able to proficiently use the passive spell chains like you showed us, we relied heavily on our namesake for food."

"How bad of a threat can they be?" I asked, turning to Dylan. "You mentioned there were a number of attuned crocs in Lake Sumter before you built the car-wall, right?"

"We killed perhaps three dozen of them over the early years, and maybe a handful in the years since," the councilman said.

"What?" Maurice said, actually jumping to his feet. "We killed that many just this year and we are barely halfway through! They are constantly raiding our wall with their dumb water cannons, ice rain, and mud shots. They probably only stayed away the last few months because of the death crows, but there have already been six sightings by our fishermen since the battle."

"Could the creatures have shortened their reproductive

cycle somehow? Traits and Quotients might have made that easy," Daniela pointed out. "An ant we fought practically threw its children at us."

"There is a simpler explanation," Clara said. Everyone turned to the demoness. She'd been quiet other than mediating, so everyone was eager to hear. "There is a gator dungeon in Lake Weir. One of those Entity-enhanced creatures is either spawning a torrential amount of the reptiles or guiding them to stationary prey in the form of the town."

My eyes widened at the implication, but it made sense. There was a lot of energy in the Metier Crystals, and if the wildlife was able to use even a fraction of it, then empowering their spawn or themselves wasn't out of the question. The spider territory and its elites seemed to have an arrangement of that sort. A visual of a swarm of alligators the size of the ant swarms we'd seen sent a shiver down my spine.

The discussion actually picked up steam from there. A new, shared threat was all the group needed to put aside their need for certain concessions before committing. Maurice still antici-pated some issues with turning Lake Weir into a food exporter, but when Sam pledged to spend some time working his skills in the fields, the thorn-haired man had practically pounced at the idea. Several hours later, after a break to wolf down a packed meal, talk had actually receded almost to zero.

"To recap," I started. "The Wild Guard, and the town of Wildwood as a whole, will focus on stopgap measures for the region. This includes crafting, food, and defense. However, their future focus will be in honing the Warriors that will ensure the safety of our people within and without the towns.

"The Bunker Institute will be established as a place where the children of elementary school age and higher will be able to gain a proper education in conjunction with some basic training on their Gifts. Graduation will line up with the acquisition of their own implant, subject to the Entities and their access to power. Specific schedule will be pending coordination with the other members of the Bunker, but the towns will be responsible for convincing families of the importance of this program." I took a breath as I flipped to the second page of the Allied Wild Towns agreement.

"The town of Lake Weir will receive assistance in order to secure the food growing capacities of the region for the people of the allied towns. Agricultural experimentation will be limited in the other towns, but more specifically allowed here in the hopes of containing any… unpredictable responses." Sam and I grimaced as we remembered the plant golem that had risen as a result of our efforts into <Infusing> living, mundane organisms. "The town of Stonecrest will lead the efforts into uniting all our territories and fortifying them in any ways they can think of. Beyond that, they will work closely with Wildwood in the development of infused items to help the fight for the surface and Lake Weir in their efforts to provide for more utilitarian needs."

"Here is the addendum," Rachael said, handing me a final sheet of paper.

"Thank you," I said, receiving the paper gingerly. The Entities had remained mostly quiet through the discussions, but they'd allowed us to keep notes in the air in the form of light swirls. The possibility to take notes and then write up the drafts for the 'official' document for the alliance was invaluable. There had only been six pieces of scrap paper between all of our group, each kept for lighting fires in case of emergency for the non-fire-attuned, but they were instead used to somewhat seal the deal on their cooperation.

Without a shadow of hesitation, I read out the last series of points.

"The allied towns will each select two representatives for the economic, infrastructure, and New Earth Defense branches of the Allied Council, based on the running structure of Wildwood. There will be a rotating seat of council speaker, whose vote will act as the tie-breaker should it be needed. Allied Council meetings will be held in the presence of Gec whenever possible.

"Further discussions on the local policies of the New Earth

Defense branch will come once the Allied Council meets and the towns have been informed of the changes. Primary concern internally will be the evaluation of the 'Misuse of Magic' clause, which is to be addressed at the earliest convenience.

"Those who have received MetierTech Implants will be required to contribute to the Allied Council for an indeterminate amount of time as of yet, but they will not be forced into combat unless as a last resort. The…" I paused and squinted at a line that had been added at the bottom after everyone had agreed on the addendum. "The Dreg Warrior Leader and co. will be free to operate for the betterment of humanity and in pursuit of the Entity's ingrained goal. Resources to be exchanged and provided at reasonable rates for their needs? What is this?"

Unfortunately, I didn't get a chance to receive an answer. A hovering pyramid of light manifested above the other Entities and pulsed in a rainbow strobe that had all of us covering our eyes.

[-] The accord has been reached. True cooperation is open. MetierTech Implants will be freely provided, as per the direction of the Allied Council, by myself. Designation of Gec is also acceptable as a means of differentiating my individual crystalline structure. [-] Gec's voice overpowered everything, but thankfully it wasn't the mind-scrambling volume that it had been outside.

It took a few seconds for everyone to realize that Gec had finally joined the conversation. Its first proclamation, however, had everyone jumping with excitement. Unlimited implants would revolutionize the way people interfaced with an Attuned Earth. Everyone but me, my friends, and Clara seemed ecstatic.

"So everyone is going to ignore my question about this Dreg Warrior Leader thing?" I said out loud. The older people in the group had the decency to tone down their excitement and look sheepish. It was actually Gec who answered.

[-] Ava and Dylan have placed the operational security of

our shared goal in the hands of the ones responsible for my freedom. As I happen to agree with this evaluation, it has been recorded as part of our accord. [-]

A poignant glance at the two showed they were caught red-handed.

"What can we say? If it weren't for you rooting out the Dreg from the town, helping your friend Alan with the weird technology, and overall shoving three collective towns into action, we wouldn't be here. There wasn't a single person that disagreed," Councilman Dylan explained, getting nods of agreements from the others.

"How did you even hide that from me?" I asked, more irritated that I had somehow missed the clause than that it existed.

<That would be a trick of the light courtesy of yours truly.>

"Bec, you traitor..." I said, holding my head in my hands.

"Someone has to come up with the crazy plans," Sam said, smirking at me. "And it sure as heck isn't going to be me."

"I actually disagree," Maurice cut in. "I've heard what you want to do with the strawb—"

A vine sprouted from the man's shirt to wrap around his mouth.

"Like I said, crazy plans. Someone else," Sam said, smiling like the entire gathering of leaders hadn't seen him cut the thorn-haired man off. When the vine came off, Maurice gave Sam a wide-eyed look and refused to expand further on the whole strawberry business.

[-] It appears that now that the Allied Council is in place, I should provide the first concern for it to address. [-]

"You *did* call us here," Daniela said, rolling her wrist in a 'go on' gesture. "We had to go through this whole song and dance before you'd actually get to the point."

—There were no musical renditions during the...— Tec was quickly cut off by Bec.

<Lets you and I have a sidebar, huh?>

[-] Dreg Warrior Daniela is correct. There is no longer a need for delay. The most pertinent bit of information is that the threat of the Dreg has not been wholly eliminated within my domain. The other is that the remaining survivors within my domain are also in dire straits. [-]

CHAPTER ELEVEN

A Lurking Threat

The news was like a bucket of cold water. Somewhere within me, I'd realized that it was unlikely the Dreg were eradicated, especially when the people that had been present in Summerfield hadn't pursued the handful of Tendrils that escaped. What exactly this meant, however, required clarification.

"Explain. How big is this threat?" I asked, staring at the pyramid hard enough that spots floated in my vision. I refused to look away, if only for the Entity to know I was serious.

[-]Perhaps a clarification on the scale of my domain is in order first.[-]

Gec exploded in a spray of light before a hovering map took the Entity's place in the air. It was a rendition of the maps that had originally been integrated in the MetierTech Implants, but now featuring the modification Tec and Bec had concocted at my suggestion. Sure enough, those additions were put to work as a pin formed in the center of the map and the boundaries of Lake Weir, Stonecrest, and Wildwood were highlighted in different colors.

[-] The growth of a domain is exponential to the Category of the Entity, as you have all no doubt experienced with my

compatriots. A further grade beyond that leaves you with this. [-]

A circular-esque area was marked as the map zoomed out slowly. All three towns, and even the Bunker, were easily encompassed. It reached further north and south than anyone at Wildwood had explored in years before it stopped. Several pins also manifested in a gold color as soon as Gec's domain stopped moving. Context clues told me that they marked Entity Clusters, as Bec, Tec, and Wec were in their respective locations. The gold pin to the west of Wildwood right smack in the middle of the spider territory, as well as the half-dozen others no one had encountered, sent a shiver through my spine. *That's a lot of dungeons...*

"I knew it!" Maurice called out, pointing at a gold pin that couldn't be more than a mile from Wec's. It seemed there was confirmation that the gators had a dungeon, after all.

[-] The situation in your immediate territories, with the exclusion of the beast-bound Entity close to Wec, is more than stable. However, the Aberrants operations to the north of your towns has hardly suffered. Your cleansing of that sullied Entity has thrown those forces into disarray, but it has placed the unafflicted Entities in danger. [-]

"You mean there are more survivors?" Clara said, herself rising to her feet. "You didn't call those other Entities 'beast-bound,' which is what I assume you called the dungeons."

[-] That is likely. The signatures of those Entities match Bec and Tec much more closely than the others. As Tec has made you aware, direct contact is necessary for me to pull those Entities into this forum. The specifics can only be ascertained by a species not...locomotively restricted. [-]

"You can't move, so you need us to do the work for you?" Daniela asked, quirking an eyebrow at the pyramid as it reformed while the map dissipated.

"Daniela," Ava said, her tone of reproach clear.

"No, Mama. This thing has been talking big this whole time. I was on board for the agreement because, honestly, it was overdue. I agreed with putting Ronan in charge of pushing the boundaries because I'd trust no one else to do it better. Ambiguous 'concerns' and unclear information is no way to have a relationship when this glorified rock is asking for our help," the brunette snapped.

The blackspace fractures spider-webbed through the air in a distinct direction toward Daniela, which caused the woman's eyes to widen even as flames enveloped her form. My body was frozen as I watched the interplay, but a sphere of iridescent light interposed itself between the cracks and Daniela. A whine like a piece of metal ready to snap grated on our ears and I watched Bec's light sputter before the blackspace fractures retracted.

<Esteemed Cluster, you must understand!>

[-] I understand that a flesh species is attempting to dictate what I should or shouldn't do, [-] Gec replied evenly.

<While I am unable to touch upon the Whispers, this could not be what the creator intended! While we've never interacted with the local species to this level, they have autonomy that we *must* respect,> Bec argued, dipping low.

All of us humans stood rooted to our spots as we watched the truly alien exchange. It had never occurred to me, perhaps due to Bec being so closely based on our human personalites and Tec being so similar to Alan's quirks, that the Entities could bring this level of conflict *against* us. The point about putting their ingrained mission first took a whole new level of seriousness.

—Agreed.—

---Thirded.---

The prisms of light that represented Tec and Wec hovered to stand beside Bec, essentially forming a wall between our group of humans and the ominous light of Gec's pyramid manifestation. I noticed that Bec's sputtering light evened the moment that other Entities joined it.

[-] Perhaps this meeting has stretched beyond its useful extent. [-]

[-] Consolidate your changes and return in a week. I will process this discussion further. [-]

Without further fanfare, the entire group of humans were ejected from the whitespace. Most surprisingly, however, was my own lack of ejection. The three lower Category Entities hovered closer to me even as Gec lowered down to eye level. The pyramid didn't really have eyes, but I felt like a tasty morsel ready to be gobbled up.

"Care to explain the whole business with the blackspace? I don't take it particularly well when my friends are attacked right in my presence," I said evenly. Internally, I was gritting my teeth in the hopes of avoiding drawing the ire of the Entity. After seeing our other crystalline allies standing up for Daniela, I knew the one with the problem was Gec.

[-] These children believe this 'Dreg Warrior' is a logical extension of our influence. A bloom of our particular abilities and knowledge melded with the ingenuity of one of your 'scientists.' [-]

"I'd say it was a success. Otherwise, we'd all be dead as the Aberrant corrupted you and leveraged God knows how many more Dreg resources against us poor, useless survivors. Oh, and, of course, that wouldn't have happened without that 'scientist' biting the bullet," I growled, unable to restrain myself any longer.

[-] Hmmm. Perhaps you are correct. Perhaps not. However, if this partnership is going to work as it has been, you will need to know more. *Understand* more. Our directive isn't blind, and the weapons of humanity were responsible for shattering the initial step of our arrival. [-]

"What are you talking about?" I asked, some of my anger turning to confusion.

<Gec is talking about the sundering event that happened before the Clusters could land on Earth,> Bec clarified.

"The missiles? How did that affect your mission?"

[-] Category. It is everything, and it is nothing, for us Entities Clusters. We are but parts of a once great whole. When our

domain can reach across the planet, then we are sent *beyond* to purge the Dreg elsewhere. By fracturing our bodies, humanity set back the clock for the next wave of Clusters. [-]

My mind was spinning as I tried to reconcile the information. I couldn't help but equate the Clusters to a virus, arriving at a host until it burst to spread somewhere else, multiplied.

"What happens to Earth when that happens?" I asked hesitantly. My anger was gone, and in its place was a concern that I'd somehow been colluding with a *different* group of crazy magic rocks that planned to abuse the people of Earth.

<I am not sure. My calculations estimate that would not happen unless the Dreg and Pith reach a cycle of balance.>

[-] What happens is that your plane of existence joins the Conflux, as well as what Bec has just stated. What humanity, or the planets we've left behind on our grand mission, do with this access is not our concern. [-]

"If your mission is so grand, then why would you need us meager humans?" I asked, frowning as I tried to reconcile the information bombarding me. Magic was step one of the conversation, and it had climbed twenty stories up to what sounded like interdimensional war on a scale I could hardly comprehend.

[-] This interaction with humanity presents an interesting amendment to our core presets. Perhaps cooperating with the planet we are sent to balance is in both our interests.[-]

"If that's the case, then you need to learn how to actually cooperate. Demands and threats are definitely not it. That's how the Dreg operated," I snarled, unable to keep cool under the Entity's high and mighty attitude. It was entirely true that the rock could probably crush my body and sunder my mind, but I felt it was better to be upfront. Knowing how the giant Metier Crystal would react before someone with less spine tried to deal with it was imperative.

I stared unflinching at the cracks of darkness that spread toward me. I braced my mind just like when I'd freed the Dreg Afflicted, and spell chain after spell chain sprung up around me.

It had been unintentional, like locking up your muscles before being struck, but in the whitespace it seemed to have a tangible effect. I was vaguely aware of three spell chains forming in the air around my waist, while two formed at shoulder level.

The arm-thick cracks shrank to finger-thin ravines and the pressure emitted by Gec's pyramid manifestation fluttered like a faulty light before they receded entirely.

[-] You and that female human are indeed at the Threshold. You knock blindly against something you could hardly understand. [-]

"Well, if you are going to keep threatening us, then I'm going to leave. Losing the implants will be terrible, but the people of Earth survived before them. There are dozens with Gifts, and I am sure we can up that number," I said, glaring at the Entity. I moved my hand back toward the back of my head, feeling the implant at the base of my neck. Its Metier Crystal was no larger than my fingernail, yet it had given me access to something unimaginable. I almost hesitated, but I wouldn't subject humanity to another form of tyranny.

To my horror, the crystalline floor exploded into translucent tentacles that wrapped around my limbs. Some of them were intercepted by my spell chains that still hovered around me, but there were simply too many and Gec was able to restrain me before I forcefully removed my connection to the Entities.

[-] Foolish behavior. Perhaps it *is* time that I impart knowledge. Select your final skill, human. [-]

"No," I said, straining with all of my Quotient-enhanced Strength. It was futile, but I could feel my spell chains revolving faster around me, stirred on by my mental state. It wasn't dissimilar to when I'd Gift Wrestled Rachael, except there was certainly no give against the Entity.

<Ronan, please. This is information that you need and I cannot provide.>

Bec's argument gave me pause. The Entity Cluster had mentioned before that despite its best efforts, there was information outside its grasp that was locked behind its Category. Even

Category 3 status, what Tec and Wec had, didn't unlock much additional information. It more seemed like Category 4 brought forth a new surfeit of knowledge. *And a case of raging narcissism to boot.*

"What guarantees do I have you aren't going to fry my mind?" I yelled, staring daggers at the pyramid manifestation.

[-] You've unlocked a spell chain you have no business possessing. It will allow you to see more than the surface of what I will impart you, and hopefully halt your childish resistance. [-]

"I will not be called childish by a thing that hasn't even been alive," I growled.

Nevertheless, I concentrated to pull up my status and concentrated on my offensive imbue skill on the list. Instantly, the world whirled as if my whole self was being flushed down a drain. Where it ended up was just as confusing. It looked just like my bedroom down in the Bunker, down to the unmade bed and the mineral samples arranged on my dresser. Without warning, Gec appeared in my doorway like a reversed bubble pop. Instead of the ominous, all-around voice we were familiar with, the Entity seemed to be speaking from its manifestation.

"For this impartment of knowledge, I figured it would be best to present a place where you were comfortable," Gec said

"How considerate of you." I said, voice dripping with sarcasm.

Instead of answering, a wall of the glyph text that manifested along with skills etched itself in the air under the Entity. My eyes swam as I tried to take in all the information. Some of it seemed to be highlighted by my subconscious, but the rest still looked like gibberish. That brief second to observe was all the warning I got before the glyphs plunged straight into the middle of my forehead and the world spun. A sixth and final 'button' lingered in the back of my mind as I gained access to a new skill.

Unlike all the previous times, however, something within me resonated between each of those connections to the skills. What it was, I couldn't even begin to guess. Nevertheless, a moment after the surge of information was locked away in my mind, text appeared in my vision with yet another barely descriptive bit of information on the skill.

<Terrasheath>

<Add the abrasion of earth at will.>

"Now let us put your true grasp of your pathways to the test," the Entity said before the world once more was flushed down the drain.

CHAPTER TWELVE

The Six Prime Pathways

The world came together like chunks of a jigsaw puzzle. Huge blocks of unremarkable terrain, woods and plains, stretched in the distance. As I tried to deal with the sudden back-to-back shifts in perspective, the annoying pyramid that was Gec manifested a few feet from me.

"If I didn't know better, I would say you are enjoying this, Gec," I said. My hostility toward the Entity's multiple threats hadn't diminished, but at the least I was still alive. My curiosity was warring with my caution and frustration.

"You—"

"Perhaps it would be best for this endeavor if I act as the mediator?" Bec's sphere blinked into existence between me and Gec.

"The Authority allows this. Satellite knowledge will be transitioned for the sake of this trial," Gec said after deliberating for a handful of seconds.

It might have been running permutations in its head, since it was one of the few times I'd seen the Entities pause to think about their response at all. Thankfully, the result was an interaction with an Entity I trusted leagues more than Gec. However, I wouldn't forget that there were some strange rules underlying the interactions between the different Category Entities, of which Bec was the lesser.

"Ronan," Bec said, hovering just in front of my head. "I am sorry that the situation devolved like this."

"You weren't the one that tried to attack me with their mind. I've seen that before, and it was when the Dreg were trying to take the afflicted people. I have my hypothesis that it was how the Tendrils were formed," I said.

"Halt. Is what you speak true?" Gec zipped closer, hovering even closer than Bec.

"Yes. I don't misdirect at every opportunity," I snapped back. "The blackspace wasn't the same as the Dreg, but it looked the same and my skills reacted the same way."

"Blackspace…" Gec drifted off. I couldn't shake off the feeling that it was staring at me even without eyes. "I leave this task to you. Full Authority over this trial has now been transferred. There are models to run."

Just like that, Gec winked out of sight and Bec seemed to double in lumens right in front of my face. The Entity manifestation almost tripled in size, shivering in the air for a full second before it said anything. "Well, that was both pleasant and horrible."

"It sounds like your boss delegated. Care to divulge why they ran off?" I asked, crossing my arms.

"I may have Authority here in this trial, but they retain it as a whole. I am only allowed to tell you what this trial was originally intended to do."

I let out a sigh. *It looks like I won't be able to eke out some answers with loopholes.* "Okay. I'll bite then. Why did your boss shove my last skill down my throat?"

"There is a purpose for the separations I generated in the first version of your status," Bec started. "They correlate to what the Harbinger called the Six Prime Pathways."

"You aren't going to tell me who this Harbinger is, are you?"

"That's right. Not authorized for that. However, I can tell you about their teachings. The Six Prime Pathways."

"Fine, go ahead. It's been a few years since I was last in school," I sighed, rubbing my temples as I leaned against a nearby tree.

"This won't be that passive of a lesson, Ronan. This is a trial, in the hopes that you meet a criterion for more information. Your first test is related to your three offensive skills. These are the spell chains binding the Turbulent Hemisphere of your soul. You didn't think the nomenclature was just by chance, did you?"

"Now I don't, but I also have no clue what you are talking about," I said, tilting my head in confusion.

A thread of iridescent mana tapped me in the middle of the forehead before I had time to react. Instantly, my mana pool stirred. Unlike normal, however, I didn't feel a drain. It was as if it clung to my skin like a thin membrane, unable to disperse. Right before my eyes, the spell chains for <Stone Spike> and <Mineral Strike> flowed out of the membrane as if they were rising through a calm pool, leaving gentle ripples of burnt umber light in their wake. Followed closely behind was a third chain, which I quickly realized had to be <Terrasheath>.

"Your Pathways for directing your will, imbuing your will, and materializing your will. Skills are the way with which us Entities accomplish anything in physical reality. As Alan, and your friend Rachael, have already started to surmise, a spell chain is a way for you to take control of a portion of reality," Bec said.

"The Gift Wrestling…"

"Correct. When spell chains are superimposed, your will and domain is tested. It can be tested in control, or directed. It can be modified, or imbued with your desire. It can be strengthened, or urged to materialize. These are the fields that Freeform allows you to adjust."

"And this test is supposed to… what? Show me how to Freeform the energy in these Pathways?" I asked, still unclear.

"These tests will determine if you have what it takes to safely progress beyond the Corporeal Limit without losing your mind. It is entirely possible for you to figure this out without our assistance, but considering all of your Pathways have been linked to skills we've imparted, it will serve you well to gain some pointers."

"Corporeal Limit..." I mumbled, remembering Gec mentioning a Threshold. "Does this have anything to do with not gaining Pith after me and Daniela made it to Quotient 6?"

"Yes. The density of your mana is sufficient for you to keep all six Pathways open, meaning you've reached the Corporeal Limit. You will need to temper your body to progress further, lest the very density of your mana cause you to burst."

"What!?" I called out in alarm.

"Think of it like this. The world is a gradient of mana. Each Quotient marks a level of Pith that empowers your mana, and your body to a lesser extent. That density is required to keep your Pathways open. When your mana exceeds what is required for the Pathways, its burden is placed on your body. If your body cannot sustain the density of energy, it will be released to the lower density environment. Hence the bursting."

"Wait, if that's the case, can't we stave that off by being somewhere where the outside mana is dense enough to stop us from bursting?" I said, suddenly much more horrified by my eighteen percent progress toward Q7.

"That is possible. However, that will not solve the issue that you are encountering right now. Your body has a density of mana sufficient to shrug off Pith from creatures of a lower Quotient. If you search for places with naturally higher concentrations of mana, you will encounter creatures of similarly higher Quotient, which would result in you gaining Pith regardless. If you don't properly temper your body, it will not sustain the leap to the next Quotient."

"Why didn't you tell us all of this when you set up the status and the skills?" I asked, trying to calm my thoughts. As unfortunate as the possibility of my body exploding was, clearly Bec had some solution.

"This is knowledge I had intrinsically; I did not have a means to share it because I did not understand how to. Interacting with Tec and Wec allowed me access to some of that information, but it also opened me up to the concept of our Authority. When Gec intervened directly, our knowledge fell within their domain and Authority ruled our actions. Mostly," Bec explained. Its hovering sphere pulsed with agitation. "Our ego remains our own, but we cannot override the compulsion of our mission. The Categories allow for qualitative leaps in our power, within limits."

"Is that why you were able to intervene as you have, but not actually direct Gec to do anything?"

"Yes," Bec sighed, defeated. "I believe Gec's intentions are correct, but my time and human-based ego tell me there is more to be gained here through a relationship rather than dominating power."

"You got that right." I scoffed. I paused for a minute to gather my thoughts before turning serious eyes on Bec's sphere. "Alright. So, I need to understand my Pathways so I can 'strengthen' my body. This has something to do with traits, no? Is that why they have a progress percentage?"

"Correct. The Dreg is not inherently bad, merely a result of increasing entropy given off by mana. It is sort of like a magical mutation fuel. However, as you have seen in the Dreg afflicted, too much of that metamorphic energy causes magical assimilation. Parts of the body become *entirely* magical instead of some facet of the two."

"Does that mean the afflicted won't be able to strengthen their bodies?" I asked, thinking of Eric's son, Billy.

"No. However, their progress will be greatly hampered. Similarly so for those born prior to magic suffusing their beings, the generation living before our arrival."

"Okay, that's a bridge we can cross when we get to it. I

suppose if I want to hear the solution to not getting blown up, I need to pass these tests?"

"As decreed by Gec, knowledge of the Corporeal Infusion will be given with the completion of the trial," Bec said, its voice becoming monotone out of the blue. It didn't take me long to realize it was likely quoting the pain-in-the-ass Entity that had caused problems already. Thankfully, that weird shift didn't last and the more animate tone of Bec came through. "Since I know Daniela is probably making a scene outside of Gec's crystal, I'll be brief.

"You will need to contest the will of Gec using your Turbulent Hemisphere and you will need to defend your domain using your Foundational Hemisphere. The tests will direct you to use each of your skills to contest individually and then all three simultaneously. You have as many tries as you can stomach, but Gec will only give you the information you need if you pass at least the two simultaneous Hemisphere tests," Bec explained.

The air shimmered and an iridescent spell chain formed in the air ten feet from us. It unspooled like fine silk on a gentle breeze. The glyphs it was made from were pristine, flawless, polished tubes of glass that hovered and spun of their own will. Some of the individual glyphs resonated with my own spell chains, but it was like comparing chicken scratches with bold computer print. There was a qualitative difference in the spell chain, even if I couldn't feel a hint of energy coming from the spell chain.

"So, I just hit it?" I asked, confused. "That's it?"

"I assure you, things will not be quite that easy, Ronan. Unfortunately, there is not much I can assist you with in this regard. The way in which you and I utilize spell chains is fundamentally different. Not least of all that I use them as easily as you breathe, and I don't think you could adequately describe to me how you are capable of breathing, no?"

"It's good to see some snark stayed under all those layers of formality after dealing with the town Entities," I said, smirking at the sphere.

"Well, being a product of you and your friends made me both extremely pragmatic, loyal, and just a royal pain in the caboose when necessary. I'd like to think it's part of my charm."

"I thought that was the shiny, polished surface," I quipped

"As much as I would like to continue affirming our friendship, Ron, the trial *is* important. I also didn't misspeak. Daniela is currently throwing fireballs and flame breaths at the side of Gec, so I think I need to intervene. I might be able to pull her into a trial of her own if Gec allows," Bec said, chilling the light mood. It was true, and I much preferred *our* Entity 'handle' Daniela than Gec even getting close. Relatively speaking, since she was probably no more than a few feet from its physical form.

"Go ahead. If I succeed, will I need to do anything?" I asked, stretching out my body as I glared at the iridescent spell chain.

"Simply call out which test you want to attempt and it will form. Best of luck, Dreg Warrior Leader," Bec said.

"Now, I told you not to—" I didn't get to finish berating the Entity before its sphere had winked out of sight, leaving me alone with the spell chain hanging ominously in the air. "Just you and me, huh?"

With a burst built up from numerous practices, I released <Stone Spike> without warning. My eyes were focused right on the lower edge, the one closest to the ground, as the spell chain orbiting around me zipped into action. However, unlike its appearance, the iridescent glyphs barely shook as my skill collided with it. My stomach twisted and I dropped to a knee the moment my spell chain failed to trigger, the appropriate twenty percent of my mana pool disappearing along with it.

"This is going to suck," I grumbled.

CHAPTER THIRTEEN

The Turbulent Hemisphere

Hours. It had been *hours*. The cycle of trying to attack the spell chain and recuperating had worn down my body less than I imagined, but eventually I was forced to take a break. One of the party's water canteens and even one of our travel meals materialized in the air the moment I slumped down for a respite. That meant either the group had left some food behind and headed back, or they were still waiting at the foot of Gec's crystal. Unfortunately, there was nothing I could do about that since I was determined to crunch through Gec's trial.

The worst I'd managed was a quiver from the Entity-formed spell chain. It wasn't even an issue of strength, because on the last attempt before my break, I'd dumped triple the mana cost of <Stone Spike> into the spell chain. My brain was screaming for rest, due not in small part to curling in on myself as the mana aftereffects pulled all of my muscles taut. Unlike the outside world, where I'd practiced <Stone Spike> hundreds of times and reduced the effect of the base cast, inside of Gec it was as if I never had gotten accustomed to mana use.

I'd stopped a handful of times to attempt using <Mineral Strike> to poor results. I'd held off on <Terrasheath> because it was the skill I had the least amount of familiarity with. There was only so much head bashing I was willing to do before I realized I needed to change my tactic. Bec said that to gain the information I just needed to, at minimum, be able to force down the spell chain using all three of my offensive skills. This meant using all of my skills in conjunction.

So, the moment I felt my mana tick over to full, I activated <Terrasheath> in the hopes of familiarizing myself with it better. Nothing. I aimed the skill at the ground. Nothing. However, when I didn't focus so much on a target, the spell chain that had been hovering around me locked into place in its lazy orbit. A shimmering tan haze covered my arms as my mana dropped precipitously, taking a full third of my mana pool. When the haze reached my elbows, it halted. The haze had specks of my usual umber mana intermingled amidst the tan dust, but nothing happened as I stared at the lazy, drifting particles.

When I moved, however, the haze changed. Like a miniaturized dust storm, the haze tightened around my hands before pushing away from my body in a facsimile of a slap. I hadn't been intending anything of the sort, simply waving my hands, but the skill had taken that as guidance. I stopped moving and the haze slowly drew back to cling less than an inch from my body. There was no drain on my mana, similar to <Earth Shell> once in place, which I should have somewhat expected since both were imbue skills.

Just that connection ticked something in my mind; it was like the first crack on a wall under siege. Instead of focusing on it, however, I kept to my original goal. I walked slowly in a circle, observing the rippling wave of sand that followed my hands. Each time my hands stopped, the haze of sand continued forward for a second before 'striking' and coming back to my arms.

I moved my hands around in various patterns and the sands followed the motions. I was no pugilist, but I cracked out a few jabs and the response was immediate. Instead of the slow roil of an incoming sandstorm, the haze turned into a chaotic haze of sand daggers. Each was only about as large as my finger, but the slight delay between my motion and the skill's response made them a dangerous tempo weapon. I couldn't help but wonder if that was where my subconscious had clobbered together the 'sheath' part of the skill, since it certainly looked like an attack completed from the draw of a weapon.

The other thing I noticed through my awkward arm-waving dance was that unlike the spell chains for <Stone Spike> and <Mineral Strike>, <Terrasheath> stuck around. The spell chain seemed to be locked around my back, standing out like an ominous umber halo. If I was honest, it was the flashiest of my skills, even if all the other ones had more bombastic effects. A little sand around the hands hardly drew your attention when there was a five-foot stalagmite aiming for your torso.

Curious about its true offensive potential, I walked away from Gec's spell chain and over toward the edge of the simulated forest. I threw out a small jab-cross combo that was mimicked a second later by <Terrasheath>. As expected, the dagger points left imprints on the tree's bark. What *wasn't* expected was the torrential surge of sand that exploded out from my arms. The motes of umber hidden within the tan sand were like faucets set into a desert as the sand blasted hunks of the tree's bark within a second. I felt the energy in the spell chain halo dim, but it wasn't completely gone.

I did a bit more testing of <Terrasheath>, and its secondary effect only seemed to trigger if the blow encountered resistance. There was a threshold that I couldn't quite pinpoint, but hitting a leaf didn't trigger the deluge of sand. When I punched the ground, though, the effect was quite impressive. The deluge of sand somehow sensed that I had and sand exploded in a circular radius around me instead of trying to burrow into the ground. Each standard cast only had enough for three follow ups, but I wasn't going to complain about the damage boost they gave.

The most exciting thing about the skill was what it represented for my fighting style. For all intents and purposes, I was meant to take an astronomical amount of damage as the vanguard of our group. If I could turn <Terrasheath> into something that also triggered when I was hit, then I would have a retaliatory skill that would wear enemies while I defended. That being said, my skill training had fallen to the wayside since the fight with Galloway, and it had only started to return. It was entirely possible that my struggles with the Turbulent Hemisphere test were due to my shallow insights into how my skills operated.

As a matter of fact, I couldn't recall a time where I'd even tried to see how my spell chains changed after I amplified them with my antler helm. The glyphs obviously had meaning and some even appeared in Gec's rendition…

"Wait a minute…"

With a wave of my hand, the three spell chains that had been hovering in the air around me since the test started halted in place. My eyes swept through the ticks, dashes, periods, and swirls that made up the glyphs. They still looked like gibberish, but not entirely. It was a building understanding of what each part of the chain accomplished. Unlike the Gifts the survivors of Earth had been able to intuit, these were crisp ways of manipulating the world. Of applying the will of the user on reality, as Bec said.

My mind flashed to my singular experience Gift Wrestling Rachael. It was an embarrassing show of strength the more I looked back on it and even despite bullying the woman with my higher density mana, she'd almost managed to blow the whole situation up in my face. This was exactly the same thing, except Gec wasn't even actively controlling their spell chain. Their formation was so pristine that their dominion where that spell chain existed was unmatched. The puzzle pieces fell into place and I knew what I had to do.

I steadied my breathing for several minutes as I visualized what I wanted. It wasn't guaranteed, but the resonance between skills could be related to the defining aspects Bec had mentioned made up the chains. If the corresponding skills of directing, imbuing, and materializing targeted those portions of Gec's spell chain, then that might be enough to destabilize the spell chain. It was still a gamble, since my understanding of the glyphs was instinctual at best. I was almost certain that Alan had already deciphered at least part of the glyph language and that was how he'd been able to neutralize the Aberrant Entity. *Maybe he had the direction and imbuement correct, but lacked materialization.*

Another layer superimposed itself over the puzzle I'd thought complete. Targeting, cleverness, and power were just as much factors in the manifestation of magic as the actual magic itself. That simple realization meant there was more depth to using skills, and their spell chains for that matter, than I thought possible. It shouldn't have come as a surprise since the Entities were living things *made up* from them, but it hadn't been a year since I'd been immersed in the world of magic.

With my thoughts now whirling from the revelations, I realized that completing every facet of the test would be impossible. My mastery of <Stone Spike> was probably the highest out of my offensive skills, yet it had lacked something to break through. I could aim the skill however I wanted, but there was more to that. I needed to understand *what* to target and *when* to target. I didn't doubt I could figure it out if I spent more time locked away inside Gec, but the world didn't stop within the whitespace.

For the first time in the test, a smirk crept its way to my face. I set my feet as I eyed the Entity's spell chain with all the animosity I'd felt toward its creature for lording over humanity. I didn't disagree that the Aberrations were something that needed to be stopped, especially if there were more nearby. That didn't mean that I was willing to buckle under the pressure of something I didn't understand.

A tingling flowed through my skin as I channeled my mana and double empowered <Stone Spike> and <Mineral Strike>. The expenditure nearly tapped my mana pool and I struggled to keep my feet under me. The respective spell chains ballooned in size, even as their position remained locked. I wasn't ready to release them. I didn't have the mana or practice to double empower <Terrasheath>, so I merely fed the skill the third it desired. I was barely able to spare a glance at my mana pool before the strain arrived.

Mana: 27%

The pain in my muscles was almost unbearable, but I locked my knees just to stay standing. I could almost hear Ava berating me since I risked passing out, but it was more likely that I would pass out from the mana side effects than from blood pooling in my legs.

"Target, intent, and potency," I managed to mumble through grit teeth. It was the three broad components I'd been able to discern for my spell chains. <Terrasheath> broke the orbit around me first, floating to encircle a portion of the Entity's spell chain that I thought represented the intent of the spell chain. Next went <Mineral Strike>, positioning itself around a section almost opposite <Terrasheath>. Instead of wrapping around the iridescent spell chain, mine directly clashed with the Entity's. A sound like shearing metal filled the plains, but I didn't relent as blood dripped down the corners of my mouth.

I took a single breath as I watched <Terrasheath> coil tighter in response to <Mineral Strike>'s friction. The gentle rotation of the nigh-impervious spell chain ground to a halt and I knew it was time. <Stone Spike> flew forward and struck an innocent looking glyph in the space between <Mineral Strike>'s grind and <Terrasheath>'s grip. Said glyph was not quite so innocent; I was almost certain it was, if not *it*, one of the keystone pieces making the Entity's spell chain so resistant to outside influence.

After having been ground down slightly by contact with my materialize skill, the iridescent sheen of the glyph wasn't flawless. It had then been trapped between my two spell chains just in time for <Stone Spike> to collide with it. The same rippling force effect I'd managed for hours manifested in the spell chain, with two notable exceptions. The glyph had been weakened, and with it constrained, I was able to visibly see the force of my skill ripple out from the glyph, only to rebound away from <Terrasheath> and <Mineral Strike> with a vengeance.

The moment the reflection arrived at the worn glyph, the tinkling of broken glass reached my ears. Motes of rainbow light scattered in the air as the rest of the spell chain fell apart. It was somewhat frustrating to see that it just disintegrated at a moderate pace starting from the broken link instead of exploding in a fantastic display of success, but ultimately it didn't matter. I'd broken the spell chain and Bec seemed to agree.

<Congratulations, Ronan. Simultaneous break condition has been achieved. Do you wish to reset the test to complete your individual skill breaks?>

"No," I said without hesitation. For all my bluster in the face of Gec, I knew the Entity was stronger and more experienced than me. There were some things I wouldn't buckle under, but if you never yielded somewhere, you were bound to break completely. "I'll work on the Foundational Hemisphere now."

Bec wasn't anywhere to be seen, but I could almost hear the grin on its face when it responded. <Very well. I would suggest dodging until you get your mind in order.>

"Wha—" I didn't get to finish my thought as a buzz saw of a spell chain came barreling out of nowhere right at me. I barely had any time to roll out of the way before the thing gave me a close shave. The simulated ground where the spell chain passed got thrown up into the air as if a small grenade had gone off the moment it had made contact with the iridescent mana. The spell chain only remained in sight for a few more seconds before winking out and appearing on the other end of the plain. It was unerringly headed for me.

"Oh, this is going to suck."

CHAPTER FOURTEEN

The Foundational Hemisphere

"Can."

Dodge.

"I."

Dodge.

"Get a moment!"

Dodge.

Like a caricature of a wheel, the inexorable spinning approach of the spell chain halted in the air for a full breath. Its perfect circular rotation wobbled under its braking power, but the moment it was back in shape, it resumed its approach.

"I meant for longer than that!" I gasped, jumping over one of the various craters the offensive spell chain had left in the simulated terrain. Thankfully, that time the spell chain actually stopped completely and even reversed to the edge of the plains. It stood poised, ready to cleave me a new one the moment I wasn't paying attention. I just knew it was.

"Bec!"

"Ronan? Are you alright?" the Entity's sphere manifestation winked into existence, flickering through the space around me.

"Yes, I'm fine but what's the deal with the murderous spell

chain?" I asked, jabbing a finger in the direction of the offender. I was pretty sure that if it had eyes, the Gec's spell chain would have been squinting at me.

"That is the test for your Foundational Hemisphere. It needs to withstand an intrusion upon your domain," the Entity explained. "As for the intensity, it is matched to the strength you've showcased so far in the trial. Calculating that was trivial for Gec. As for why it seems so murderous… I would hazard more than a guess that you and Gec aren't exactly buddy buddy at the moment."

"You think! Am I okay to at least gather my thoughts before that thing blows me to bits?" I asked, trying to get my breathing in order.

"I have modified the parameters to attack when you direct it. Oh, I need to go. Daniela is not having a good time herself, and I think she is less understanding than you. Good luck!" Just like that, Bec was gone in a wink. If the Q6 people in town were going to need to pass this kind of trial for further guidance, things were going to be a tad rough moving forward. *Hopefully they install Bec as the trial administrator. Gec does not have good people skills. Or skills, for that matter.*

Without having the pristine spell chain bearing down on me, I was able to get my thoughts in order. For the sake of myself, I used <Mudpit> to restore the space around me from an exploded battlefield to a smoothed-out circle of packed dirt. I was somewhat tempted to see what the spell chain would do if it collided against a compacted <Earthen Barrier>, but I had a sneaking suspicion that it would blow up in my face. Literally. The line between metaphysical magic and reality was getting hair-thin and after taking so long to pass the last test, I didn't want to waste time.

Instead of trying to slam my head at the problem, I opted to start practicing for the simultaneous attempt. Thankfully, with my tank fighter focus, I was much more confident with my defensive skills than my offensive skills. With a nudge, that strange film of mana reappeared around me. <Mudpit>,

<Earth Shell>, and <Earthen Barrier> flowed out of my body to orbit around my waist like shields at the ready.

If I thought about the spell chains as the skills they represented, I could get myself in trouble. The whole test had been one of understanding the three variations for the Pathways. With my success in the Turbulent Hemisphere test, I had a much better idea what directing, imbuing, and materializing could do. Something told me my understanding was crude, but it would do.

"First, a test to see where we stand…" I nudged <Mudpit> and <Earth Shell> to the side before placing <Earthen Barrier> front and center. I fed the spell chain triple mana in the hopes of getting a good representative sample of the test. I doubted it would be enough, but I didn't have anything to lose. The pain was immediate, but I was already down on one knee to stop myself from falling. With how much I'd struggled during the first part of the test, my pride was already a non-issue.

"Come on!" I said, urging the Entity's spell chain forward. It was more than happy to comply.

The gentle rotations of the iridescent spell chain revved up considerably. The glyphs were nothing more than a blur, making the whole thing look more like a disk than a spinning array of script. I braced and I could almost feel my spell chain respond similarly. Instead of swelling like my offensive skills had, it deepened. The glyphs took on a more substantial density, going from burnt umber in color to hickory. The change was so significant, I swore I could feel a palpable pressure from the spell chain and it was almost like I could touch it if I tried. This went on for the handful of seconds it took the Entity's spell chain to arrive.

Unlike all the times the spell chain had rushed me down, I was ready. <Earthen Barrier> in its new condensed form met the spinning edge on its flat side. A ghost of a proper shield manifested in the air, taking the brunt of the spell's momentum before it collided against my spell chain. A rumble filled my ears as my denser skill clashed with the iridescent one. The spin slowed enough for me to be able to see the individual glyphs again and they looked the worse for wear. Ground down by my spell chain, their glass-like surfaces were pitted and scarred, as if their polish had been wiped off with a thick grit sandpaper.

Despite all the wear, the rumble turned into a crumble and I watched my densified spell chain fold like a cave in. Wisps of umber mana turned into physical stone before blowing away in the wind around me. Then the spell chain struck. Thankfully, the spell chain wasn't anywhere close to maximum power, but it didn't seem to care. All of my traits resonated with the blow, but even with a decent chunk of it being redirected to the soil, it still had plenty of oomph. My simulated body flew almost twenty feet back to land in a heap on the ground.

Nothing was actually broken, but the simulated injuries sent waves of pain through my body. I was only barely able to mumble for a reset before the offensive spell chain blew me across the plains again. It reversed its spin from where it stopped five feet away, and I was certain it was giving me the stink eye. The damage I'd inflicted was restored at a visible rate and it was back to full power even by the time the glyphs were too far to differentiate.

Despite all of that, a grin split my face. I could feel it; the chain had almost broken just with <Earthen Barrier>.

I was almost certain that was why the spell chain had gone in for a follow up so quickly, even faster than when it had first manifested. All the manipulations, adjustments, compactions, and amplifications I'd used <Earthen Barrier> for had counted for something. It wasn't enough to accomplish the task by itself, especially when I took into account that I'd triple empowered the skill, but it showed that I had a few foundations I could rely on.

I stayed right there on the ground for almost an hour while my mana recovered. Each silent ebb of energy filled my body and soothed the strain on my muscles as I worked through my plan for dealing with the offensive spell chain. The overall shape and function of my defensive skills, the spell chains that bound my Foundational Hemisphere, flitted through my mind in numerous ways.

It was unavoidable that I also thought about how I could work on blending my offensive and defensive skills. While I wasn't very experienced with <Terrasheath>, I could definitely picture the sandy halo turning into my armoring skill and vice versa. The two skills had a... flowing nature that I felt bridged my thoughts and desires better than even <Earth Wall> as one of my most practiced skills.

I allowed the deviation for only a few minutes more. Since the connection between <Terrasheath> and <Earth Shell> had helped me realize how I could change the intent of the spell chains, I knew I would need to practice with those skills more. Ultimately, however, I had to look at the defensive skills as if those were the only things I had available. It framed my mind around what would make me unmovable and unbreachable so that I could stand at the front of the things I wanted to protect.

With those thoughts entrenched in my mind, I spun up my spell chains once again. <Earthen Barrier> once more took the front and center position. Unlike the previous attempt, <Mudpit> encircled me with its spell chain. Having reached Q6, the unempowered cast of the skill produced a truly horrifying mess of mud and I was counting on just that reach. As a lynchpin, <Earth Shell> orbited inconspicuously around me.

I cracked my knuckles before waving the spell chain toward me. I didn't have to come across like a cocky bastard, but I was ready for some answers. My path to power was in Gec's hands and even if I could forgive the Entity for its behavior on the basis of species differences, it didn't mean I didn't want to show it up.

Sure enough, the buzzsaw of iridescent magic ripped through the air in my direction. I took a deep breath before I fed mana into the spell chains. In the blink of an eye, my mana was down to thirty percent. I did notice that the strain on my body wasn't as bad when it was singular, more expensive skills, as opposed to the same expense of my mana pool but from empowering a specific one.

Nevertheless, I didn't really have time to ponder on that realization before the spell chain reached the boundary of <Mudpit>. As if the attack was cutting through molasses, the motion of its spin lost at least half of its speed. That was only enough to get the solid-looking band to turn into a blurry circle of glyphs, but it was a good start.

A breath later, the spell chain struck against <Earthen Barrier>. Similar to before, a rumble filled the air but much weaker than before. I saw signs of the spell chain crumbling, so I let free a trickle of mana to patch up the damage of the two skills grinding into each other.

Each crack in my glyphs was filled with the darker brown of densified mana, showcasing a kintsugi of magical proportions. Thankfully, the discomfort of the mana side effects drew me away from the beautiful transformation occurring live to my skill. My eyes locked on the growing damage of the glass-like surface.

The moment I was able to discern the individual glyphs on the Entity's spell chain, I knew it was time to pounce. <Earth Shell> snaked down the middle of <Earthen Barrier>'s vertical ring before glomming onto the Entity's attack. Very quickly, the skill matched the diameter of the attack at the expense of all but five percent of my mana. As soon as the iridescent glow was clouded in sludge brown, I clenched my fist. <Earth Shell> triggered, expanding and wedging itself in the space between glyphs.

The actual increase in size of the Entity's spell chain was less than a foot in diameter, but that was enough to destabilize the attack. Miniature bursts of light flashed as mud rained down around me where pure mana and earth mana collided.

It started as a giggle, but it quickly climbed to a cackling laugh as I plopped on my back. I had no delusions that I could pass the individual parts of the test, but both of my plans had worked out as I hoped. The very same flaws I'd seen Gec's spell chain exploit in mine I was able to replicate. The process and application were magnitudes more elaborate, but they had both succeeded. I'd subverted the Entity with my will and defended my domain. *Another step forward…*

I wasn't sure when I'd fallen asleep, but a gentle chime brought me back. The simulated terrain had been replaced by whitespace except for the conference table the group had utilized on their first arrival. As a contrast to the last time I'd been in the room, only Daniela was present. She seemed to be glaring at everything and anything, her feet propped up on the table.

"Took you long enough," the woman huffed.

"Had to get the hang of the whole spell chain thing. One wrestling match did not prepare me for this," I replied, somewhat defensively.

"Me and Mama told you to spend more time on control," she warned, sucking her teeth and wagging her finger in my direction.

"Sorry, I was too busy taking fireballs, frost daggers, acid clouds, and a variety of other ailments to the face for you."

"I never asked you to—"

[-] Perhaps I should reconsider my trial, if the two to have successfully passed it act in this way. [-]

"You don't get a say," me and Daniela shot back toward the pyramid manifestation that winked into existence over the table. The Latina and I shared a look before turning away from each other and pinning the Entity with a glare. It was enough to say 'this conversation isn't over yet.'

[-] My projections indicated that you both should have been worn out by your trials, but it appears I miscalculated. Again. [-]

"Humans have a tendency to surprise, for better or worse," I said.

[-]Indeed. I have opted to leave you as free variables in my future predictions, as a courtesy for your efforts. The conviction

you showed in your trials is sufficient for me to be guaranteed of your commitment to this effort.[-]

[-]My prior words stand. Our goal is superior, but I understand that is not the case for humans. As the core of our ultimate objective coincides, I shall accept a supporting role in the Dreg Warrior Initiative formed between you and Bec. [-]

"Does that mean you are going to tell us how not to blow up?" Daniela asked, quirking an eyebrow.

[-]Perhaps Bec was somewhat selective in the information they provided. Catastrophic accumulation is not the main problem when contemplating your path moving forward. [-]

"Can we not be cryptic here? I've tapped my mind for all it's worth today," I said. Daniela snorted, but thankfully didn't follow through that easy laid up insult.

[-]As you are familiar with, Leader Ronan, the Dreg are interfering with the Quotient growth and trait acquisition of local species, most concerningly in humans. The natural order would lead to a consolidation at the sixth Pathway threshold, either to holistic advancement toward the Mortal Limit, transcendental shift into an elemental species, or combustion. [-]

"I gotta say that only one of those sounds appealing at all." My level of concern for what the Entity was implying rose sharply. "Based on your tone, this isn't what the Aberrations want."

[-]It appears they have constituted some further deviation from these paths. Considering the mental openings that unpurged Dreg accumulations cause in the psyche, I would imagine that the Aberrant have been 'pulling the strings,' as you say, of humans for some time. I cannot verify this without further access to data. Early models would suggest tampering on a level much more fundamental than the one we are providing with your MetierTech Implants.[-]

"Wait a minute. Are you saying that the Tendrils have a status just like us?"

CHAPTER FIFTEEN

Corporeal Infusion

[-] That is my hypothesis. The structure seems formulated around a dependence of Dreg sources as opposed to mana. [-]

"Kirby…"

"What about Kirby?" Daniela asked, turning at me with confusion. "I thought you said he died."

"I did, but it didn't make sense. Why did he die when he was perfectly well taken care of? The others in the squad that helped him, though they also looked like they weren't doing too hot," I said, leaning back into my chair as I ran his final words through my mind. "Is it possible to have partial access to this Aberrant status?"

[-] Anything is possible within the Conflux. [-]

"Then Kirby…"

"That bastard probably had access to it. He was already taking advantage of the people in town, what's a little extra power on top of it?" Daniela said.

"Wait, how would that dependency work? Is it reversible or manageable, like with the afflicted?" I asked.

[-] There is insufficient data. As of right now, they are still bound within the Six Prime Pathway Thresholds, but it

wouldn't be out of the scope of possibilities that they could deviate. Your experiences and the information I acquired from Tec on the afflicted is not expansive enough to build a profile. The sensory system overlay built into the implants is capable of sensing energy concentrations, as was its original intent, which are then filtered by the subsystems created by Bec to provide you information. [-]

"The attunement, refinement, and quotients…" I mumbled. That explained some of how Alan had been able to isolate the purging crystal. He'd already been collecting data and studying the frequencies; the implants took the next step and produced 'clear' results.

[-] Correct. This is one of the primary warnings I wanted to convey prior to our… discordance of goals. The Dreg creature you encountered when freeing me was physiologically superior, but it was ultimately a pre-mana creature. It could only bind its Pathways, not channel mana into spell chains. [-]

"Galloway wasn't Fallen," I whispered, my mind running a mile a minute. That was likely the only reason we'd been able to win at all. If a Q7 creature had blasted us with magic, it was dubious if we would have been able to resist it. Based on the recounting of the fight against the death crow, I was inclined to believe it was also lacking access to mana. Its physical power and that aura of death were the only things it showcased, and those could easily be explained as effects from traits.

The truth of the growing mana density was ever more apparent, especially after the Turbulent and Foundational Trials. Quantity would only be able to breach boundaries up to a certain level. If someone with spell chains showed up and deflected all the lower Quotient skills we threw at it, the numbers advantage would turn into mounting losses.

"You think we were being cocky?" Daniela growled.

[-] No. However, it is important to highlight your deficiencies if this initiative is to succeed. Hence, the skill I plan to impart on you both, *and* to further Warriors who reach the Corporeal Limit should they pass the trial. [-]

"We are ready," I said, cutting in before Daniela could argue about us having 'deficiencies.' "Do we need to do anything?"

[-]You will need to develop your own system depending on your traits; this is merely the tool to achieve it. Each attunement will also respond differently. Your goal should be to absorb Dreg from foes or otherwise while directing the volatile energy into developing and strengthening your traits. Should you flag or be overwhelmed, you risk converting your traits into afflictions. See that you do not. [-]

"We can handle it, you over-inflated pebble," Daniela growled.

[-]Very well. Moving forward, you will be able to interface with any one of the Entities within my domain for the Hemispheres Trial. I will impart to you the skill and knowledge you need to begin reforging your body. Recall that there are more humans within this domain that are ignorant of the true enemy. They are now as much your responsibility as the Entities.[-]

A rainbow of light strobed out of the pyramid, blinding me even as it transitioned us back to the cave outside. The world was awash with that light for several seconds until I was able to blink the spots out of my eyes.

Somewhat unsurprisingly, there was an impatient Samuel lingering in the cave. His furrowed brow vanished the moment he laid eyes on us. His relief was evident. "Are you guys—"

Another strobe of rainbow light once again filled my mind until only white remained. I tried to fight the sudden bout of vertigo, but the last thing I felt was the lukewarm touch of the cavern floor pressed against my cheek. A notification, black letters bold against the whiteness, at least told me I hadn't passed out from exhaustion or some other magical ailment.

<Corporeal Infusion>

<Your mind and body are one with the energy of the Conflux.>

In the recesses of the impromptu whitespace, I could feel four throbbing masses of energy. They each had individual signatures; one wobbled with each pulse, another left a grinding sound in the wake of its passage, while the last two reverberated with echoes of different pitches. My thoughts were in disarray, but I could feel my new miscellaneous skill coming into play.

Six spell chains appeared in the air around me, orbiting not unlike they'd done in the Hemisphere Trial. I quickly picked apart my Turbulent and Foundational skills. However, I watched as snakes of mana spilled out from various parts of them to form two smaller spell chains and two much larger ones. The largest of the two chains took to the air around me, spinning and rotating like a gyroscope with me at the center.

As I focused on these extras, I could see that each of the four additions had portions that were akin to the form spell chains took for individuals with Gifts. Glyphs *and* natural formations worked in conjunction to give those skills shape, meaning, and strength. The longer I spent trying to piece together the picture floating before me, the clearer the skills became and alignments started to show. Very helpful bits of information outlined the smaller skills, identifying them as <Pith Mana Lock> and <Infusion>. These two were almost entirely composed of glyphs, but I did note that <Infusion> almost looked like it was transforming from the rigid glyph forms into a Gift. *That's definitely something to keep an eye on.*

My eyes kept following the myriad symbols and shapes around me and the second largest spell chain was identified as <Memory Canal>. In contrast to the smaller skills, it was made up almost entirely of formless mana. Branching lines of pure mana radiated out from only a handful of glyphs, and I couldn't help but to think of neurons reaching out with their axons and dendrites to connect to other neurons. It was the first time I'd seen the spell chain and it was honestly a thing of beauty.

The visualization of <Memory Canal> was disturbed as the fourth and final skill crashed through it, only for the spell chain to reform from a mist-like substance. I traced the offending, gyrating spell chain and its name appeared at the edge of my vision. Unsurprisingly, it was <Corporeal Infusion>. My newest skill almost looked like a backward version of <Memory Canal> as nodes of swirling wisps equidistant from each other were bound by glyphs in various alternating geometric shapes. I could hardly tell if the whole spell chain was consistent or if it was just moving too fast for me to pinpoint its pattern.

With the ensemble of skills, and the strange throbbing pulses coming from the distance of the whitespace, I couldn't help but feel more connected to the changes I'd undergone since arriving at the surface. Fights and injuries, overdrawn mana, yanking the afflicted out of their own entrapped minds, gaining a new sense, and now whatever step I was meant to complete with my new skill. All of the changes culminating toward a cohesive whole.

Gec had said we needed to transfer the Dreg energy into our traits, but I had no clue where to begin. It didn't take much for me to guess the strange pulses were originating from my four traits, but other than being suspended in the air and being able to move my eyes, I didn't think I could locomote. I almost felt hollow in the whitespace. It was very much a contrast to when I'd connected with the afflicted, where I felt *larger* than I actually was. *Maybe that was because you were larger, smarty pants. Your mind was literally connected to that of others.*

Even if the state wasn't the same, I had an idea of how to control things in the whitespace built around my mind. It was crude, but it was definitely a place to start. I focused on the direction of the wobbling pulses with my mind, urging <Earthen Barrier> to connect the space between us. It didn't look pretty, but a muted string of brown mana spiraled out from my body to pave a metaphysical path toward the pulse. The spell chain corresponding to the skill lit up, halting its orbit right in front of me. The longer I fed the skill, the brighter it lit up, taking on that denser coloration I'd seen during the trial.

While I didn't get the mana side effects in the whitespace maintained by <Corporeal Infusion>, I could feel my mind wearing down from controlling the spell chain and directing the effect. It wasn't a huge drain, but it was noticeable. *Maybe infusing traits will work similarly to infusion crafting.* The thought was all I needed for energy to coalesce from the very air within the boundaries of <Corporeal Infusion>. It sparked and jerked like a contained bolt of translucent lightning even as I tried to 'grab' a hold of it with my mind.

Several minutes of unsuccessful mental groping left my mind winded. It was quite literally like catching lightning. With a growl of frustration that seemed to reverberate through the whitespace, the translucent bolt crashed into a solid wall of tan energy before it got locked down by the spell chains of <Earth Shell> and <Terrasheath>. The two skills rotated perpendicular to each other, forming some kind of invisible barrier for the lightning thread as it bounced around its new prison. As the bolt of energy struck the mana barrier, I felt a minute drain on my mind.

The most surprising thing was that I hadn't given them any commands. The skills had reacted in response to my frustration. Like a lightbulb going off, I realized the connection between both skills being my imbue skills. They were responsible for making my will and domain manifest.

It was an important reminder that while things appeared similar to my regular <Infusion>skill, and to when I'd freed the afflicted, things might not work the same. The path formed from <Earthen Barrier> and the energy cage formed by my imbue skills was proof enough of that.

Unsure of what to do with the trapped energy, I followed the path that my materialize skill had been working on the whole time I spent trying to suppress the translucent bolt.

It was a strange combination of floating and walking because I didn't feel my body moving, yet my perspective shifted as I moved down the path further from the point of origin of the whitespace. The wobble grew in intensity from a faint echo to a deep thrum that forced me to stop at the start of each pulse. When the pulses felt as physical as they could get in a mental world, I stumbled upon a humanoid avatar of myself.

It was uncomfortably detailed in its depiction, floating in the air as if it were suspended within a tank of water. Invisible currents tussled my overgrown mop of hair and growing beard as I stared into a pair of blank eyes. If the discovery wasn't unnerving enough, when the pulse came, I watched as my entire body *rippled* like I was the water on the surface of a still pond.

The source of the wobble to the pulse became evident as my skin undulated, adding its own flavor to the drumming pulse. After observing that peculiar behavior, a notification told me what I'd managed to pull together through observation, with some flavor adding to the confusing situation.

<Trait Paradigm>

<Limestone Skin>

<Sublimation Threshold: 12%>

<Macrostructure Impact: Skin>

<Refinement Catalyst: Force>

I watched for several minutes with a certain level of morbid fascination as the model of my skin shifted before my eyes. Other than moving with the sourceless pulse that caused the ripples, there was only one thing that changed. The section marked under <Sublimation Threshold> seemed to be a constantly moving value. Sometimes it showed as high as fifteen percent or as low as nine percent.

There was no other information shown or instructions given, so I could only stare at the trapped energy I'd dragged along with suspicion. With a wave of my mental hand, the mana cage floated over close to the trait paradigm. The next pulse rippled out with enough force to cause my spell chains to dissipate into smoke for a second, releasing the translucent lightning. The next moment, the pulse came again and the bolt froze like a deer in headlights.

Like a drop of ink in a cup of water, tan-colored mana diffused through the bolt until it matched the shade of my skin perfectly. Several splashes went through the bolt, filling it with more color. When the whole thing didn't look like a watered-down version of my mana, but something actually more vivid, it zipped into the abdomen of the paradigm.

Before I had enough time to wonder what had just happened, the world blurred with color and I found myself back in the cave. Instead of just regular exhaustion after enduring the Hemisphere Trial, I had a pounding headache that warranted an immediate nap as well as an uncontrollable itch. It crawled up my fingertips and left me squirming in the ground, pressing myself against the ground for a full minute to try to scratch at the silent torturer.

CHAPTER SIXTEEN

Getting the Gang Back Together

After writhing around on the ground for what had to be a full half hour, the itch finally subsided. A relieved sigh escaped me as I slumped to the ground, true exhaustion threatening to claim me right into sleep. Unfortunately, I had a very concerned friend that immediately rushed to my side and blasted amplified healing right into my brain cavity. It was like crunching through seven of those chocolate coffee beans from the Bunker all at once and my eyes snapped open.

"I'm awake!" I snapped, blinking rapidly to clear the last hints of sleep from my eyes.

Samuel, hair matted and plastered to his head from sweat, let out a nervous chuckle as he slumped back to catch himself on his elbows. "Thank God you two are alright."

"I was fine before you rebooted my brain, Sam," I said, rubbing my eyes. However, somewhere deep inside, I wasn't entirely sure about that.

"He needed it," Daniela groaned from somewhere behind the blond.

"Oy! I don't want to hear anything from you. Why did you

have to be so confrontational with the giant crystal that could vaporize our minds?" I snapped, exhaustion ignored for the sake of taking a shot at Daniela.

"Well, if *you* weren't going to do it…" the Latina drawled.

"I wasn't going to let it—"

"Enough! Before you two are back at each other's throats, can I get a proper answer for what the hell just happened for the last two days?" Samuel said, sitting up and putting a hand in front of both of our faces to cut us off.

I did a double take as I processed what he said. "I'm sorry, did you say two days?"

"Yeah, there was even enough time for Lake Weir to send one of their scouts to relay a message to me. The Allied Town Council is doing fine, by the way, no major waves upon that shore. So to speak. The problem with the gators is getting worse quickly, but that's neither here nor there. Details. Please."

Daniela and I shared a surprised look, but we both recounted the series of events that had happened after the big meeting. Daniela added the bit where Bec plucked her back into the Entity after printing out a somewhat cryptic message for the others telling them about the trial. Samuel also took the opportunity to tell us about the group leaving, and him refusing to leave until we'd returned from the trial. Ava had eventually convinced the other town leaders that getting the changes started would be the most beneficial course of action; the Bunker Busters had proven themselves capable more than once and the trip back wouldn't be too dangerous even without us to muscle through.

We explained the general gist of what we encountered in the trial and how tenuous the situation after Quotient 6 became. That part was news to Daniela, who'd opted to completely concentrate on her trial instead of asking wider questions. She'd gotten the tail end of the discussion after we both passed the tests, but not the details on the bit about exploding, turning into an elemental, or getting corrupted by the Dreg.

"I don't know if I should rush to Q6 or stay at level 5 as long as I can," Samuel mumbled. "You all know the death crow took me right to the cusp of Q6, even after it was spread across all the others raiding Summerfield."

"I think you should advance to Q6. I don't know exactly how creatures progress, but their physicality has always been greater than ours, and any advantage will matter," I said, pausing to stroke my beard. "Gec mentioned areas with higher energy concentrations, which means stronger creatures. I know it seems hard for us, but I can't imagine there aren't more things past the Corporeal Limit that have lived on the surface longer than us. Progress at this Quotient, for me, is the equivalent of four levels if my math is right."

"That's going to take forever," Sam frowned.

"Your traits are supposed to evolve in the process though," Daniela said. "Should help bridge that gap. Not to mention getting better with using our skills."

"Wait, what about that extra skill point you guys have? Isn't Bec able to upgrade one of your skills right now?" Samuel asked.

"I ain't touching that with a ten-foot pole," Daniela said.

"Agreed. After that trial, there is so much more to do with what we have available that it would be pointless to complicate it. I don't think this is a 'more is better' type situation," I clarified. "It's not like I don't already have enough mana-hungry skills to feed."

"I finally get why Bec didn't want to cram those things into our heads as fast as we were leveling early on," Daniela mumbled, shaking her head slowly.

"Okay, so what now?" Sam asked. "Did you guys figure out how to use this <Corporeal Infusion> thing?"

"Kind of?" I said, recalling my experience in my personal whitespace.

Daniela echoed the experience, if a bit different in the way that she chose to move and contain the energy. I tried not to look too jealous when she said she used her skills to rocket boost freely in her whitespace, because that sounded pretty awesome. I did finally get an answer as to why Samuel was sweating as if he was in a sauna; because he kind of had been in one.

Similar to my response after feeding Limestone Skin, Daniela had reacted in the physical world. Unlike my bout of twitching and itching, she'd done her combustion routine again. Samuel had been able to put her out at the cost of his canteen, but that had released the steam cloud that gently cooked my blond friend. Of course, injuries of that level were only a mild inconvenience for the most powerful healer in the Allied Towns, but the manifestations were something to keep in mind when using <Corporeal Infusion>.

Curious to see if anything had changed, I opened my status completely.

Subject: Ronan Terrigan
Health: 100% (Unafflicted)
Mana: 100%
Metier Quotient: 6 (18.75%)
Dreg Accumulation: 0%
LPS: Wildwood Bunker, FL
Communications
Party
Skills - *(1) Selections Available*
Traits - *(0% Banked)*
Attributes - *Growth Quantified*
Skills:
Offensive
- <Stone Spike> / <Terrasheath>/ <Mineral Strike>
- <Freeform>
Defensive
- <Mudpit> / <Earth Shell> / <Earthen Barrier>
- <Freeform>
Misc
- <Pith Mana Lock>
- <Infusion>

- <Memory Canal>
- <Corporeal Infusion>
Traits:
Limestone Skin (12%) > (12 [+2]%)
Quake Osseum (24%)
Slurry Ichor (8%)
Harmonic Sinew (31%)
Attributes:
Strength: 1.93 > 1.94
Mobility: 1.68
Perception: 2.20
Refinement: 1.54
Containment: 2.41

There were a handful of expected changes, like the addition of <Corporeal Infusion> to my miscellaneous skills and <Freeform> under the offensive skills category. Especially after the Hemisphere Trial and <Corporeal Infusion>, I was much more aware of what the miscellaneous skills were and how exactly <Freeform> operated. It was something that would require a fair bit of training to internalize, but I wasn't daunted; it meant the ceiling for power even from where I stood was much higher.

The more surprising changes were for Limestone Skin and my strength attribute. It wasn't entirely out of the scope of reality that I had improved my strength during my routine training back in Wildwood, but I doubted it. I was fairly sure it had to do with the strange line of information attached to my Trait.

Traits:
Limestone Skin (12%) > (12 [+2]%)

How am I even supposed to interpret that? "Danny, do you have something weird attached to your trait progression?"

"Huh?" she said, her eyes glazing over as she looked at her

status. "Yeah, it says my Gills have a segregated percent, but it also progressed at the same time?""

"I have no idea what you two are on about," Sam said, looking between me and Danny.

"We've got to make a note for Bec to add status sharing to the implants," I said, shaking my head. "The <Corporeal Infusion> worked, but it's almost like the progress hasn't been applied? I'm not sure how to describe it other than how Daniela did. It says twelve percent plus two percent without actually summing it."

"Odd..." Sam said, scratching at the scraggly goatee he'd been growing. "I could try to check you guys."

The external nerve webs flowed out of his hands like hundreds of tiny snakes. I had a flashback to when Alexia, Ava, and Sam had examined me before leaving the Bunker and I couldn't help but shiver. Samuel frowned at my response but didn't lower his hands. Reluctantly, I agreed and stepped forward. The most horrifying thing about the check, though, was that I couldn't feel it. The nerve probes struggled to pierce my skin, but when they eventually did, there was no sensory response from me. Nevertheless, the sight of a millipede's worth of hair-thin white filaments crawling up and down my arm as Sam moved had caused more than one nightmare. *Not that I told the healer that, but for such a beneficial trait, why did it have to look so horrible?*

"This is... weird. It's like some of your cells have extra layers. This by itself isn't surprising, since that's how your Limestone Skin manifested, but now some of them have a caked-on layer instead of it being dispersed evenly," Sam said, eyes closed as he continued to run his hands over me.

"You can go ahead and check Daniela," I said in a hurry as Sam started to reach toward my neck-face area with his free hand.

"What a baby," Sam said, shaking his head before turning to Daniela. I didn't comment on the fact that the brunette had taken several steps back the moment Samuel started to turn; her mobility could hardly hide from my perception. However, I wasn't going to begrudge her a slight delay from the horror of the scanning trait.

"Curious…" Sam muttered.

His eyes were closed as he held Daniela's neck between his hands. The woman couldn't see it, but I watched as the spindles probed the space between her gills, essentially tickling the inside of her trachea. I couldn't recall having goosebumps since gaining my skin trait, but they were full-blown as I watched my friend check Daniela. She let out a deep sigh in relief when he eventually retracted his hands.

"What's up, doc?" I said, trying to lighten the tension in the air as Sam scratched his goatee again, except he used the trait's nerves like tiny combs. It was a sight I never wanted to see again, but he continued to do it as he contemplated whatever he'd sensed from both of us.

"Daniela had something similar to you, but hers was like microfilaments trying to reach out from the cell walls. Her trait gives her that already, but these were curled up tight, unlike the others. That trait paradigm page, what did it say again?"

"We only saw it when <Corporeal Infusion> triggered," Daniela said.

"Hmmmm. I have a few hypotheses, but I'll need to see you two in action before we confirm it. Other than that, how are you two feeling?" Sam asked.

"Better than ever, honestly," Daniela said, uncurling her legs and rising to her feet in one smooth motion. Compared to her, my stooped way of standing made me look like a Neanderthal, but I didn't think my mobility was built for that fluidity of motion. Instead of grumbling, I agreed with the brunette. The cloudiness of exhaustion had actually been banished the longer we spoke. I wasn't sure if it was a result of Sam's amplified heal or the effects of <Corporeal Infusion> settling in.

"Then I suggest we try to hunt something on the way back

to Lake Weir. Quotient 6 is calling for me, and I need to check something with you two. We can talk about what we should do while we travel," Sam said.

"Just like back at the start, huh? I'm more than fine with that," Daniela said, an easy grin appearing on her face.

"Could be tough. Maybe we should save our energy for those gators before we do anything rash," I argued. Weakly.

"No. We need to do this and there is no better time for me than now. When we get back into the towns, one thing or another is going to show up to take up my time. The hunt needs to be now," Samuel said, nodding seriously.

The moment Sam, our introverted healer, had displayed a smidge of bloodlust, Daniela and I were already itching. It could have been a result of an infinite number of things, not least amongst them the fact that I knew Sam blamed himself for not being able to save more people during the assault on Summerfield. The glint in his eye as he considered taking the final step to Q6 and joining us as we pushed for power was enough to send adrenaline coursing through me. It was the same glint that had appeared in his eyes when Daniela told us about the MetierTech Implant prototypes years before.

While I was the shield and Daniela the sword, Samuel had always been the spine of our little group. He was the glue and insulator that kept me and the brunette from blowing up on each other when cooperation would give the best result. The blond had been an unerring moral compass despite the maelstrom of new things the surface threw our way.

At that moment, I realized that while I'd been lost in my head, he'd kept at it. Knowing him, he'd turned his pain into strength to support others. I hadn't even spoken to him about what he'd been working on, how he'd dealt with the aftermath of Summerfield, or what his goals for the future were after the Dreg were handled. Despite all of that, Sam had welcomed me back with open arms. The healer had even run interference between Daniela and I as our tempers continued to flare, regardless of how dangerous being the intermediary became as our individual power grew with the addition of magic.

So, I made a decision.

"I'm sorry," I said, drawing confused looks from both of my friends. "About the funk I've been in and just being generally absent. I guess being stuck in your own head is easier and I've taken it out on you guys."

"Don't I know it, you entombed me!" Daniela yelled, redirecting her bloodlust with practiced ease.

"You're right," I said, not rising to the words. My mind wasn't always in the best place, but I could admit when I'd been the asshole. That, by itself, seemed to cause Daniela to deflate slightly. Samuel put the nail on the coffin.

"We know you are, Ron." He turned an upturned eyebrow on Daniela. "I'm just glad that you are willing to talk about it. I know we tease you about plowing straight through all our problems, but we know why you are the tank of the group. Unfortunately, there will be times where you cannot protect us, despite how hard you try."

There were a few seconds of contemplative silence before Daniela groaned. "Now I can't rightly be mad at him anymore. Thanks, Sammy!"

"You are most welcome," the blond said. He tussled my hair before flicking me on the forehead. Instead of what he expected, he flinched as he sanded the end of his nail. It couldn't have been painful, but the goosebumps must have been something else. "Well, I was going to make a point about being more vulnerable with us, but apparently that's difficult just on a baseline."

I couldn't help it, I laughed out loud. Some wetness reached my eyes, but I felt it was more thanks to the relief of knowing that my friends were here with me regardless of how I blundered. It wasn't that the chains of responsibility got any lighter, but having a pair of friends like Samuel and Daniela to lift me up should I falter made things just a tad brighter.

Channeling my uncle, I pulled both of my friends close. Daniela grumbled as I held them in the crux of my elbows and Samuel gave me a crooked smile.

"I think it's time we remind the surface that we didn't leave the Bunker to settle."

CHAPTER SEVENTEEN

Pink Not-Ducks

After our brief bout of bonding, we headed out of Gec's cave. The three of us speculated about what the Q6 threshold, the Corporeal Limit as Gec called it, would mean moving forward. The conversation didn't get the chance to build before a massive gelatinous blob collided with me, flattening me to the ground. Vibrosense had been quiet, as it always was with my companion, as Blobby jiggled and wobbled on my chest like an excited puppy.

"Oh, right! I forgot that Blobby was up here," Sam said, scratching the back of his head awkwardly. "It couldn't go through that membrane into Gec's inner area, so it came back topside."

"I can... see that... Sam," I managed, squirming to keep my face out of the slime's insides. With the Metier Crystals inside the slime, and apparently a few days in the wild, Blobby had regained a significant portion of its bulk. "Down, buddy! I still need to breathe!"

The slime rolled off of me smoothly, keeping a small appendage protruded out of its main body as it prodded me with it. The slime poked my arm some more, before it did

FRANK G. ALBELO

something none of us knew it could do. With concerted effort, the slime pulled its body tight to form a vertical tube roughly my size. Two appendages split from the main body to either side, looking not unlike arms. If I followed that assumption, the slime then proceeded to 'flex' in front of our dumbfounded group.

"I think your slime is telling us it thinks you are stronger," Sam said, unsure. Out of all the creatures the life-attuned could interact with thanks to his traits, the slime was not one of them. The gesture, however, was pretty clear.

"How did you know that, Blobby?" I asked, surprised. The humanoid-shaped slime had the audacity to *shrug* before spilling down into its more *blobby* shape. "What am I going to do with you?"

"Take it hunting with us, that's what!" Daniela said, patting the slime. "I've seen it in action, and I think it's a better defender than a certain rock brain I know."

"You wish," I scoffed, rising to my feet and wiping the thin layer of slime that covered me onto the ground. Blobby rolled over the spot where it fell, reabsorbing it into its body before taking off for the thick forest around us.

"Think it knows where there is something to fight?" Sam asked.

"My bet is on yes," I said, shaking my head.

I readjusted my grip on my chitin scutum and tightened my antler helm. Both bits of armor had actually been left outside of Gec the moment the Entity Cluster pulled us into the white-space. It was a new development, and I wondered why the stronger Entity had done that but not Tec. Sam and the others that had traveled with us to the death territory had also been relieved of their infused gear, only finding it scattered on the cave floor after exiting.

Reequipped and with a 'bloodhound' to lead us, we took off after Blobby. Now not within the simulated existence of the whitespace, vibrosense spread wide around me. I didn't try anything fancy with it, instead just using it to navigate through the thick forest more easily. Daniela had the mobility to weave through the trees, barely slowing down, while Sam looked perfectly capable of reading the foliage somehow. It was a reminder that while I knew their traits, they might have more minutiae that I wasn't even aware of. My Harmonic Sinews were certainly a gift that kept on giving.

Those thoughts were brought out of mind as vibro stirred from a scuffle ahead. A trickle of energy entered my shield and my strength jumped at the same time I did. A divot was left on the ground as I picked up speed and relayed the development to the others through the comm-plant.

The trees thinned over the next few seconds and a small lagoon was revealed. Some of the vegetation, short shrubs and reed-like grass, of the proper death territory remained at the edge of the lagoon. The things in the water were what gave me pause. It was like some kind of mix between a duck and a flamingo, with vibrant stripes of pink clashing with gray highlights on their plumage. Each was easily the size of a human, which was highlighted by two mitosed Blobbys clinging to the stick legs of the creature. My perception easily highlighted its information as a whole flock of them came into view the next moment, clearly agitated by the sudden attack.

<Roseate Spoonbill>
<Attunement: Air>
<Refinement: Squall>
<Perceived Metier Quotient: 2>

There were easily a dozen of the creatures that had been pecking at the waters, but now they converged on my gelatinous companion. With a grunt, I focused on a single <Stone Spike> and used my newfound control on the spell chain. Instead of doing anything complex, I focused solely on one thought. *Reach.*

The skill chomped through ten percent of my mana, but it manifested much more differently than before. It still pinched the muck-filled earth on the bank of the lagoon, but instead of going for wide, it went for long. Like a javelin thrown out of the ground itself, the <Stone Spike> impaled all the way through the spoonbill nipping at Blobby. The structural integrity of the spike was nowhere its usual, breaking at the middle length, but that just benefited the slime as the spoonbill seemed unable to keep itself airborne with the extra hunk of stone in its body.

I was so surprised by how reactive the skill had been that I stopped long enough for one of the flock to reach me. A hair-tussling breeze was all I felt before the creature's stick-like, but still Quotient-enhanced, legs tried to pulp my chest. The wind was knocked out of me by the attack, but my Quake Osseum practically laughed at the force behind the attack. Compared to Galloway, it was a tickle. The impact with the tree at the edge of the lagoon was a slightly different story.

My health dipped a full fifteen percent from the attack and collision, but the more worrisome part was the branch sticking out of my shoulder. My trait-reinforced shoulder blade had deflected the wood right to my deltoid muscle.My shield arm sagged as the muscles failed me when they tore under my weight, dropping to the ground. The pain was significant, the world going black and white and my mind scrambling from the vibro feedback.

The wind in the lagoon battered everything, picking up mud and water as the bulk of the flock started to work in concert for something. My Slurry Ichor worked overtime to close the torn muscle with a sludge scab and I blinked the dirt out of my eyes. Samuel was encased in a cage of bushes as vines reached up from the ground to slap down the spoonbills. Daniela was a red blur intertwined with her wisp as she almost seemed to ride the same gusts the birds were building. A trail of fire seemed to follow her <Heat Touch>. One of the spoonbills combusted as her <Flame Blast> collided, the fire feeding off the air that circled it before it was smothered.

"God, I hate flying enemies," I muttered through grit teeth, struggling to my feet.

A vine rose out of the ground and shot <Health Bump> into my wounded arm, the pain lessening thanks to the cool, refreshing energy. Instead of bothering to wait for it to heal all the way, I locked the elbow close to my body and held it with my right arm. My tower shield left just my eyes and shins exposed as I forced my way closer to the buffeting winds. Eight of the birds still circled the lagoon and I could see their mana spilling liberally into the growing tornado.

The force of the wind was even enough to push Daniela far enough that her range advantage was neutralized. It was an impressive response from a bunch of Quotient 2 creatures, and a good reminder that we hadn't encountered everything possible with magic. However, that didn't mean that the power of our Quotients could be ignored.

"<Crystal Cascade>!"

My mana dropped right to half as a double empowered, amplified <Mineral Strike> formed in front of me. While the hunk of what had to be felspar grew, it was light. The gusting winds grabbed the attack and took it away. The mana continued to crystalize until the wind wasn't able to lift it any higher and the attack ruptured. The first bout of mineral fragments didn't strike any of the spoonbills, their winds easily letting them dodge the attack, but they couldn't dodge the hundreds of razor-sharp projectiles from the subsequent explosions.

Three of the remaining eight birds went up in a puff of feathers, their bodies thrown out toward the trees with the rotation of their own attack. Having seen the result of my own attack, Daniela grinned and threw her hands forward. <Flame Blast> after <Flame Blast> joined the weakening tornado. Even when they were snuffed out, the heat in the area quickly turned stifling as the brunette unloaded her mana pool into the tornado. Thankfully, it didn't light the whole thing aflame like one might have expected in a movie, but it was enough to force the spoonbills to disperse.

The creatures, having seen they were unable to take down their attackers, tried to flee over the trees. Only for said trees to come alive. Branches way up grasped like verdant hands, easily crushing the remaining creatures. Samuel didn't waste mana releasing them, instead leaving them up in the air as the man squeezed through his defensive bushes.

"That went terribly," our healer said.

"I don't like flyers," I responded.

"Nice call on the crystals," Daniela said, slapping me on the shoulder. I let out a grunt of pain, glaring at the woman as she chuckled and went to check on Blobby. She started plucking sticks and rocks out of its gelatinous body. The slime had more than a few pieces of debris stuck within its body, but it seemed to be happily digesting the spoonbill I'd helped it kill.

"I think we are a bit rusty working together," Sam said, scratching his goatee. "Do you think we should have trained a bit before jumping into a fight?"

I was one hundred percent sure we'd seen Ava's frowning face in our mind's eye. The three of us shared a look before we started laughing. Mine was more of a pained series of huffs, but I still joined in. There was something about the pump of the moment, about being the attacker instead of the defender, that left us all jittery for more. We weren't dumb enough to act on that, especially after the debacle of the engagement, but we weren't going to beat ourselves up for it. The numerous fights against the Fire Ants had shown that knowledge of the creatures and their behaviors were invaluable, so engagements against new creatures with unknown abilities would have a cost. It was simply the risk of the surface and it had been months since we'd acknowledged it.

We agreed to reconvene when we returned to Lake Weir or Wildwood, and discuss what we could have done better, but that was something we did after the adrenaline of the fight had settled.

I did my best to wait patiently for Sam to regenerate his mana while Daniela and Blobby kept watch. I was also technically keeping watch as vibrosense extended out between the trees all around us, but I wasn't in any shape to respond. Instead of wasting my meager focus training vibro like I usually did, I took stock of the spoils of the battle.

The gluttonous slime somehow managed to digest most of his bird—they were mostly feathers, it seemed—and snagged another from the edge of the lagoon. That left ten total for the rest of us to dissociate. I did some quick math based on my power-of-three model for Quotients, which netted me something in the range of one-point-three percent for my Dreg accumulation after splitting the Q2 flock between us. Not at all groundbreaking for a fight where I'd torn a muscle, but unfortunately that was how the cookie crumbled.

For Samuel, however, that netted him almost four percent. When I told him as much, the Q5 healer sent frowns at all the birds like they had insulted his father personally to his face and I didn't think it was because most had managed to avoid his <Vine Whips>. When I asked him as much, he had a simple answer. He would be one percent short of his goal.

Naturally, Daniela laughed at him while Sam grumbled the whole while. I made the tactical decision for Blobby's sake not to remind the blond that he might have made it if Blobby hadn't eaten two of our winged targets. The man probably wouldn't hold it against the slime, but no need to throw fuel on the fire.

After a good fifteen minutes, Samuel finally hit my injured shoulder with his amplified healing skill. <Restoration Surge> wormed its way through my muscles, and I watched it take hold of the strained fibers that my Slurry Ichor held together and repair the damage. Flakes of hardened blood-mud fell to the ground as my Limestone Skin regenerated over the injured shoulder.

He topped me off with a <Health Bump> and I felt the last bit of the pain drain away into a stiff soreness. My arm didn't want to lift all the way, but Sam assured me that my passive regeneration would have me good to go before long. A glance at my health showed a steady three percent missing, with no afflictions, but it certainly felt like I had one.

Nevertheless, our group was back to more than reasonable shape. Instead of risking another fight, I managed to convince a frustrated Sam and fight-pumped Daniela to hold off and instead make the final step by taking a trip to the spider territory dungeon. That was, of course, with the assumption that something in the wild didn't try to take a bite out of us.

Now healed, we turned to the bit that Daniela and I were most hesitant of. Dissociating stuff as Q6'ers.

CHAPTER EIGHTEEN

Assimilating Catalysts

"So, how do you want to do this?" Daniela asked, hovering over one of the spoonbills she'd charbroiled.

"One at a time?" I answered, slightly unsure. The absorption wasn't the worst pain I'd endured since arriving at the surface, but there was something about willingly 'poisoning' yourself. It could be argued that overdrawing mana had a similar result, but that often just felt like nausea or a strained muscle, *not* like you were being ripped up from the outside.

"I was thinking all at once, but I suppose it's best to get the hang of the process rather than just passing out," Danny agreed.

The woman gave me a nod and I nudged the dead spoonbill with my boot. The response was immediate as it crystallized faster than I'd ever seen them. I wasn't sure if it was due to the disparity in Quotients or something else, but it was wholly covered in less than five seconds. With the tinkle of breaking glass, the corpse turned into the usual Pith cloud. The shimmering energy hovered in the air for a beat before splitting three ways. I tensed my whole body as I watched the finger thin cloud flow into my chest.

Instead of leaving behind the warmth of Pith, I saw the iridescent stream get filtered as it got within a foot of my body. Like a current splitting on a rock, the Pith parted around me and a hazy brown flowed into me. The sight reminded me of what Bec had said long ago about attunement being related to the type of Dregs remaining in the body. That was all the time I had as my already tense muscles groaned against the energy being fed into them. It was less of a strain than when we fought the luminous panthers, but it was uncomfortable nonetheless.

The next moment, however, <Corporeal Infusion> took form around me. Glyphs sprouted off my skin, drawing in the Dreg that had been flowing into my body like a magnet and the discomfort abated. I saw a similar response from Daniela as her fiery mana swam through the air. Sam stood mute between us, eyes reflecting the light from the two spell chains.

"That's pretty awesome," he whispered as the last bits of energy faded away with <Corporeal Infusion>.

"I'd say it's an improvement over the last time," I said.

"Ditto," Daniela answered. "You think that there are other ways to handle those Dregs? Obviously we absorbed them more or less fine the last time, fever spike and seizure aside."

"I think you might be right," I said, nodding at her words. "Gec mentioned that it was a path built around us since our Pathways were imprinted with the glyph-based skills, instead of the more organic Gifts that some of the surface survivors have. How that shakes out, we'll have to see. There are too many unknowns up in the air and, as far as our group is concerned, we are breaking new ground."

"Alan is going to have an aneurysm, isn't he?" Sam said, shaking his head while releasing a sigh.

"Alan is probably our best bet at getting some answers as to just what the heck is going on. We still have that weird segregated progress on our traits," I replied.

"Oh! Yes, let me check what I thought about," Sam said, rushing over to me without delay. His nerve spindles flashed out, probing me through my torn shirt. The healer mumbled to himself for several seconds before nodding. He didn't say anything, instead he spun and pounced on Daniela's trait. He went back and forth between the two of us for a few minutes as he mumbled to himself.

"Well? Care to share your thoughts with the class?" Daniela said, halting Sam in place before he could start probing her neck again. The blond seemed to snap out of his strange trance, his eyes opening and blinking as if blinded by the shaded light in the lagoon.

"You two have assimilated those changes. Most of your gill filaments have extended, and Ronan, your cell walls have evened out more. Check your progress on the traits," Sam said, the edges of his mouth curling up.

I stared at the man skeptically, but opened up my Status regardless. Most of it was unchanged, but sure enough there were two small, but significant changes.

Metier Quotient: 6 (19%)
Traits:
Limestone Skin (12 [2]%) > (13 [1]%)
Quake Osseum (24%)
Slurry Ichor (8%)
Harmonic Sinew (31%)

My Limestone Skin trait had integrated *one* of the two percent that had been isolated. Along with that change, the progress that my Quotient Level had been locked at since the fight with Galloway had finally changed. Considering the two events happened at the same time, it couldn't be a coincidence. Gec's words about our progress being tied to our body made a whole lot more sense. I wasn't clear on what advancing our Quotients *without* building that energy into our traits would entail, or how we might go about it, but I was at least glad to see tangible progress from our efforts.

"Okay, that's somewhat good news, but care to enlighten us

as to what happened?" I said, spinning my hand in a 'go on' gesture.

"I'm not sure of the specifics, but it looked like your bodies needed something to instigate the assimilation. Perhaps it's not enough to slap some of that evolutionary potential you described, but you need to give it a nudge," Sam said, shrugging. "Or it could be magic. That's always a reasonable answer, I've found."

"All I did in that last fight was cast two skills and get my ass thrown at a tree," I complained.

"You know, there did seem to be more of the assimilated cells on your back and chest than anywhere else. Even from the parts I helped you heal," Sam added, his finger wagging in consideration.

"That pebble could have given us a better lesson on how this damn skill works," Daniela growled, her voice rising to meet her irritation. She flicked her middle finger in the general direction of the Entity's crystal before focusing back on our conversation. "Anyway, so I have to, what? Torch myself every time I want the change to stick?"

"Perhaps? Your gill filaments do seem to be temperature sensitive."

"Hold on, give me a second," I said, plopping on the ground. I'd meant to do that for the sake of resting, but the conversation had jumped topics and revelations much too fast. My thoughts drifted as I scoured the space in my mind where my skills lurked.

Instead of the 'button' I'd always pictured in my head, the skills were clustered as a series of knobs with a matching level for each of them, miscellaneous or not. It was almost a subconscious change, but the fluctuating parameters I accessed during the Hemisphere were indelibly part of my mind. On top of that, the skills were organized just as I'd seen them in <Corporeal Infusion>'s whitespace. Smack dab in the middle of all of that, however, was the latest troublemaker.

Tensing slightly, I triggered <Corporeal Infusion>. The

perspective in my mind didn't actually change much, but the featureless void of my thoughts suddenly looked like someone had turned on the lights. The imagined console panel with levers and knobs was replaced by the living spell chains for my skills as the gyroscopic, trait-manipulating skill started up.

Everything was the same; pulses echoing in from beyond my perspective, orbiting spell chains, and even the path of mana leading off toward Limestone Skin's Trait Paradigm. Since that was what I was looking for, my perspective shifted as I started to move toward my trait faster than the first time.

As I drifted, I could feel zinging particles of dust in the air. I wasn't sure what they were, but I had a good guess it was the smidge of Dreg I'd acquired from the spoonbill. That tangible change sent a trill of excitement through me again. It was like I was actually in control of everything going on in my body, instead of being set upon by the winds of change that came with the magic on the surface. I was perfectly aware it was an illusion of control in a sense, since it stemmed from Gec's given skill, but I opted to think of it as a tool. *True* control would come along with my proficiency.

Ignoring the energy for now, I focused on the rippling effigy of myself hovering in the air.

<Trait Paradigm>

<Limestone Skin>

<Sublimation Threshold: 13% [+1%]>

<Macrostructure Impact: Skin>

<Refinement Catalyst: Force>

Bingo. The nomenclature wasn't perfectly clear, but with Sam's observation, it was easy to confirm. The <Refinement Catalyst> was the requirement to assimilate the energy given to the trait. Daniela had cooked herself in the tornado, hardly an inconvenience for her really, while I'd been slapped against a tree. The impact was easily managed; the injury to my shoulder was what had slowed me down during that fight.

With my question answered, I focused on pulling back the mental 'lever' for <Corporeal Infusion> and my mind returned to the flitting soup of my thoughts. I opened my eyes and blinked them for a second in order to focus on my friends.

"—check out," Daniela complained.

"I'm sure he had a good reason, Danny," Samuel answered, putting on his patented calm-down-Daniela voice.

"He always has a good reason, Samuel. Did he even realize that we've been relying on his senses more and more? The only reason that I'm still the scout of this group is because he's a turtle in human clothing!"

"I'm right here, you know," I said, cracking my neck and standing up.

"What?" Daniela said, spinning around to face me. Her brown eyes burned, fire-attunement notwithstanding, as she met my gaze. "You've been sitting there like a moron with a stupid grin on your face for over thirty minutes, Ron!"

"What?" I asked, my snide shot back dying in my throat. That same stupid grin on my face slipped into a concerned frown. "I felt like I was gone for maybe a minute…"

That seemed to finally give Daniela's ire some pause. She turned to Sam, asking a pointed question about how long we'd been unconscious after exiting Gec's whitespace.

"Something like an hour? I figured it was exhaustion or something because your vitals were normal. Of course, that was before you two started doing your magic twitches," the blond answered.

"It was only a few minutes…" Daniela whispered, her anger replaced with concern. I didn't plan to ignore the words she'd said before, but right then wasn't the moment.

"All I did was activate <Corporeal Infusion> and check on that statement for my Trait Paradigm," I said, drawing back the attention of both my friends. "I didn't know there was some time perception shenanigans going on, but can we really be surprised?"

"I suppose not, considering you are basically blasting your cells with the equivalent of magical radiation hoping they change productively," Sam stated matter-of-factly.

"When you put it like that, it makes me not want to do it again," I said, frown deepening.

"Then by all means ignore me. Please, do tell us what you confirmed."

Despite my worry about the lost time, I couldn't help but snort at Samuel's display of confidence. "I think you were exactly right, Sam. More specifically, the <Refinement Catalyst> portion I think refers to the kind of stimulus required to assimilate the Dreg once it's been fed to a trait."

"Wait, my gill's was heat," Daniela said, slapping herself on the forehead. "Of course it's heat."

"I haven't checked my other traits, but I would be surprised if it's not the same or something similar. The premise of each is all around mitigating damage to my body," I added.

"Same with overheating for me," Daniela said.

"Now I'm curious what mine are," Sam said with a nervous chuckle. "Mine are all about feeling and connecting to things."

"Breaking new ground," I repeated.

"I bet Clara is going to have to sniff some farts or something," Daniela wondered aloud.

"Danny!" Sam admonished.

"No, no. I think she's on to something," I agreed.

Samuel groaned loudly, eliciting a round of laughs from us. Blobby, who'd been quiet a little way from our group, exited stealth long enough to jiggle its body as if it were laughing as well. This, of course, reignited our bout of laughter, and some of the tension of the day's fast-paced developments drained away.

Things were getting more and more complicated while Daniela and I were on the cusp of butting heads like never before. But despite all of that, I knew that my friends were there for whatever came. I could only hope the situation didn't boil over at the worst time.

CHAPTER NINETEEN

First Report Back

After the initial slowdown with the first spoonbill, we worked our way through the rest quickly. Each gathered bit of Dreg struck our bodies for a second before <Corporeal Infusion> kicked in. Fortunately, once Daniela and I figured out how to keep it active between dissociating corpses, the wear on us vanished almost completely. Unfortunately, it was only for the last few dissociations. The trick was to rush getting the energy while focusing on the skill to keep it active. It was like juggling with a limb you didn't know you had, but it was much preferable to the flicker between well and seizing that happened with each corpse at the start. However, after experiencing the stinging of the dust during my 'brief' visit into the Trait Paradigm, I knew those few we managed to deflect would be back for a vengeance during our next proper activation.

The last corpses we dissociated were the ones Sam had trapped up on the canopy. To impress us, he actually channeled his <Arboreal Grasp> and triggered the dissociation at range. The man was very smug... up until I pointed out that the infusion and material loot was still up in the trees.

With a snickering Daniela in the background, Sam deposited the last of our loot on the small pile we'd created. Ten Q2 air infusions and over half a dozen feathers the size of my forearms. One of the spoonbills that had been killed up in the trees actually dropped its beak. That particular material shone with a green outline, marking it as a potential component for an amplitude infusion item.

The thought of crafting made me *want* to craft, not least of which because I was still barehanded. It didn't mean I wasn't happy to punch or shield bash things, especially with the addition of <Terrasheath> to my repertoire, but I was a fan of having at least a tad bit of range in combat. The thought of what the Allied Council would need, the looming threat going on north of Gec, and progress at the Corporeal Limit easily crushed any chance of me finding an opening to work on infusion crafting. Nevertheless, I vowed to sneak in some time for it while in Wildwood.

I have a working budget now, don't I? I wondered as we made our way back toward Lake Weir. There wasn't anything in particular that we needed from there, but I was looking forward to at least a day to process everything. Plus, if the threat of the gators in the lake was truly expanding, then I was sure that would be the next target for the Wild Guard and our own squad.

The three of us traveled in silence and, after just under an hour of travel, we arrived at the Weirdian wall. A guard called out in greeting, motioning to the gate and letting the three of us in. To my surprise, people were primed to greet us as they asked a million questions about a million things. From tips on infusion crafting to proper flight technique to mana horticulture. The last set was almost solely directed toward Samuel, who had the biggest part of the audience. Daniela and I looked around confused, but Samuel explained that he'd been in correspondence with the active guard due to the scout rotation that checked in on the death territory.

"Why are these people asking us all these things?" Daniela

asked through the comm-plant, not wanting to offend anyone as she kept a strained smile on her face.

"They see us as the epitome of what the council is looking for. Crafting, combat, and infrastructure. Not to mention, we are extremely well-known and popular, especially with the kids," Sam said matter-of-factly. For an introvert, he handled a slew of questions about horticulture with aplomb.

Thankfully, a skeletal-limbed man parted through the crowd, dispersing them back to their various responsibilities. There was more than one grumble, but the huff from the vine-haired man behind Ian set the whole lot scrambling. Only the guard who'd let us in remained, looking sheepish. Maurice raised an eyebrow in his direction, and the man double-timed it back up to the wall. He bowed and excused himself profusely the whole way up to the small ramparts.

"Hard to find incorruptible help these days," Ian joked.

"Hard to find any help at all, Dad," Maurice countered.

"Yes, Maurice, we are all aware." Ian let out a suffering sigh before turning back to our group. "Welcome back."

"Something about being behind a wall is very appealing," I said, smiling at the old man.

"Especially when it's inspired by your handywork, I imagine."

"That doesn't hurt," I said, shrugging.

"Come on, we can talk in Wec's crystal," Ian said, waving his hand over his shoulder.

"Actually—"

"If we could—"

Daniela and I both interrupted each other. The Latina waved her hand, motioning me to continue. "Actually, I think we've had enough of the whitespaces for a minute. Your office will work just fine. It's not like Wec doesn't know what we plan to tell you all already."

"Very well," Ian said slowly. "Maurice, see if you can't scrounge up something to eat that isn't dried rations. A few days in the wilderness couldn't have been comfortable."

"You have no idea," Daniela mumbled as we walked toward the pre-Fall school building.

If it was possible, Lake Weir looked even more vibrant than when we'd left for Gec. The fruits looked more saturated with color and the bushes were forming natural walls to segment the open areas of the town by grow zones. With so much growth everywhere, the pathways that had originally been built for defense were now used as the main thoroughfares of the town. I couldn't help but think of them as a road system. *If the town grows much more, then it will become the only means of moving about.*

My musings about the infrastructure of Lake Weir were cut short as we passed by Wec, a gap in the hanging vines exposing its shimmering surface. The Entity's crystal was visible from beyond the walls, but now finally being close to it brought its growth into perspective. From the small, wagon-sized chunk of Tec that our excursion had brought, the Metier Crystal had grown to incorporate itself into the old school structure.

Where Gec bloomed into several tetrahedral peaks, secretly reaching deep below ground, and Tec towered over Wildwood with its massive singular bulk, Wec had followed Bec's route.

Through its transparent crystal, I could see a few people climbing stairs to reach the watchtowers built into the roof of the school. Some even moved straight through where there had once been a wall just to flow down to ground level like a fancy magic elevator-tube slide combination.

The development left me excited for when Bec, who'd started our collaboration with the Entity Clusters in the first place, would be able to grow into the next Category. It was already incorporating itself into the keep I'd been constructing over the Bunker, and having it assist with magical amenities would be an awesome sight.

One such amenity that Wec had implemented while expanding over into the school was lights. Where there had once been torches and a number of candle-brazier-barrel sources of light in the building in the rooms with no windows, now there were hanging crystals in the ceiling. Usually one or two per room, but they shined a soft white light not unlike the LEDs in the Bunker. If the computer systems, data banks, and simulation classrooms weren't set up in the Bunker, I would have almost suggested that they return the building back to its original function before the Fall. It was part of the way there already.

Instead, it was still the primary source of housing for the Weirdians. Their small council had designated spaces for the various crafts and storage necessary to survive the decades after the Fall. It was yet another testament to human ingenuity and perseverance to see the different ways in which the towns had survived. Combining all the strengths of the groups in the Council was the first step into truly forming a cohesive front to regain the surface for humanity.

Before long, Ian led us to his office and the three of us practically collapsed into the worn couches stashed within. Ian gave us a bemused smile as he waited patiently for his son to return. A half-hour later, Maurice returned with a spread of fruits and vegetables that had me salivating. Since coming to the surface, I'd realized that I'd always craved to be a carnivore instead of the pescatarian-vegetarian blend that us Bunkerborn had been raised on. That did not mean that I couldn't shovel an inhuman amount of fructose and veggies when they were presented. The tough bread and flavorless bean paste that was standard fare for the Wild Guard were a far cry from the insta-meals available in the Bunker, but I didn't think it was physically possible for me to reject fresh food since the moment I tasted it.

When we finally retreated from the ravaged tray of food, Ian's expression was slightly more strained. Maurice was holding back laughter as he stood over his father's shoulder. Ian cleared his throat before proceeding to ask for updates.

And update him we did. The trial, the preliminary testing we'd done, as well as all the bits of knowledge we'd acquired about <Corporeal Infusion> were passed on. Ian and Maurice both started taking notes on some pads when they realized the deluge of information coming their way.

While it was just a short amount of time since the trial, the three of us had already spent a lot of time contemplating the data we had available. Our combat bout and slips into our whitespaces weren't scientific in nature, but that didn't mean it couldn't be structured as such. It was a side effect of being raised by in-field experts and then subsequently surrounded by other talented people in the Bunker.

None of us had discussed our theories, but many overlapped with our fields of expertise. It was the key reason why I was still requested to give lessons on infusion crafting and Samuel was sought out for anything healing or horticulture related. There weren't any universities or trade schools left on Earth that we knew of, but the Bunker had a pretty good information base and we'd had nothing but time before coming to the surface.

"That was certainly...extensive," Ian said, finally putting down his pencil after almost an hour of writing.

"We like to be thorough," Daniela said, crossing her arms and leaning back on the couch.

"Yes, you can't be faulted for that. Especially when it comes to something like this," Ian started. "As a matter of fact, one of our fighters actually hit Q6 while you all were away. We pulled him from patrol the moment he did, but it's good to know he might be able to join back up. He's able to handle one of the crocs singlehandedly."

"How's the situation there?" I asked, leaning forward.

"Stable for now. With the hanging gardens, we haven't needed to rely on fishing as much to hold up our food stores. This let us dedicate more people to the lake defense. Not to mention the guard's contribution in squads, and Wec's presence easing the pressure from the other parts of the wall," Maurice explained.

"Does the Allied Council have a plan they are looking to implement?" I asked.

"Currently, they are trying to get Gec's guidelines in place. It's not a leap, but there are a handful of people pushing back.

They don't think we should be listening to the 'alien rocks that caused this problem in the first place,' I quote."

"Unfortunately, they have a point," Ian added. He raised his hands to cut off the argument already rising to my mouth. "*I* understand, Mr. Terrigan. The fighters and the farmers do as well, especially after they have seen what the implants do. We are close to the level of communication we had before the Fall, which has helped relieve a lot of the stress being isolated caused. But there are a few tough nuts to crack. As much as I see the benefits, if Maurice hadn't survived through the Fall, I think my view would not have been as amenable to the Metier Crystals."

My mouth shut with a clack as I was forced to accept his point. It wasn't something I'd considered since we'd been working together with Bec for so long I often forgot that their arrival had been a fundamental shift in the laws of Earth. Even when the world was 'civilized,' there had been disagreements. A high stress environment with death lurking around every corner would likely cause many times more.

"Let me know who they are; I'll pay them a visit and see if they are still willing to cause trouble," Danny said casually.

Thankfully, I didn't have to be outraged alone because Sam jumped up.

"Daniela! They are entitled to their own opinion. As long as they don't impinge on the rest of the group, we are *not* going to strongarm them," the blond said.

"Fine, fine. It was just a suggestion," Daniela mumbled in response, sulking even further back in her seat.

"We'll pass the Q6 information on to Stonecrest," I said, shifting the topic back. "Then Wildwood. Be prepared to be called forth for another Entity conference call once we've got everything arranged. I'll reconvene with Sarah on the subject of the gators, and we'll focus our efforts there. Gec was vague on a lot of things, but *not* on the fact that there was more Dreg to fight. If there are people out there that need our help, then we need to *reach* them."

"You three really know how to light a fire under someone, eh?" Maurice said.

"What can I say? When you spend your whole life idling, the first thing we want to do is go full throttle." I chuckled. Samuel and Daniela matched my smile as we parted from the Weirdians. There was plenty of work left to do.

CHAPTER TWENTY

Live Load

"You know, the world is very much a fantasy one now," Sam said out of the blue.

"Your point?" Daniela asked as she dropped from her perch up on a tree. Even as she walked close to the group, her eyes scanned for anything that had the guts to attack one of the highest leveled squads in the area.

"I'm sure we can figure out a way to make Bags of Holding," Samuel said, tapping the straps of the three travel rucksacks on his shoulder. "I'm tired of carrying stuff."

It wasn't possible for me to be outraged because I was just speechless. In the process of leaving Lake Weir, Samuel had been halted by Maurice. The Weirdian had led the group to a wagon stacked high with grapes and strawberries in crates. Since we didn't have Anthony, or one of Wildwood's oxen, the beast of burden role had once more fallen to me. Daniela took point as our scout and damage dealer, while Samuel carried our original subset of supplies and healed me for the sake of refreshing my stamina.

I was distinctly unhappy about being used for my strength, but Samuel and Daniela had been improving other attributes as a result of their attunements so I couldn't blame them for that. What I *could* blame Sam for was the nonsense he was spouting.

"Samuel, you ungrateful piece of—"

"Shhhh, we are almost at the wall," the blond said, grinning as he took the lead of our little group. Daniela was equally as surprised as I was by Sam's boldness, but he wasn't out of the dog house yet. She shook her head, silently taking my side, but just followed after Sam to make sure something didn't get the drop on him over the last quarter mile to Stonecrest.

"I don't think my contributions are appreciated in this group, Blobby," I told my slime companion. Said gelatinous blob was rolling just to the left of me and it wiggled in agreement before following after my friends. "Traitors, the lot of you."

Despite all my grumbling, I arrived at Stonecrest in less than fifteen minutes. The sight of my arrival stirred up the guards and I watched with curiosity as two Stoneshapers appeared on the wall. The two mirrored gestures where they pulled their hands apart as mana flared over their skin. To my surprise, a gap formed in the smooth stone leading into the Walmart-turned-shelter town. I wasn't sure if it was a new skill, or a trick of Freeforming their Gifts, but it was an impressive show of their control.

As I pulled the wagon into the town proper, the Stoneshapers repeated the gesture and shut the wall behind me.

"Impressive," I said after spotting Angel, Rachael's second in command, approaching me.

"They're trying their best. Someone had to go out of their way to make one of the bases look like a spider, so the Shapers have gotten a *tad* ambitious," the man said, an easy smile on his face. It was a big leap back from the nice-guy-into-more-hostile-guy approach he'd taken when Rachael and I had Gift Wrestled.

"That got around, did it?" I said, chuckling awkwardly.

"Oh, it certainly did. Especially when this one very talkative elf boy shouted your praises to the wind," another voice added.

Jasmine, the chief healer of Stonecrest, dropped easily to the ground from where she'd been approaching.

I turned, surprised. I hadn't actually sensed her approach and I quickly realized it was thanks to the mana-based properties of the Shaper's work. Unlike the ground, the wall they'd surrounded the town with was constructed with their Gifts, and my vibrosense was muted from the steady thrum of energy within the conjured stone. *Something to watch out for. Maybe I can learn to read that feedback better?*

Jasmine seemed to realize I was running through something in my mind because she rolled her eyes and turned to Angel without missing a beat. "Is Rachael out of her seclusion yet?"

"That's a negative," Angel said, concern flashing on his face.

"Wait, what? Seclusion?" I asked, refocusing on the conversation instead of the ripples of the world around me.

"She dropped a load of work on Angel the moment she got back and pushed to Q6 despite our best warnings. She said something about 'I can feel it' and then off she went," the healer said, making a dismissive motion toward the building. "She's been holed up since. Literally. She dug herself a hole and hasn't come out from there."

"Hmmmm," I said, trying to figure out what the dwarven woman had felt. Considering she was the best Gift Wrestler out of the Allied Towns, by the admission of most *and* myself, then it was entirely possible she'd touched upon the concepts Gec had imparted to us. That is, touched on them *without* the Entity's skill to help. "Have my friends caught you guys up?"

"No? They mentioned you had news. Daniela is getting up to speed with a Wild Guard squad in town for help with your trip south and Samuel went over to the gardens," Angel said. "I'm surprised they didn't wait for you."

"They are being difficult. You guys wouldn't happen to have an ox to spare, would you? My slime isn't physical enough to pull a wagon," I said, half-joking.

"Your... slime?" Angel asked, confused.

"He means the thing that's been lurking over there by the wall," Jasmine said, pointing over her shoulder at what seemed to be another patch of dirt road.

Angel and I looked at the spot for several seconds before Blobby jiggled into view, the perfect color-matched dirt being replaced with his darkening lime-green gelatinous body. The slime formed an appendage and seemed to wag it in admonishment toward the healer. At least *that* seemed to catch her by surprise. Blobby returned to ball form and rolled away down the road deeper into town as if it was perfectly normal.

"Alright, I'm out," Angel said, throwing his hands up in the air. "You can tell Jas whatever and she'll pass it on to me. I've about had it with magic today."

Angel headed straight for one of the Shaped buildings closer to the warehouse in the center of town without even looking back. The healer and I shared an awkward look before she chose to break the ice formed in the wake of Angel's sudden departure.

"I didn't realize your... follower was so intelligent," Jasmine said.

"Sometimes I feel like it's smarter than me," I said, shrugging. "I'm more impressed that you managed to spot Blobby I can hardly spot him and he has to be moving for me to do that."

"Blobby, huh. Well, it has a life signature," the woman said, as if that explained everything.

"Oh yeah, totally."

"You have no idea what a life signature is, do you?"

"Not one bit."

"It's similar to an aura projected by living things. The MetierTech Implants tell me it's some enhanced Pith sense, whatever that actually means. It does seem to correlate to the Quotient of people, but not always."

"The descriptions do tend to be fairly vague. I'm starting to realize that was mostly on purpose because..."

For the better of an hour, I proceeded to share the same

information with Jasmine that we'd given the Weirdians, in addition to the tentative meeting invitation. Her feedback on the adaptability of Gifts was actually very beneficial, and I vowed to add Gift Wrestling to my training repertoire if the time somehow spontaneously generated itself; I was busy enough as it was.

While I hadn't been successful at the individual skill tests of the Hemisphere Trial, I suspected the people of Stonecrest would have an advantage. That train of thought also plowed through my mind as I considered what fighting other Q6 individuals would entail. If I needed to handle an empowered skill from a damage dealer, wouldn't it be easier to contest the spell chain than to just block the attack?

Of course, I kept all those thoughts to myself while giving the healer the rest of the information. She was particularly invested since she'd been close to Q6 now for a while. At one point during the discussion, she led me to another of the nearby buildings which seemed to be their medical area since I only saw fae, satyr, and beds nearby. Jasmine actually had the entire group join us, and I gave the healers of Stonecrest an abridged version of what we'd learned. The two fae and three satyr looked dead serious as they left to discuss something about blending skills and Gifts.

"I think when the Shapers hear about this, they are going to lose their minds," Jasmine said, chuckling.

"Oh?"

"They aren't fans of fighting, but if Q6 and the trial offers them a way to test and challenge their abilities, they are going to eat it up. If Rachael wasn't doing her own thing right now, she'd be front and center."

"I'm just happy we have a path forward."

"We would have figured something out," Jasmine said, shrugging. "Just like we've figured out enough to survive until you guys came about."

"I wouldn't put so much stock in us. Sure, we brought the implants, but the work you all are putting in is what is making this collaboration work at all," I said, shutting down any further argument. The woman gave me an assessing look before nodding. She excused herself to check on the status of the others and left me to hang out with the berries in the wagon, which I totally didn't snack on.

Almost an hour after I'd debriefed Stonecrest, my friends returned. Samuel was loaded down with what looked like another rough sewn sack, but I didn't feel bad for him in the least. Daniela was trailed by a one-armed orc and his scarred ragtag squad.

"Good to see you, Igor," I said, slapping the hulking man on the shoulder.

"Likewise, Vanguard," he rumbled. "The Wild Fists will lend you a hand."

"Your humor is as dark as ever, isn't it? I see you are all doing quite well," I replied, eyeing the five members who were now all Q5. Hilda, the chipped-tooth, haymaker-throwing, no-nonsense dwarf sent an exaggerated 'dainty' wave of her calloused hands my way before engaging Daniela in conversation.

"Your little friend told us about the jump at Q6. Only rational for us to get there quickly. Perhaps we would have crossed the threshold, had your plant-twisting companion not hogged the crow," he huffed.

"Perhaps we wouldn't have had to clear our noses of the smell of charred flesh if you knew how to cook," Sam shot back, a mock look of disdain on his face. The tusked man in front of me chuckled, matched by the few other members of the squad that had been listening. Clearly there was a story there, but neither Samuel nor Igor seemed to be ready to share.

Our joined group caught up for a few more minutes before Angel appeared again, followed by a cadre of kids. Quite liter-ally kids. There were two women following behind them, wran-gling them while Angel approached us. Nine of them total, ranging from five years old to early teens. The two teenagers had reached Quotient 2, but the others actually showed up as mundanes when their information appeared through my implant. The whole situation had us all raising an eyebrow in question.

"Maurice didn't tell you?" Angel asked, having noticed the confusion on our faces.

"Tell us what?" Daniela shot back, annoyed.

She was holding back one of the tykes that snuck away from the two caretakers. They were trying with their all to grab hold of the fang daggers on her belt. We'd discovered early on after arriving in Wildwood that while Daniela didn't much like children, they were *obsessed* with her for some reason. Which, in turn, led to the comical development as Angel rushed over to pick up the child before it learned not to touch the stove top. Or The Torch, in that case.

"The parents were wholly on board with sending the kids to the Bunker," Angel explained. "Everyone knows you three were born there and now here you are, leading an expansion effort that hasn't been seen since the Fall. Really, it was a no-brainer even if they wanted to send their current teachers with them."

The two women waved meekly as they resumed their wrangling. *That looks really stressful. I am even more impressed that people managed to raise children after the Fall now.* For all that we gave Daniela grief about the toddler magnet she was, Samuel and I were glad it wasn't us. The young kids were fascinating and they lifted my heart when I considered what they represented for the future, but…*I'm getting tired just looking at them, and I've spent the better part of a day pulling a loaded wagon.*

"Complicated," Igor huffed, his prominent brow furrowed as he looked at the toddlers.

"Since Rachael knew you three would be coming through on your way down, she figured it was safest to send them with you for the long stretch," Angel said, smiling as he handed the small child to one of the caretakers.

"Intentional," the orc rumbled, frown deepening. Angel could only cough to clear his throat as the one-armed man stared him down.

Samuel tugged on my arm before tapping the back of his neck. *Comm-plant.* "This is going to be hard. How are we supposed to keep these kids from getting eaten? We are even going to be traveling through the portion adjacent to the predator territory!"

"Just leash the little brats," Daniela said, joining our mental conversation as Angel tried to explain the situation of the Bunker Boarding School—again from the sounds of it—to the children. Each had a small sack that presumably held their possessions laying discarded with the attraction that was the armed and armored squads right before their eyes.

"You can't just— Actually, we may need to depending on the situation," Samuel said, sighing. Daniela chuckled at the despondent healer.

"We'll see how it goes. With more help, though, I have an idea," I said, glancing over my shoulder toward a certain red-skinned fae in Igor's squad.

I switched out of the comm-plant and placed a calming hand on Igor's shoulder. It almost felt like the orc just wanted to turn Angel into puree and be done with the whole situation. "So, Angel, I'm going to need another wagon."

CHAPTER TWENTY-ONE

Next Steps

As it turned out, my plan was genius. Angel did indeed have a spare wagon, even if it wasn't one of Sam's make. My life-attuned friend still made some modifications for the sake of comfort and safety, turning it into a magical covered wagon.

Angel didn't look particularly happy with our sudden commandeering, but since he had thrown the batch of children at us at the last minute, he hardly had a leg to stand on. With some coordination between Sam and I, we were able to turn the wagon into the first official-unofficial 'school bus' for the Bunker boarding program. It was nowhere near as fortified as one of Sam's tank models, but it was much more comfortable and roomy.

In addition to that, I put the Wild Fists in charge of hauling. With the handful of children and the adults wrangling them, that wagon actually turned out heavier than my own, but the load was spread between two of the strength-focused squad members. The children were initially very interested in the covered wagon, but that faded fast once we got on the road. That was when the secondary part of my plan came into play.

Fowler, the healer of the Wild Fists, had a light refinement to his life attunement. His healing Gift manifested as little motes of light that helped the body recover. Instead of actually serving his key function as a healer to the squad, he was relegated to be the entertainment. Shouts and grunts were heard regularly as the small children bounced around in the covered wagon, trying to catch the motes of energy. When they did, the tickling warmth of the mana caused them to burst into silly giggles.

Of course, the older kids in the group seemed less than enthused by the childish entertainment, so they walked on the outside flanks of the wagon as our group traveled south. They looked quite serious about the whole thing, as if they were heading to a fight instead of to a place with more comforts than they'd encountered in their lives.

Throughout the trip, I got the distinct feeling that the Wild Fists wanted to use their namesakes to beat me up for rooking them into pulling wagons. Thankfully, I was in the same boat with Sam's goods so they could hardly complain. *A lot of that going around on this trip*, I thought with a chuckle. Daniela once again took to the trees now that there were many more people around the core of the group. My minimap occasionally lit up with an enemy when she encountered it, but almost as quick as it appeared, it winked out. She made it a point to 'gift wrap' a spider and some caterpillar-looking thing for Samuel to finally cross into Q6, to the joy of the blond. The blatant Quotient grind seemed to leave a sour taste on the Wild Guard squad, and their speed took on another level as their trigger fingers demanded attention.

I sighed, focusing on my own pull and sensing our surroundings with vibrosense. Jasmine's comment about her life sense reminded me that it was entirely possible for people to develop any number of magical senses, making my honing of Harmonic Sinew jump up in priority. If I wanted to progress the trait, I needed a full handle on the sense. Something told me that I would lose some of my control over the sense the moment it progressed, which was going to be enough of a problem.

For the sake of keeping my mind clear, a steady stream of

my mana went into my shield. The strength went a long way to keeping up with the school wagon, and it freed me up to focus on filtering the world around me.

Just like that, immersed in the ripples that marked everything around us, we arrived at the car wall. A guard called down when we were in visible range and some of the vehicles were moved in anticipation of our arrival. A few minutes later, we were crossing the bridge into Wildwood proper. I pushed vibrosense to the background as I looked out over Lake Sumter and the handful of rafts working through fishing and trapping the lake.

On one of the fishing vessels, I spotted a familiar auburn head of hair rising out of the water and my speed ticked up. The rest of the group was confused by my sudden burst of speed, but nonetheless matched it as the trees near the other end of the bridge hid us from sight of the rafts. Daniela and Sam gave me weird looks, but opted not to say anything. Before long, we'd made it to the central area of town where the pre-Fall buildings remained.

"I'm going to find my mom," Daniela said as the group pulled to a stop. "She'll want to know to focus on training the spell chains."

"I need to get to Tec and snag that final Prime Pathway skill. Leave the wagon with Irwin, Ron, and I'll touch base with him," Sam added, giving Danny the bags. "Can you drop these off at the apartment while you go?"

"I suppose," Daniela said, rolling her eyes.

"You are just going to leave me with this?" I gestured not subtly at the school wagon and the Wild Fist squad that was slowly making their way *away* from that wagon. By their trajectory, it didn't take much to guess they were heading either to the spider dungeon, or maybe their designated house. The latter was doubtful.

"You are going to go talk to Dylan and Irwin, aren't you?" Samuel said.

"Well... yes, but—"

"Then you can pass that on to them. Delegation is the name of the game, Ronan," Sam said. "With my experiments, I've come to realize that more than ever. I know you want to help with everything, but this is exactly how you found yourself in a rut. It's okay to do your own thing, you know?"

"As much as I hate to agree, he's right," Danny said, looking at the school wagon. Her face scrunched like she'd eaten something sour before she sighed. "But I suppose I can give you a hand before I find Mom. Let's find that walking bonfire and offload these critters on him."

"You are talking about children, you know?" Sam questioned.

"So?"

"Let's just go. Now you just made me feel guilty about leaving. It's not like Tec is going anywhere," Sam grumbled. I couldn't help but grin and shake my head at my friends. Even when they were trying to shed themselves of responsibility, they still came through. *No sense pointing out how much it seems like pulling teeth.*

I spoke briefly with the two teachers, telling them we would be heading to find the Wildwood Council. They were thankful for our assistance on the trip, but were more than eager to get some proper help. Considering it was the children's first 'field trip,' they were all burning energy faster than was sustainable and it wouldn't be long before they devolved into balls of cranky fury. With their urging, Sam took over entertainment for Fowler while Daniela and I headed toward the council's office.

I didn't know what the plan for the trip to the Bunker was, but I didn't intend to be a part of that effort directly. Not because I didn't want to return and see everyone, but because I was already feeling the pressure of idling. The trip to Gec and passing the information on Q6 wasn't a waste of time by any stretch, but now that we had a path, I could feel the itch to take further steps on it. There was also a dungeon full of alligators calling my name, unknown territories to explore, and people to save.

With my implant, I sent a ping message to Dylan and Irwin about where we were headed, and the two councilmen, plus Sarah, were already outside when we arrived. They seemed surprised to see me hauling yet another wagon, but they didn't comment on it. I passed along Sam's message and Irwin immediately started to tally the contents of the wagon. Leaving the man to his inventory, the rest of us went inside. It only took a few minutes for me and Daniela to break down what we'd learned, now having repeated it a number of times. The only thing that seemed to throw him was the live passengers we'd brought along.

"This is… unexpected," Dylan said after some consideration.

"Didn't expect them to send you almost a dozen pairs of grubby hands?" Daniela asked.

"No, I did not. We didn't discuss our current population distribution," Dylan answered, brow furrowed as he thought. "Lake Weir only had two; most of the others were old enough to stay and work or join the Guard. We brought them along when we headed south. Maybe we'll have to expedite the school process…"

"Talk to Ava," I said. "She was the Bunker representative at the Allied Town meeting, and I'm sure she'll be able to tell you what you want to hear; that the Bunker is ready for them. Which, in all honesty, it might be if you can send a life-attuned to help manage Sam's first garden."

"Really?"

"It was pretty close to blowing the hydroponic floor out of the water—pun intended. Plus, other than building up the Bunker camp on the surface, the population of the Bunker has been free of responsibility since we stopped our schooling. Something worthwhile should give those old farts a second lease on life."

"From what I understand, those 'old farts' aren't much older than me, Ronan," Dylan said, giving me a disapproving look.

"Hey, I reckon that increasing attributes will also extend

people's lives, so it might be true you aren't old farts anymore," Daniela added, not really helping the problem. Dylan looked like he wanted to argue more, while Sarah was holding back a laugh. Somehow it reminded me of another parent-child duo.

"That doesn't matter right now. I'll get the kids settled in one of the buildings downtown and I'll talk to Ava," Dylan said, spacing out as he surely focused on the comm-plant. Daniela and I stood awkwardly while he worked, so Sarah stepped in.

"He'll get you sorted," the orc woman said.

"Did you have anything for us?" I asked. In all honesty, I was ready to collapse from the non-stop days, but I knew some things were time sensitive.

"We have updated information on a number of things. I can go ahead and share the map with you, but I think you'll want to be involved with this next bit," she said.

"Something to do with some reptiles in a lake, I presume?"

"That's right. Come on inside. I took over one of the rooms here." Sarah pointed a thumb over her shoulder into the building.

Not much had changed since the last time we'd been in the offices of the Wildwood Council. Three desks, one of which once belonged to Councilman Kirby, were pressed up against the sides while stacks of papers and reports covered the walls. The wide glass windows on the front were still there providing light, but I actually noticed sconces set into the corners, giving everything a slight yellow shade. The moment my eyes focused on the sconce, information blipped onto my Implant.

<Quotient 1 Radiance Sconce>

<Attribute: Refinement>

<Trait: Brilliance>

"Woah, that's a new one," I said, unable to stop and point.

"Ah yes, quite a few useful products have been coming from your crafter's hall. It isn't too common, since there aren't that many life-attuned spiders coming from the dungeon, but I imagine before long there will be a whole product line of 'radiance' items," Sarah said. "Plus, if you like *that*, you'll love *this*."

With a bit of a flourish, Sarah pulled open a heavy curtain that had been separating the main office from the rest of the building. Lying there was an enormous relief map of the immediate area around Wildwood and the Allied Towns in general. Vibro told me that the whole thing was set up on a number of stumps that had been nailed together like a weird, segmented table underneath what could be seen. The relief map had then been separated into grids. Three different colored lights shone from dozens of pins over the relief grid boxes in green, yellow and red.

"This is my baby; the threat map!" Sarah said proudly. "It was not easy to get Marie to come here on her off time to shape this thing, let me tell you."

There wasn't a crazy amount of detail other than for the major features; Lake Weir, Lake Sumter, AE-1, and the actual towns were done up in a much neater fashion to what I could only imagine was a quarter mile scale for each grid box. It was quite the undertaking, and it made me realize that Sarah must have started working on her threat map even before I'd even conferred with Bec on creating the map features of our implants.

"Impressive," Daniela said, stepping forward and running her hands over the gentle dips and swells that marked the Bunker's location. A handful of the town's scouts had already made their way there, and sharing the map information wasn't terribly difficult. With Kirby gone and the Aberrants pushed back, it wasn't as much of a concern to keep the Bunker's location under wraps.

Beyond the geography, the colored lights showed the suspected threat level of things in certain areas, Sarah explained, hence the name. There was a gentle gradient from Wildwood all the way to the spider dungeon, ending in a ring of red almost a mile wide. There was also a green band around Wildwood proper that seemed to indicate Tec's area of influence before switching to alternating yellows and greens. Rings of red seemed to outline the core areas of the spider, ant, predator, and gator territories, even going so far as to clash at the edge of Wec's area of influence bubble for it to be marked yellow to the east.

As I peeked closer, yet another infusion item notification appeared in my vision. The little sources of light were apparently named radiance pins, preceded by the color they lit up. Unlike the sconces, they were Q0, which was an interesting study in scale for the amount of energy jump between the Quotients. I plucked one out and noticed that it was indeed a metal pin about the size of my thumb that glowed as if it were radioactive.

"I see you weren't joking about that product line," I chuckled. "We gotta get some of these."

"I'll have some sconces installed in your apartment," Sarah said dismissively as she took the radiance pin from me and put it back in its place. "For now, I am more interested in what is going on here and here."

Sarah pointed out the same area I'd noticed where the gator territory in the lake clashed with the town, as well as the region to the north of Gec where no pins were placed. While we stood over the map, Sarah seemed to freeze mid-word. She stayed that way for a second before quickly adjusting a handful of the pins from yellow to green in the area between Wildwood and Stonecrest.

"Sorry, scout update from Devon and Dai. They are part of the reason I wanted to talk to you," Sarah said, turning back to us.

"What are those two up to?" Daniela asked, suddenly very interested in the conversation.

"I sent them to scout north of the death territory. They'll be relaying their progress to one of the other scouts near the towns until they are out of range. They'll keep going until something noticeable crops up or things get dangerous, whichever happens first. Based on the report they just sent and the information I passed along, I would imagine they are going to hit up Wec or

Gec for the Hemisphere Trial before going into the uncharted terrain. They are both Q6 now, after all."

"Do you think just two people is enough for that job?" Daniela asked, her face scrunching into an unusual frown. I could practically, and literally, *feel* her concern as her foot began to tap on the ground.

"They have been doing this sort of thing even before we had the leeway *not* to send them," Sarah said. Her tone left no room for argument, and I watched Daniela swallow her retort when the orc met her eyes. *Clearly, this had been discussed before.* "I know you're worried, and you are right to be. This is the furthest any of us have gone, but they are our best scouts. Devon can outrun pretty much anything, and Dai could hide and outmaneuver just about everybody in the guard."

"Sarah's right, Danny. We can't drop everything just because someone is doing something dangerous. We are *all* doing that when we leave the towns," I said, trying to give the brunette a reassuring look even if she didn't want to hear it. When she huffed, I knew she'd at least gotten the point, so I turned back to Sarah.

"Before they get out of range, I *would* tell them to be wary of high mana areas. Gec was as ambiguous as always, but the Entity pretty much confirmed that there should be some close by. Now that I think about it, I feel like we witnessed the formation of one of these areas during the memorial."

"You think that's what that was?" Sarah asked. She tapped her tusks for a second before holding up her finger to tell us to hold on. She spaced out again before rejoining the conversation. "I asked Clara to investigate further. She'll get whichever New Hopers are free to join her."

"So that means we'll have some information on the north in a few days," I said, running the travel math in my head.

Since Gec's senses spread even to the Bunker, then its range was somewhere *at least* in the fifteen-mile radius around the Metier Crystal. Fifteen miles wouldn't be tough to travel in a couple of days even without our Quotient-boosted bodies, but moving through uncharted territory made the risk of encountering creatures jump significantly. If there weren't three towns actively hunting the area, then it only made sense that the wildlife would have more freedom to prowl. The chance that they encounter a proper territory for a group of creatures wasn't out of the question, especially with four Metier Crystals unaccounted for to the north.

Beyond that, the biggest threat of the scouting mission was that the pair found their targets or were caught unaware by some rogue predator. Said targets being Appendages or the Aberrant Entities Gec hinted at. Unfortunately, none of those things could be anticipated, as they were mobile threats. *I just hope they don't step on the metaphorical ant pile without being able to back away.*

"That's right. Assuming that they stop at Lake Weir for a day or two, then I expect to hear back from them within eight days. If not…" Sarah's face hardened.

"We go find their asses and drag them back," Daniela growled.

CHAPTER TWENTY-TWO

Dense

Daniela's vicious response was matched by both of us. Unfortunately, there wasn't much more we could do about their situation short of going along with them. I didn't even bring that up, lest Daniela fly off and do just that. With the mission already on its way, the guard's leader brought our attention to the next pressing threat.

"Now for Lake Weir…"

Sarah spent a few minutes breaking down what information they had on the gator territory. Other than the spread of water-, air-, and death-attuned beasts, no one had been able to get to the core of the territory to lay eyes on the creature holding the Metier Crystal. It was almost certainly a gator, but stranger things had happened. Despite that, perhaps for the first time, I was given a thorough breakdown on what were some key weaknesses of our enemies. Particularly, one they'd retained from their pre-Fall nature; the core of their strength was their biting power. This, combined with their death roll, was the biggest threat. Obviously, the creatures were several times stronger than their mundane counterparts, but negating their bite was the easiest way to disable them.

The orc woman also walked us through some of the more common magical abilities the creatures could muster, like ice blades, ice dashes, and debilitating auras. On land, they were easily outmaneuvered, but in the lake or shores, they were a threat hidden until the last moment. Only a handful of extra sensory traits, like Jasmine's life auras or some of the water-attuned with electromagnetism perception, were able to penetrate the water when they hid. *Vibrosense won't work in the deeper water, but maybe I can figure something out like in the swamp.*

I was broken out of my musings when Dylan returned, letting out a sigh of relief. "Oh, good, you are all still here. The kids have now been rounded up by your mother, Daniela. She plans to take them to the Bunker along with your researcher friend Alan."

"When?" I asked, surprised at the quick turnaround. *Ava does have more experience with children, considering how much trouble the three of us were.*

"Two days. She's running it through all the parents that agreed here in Wildwood tomorrow before leaving. Some of the parents will be accompanying, I would imagine, since she said she'd love to do a tour. I was hoping you had a squad or two to spare, Sarah," the councilman said.

"I can wrangle one. Plus, I might attach all the trainees and make it a trip," the orc said, nodding her head as a plan formed.

Daniela excused herself, giving me a glance, before going after her mother. The Sage family pair continued talking for a few minutes before Dylan also left. Me and the orc woman were left alone, each of us contemplating the information at our disposal.

"When are we attacking?" I said, cutting right to the point.

"Three days. It should give the squad and the combat ready trainees time to return from your Bunker."

"Can we delay for a day? I want to make sure that we are all on the same page about what we are doing here and what Gec's nonsense means for us. They didn't necessarily simplify the situation, but I think our goals have crystalized some."

"I'm going to ignore that pun," Sarah groaned. "But I don't see why not. Who did you want to have part of that meeting?"

"Everyone that needs to know. If Ava is going to the Bunker, then maybe she can get Elias, our acting major, to join."

"Timing will be tight, but I think we can manage. I'll confirm with Ava and then send runners to the towns."

"Great. Now the only thing we need to do is kill us some oversized lizards," I joked, getting an eye roll in return.

Sarah paused before her expression turned serious, gesturing toward the spider dungeon and the suspected location of the ant dungeon boss. "You know… This is the first time we've considered clearing a dungeon completely."

"We cannot ignore it. I've been thinking about the balance of the ecosystems here on the surface. They seem much more… fluid than they did in the world before; this is especially the case when the creatures with the help of a Metier Crystal are replicating like they are."

"Should we consider clearing the ants and the spiders, then?" Sarah asked.

"No. There has to be a balance, and there is more to it than the potential gains. What happens after we clear the gator dungeon?"

"Not sure what you are getting at," Sarah asked, confused.

"It's like with the Dreg before you kicked them out. You aren't paying for their protection anymore, so the Wild Guard had to take over. It hasn't been as much of a burden because you've gained access to the implants and the infused items to improve everyone's strength and survivability. However, you are ignoring the place that the Entities hold in the balance. Tec, Wec, and Bec are keeping the towns safe by pushing back weaker creatures and discouraging stronger ones. The dungeons are doing the same, while presenting a concentrated threat," I said, voicing something I'd considered for a long while.

"A buffer," Sarah said, her thick eyebrows bunching on her

face. "If we eliminate a dungeon, it leaves a gap like when we stopped relying on the Tendrils. A gap that was immediately filled by spiders, the predators, and the gators."

I nodded. "That would be my guess. The gator dungeon is causing active conflict and we cannot avoid dealing with it, but that will open up the Allied Towns to whatever *they* are keeping at bay further to the east."

"That… is certainly concerning, especially when we are looking toward the north," Sarah said, plopping into a nearby chair. "As far as we know, there is just wetland to the east that gets swallowed more and more with each year that passes."

"Not to kick you while you are down, but another thing to consider is the dungeons themselves growing in power beyond what we can handle if we leave them alone for too long. I don't think this is as much of an issue if we cull them regularly, like with the spider dungeon and the ant raids, but it will come up. If we hit a high mana area, or a rogue creature past the Corporeal Limit, things will get dicey."

"You are truly a beacon of hope, Ronan," Sarah said, the sarcasm dripping off her words.

"The time since my fight with Galloway was… contemplative," I said, leaning on the wall beside her. "I wasn't doing well, but it gave me a lot of time to think. Once you all slapped me out of my funk, well, things have been falling into place. I think Gec opening the path past Q6 was the last piece I needed to know where to go."

"I kind of wish I *had* slapped you now," the orc grumbled. When I asked her to repeat that, she ignored me and forged on. "So, we kill some lizards and buckle up for something else to show up?"

"Yep. I think this network of scouts you are building will serve everyone well," I said, gesturing to her threat map.

It was rough, and incomplete, but it showcased what our pocket of humanity had accomplished. A vision of a whole building dedicated to the different dungeon reports flashed through my mind, Sarah shouting directions while a monitor blipped whenever a significant threat appeared in their territory. Squads dispatched through tubes to the outside, landing on mounts or vehicles to reach their target. It brought a smile to my face, prompting me to pat the woman on the shoulder.

"We'll be ready. But for now, I need a nap," I said, letting the exhaustion I'd been holding back artificially with Sam's help show. I'd gotten the <Overhealed>affliction not long before arriving in Wildwood, but I'd used my prodigious strength to ignore it. The watchfulness I'd pushed for while caring for our tiny human cargo had been responsible for most of that, but it wasn't their fault.

"Make sure you talk to Arnold, he said he had something for you," Sarah said, almost absently as she crossed her arms and glared at her threat map.

"Good night, Sarah."

"Thanks, Ron," she added quietly as I stepped out of the building and into the night.

Fires burned outside of a few buildings, with people speaking quietly around them. I saw a group of demons trot through the town with purpose before splitting off to what I assumed were their night time tasks. Tec's glow suffused every-thing near the center of town, the shimmering bubble marking the edge of the Blessing of Magic visible without the sun's rays to overpower it. I took a deep breath of the earth, smoke, and life around me, vibro rippling merrily into the buildings around me. Despite all the loss and the weight of responsibility, it was damn worth it.

— + —

Since I knew the crafters were early risers, and I wanted to make as much use of the time before the raid on the gator dungeon as I could, I'd opted to force my body into action at the crack of dawn. Thankfully, Samuel had been able to augment the coffee growing speed for the people of Wildwood to an unprecedented level, and pots of watered-down coffee were becoming much more commonplace. Daniela had percolated some espresso just that morning before everyone in the dojo dashed off their separate ways. It had been late when everyone returned home, and other than a brief update, we'd all crashed in bed.

"He's back! Surprised you are up this early, sunshine!" Arnold the dwarf roared with laughter from his spot on the top of the crafter's hall. The handful of tradespeople around him glared as he disrupted their work.

I had to do a double take as I approached what was growing to be the largest building in Wildwood. The expansions I'd helped the other workers with had been completed and a second, open concept floor had been erected on the new wing. Thick, reinforced pillars held up a smooth sheet of stone that blocked out the stinging sun as a number of people worked on several crafts in the open air. It was somewhat reminiscent of when the crafters of Wildwood had operated in several roughly crafted pavilions. Except, the crafter's hall would likely be able to endure more than ten times the abuse the old buildings could have.

A new set of steps and what looked like a ramp went all the way to the second floor from the road. Less than a minute later, I was pulled into a rough hug by my fellow crafter. The rough part was mainly because the man only came up to my chest, but neither of us dwelt too much on that.

"It's looking good up here. With those light sconces, Wildwood will be running day and night!" I joked, waving to the other tradesmen and women that had opted for the open workspace.

"Yah, you're right about that. That right ol' Rommel, I thought he was a weapons man, but it turned out he has a soft spot for utility," Arnold replied, huffing as if working on dangerous magical cannons with your squadmate and this other man that used to live underground didn't put him squarely in the 'weapons man' territory.

"Hmmm, perhaps I seek elaborate works as opposed to big

hunks of metal," a voice carried from below them. The both of us turned to see the large orc making his way to the second floor, a small wooden wagon pulled behind him. He offered me a nod and snorted in Arnold's direction before moving to one of the nearby worktables.

"What are you doing here? I thought you had time off from work," Arnold complained.

"One can't spend his time off doing something he enjoys?" Rommel asked, raising an eyebrow in question before he started to pull things from the handcart he'd been pulling up the ramp. Infusions, various colored rocks, bits of metal, and different pieces of wood were lined up on his table. I recognized two of the sconces in question as he laid them out on Arnold's table.

"Dang tusk-mouth, making me look bad," Arnold grumbled as he turned back to his own table to install one of the sconces in the corner. Rommel shook his head, a slight curve at the corner of his mouth showing more of his dental hardware.

"I am very much interested in how you managed those, Rommel. Unfortunately, I haven't had as much time to work with infusions. With the Gec stuff sorted, I do now," I said, drawing the attention of both of the men. "Well, quite literally *some* time. We'll be heading to Lake Weir in four days."

"Indeed. Clara has told me of this deployment. And, I would like to thank you and your friends for watching out for her in my absence," Rommel rumbled, eyes serious as he spoke.

"It's not a problem. Seriously. You guys have pulled our asses out of the fire more than once. Plus, it was like you were there with me," I said, tapping the shield that was affixed to my back. "Wouldn't be much of a frontliner without this bad boy you made me."

"That thing is serious defense indeed," Arnold said. "Now the real question is what are you doing about offense?"

"I was planning to borrow something you guys crafted recently, actually. Figured that's why you asked Sarah to pass your message. It's not like my lack of a weapon is unknown to the offensive trainers," I said, shrugging.

"Something like that," Arnold said, glancing over to Rommel.

When neither said anything for a full second, I asked what the deal was.

"We've had… a development of a sort. It happened while you were away to Gec and we added this second floor," Rommel said.

"Out with it then! I'm not planning to beg, now am I?" I said, gesturing for either man to say something. *I would almost beg, if I thought it would make a difference. Neither Arnold nor Rommel are prone to suspenseful pauses, so now I really want to know.*

"Come on, I'll take you," Arnold said.

"I shall come along. Ronan's perspective on this will be most relevant," Rommel said, rising from his own workstation. He barely spared a look toward the items he'd brought along, instead using his long strides to catch up with us on the way to the original building of the crafter's hall.

Both men remained silent as we walked, and I tried to push my vibrosense out in search of anything strange. Other than the steady—if more intense than I remembered—thrum of the mana-created rock the building was made of, nothing came up. My anticipation kept climbing as the three of us walked into the first testing room, which was surprisingly empty of people. Some of the radiance sconces had already been installed in the corners, washing everything in a slight yellow tone, but making the room near as bright as the outside.

It didn't take long to find the thing they were talking about once we were inside. Not but five feet into the room, close to the center, was a shimmering barrier of almond-colored light. Not unlike the grayspace I'd witnessed within the afflicted, the aura seemed to shift and blend with the space around it, becoming more stable the further in you went. My feet took me forward of their own volition.

As if I had crossed into the Blessing of Magic from an Entity, wisps of earth mana peeled off the world around me. Tan, beige, brown, and umber danced around a fragment of stone on the ground at the foot of the strong wall. It looked just like any other part of the wall, perhaps a slightly darker shade of brown than the rest, but the slow orbit of visible mana highlighted it. Vibrosense spazzed out, going silent the moment I crossed the boundary and leaving me disoriented in its absence before it returned an astounding amount of information. It was so much information, I had to forcefully focus on my sight and hearing so that I didn't hurl right on the spot.

"I'm assuming that's it?" I managed.

"That's right. Scared the piss out of me when the whole floor shifted toward it like a sinkhole. It was part of the reason why we built that second floor; no one wanted to mess with the weird magic rock," Arnold explained. *I hadn't noticed that.* A look around confirmed that the floor was sloped slightly; I'd been too engrossed in the fragment to notice.

"Not *one* of the people that have been working with magical infusions with the power to transform and reshape materials in ways impossible before the Fall of society fiddled with this?" I asked, an eyebrow raised in question.

"Well, we did try to mess with it a little," Arnold admitted, averting his eyes in embarrassment. "But it didn't react other than to stir the mana in the air."

"I have attempted to use my <Flame Discus> on it, but it actually snuffed it out faster than I expected," Rommel added.

"Same with the other elements. Only earth seems to do anything, but it just breaks down stuff back into those wisps. There were hardly any before we started," Arnold said.

"Have you tried…well, touching it?" I asked. "Instead of blasting it to kingdom come?"

"No! Oh, great crafter, your wisdom is truly at the height of our— Of course we tried!" Arnold growled.

"No need to be so touchy. Just a question," I said, lifting my hands in defeat.

"Any ideas?"

"If I had to guess, and that's exactly what I'm doing, this is one of those high mana areas we've been hearing about. A budding one at least."

"High mana areas?" Rommel asked.

"Gec talked about them. Sarah sent Clara to prod the place where the memorial transformed," I said.

"Wait, if that's a high mana area… then that was for death mana, and this is for earth mana?" Arnold asked as Rommel took on a contemplative expression. They had both been there at the memorial and watched the strange energy development.

"That would be my guess. Gec did say that we would encounter more of these as we go up in level and draw more mana to an area. I gotta be honest, I wasn't quite expecting one to show up *right here*," I said, gesturing at the spot on the ground.

"Should we…leave it alone?" Arnold asked.

"Don't see why n—"

"No," Rommel said, cutting off my suggestion. I wasn't mad, but I did look at the orc curiously.

"I noticed something while working," he started. "Infusing my sconces was more difficult the last two days since we found this thing."

"Hmmm," I said, making the connection. "You think the mana from this thing is affecting your crafting?"

"That is my observation. It might be weakening the threads from the infusions like it did to the spell chains from other attunements used within."

"That's easy to check," I said. I walked over to the far wall where a small set of baskets held some low-level Quotient infusions. Earth infusions always seemed to be in short supply, but I plucked a pair of them, as well as a pair of air infusions. Arnold seemed to get my idea and retrieved a handful of spider drops from an adjacent room.

I hadn't seen the unprocessed material loot before and gave it a curious look.

<Araneid Chitin Plate>

<Attunement: Air>

<Quotient 1 Density>

Nothing too crazy, but I'd seen it used for a few of the armor variations the crafters made. There wasn't an infinite supply of fire ant chitin, even if it proved one of the best types of armor for direct damage tanks such as myself. The other attunements tended to form items with deflection, mobility, or obscuring traits. I had a sneaking suspicion that wasn't always going to be the case, but our early testing had only manifested those types of traits. Curiously, the spider chitin from fire spiders didn't produce the Force Dispersal trait either. That had opened up an entirely different line of study in traits and their connection to the creatures the item was formed from.

I pushed those idle thoughts out of my mind before focusing on my 'test.' I set one of the spider plates within the mana zone and activated <Infusion>. The earth blob in my hand unspooled much faster than I'd ever seen, hosing out like a spray can before I even had a chance to 'grab' it with my own mana.

The concentrated attuned Pith spread over the plate for a full second before I could get it under control, essentially emptying the infusion. The spider material shuddered as hair-line fractures formed all over it from the sheer pressure of the infusion, then it *shrank*. Some of the wisps of earth mana in the air were sucked up, glowing a rich caramel as they filled up the cracks.

Within the blink of an eye, it was at least ten percent smaller and the fractures were no longer visible. The whole thing had stabilized instead of crumbling into little itty-bitty pieces. It had managed to feed a whole extra Quotient's worth of Pith into the material successfully.

"Well, I'll be…" Arnold whispered as we stood dumb-founded.

CHAPTER TWENTY-THREE

Fiddling with the Field

I pulled the spider plate back out of the concentrated ambient mana. Unlike before, the material had almost no give. However, it wasn't brittle. I hammered it with my fist, causing it to explode in a spray of sand that would have scraped my skin were it not partially made of stone. Arnold sputtered as he got some of the grains in his mouth and Rommel groaned as he swatted the stuff out of the air.

"Curious…" I whispered, unable to stop myself from grabbing the other plate before walking back into the bubble.

Now prepared for the increased force of release, I was able to 'catch' the Pith thread before it splattered onto the material. It coiled and writhed like a worm within my mental grasp and I felt a headache forming just from a few seconds of crafting. With a sigh, I released the thread which practically dove into the material. Once more it fractured, shrank, and was stabilized by the wisps of mana in the air.

Watching the whole process and holding the energy in hand caused many things to slot into place in my mind. Primarily, where the laymen of Wildwood had been able to gain their levels and traits. The obvious answer had always been Tec.

Now, however, I could postulate *why* it was Tec. If the concentrated ambient mana attuned to the wall fragment could affect materials, then why couldn't that also be the case for the full spread the Blessing of Magic produced?

Even as my mind spun a million miles a minute, I snagged another plate from a speechless Arnold and repeated the process with the air infusions.

Molasses, that was what it felt like. The moment the thread was released from the infusions, I practically had to tug it from the cotton-like blob. Once I had a good grip on the thread, I was able to guide it into the plate, but it was almost like the plate was covered in an oily film. The thread slipped and slid for several seconds before I was able to push it into the material with enough force for it to stick. I was covered in a light sweat by the end of the infusion just from how tense I'd been.

"Are you alright, Ronan?" Rommel asked, placing a hand on my shoulder.

"It's...well, confirmed. Much harder to work with stuff outside of earth with this thing," I replied.

Does the amount of ambient mana affect which attunements people will have? What if we'd been born in an earth-heavy environment? Would me and my friends all be dwarves instead of the distribution we have now? Is that why there are more non-death-attuned in Wildwood? Because there wasn't much of that in the atmosphere? Did the Entities make that a null point? Is that why there are going to be higher-leveled creatures in higher mana areas? These concentrated bubbles are amplifying the process?

Question after question floated through my head as I prepared for my final test. I stepped out of the strange bubble and used <Infusion> to push the final air thread into the plate. The difference between the outside environment and inside the bubble was night and day, but I could still feel a noticeable strain from using the non-earth infusion.

"You are right, Rommel. Even outside of the bubble, using the other infusion was harder," I said, confirming the orc's hypothesis. A magical application of the scientific method, how far have we come...

"So… Isn't that a good thing though?" Arnold asked. "If we can make stronger earth stuff, then that's great… Right?"

"What about the other crafters?" Rommel asked, gesturing at himself and the other rooms beyond our current walls.

"Arnold, if we leave this here, it would detrimentally affect the people experimenting with other attunements. The pendulum cannon, for instance, would have been much harder to develop with this thing around to interfere with each craft. Not to mention all the testing we did," I said.

"Dagnammit… Could we…isolate it to this room somehow? I mean, it just sort of formed here. Who's to say it won't again?" the dwarf said, clearly unwilling to waste the opportunity presented.

"Maybe? That would be a question for Alan, or maybe the Entities if they can talk about it," I said. The man looked immediately less enthusiastic about the prospect.

"I'm sure we can figure out something to do with it," I said, trying to cheer up the frowning man.

"Yeah, yeah. It's fine, not like I wanted to make some crazy equipment in here. How do we do this?"

"I can try to use <Mudpit> to liquify the wall around it," I suggested.

"Better than me making it denser, or Rommel throwing some hot wind at it," Arnold said, shrugging. Rommel growled at the insinuation that his staple Gift was 'hot wind.' The dwarf didn't look perturbed. He waved me forward and I stepped back in, bracing for the scramble of my vibrosense, even as repressed as I'd forced it.

Just like everything else within the mana bubble, my spell chain snapped out in a blink. Normally it took a second for the glyphs to form before the skill could manifest, but it was instant within the amplified space. Thankfully, I'd been bracing for a development of that sort, otherwise I'd risked liquifying a larger portion of the wall.

My abdomen curled as I restrained the size of my skill to less than three feet. The underpowered casts, just like overpowered casts, took more mental faculties and triggered the side effects more than just expending mana normally. If I hadn't practiced as much as I did with reshaping the skill to build things, the passively amplified skill would have put me out when it sucked up my mana pool like a vacuum.

Twenty, then thirty percent of my mana went down the drain. It was more than the small cast had any right to take and yet still the wall refused to liquify properly. Gritting my teeth at what was coming, I channeled mana into my helm.

<Mudpit> leapt into <Landslide>.

With my improved understanding of spell chains, I was able to discern the change. A secondary dimension was added to the skill, but it wasn't anywhere near as complex as the first set of glyphs. Instead, it twisted around my base chain before sinking into the strong wall.

The building rumbled. Dust dropped down from the plant woven ceiling as the wall finally reacted to my skill. Very slowly, the stone took on a wet sheen before seeping toward the ground.

Too slow! The thought roared in my head as I doubled over from the pain of my mana side effects. I was vaguely aware of Rommel and Arnold shouting at me, both slamming their fists against the mana bubble. The near invisible membrane had coalesced somehow, blocking the two men from approaching me as I watched the precipitous fall of my mana.

Thankfully, I wasn't one to hesitate when faced with the unknown. My hands plunged into the wall. The stone was just shy of being solid and my muscles strained to push deeper than my elbows. Warning after warning flashed by at the edge of my vision and it wasn't until my mana crossed the twenty percent mark that I felt it. Something that had no place within the wall; a small octahedral structure.

With a mighty sucking sound, I grabbed and pulled the thing out of the strong wall. The moment my hands weren't making contact with it, my skill went into full effect. A full five-foot section of the wall immediately turned into a puddle before hardening on the floor when the skill stopped receiving my mana. Very slowly, the mana bubble started to recede toward my hand. The three of us watched in silent fascination as the whole thing disappeared into the sludge trapped between my fingers.

With the flash of adrenaline gone, I slumped back, feeling the breeze coming in through the hole in the wall relieve some of the tension in my muscles. Unfortunately, just like how the wall's mud had hardened again, so had the small amount I held in my hands. My fingers were trapped and my mana was tapped.

"Any of you got a chisel?" I asked, out of breath.

— + —

"What is it?" Arnold asked when he returned with a chisel and hammer from his smithing station.

"No clue, but it had no business being inside a wall," I said. "I wonder why it formed."

"Perhaps it was due to the large amount of condensed stone," Rommel proposed. "If it is a similar situation to the memorial, perhaps there is a threshold required for it to turn into a mana zone."

"That makes sense, as much as magic can make sense. Not that it isn't a bit morbid, but we did inter many people in that area. Why did it focus on the memorial stone? And why now?" Arnold asked, placing the chisel tip over my hands.

Each blow vibrated through the stone, but my traits made it nothing more than uncomfortable instead of the finger-numbing it should have been.

"Maybe it was intent or maybe it was something to do with the number of people around," I thought aloud. "What came first, the high mana area or the high Quotient people? Perhaps a bit of both?"

"I think you are going to give your poor science friend a heart attack, Ronan." Arnold chuckled as he worked the hammer methodically. It wasn't for no reason that we called it a 'strong wall;' even though it was smaller as it clumped on my hands, the stone took several minutes to yield and free me. It took almost a half hour before the object in question was completely free.

It rolled on the ground with a fragile *tinkle* before settling. To my immediate dismay, the bubble of mana started to form up around it. The ground once again gained the liquid sheen, as if I was once again channeling <Landslide>. I dove, ignoring the chips of rock that dug into my chest, and plucked the thing off the ground. The mana field receded.

"I don't think this thing likes being exposed," I groaned, peeling myself up from my belly flop.

"You can say that again," Arnold said, setting his tools on a nearby worktable and glaring at the hole in his strong wall. "This is going to take a whole day to patch properly!"

"Hmm. Perhaps you should be happy it is magic stone and not mundane. An ordinary wall would have collapsed with a hole like this in it," Rommel said, gesticulating at the shrinking cracks that spread when the mud hardened. I hadn't been able to smooth out the edges of the liquid stone, hence the natural faults in even Arnold's <Stone Anvil> blocks being put on display.

"Yeah, yeah," Arnold said, waving his hand dismissively. "The more important question is what are we going to do with that thing?"

I finally opened my hand to look at the octahedron. Information and gibberish floated through my implant until a golden and purple glow highlighted the object in my hand.

<Mana Shard>

<Attunement: Earth>

<Category 1 Density>

<Ambient Propagation: Inactive>

<Stability: 100%>

"What the hell?" I whispered.

The information had the same arrangement as a piece of

dissociated material drop, but appeared to be more of an infusion-type object. It was probably a rare object, based on the coloration it was highlighted in. I hadn't seen anything other than green before. If Bec had based this on our subconscious knowledge of magic systems, then this would be something Epic rarity or more while the amplitude item candidate materials were uncommon with their green glow.

"Woah, why is it glowing purple?" Arnold asked. "I've only ever seen green."

"I think it's because of its rarity. I'm not sure what this thing is, but it must be pretty nice for the Entities to highlight it like this. We'll have to go see Tec to maybe get some answers," I said.

"Perhaps it would be best to come up with another alternative. It is destabilizing," Rommel said evenly, pointing at the shard. Sure enough, in the minute we'd been talking, the stability had ticked down two percent. I had no clue what that meant and I didn't particularly have any interest in finding out. Stuff destabilizing only brought the mental picture of the old world's nukes to mind and I didn't want to think about the Attuned Earth's version of that.

"But we don't know what to do!?" I asked, suddenly not nearly as happy to be holding the shard. I didn't dare set it down, since it would probably try to sink back into the ground, nullifying my efforts.

"Maybe… You can craft something with it?" Arnold suggested.

"What?" I asked. "We don't even really know what this thing is!"

"Did that stop you from using infusions?" the dwarf asked, raising an eyebrow in question.

"I mean, technically not, but I at least had a miscellaneous skill for that," I countered.

"It just went down in percent again," Rommel interjected.

"Oh, for God's sake," I groaned. "What do you have in mind? My guess is that whatever we use this thing on will produce that field of mana. Heck, it tried to produce it from the ground."

"We could try to meld it to an existing item," Rommel said.

"And waste possibly the strongest material we've been able to get our hands on? No thanks," Arnold snorted contemptuously.

"Then perhaps we build that weapon Ronan was looking for."

"Now you're talking," the dwarf replied. A grin split his face so wide I was able to see his teeth through his enormous beard.

"I don't know if I can really craft while I hold this thing," I said, looking at the shard on my palm.

"Try your pocket?" Arnold said with a shrug.

"There's no way a magical material of this unprecedented caliber is going to be just fine being in my—Oh, look at that. It works." There was no overt reaction from the shard, and no mana bubble formed out of my pants.

We all shared a nervous snicker before the brainstorm started. It was a slowly building crescendo. Normally we weren't in a time crunch while crafting, even with the strain of controlling the Pith threads, but the shard was presenting a unique opportunity and challenge. It wasn't a stretch to say that Arnold, Rommel, and I were at the cutting edge of infusion crafting, even with my combat-related sabbatical. However, with the object we'd acquired, we didn't know the potential heights we could reach.

CHAPTER TWENTY-FOUR

Field Anvil

"Do we want to test what happens if we feed it an infusion?" Arnold postulated.

"I think that's a negative. Let's focus on what could benefit from a strong earth connection first and then we can muck about with the actual shard," I said, pulling us back to the sketches on the table. The time crunch remained a silent guillotine.

"You sure you don't want to go back to a pickaxe?" Rommel asked. "You did some *work* with that, if I recall."

I shook my head. "Manipulating it and making sure it hits just right takes a lot of finesse. As you've both seen, I'm more on the 'smash until solved' side of things when it comes to problems."

"That puts out another naginata," Arnold said, running his hands through his beard. He absently braided and unbraided one of the strands as he considered the table. "Maybe we shouldn't just focus on the shard connection at all. What about making sure we have the materials that can do a regular weapon justice in the first place?"

"Hmmm. You're right. It isn't like we know how the shard

will react, anyhow. So, just make a bad mamma jamma weapon and slap a radioactive chunk of concentrated magic onto it?" I asked.

"Sounds like a plan," Arnold said, smirking through his beard.

"Let's all dive into the stockpiles and fish out the things we think will make the weapon the strongest, then reconvene in… ten minutes," I said, glancing nervously at the shard and its sub-ninety percent stability.

My fellow crafters didn't need further prompting and they rushed out of the room, me right on their heels. The storage bins that had been set up outside of the crafter's hall had been refined somewhat since the first time Wildwood actually dipped its toes into infusion crafting. The main road leading to the hall was now lined by three, ten-foot tall, wooden rectangles on the north side and six on the south. A woodshaper—probably Marie, based on the quality of the wood joints—had made partitions for the plethora of infusions and material drops. With most of the crafters, and even the civilians of Wildwood, having gained the implants,they were able to differentiate the Quotients of the infusions. It was a testament to the resurgence of the Wild Guard and their efforts that only the crates labeled for Quotient 5 and 6 loot were empty.

Rommel dove into the Q4 fire materials, while Arnold dove into the earth ones. Shaking my head at the obvious bit of bias, I actually made my way to the life-attuned section. It was one of the least filled, even at the lower Quotients, but there were four objects therein. A femur, a human jawbone, a fang that glowed with a strange inner light, and what looked like a dried bamboo stalk. Just to confirm my suspicion, I identified the fang as one of the bioluminescent panther drops. The last material reminded me of that water-attuned patch that Sam had found during our first day on the surface. Nostalgia aside, however, I moved over it, the fang, and the jawbone to the femur.

The selection was easy, really, since whatever weapon we created would need a handle. It would be possible to create one with the bamboo, but if it was anything like the bamboo from before the Fall, it would be much too bendy. Even with the femur tucked under my arm, I couldn't stop my curiosity and tested just that. The bamboo could fold almost entirely over! It was practically rubber, like some movie prop version of the true plant. I could almost see how the living plant had attacked and a grimace crossed my face as I pictured whip-like motions. *I want to hear the story behind that one. Maybe I'll tell Arnold to add little tags for the rarer drops, so you can know who contributed to the crafters.*

Even without that quality-of-life suggestion, there was another big change to the storage area. The accountability clerk. A somewhat unfortunate position, considering all the magical stuff that was going on in Wildwood, but a necessary one nonetheless. The task was rotated by some of the oldest members of Wildwood as a means of giving them a break from the relentless pace the youth in the town had set with their Gifts and skills. Since most of them didn't have access to those, they'd opted to learn the minutiae of the trades and share their wisdom with the others. As well as fill in positions in the bureaucracy of the council's scope.

"Margery," Arnold said as he joined me at her small sheltered hut that had been built with a perfect view of the storage area.

"Mr. Gram," the older lady replied. "It seems you never did learn any of those manners your mother tried so hard to ingrain into you."

"Normally I would be delighted to trade veiled insults with you, Marg, but we are in a bit of a hurry," Arnold said, glancing at my pocket but not saying anything.

"Well, Mr. Terrigan has already logged his withdrawal. Perhaps if your mouth didn't move so much, you would have already put your name here."

The woman retrieved a clipboard from the folds of her dress using her seemingly adhesive hands to present it vertically to the dwarf. I heard a quiet grumble come out of Arnold, but he obliged her. With the tiny stick of charcoal, he'd officially marked himself as the new owner of a Q4 earth tortoise shell plate. A few minutes later, Rommel joined us, carrying a Q4 fire ant chitin plate. Unlike the cantankerous dwarf, the orc inclined his head in greeting to the older woman as he filled in his name. I didn't miss the slight flush on her face as she looked at his impressive figure, but I quickly put it out of mind as we shuffled back to the test room.

"Never knew you were a hit with the older ladies, Rommel," the dwarf said, unable to help himself. Arnold wagged his eyebrows suggestively. Rommel let out a sigh, doing the smart thing and ignoring the dwarf's bait.

"Perhaps we should discuss what we acquired?" the orc said.

"Let's," I said, glancing at the shard and seeing the stability tick down once again.

"Alright, I want to make you a hammer with this bad boy," Arnold said, slapping the tortoise shell plate. "If I infuse it with earth, it sprouts crystals. If I turn it into an item, well, it will be like a meat tenderizer."

"What? Shouldn't it have crystals already?" I asked, surprised.

"These big crystal bastards? Not really. They are pretty rare, but their shells aren't actually covered in crystal. They only show that stuff when threatened."

"I suppose getting shot at and being exposed to a wildfire would threaten me too," I mumbled. "Okay, I'm not opposed to the idea. A hammer would be a fairly straight forward weapon, and I very much like the idea of poking holes in my enemies. You've both seen <Stone Spike> and <Mineral Strike>. Just wait 'til you see <Terrasheath>."

"What would you use for the hammer's head?" Rommel asked, eyeing the tortoise shell.

"I was going to make a <Stone Anvil> for it," Arnold replied. He gestured at the strong wall. "I've come a long way from this building, and I'm fairly confident it's at metal levels of strength while also being drowned in my mana. Can't help but think that might help with the shard situation."

"Fair enough," Rommel conceded. "I was hoping to craft a similar thing, but more on the bladed side rather than blunt."

"How're you gonna get a blade out of that!?" Arnold huffed, gesturing to the chitin plate.

With a surprising amount of grace for a man almost a head taller than me, Rommel reached behind himself and produced what I could only identify as a chakram. A central S-curve acted as the handhold while Rommel slammed it down on the work table only a few inches from where Arnold's palms were resting on the tortoise shell. A gust of heat swept out from the impact and I saw the red veins of a fire attunement bloom through the weapon's edge.

"Perhaps it isn't wise to question things simply because you do not expect them to be possible. Present company is a good example of that," Rommel said, gesturing with his head in my direction before letting go of the weapon. It remained propped, its blade having cut a good inch into the rocky surface. "This is made from chitin."

"Ah, bloody hell. You didn't have to make me piss myself to make a point, did you?" Arnold grumbled, stepping back from the weapon that the Wild Guard could have used to maim him. Easily. My perception had screamed at me, warning me of the draw, but Rommel's speed would have left me in a tough place to block if the orc had tried to attack me. *Seems Devon and Clara aren't the only ones with tricks up their sleeves.* The thought caused my respect for the New Hopers to once again rise, and it was pretty high already. Sans Devon, but at the least I knew the elf was reliable.

"Okay, so… hammer or a blade? Clearly you have the handle there," Arnold said, pushing past the fright to focus on the battlefield where he *could* contend. "What weapon are we gonna craft?"

Of all the things that could have been going through my head, I did not expect what surfaced with that question. There was a potential magical reaction brewing in my pocket, my friends were asking to help build a weapon that would go with me to kill magically 'roided up beasts, and the thing that came to mind was… tacos. One single joke video amidst many that managed to make it into the simulation databases, and it lived rent free in my brain for over ten years until that moment. However, I didn't begrudge that memory. No, it had provided the perfect answer to the question.

"Porque no los dos?" I said, a grin splitting my face. Obviously, Arnold and Rommel had not even an inkling of what I was saying, especially when I threw in a sudden dose of Spanish into the mix, but I did. For the sake of clearing the befuddled expressions off their faces, I repeated myself in English. "Why not both?"

"Both? How are you going to build both?" Arnold asked, looking from the shell to the piece of carapace.

"Axe hammer," Rommel said, nodding his head as I pointed at him.

"Ambitious… I love it!" Arnold roared, thumping his hand on the table. "Say no more. What's the plan?"

"We do what I did when I first started using infusions," I said simply.

"Oh?" Rommel asked, raising an eyebrow in question.

"Slap it together and hope to God it works!" I wiggled my eyebrows, *hoping* for some kind of reaction. The two looked at me for a second before they had to chuckle and shake their heads at my attempted comedy. *Maybe I should take my uncle up on some of those comedy lessons…* They didn't need to know about the sweat dripping down my back or how my thoughts kept flipping to the shard, doing my best not to check the stability counter obsessively.

Thankfully, that wasn't actually my plan. Instead, I planned to have each of us focus on what they were more practiced at. Since it was just a combination of two weapons into one, I figured it made sense to build it just like that. I asked Arnold to create his <Stone Anvil> to serve as the base while he molded the shell to be able to fit the hammerhead he created. Rommel would work on making an axe blade sturdy enough not to break due to the sheer weight of the hammerhead, sharpening it in the process. I planned to concentrate on modifying the femur and shaping the hammerhead itself to receive all of the parts.

Without fanfare, the three of us got to work. Rommel took over a workstation beside me and several fire infusions uncoiled from his hands into the air within seconds. I'd never tried to use <Infusion> on multiple threads at once, but there was no reason why not. I was curious about what he planned to do, but I had my own work to do until Arnold finished his cast for his compressed <Stone Anvil>.

The femur I'd selected for the handle was a significant specimen. The other Tendril drops, the only source of human bones that I ever wanted to have, had been fairly close to pre-Fall human dimensions. Galloway seemed to be an exception, and it was perhaps due to his transformative traits. The femur I held was firmly in that exceptional category at roughly one and a half that of a normal human's. Close to two inches thick at the thinnest portion and almost three feet in length, it would have made a decent haft as it was, if I carved a handle. Instead, I opted to get fancy.

All my practice making equipment, shaping and shaving stuff with fire infusions, was put on full display as I carved up from the knee joint portion of the femur with the threads of Pith. I was actually forced to use Quotient 1 and 2 infusions, since the Q0 ones barely scratched away any material. It wasn't anything too crazy, just a helical swirl up the length of the bone, but it was the first time I'd worked an embellishment into a crafted weapon. Something tickled at the back of my mind, guiding my hands absently until Arnold tapped my shoulder.

"Anvil is done," he grunted.

There was sweat dripping down his forehead as he dropped what had to be fifty pounds of rock in a rectangle in front of me. It was a mind-boggling weight for something that was maybe the size of my head. When I put my hand on it, vibrosense also spazzed out. The thing was chock full of mana. I looked at the dwarf, somewhat unsure of how to proceed.

"Use that liquid stone trick," the man huffed, grabbing the shell from our planning table and getting to work feeding it earth infusions before he'd even made it to his work area.

A glance at the shard and the just over fifty percent stability was the fastest way of vanishing any hesitation I had about working the weapon. I wasn't sure how I was supposed to swing fifty pounds of stone, even with my increasing strength. Nevertheless, that was a problem for another time! With renewed vigor, I fell back into my crafting trance. Instead of trying for <Mudpit>, I jumped straight to <Landslide>. My mana roiled inside me, and the spell chain protested when I bound it around my finger. The pressure of the mana was so much, I actually felt the muscles of my finger *curl* in protest. *This isn't going to work! How do I make the opening for the haft?*

The answer was simplicity itself as I looked between the spell chain around my finger and the femur ball socket. Just put it there instead. The spell chain resisted being applied to something. The image of the switchboard linked to my skills in my mind went haywire as sparks flew, but I forced the lever to trigger the skill with both mental hands. With a sucking sound, the spell chain orbited the femur even as my mana went out the window. Eighty, seventy, sixty percent it drained to keep the slapstick cast I'd made active.

As if I were stabbing Galloway with the spider naginata, I plunged the femur into the <Stone Anvil> just off center. There was immediate resistance, but I was already committed. Mana flowed through me into the femur, my muscles strained with the side effects, and the stone was as stubborn as Daniela sharing a dessert made by her father. Nevertheless, at turtle speed, the anvil yielded and the ball socket *popped* out of the other side.

I dropped to the ground and let out a breath I didn't realize I had been holding. My mana flashed a warning at thirty percent and spots floated in my vision, but I'd managed it. Gec's Hemisphere Trial had already lit the importance of malleability in the use of spell chains into me; being able to use it so tangibly was the icing on the cake of that lesson, and crafting ideas already ran rampant in my mind. Until Rommel and Arnold shook me out of my daydreaming.

"Ronan, are you okay?" Rommel asked, leaning forward.

"Peachy. Why would you ask?" I managed.

"Because you are curled around the hammer like you want to make love to it? I know we are sort of in a time crunch, but if you need a moment for your... crafting process..." Arnold trailed off as he looked away from me.

"Very funny, you buffoons," I said, uncoiling myself from said hammer and rising to the sound of my popping joints. "What've you got for me?"

"Made a rough cross out of the shell, but I wasn't able to get the slight curve of the plate out of it," Arnold said, handing me something that *wanted* to be a cross. It was more like a square with small squares cut out of the corners. Regardless, those could help fit the shell to the hammer side of the weapon.

"I folded the plate and welded it from the center to the outer edge. Sharpened, of course," Rommel said, gesturing to an astoundingly honed piece of ant chitin. The slightly bowl-shaped plate had been folded *against* that curve. This, in turn, left a small, triangular hollow tube near the fold after the orc had welded it with more infusion work. The chitin edge had then been flattened and sharpened to provide a wedged blade, flaring wider than the original piece of carapace like half of a battle axe.

Both pieces could have made frightfully good weapons of their own right. Even the femur could have been used to provide a strong base for a weapon—common rarity or not, Q4 was Q4 in terms of the attributes it provided. Yet we stood together, and in agreement, to use three of some of the best pieces of loot at our disposal into a single weapon. *Daniela is never going to let me live this down, especially after I broke her naginata.* A mischievous grin split my face.

"Let's do it." With the help of <Mudpit>, I was able to make the stone block pliable enough to sink the shell and chitin blade onto opposite heads on the weapon. It looked like utter trash. They weren't secured nearly as tightly as the femur, even with the stone hardening overtop, but I was confident the item creation process would shore up any weaknesses. *Plus, I'm pretty much out of mana and there's only twenty percent stability left on this shard. Stop thinking, focus, Ron!*

I shook my head and refocused on the brief discussion between Arnold and Rommel. They weren't sure what infusion to use as the one to power the item transformation process. Through testing, and much failure, we'd come to discover that mixing infusions during the item transformation stage of the crafting resulted in chaotic reactions. From a fizzling waste of the infusion used to an impressive conflagration of elemental clashing. Thanks to that, there had been a silent consensus *not* to mix them and instead let a single attunement guide the item transformation.

"If we double down on the earth, then this thing will really pack a punch," Arnold argued.

"This hammer is the weight of a small child; it does not need more 'punch,'" Rommel countered, surprisingly heated for the normally stoic orc. "The possibility of getting the Lightweight trait by using an air infusion is much more important. Making the weapon usable will be much more important than having a fancy statue to decorate your home because you can't swing it."

"As much as I like earth, Arnold, I'm going to have to agree with Rommel on this one. As is, this thing is at the edge of usability," I said, drawing the argument to a close. All I had to do was gesture to the large shield propped against the wall of the test room. It wasn't heavy, courtesy of the material it was made from, but wielding it *and* the axe hammer would be a task. The dwarf sighed, but raised his arms in defeat.

Without delay, I rushed back and retrieved a handful of Q3 air infusions. I passed one to Rommel and Arnold, getting odd looks back. When I explained that I wanted to attempt to <Infuse> the item together since we'd worked on the parts together, they were surprisingly touched. They also told me they'd never tried that before. I hadn't either, but I couldn't help but feel my heartbeat rise. Just like the sudden urge to carve the helix on the femur, or the manipulation of my spell chains, something in my subconscious was probing for *more*. More connections, more trials, more understanding of the way the world around me connected to the magic that suffused it, even the inkling that existed before the Metier Crystals arrived on our world.

If my math was correct, the three Q3 infusions would be enough to finish off the item in one go. We didn't hesitate. The moment I pulled the mental lever for <Infusion>, so did my fellow crafters. Dust gray threads of air Pith unspooled and we each grabbed ahold of them. The air around us swirled, drawn through the opening where I'd melted the wall to dance around our bodies as we manipulated the energy of their element. With a shared nod, I doused the amalgamated hammer with my Pith thread. Two others followed a second later.

A dull glow flowed through the entire item. I didn't miss the way my carved helix was refined and realigned where my cuts were suboptimal. The straight femur gained a slight *kink* toward the bottom as the yellowish bone darkened. The darkening was also repeated about halfway up the haft. The femur, however, experienced the least amount of change out of the whole item.

Whereas my Pith thread had struck the bone itself, Rommel and Arnold had subconsciously aimed their own threads to the parts of the weapon they'd worked. As the waves of energy from the handle, axe blade, and strike head met, the world around the weapon seemed to *twist*. The vibrations that took over the weapon were so strong that the entire thing warped and flexed as if the inherent properties of the materials we'd put into it didn't matter. Stone rippled like water, the shell crinkled, and the chitin flexed and warped like a flag in the wind. The femur dancing the worm was what forced us to take several steps away from the workstation.

The three of us watched in mute astonishment as we watched our hard work threaten to rip itself apart. As the vibrations continued to feed on each other, the whole weapon just became a blur of motion. Seconds ticked into minutes and yet we didn't utter a word. We couldn't. For all the item transformations we'd witnessed between all three of us, this was on an entirely new level. *Was it the joint effort? Some unknown synergy between the materials? The fact that we incorporated mana-created materials?* Like usual, I had more questions than proper answers.

A full ten minutes after we started to infuse, the transformation ended abruptly.

The first thing that hit me was disappointment. Hair-thin cracks spiderwebbed all through the stone hammerhead and just into the edges of the two materials. The femur was spared, somehow, but that didn't raise my mood much. If I ignored the cracks, the result of our efforts were something to behold, however.

The poor binding job I'd managed for the blade and shell had been perfectly corrected by the item's transformation. Where before there had been a roughly rectangular hunk of rock, misshapen by my antics in pushing the femur through it and exacerbated by glomming the shell and chitin to it, now there was a piece of deadly art.

The slight cross-shape that Arnold had been able to cut out of the shell fit perfectly onto the side of the hammerhead. Stone had filled in the concave bowl of the shell plate, leaving it flush with the head. Furthermore, rock seemed to have flowed through the gaps in the bone of the shell, securing it further onto the <Stone Anvil>.

On the opposite side, the stone had stretched and flattened to flow smoothly to the thickness of the chitin. Three deep ridges of stone seemed to intrude and displace the fire ant material to truly wedge it in place. Not only that, but with the flattening of the stone had also come a bit of flattening of the ball-socket joint on the femur. The bit of the weapon that had poked out of the top of the hammerhead hadn't made it through the transformation process unscathed. I'd intended to keep it pointing away from the bladed side, but the transformation had taken that one step further by sharpening the bone into a wide, slanted spear point.

As if it had been waiting to drop the bad news until I had gotten a good look at the axe hammer, its information floated into my vision. It confirmed what my observation told me.

<Quotient 4 Fractured Axe Hammer>

<Attribute: N/A (Mobility)>

<Trait: N/A (Ballast)>

"That... doesn't look good," Arnold said, his voice barely above a whisper.

My heart fell. Probably due to our manic rush, and despite unprecedented team work, the item had come out...*lesser.* I couldn't help but think it had been my fault. I'd been driving the whole craft with a desperate air, running against a silent clock for something I wasn't even sure would turn out badly. On top of that, I'd pushed the others to attempt something entirely new by infusing together, and I couldn't help but feel that *that* was the reason for our failure. Whether it was inexperience or incompatibility or some other of the hundreds of factors we probably didn't account for, the result was inert before us.

I could have left, relegated the shard to the wilderness, and rushed back quickly. I could have installed it, if it let us, somewhere out there. If the concern that it would have had a critical reaction had truly been there, I could have contacted Daniela to take it further than my own mobility would have allowed. Yet... I hadn't. The shard had felt... right, in my possession. I wasn't sure if it was my earth attunement resonating with the earth shard, or any number of other things, but I'd wanted to secure it close to me.

I pulled out the shard in question and stared at the information as it almost seemed to taunt me. The line that even now caused my heart to skip a beat got my strongest glare.

<Stability: 16%>

"What should we do?" Rommel asked. The orc practically had to tear his eyes off the item. I couldn't manage a response and just shook my head.

"Maybe we can revisit it once we've got more experience crafting. Now that it's done, I must admit it was quite… ambitious," Ronan said.

"Nothing to it. You gotta take it on the chin and keep going. I suppose we should at least reinstall this thing and see if it doesn't kill us all in the process, eh?" Arnold said, grumbling. The dwarf was making a concerted effort not to look at the axe hammer.

I nodded, absently walking toward the portion of the wall where I'd extracted the shard. The actual spot wasn't there anymore thanks to my amplified skill smoothing it out, but if it could reset its mana bubble, then it had the best chance of doing so near where we'd found it.

The shard, however, had other plans.

Before I had a chance to react, and even faster than my perception, the shard took to the air when I got close to the axe hammer. An invisible thrum of power, not dissimilar to when Bec extended his area of influence to ward off creatures, exploded from the shard a moment before it plunged into the hammer like it wasn't a solid object. I stood like a deer in headlights, Rommel and Arnold similarly frozen. Nothing happened for several seconds until the familiar caramel light blazed out from within the hammer.

The radiance climbed steadily until I couldn't stand to look at it. With my eyes closed, vibrosense surged to fill in the gap in my vision. Just like the constant tippling strobe of the mana bubble, the hammer was a pulsing mess of energy that also lit up like a Christmas tree in my sixth sense.

Even as the waves of energy petered off to a handful a minute, they seemed to refuse to go out. A strange heartbeat of mana caused energy to flow through the weapon and I finally dared to open my eyes.

The hammer was much the same, except the cracks no longer seemed like a weakness. That caramel light had coalesced into a binding agent, securing the weapon to itself and filling in the helical groove I'd carved along the femur.

It had been flawed, fundamentally, but that made it perfect. It had left a gap for something new to pull together the weaknesses and forge it stronger yet. My eyes unfocused as I read the *new* item description.

<Quotient 4 Asymmetrical Field Anvil (Axe Hammer)>

<Attribute: Mobility>

<Trait: Ballast (Q4)>

<Shard Trait: Arcane Sink (Unbound)>

The purple highlight that outlined my weapon had never looked so wonderful. The whole thing laid inert on the table, but I could feel a draw to it as the mana pulsed within. It was as if a wisp of my mind could reach toward it, even without making contact with the weapon, and wield it. It was unnerving and comforting at the same time. I didn't wait for either of my companions to respond and grabbed the bone haft.

CHAPTER TWENTY-FIVE

Soulbound Shard

Power. Growth. Stalwart. Those concepts erased everything in my mind for a full second before I could take a breath and the world came back into focus. The caramel intrusions in the weapon flared with energy before settling to mute pulsing glows along with the heartbeats of mana I sensed. It wasn't as frequent as my own, but they were in time with the pumping of my Slurry Ichor. It was as if the energy in my veins was also the energy within the axe hammer.

Hand still firmly planted on the haft, I focused on it so its information would show again. Things had changed just from that brief interaction.

<Quotient 4 Asymmetrical Field Anvil (Axe Hammer)>
<Attribute: Mobility>
<Trait: Ballast (Q4)>
<Shard Trait: Arcane Sink (Q6)>
<Soulbound: Ronan Terrigan>

Not that I know what the Arcane Sink trait does, or even Ballast for that matter, but now the weapon is Soulbound?

"Huh, I can't see the description anymore," Arnold said, snapping me out of my staring contest with the weapon.

"Really?" I said, turning to the others. I turned just fast enough to watch their eyes widen. "What is it? What now?"

"Ronan, isn't that… a tad heavy?" Rommel asked, pointing at my side.

Confused, I turned to follow his finger and saw that the axe hammer was held firmly in my hand. The weight was so inconsequential and the grip so comfortable I'd hardly noticed it had come along when I turned around.

"Woah," I replied eloquently.

"What happened!?" Arnold asked, hands gesturing wildly. "Speak words, man!"

"Uhh, it says the weapon is 'soulbound' to me now? And that Arcane Sink that was blank is now Q6."

"Hmmm. Too much for coincidence," Rommel said, as if that explained his entire train of thought.

"Not you too. Come on, Rommel! I can't deal with another of you going braindead on me," Arnold complained. "Are we all going to blow up? Did we succeed? Blast! Can I get a straight answer?"

The dwarf was a tad agitated, his entire face turning a slight red as he glared at both of us. I was still somewhat in shock at the development, while Rommel seemed to be in deep contemplation of *something*. Not the most conducive environment for the cantankerous man.

"I don't know what happened, Arnold," I said, making a placating gesture with my free hand. "The description changed, I felt energy flow through me, and then bam!"

The dwarf fiddled with his beard angrily, grumbling all the while. He was glaring both at me and at the weapon. Before I could try to say something else to Arnold, Rommel rejoined the conversation. "Are either of you familiar with this Ballast trait?"

"That's a no from me," I answered, focusing on the easy topic of conversation. "Haven't messed around too much with air infusions other than the spider naginata."

"Hmmm, me neither," Arnold rumbled. "Air doesn't tend to like the worked metal."

"Anyone that might know?"

"Devon," both Rommel and Arnold answered at the same time. They shared a look, but the dwarf let Rommel speak. "Ever since the cannon, he's been interested in making multipurpose cannonballs based around the attunements. He's worked a bit with all of them, so he would have been my first pick to ask, but…"

"He's off on the scouting mission and doing the Hemisphere Trial," I finished for the orc.

"You think them big rock friends of ours will be kind enough to answer some questions? What with the hammer not looking like it's going to blast us to smithereens, I reckon we might get some answers," Arnold asked.

"Worth a shot," I said, placing the axe hammer on my shoulder and taking a step forward. Or I tried to, at least. My leg was lead, and it did not move as I'd expected it. The strange extra weight cut my stride in half and tripped me forward on my face. I reached forward with my hands to catch myself, but the oddity left me blinking on the ground.

"Ronan?" Rommel asked.

"My legs…are heavier," I replied.

"Like tired?" Arnold asked, confused, as he helped me to my feet.

"No?" I responded, unsure.

I wiggled my toes in my boots, but they felt about the same. However, when I lifted my leg as if I was going to take a step, my calves were much heavier than they had any right to be. Frowning, I set the axe hammer back on the table, releasing the haft for the first time in the conversation. The pulsing heartbeat faded from my senses, but I was still vaguely aware of where it was relative to me. It was like a magical compass pointed right at the weapon.

When I tried to take a step, my body moved as I had expected it to.

"That thing was making my legs heavy," I said, pointing an accusatory finger at the axe hammer.

"Were you feeding it mana?" Rommel asked, approaching closer to examine the weapon again.

"No, I was just holding it as is."

"Curious… May I?" the orc asked, using his palm to point at the hammer.

"Go for it," I said, shrugging. Considering the definition of the word 'ballast,' I had an inkling of an idea what the weapon was doing when I wielded it. How that translated to the trait activating by itself without any stimuli, I didn't know.

Rommel gripped both of the darkened bone spots on the haft and pulled. The weapon was a slight strain, even with the orc's great strength. A flash of red spun out from his palms into the weapon, only for the caramel accents to flare in response. Like a sinkhole swallowing a house, the fractures gobbled up the energy and Rommel grunted as the weight of the hammer *increased*. He set the weapon down a second later.

"It swallowed a chunk of my mana," the man said evenly. I could see a sheet of sweat rolling down his brow and his green skin was slightly flush. It wasn't due to the strain of lifting; somehow the axe hammer had triggered the fire-attuned's side effects.

"Oh? Think it will do the same for me?" Arnold asked, not bothering to ask for permission as he grabbed the axe hammer. The energy flowed out of his hands and into the weapon. The brown of his internal mana mingled with the caramel of the cracks until they were pushed away by the caramel. I wasn't sure why, but the mental image of a child being a picky eater flashed through my mind as the caramel energy retreated back into the weapon. Arnold looked like someone had slapped him in the face.

"This cheeky thing took your mana but not mine!?" he said, much too outraged by the inanimate object.

Or is it?

"I suppose we can see if it's biased," I said. Grabbing hold of the haft once again, I fed it mana in the hopes of activating the item. The response was immediate.

The mana bubble that we'd encountered in the room bloomed around me. It spread with a good ten foot radius to encompass my two companions. Then came the sensation of increasing my mobility attribute, a slight jittery need to move and a flexibility to my joints that was quite noticeable from a Quotient 4 item. Lastly was the drain. Nominally, the lack of one outside of my initial probing wisp to activate the item. Somehow I could tell the effect wouldn't last, however, as I felt the density of the mana within the bubble drop quickly the longer I held the flow.

Before that happened, I set the weapon down on the table and released its activation.

"So, that's new," I said.

"Magic rock. Let's go," Arnold said, pointing over his shoulder. The dwarf pivoted on his heel in one smooth motion and trundled off. Rommel seemed to have been in agreement because he was already making his way straight through the opening in the side of the building and waving us through.

I gave the weapon a look, then I gave my feet a look and sighed. The idea of going through the learning curve for moving when your legs were twenty pounds heavier wasn't an issue itself, but it definitely hurt my pride. After stumbling around dealing with vibrosense, to go back to that right in the middle of town because of the weapon left me throwing glares at it. Nevertheless, we cut through the handful of carts near downtown and past a very confused Irwin to make it to Tec in record time.

The Blessing of Magic rippled as Rommel and then Arnold crossed the threshold like stones tossed in a calm lake of rainbow water. My leg, thigh, and left arm went in just as well, but the moment the haft of my weapon tried to cross the threshold, it was like I'd hit a brick wall. The momentum of my jog, and the strange need for me to hold the weapon tightly, caused my legs to flounder out. My much-heavier-than-before-I-came-to-the-surface body dropped like a stone onto the wooden dock that had been built at the edge of Tec's crystal.

I blinked as the sun shone in my eyes, surprised more than injured by the fall. The other *buddies* in my group finally realized that I wasn't there with them and turned around to see me half out of the Blessing of Magic.

"What happened?" Arnold asked as he helped me to my feet. *I guess being shaped like a teapot had its benefits from time to time. Picking stuff up must be a breeze from down there.*

"Not sure. The axe hammer doesn't want to," I grunted as I tried to pull even the haft through the membrane of the Blessing, "come through."

"Strange, maybe Tec will tell us why? Why don't you stash i—"

"No!" I yelled, surprising myself. I did a double take at the intensity of the reaction, as did my friends. I whispered to myself. "What the hell?"

—ACTIVATE THE SHARD BEFORE YOU ENTER.—

The volume was bone-shaking and we all did our best to cover our ears. Arnold and Rommel were more successful, what with their access to both hands, but even with only one free, I barely managed to only get half deaf. There was no question who had spoken, and I could see several people deeper into town giving us strange looks and a few glares. Just because we were the closest and most affected didn't mean that the Metier Crystal talking wasn't a spectacle that rarely happened in Wildwood. For good reason, since no one wanted to deal with the proportional increase of volume due to size the Entities seemed to suffer from in day-to-day conversations.

Taking Tec's word, I trickled my mana into the weapon. The bubble immediately tried to expand, but the Entity somehow suppressed the size and it extended less than an inch around the weapon like a thick film. The part of the haft where I'd been holding it against Tec's barrier slipped easily through. I had to blink as I watched a *second* membrane, this one made from iridescent energy, overlap the shard weapon's bubble.

The three of us waited for several seconds to see if there would be some further reaction. Other than the caramel-colored field around my weapon dimming slightly, nothing happened and we headed toward the crystal. Arnold glanced at me before slapping his palm onto the crystal, followed by Rommel, and finally me.

The world shifted as the crystal swallowed us, depositing us not in the whitespace but in a long, featureless hallway. Macabre and familiar crystal jail cells lined the sides. While they all looked identical, I'd seen them hold Kirby and the other traitors. Considering those people had passed away… Arnold and Rommel looked mightily confused, and I felt a chill down my spine as I considered that bringing the hammer might have been a terrible idea. Thankfully, glowing lines of energy spelled, 'Deposit Shard Here.' Oddly, the urge to not let go of the axe hammer wasn't there anymore, and I easily let go of the weapon.

"Couldn't do that before we got sent to prison, could yah?" Arnold asked, heat climbing a bit to his cheeks.

"I… uh… didn't need to fight it in here," I said, unsure of how to treat what felt like my mind being manipulated.

"Fight it?" Rommel asked, a frown creasing his face.

"It almost felt like you'd asked me to cut my arm off and leave it on the ground," I said, recalling the brief but intense emotions that followed the suggestion.

"Okay, maybe we should really talk to the crystals," Arnold said, irritation replaced with what looked like genuine concern.

As if they had been waiting for our conversation to close, the walls closed in around us and we were pulled into the whitespace in a blink. Except it wasn't exactly the whitespace we were used to. Cracks of black void covered the whole space around us in a dome and I spotted the one responsible quickly.

"Gec," I said, nodding at the pyramid manifestation hovering in the air.

[-]Warrior Leader, when I spoke previously about areas of high mana, I did not intend for you to supplant them and bring them with you into purged territory![-]

I'd hardly heard Gec agitated. Even when the Entity had

threatened to splinter our minds, it hadn't really raised its voice. Now, however, its voice thundered across the space, causing more cracks to flicker in and out of existence. I saw a frantic geometric shape floating about, leaving trails of iridescent light that held back the cracks.

"Is this perhaps a conversation better had in person? Tec doesn't seem to be particularly enjoying your efforts at polite conversation." My words dripped with sarcasm. Even if I felt bad for the other Entity, being direct with Gec had served me the best.

The Entity's manifestation flared at me for a full three seconds before it shrunk in radiance. The black space cracks receded as the higher Category Entity retracted more of its power from Tec's body. Their manifestation didn't let out a sigh, but I saw the geometric shape sag in relief against the floor of the whitespace.

[-] You have brought a threat of corruption to their doorstep. [-]

"That doesn't sound great, but do you care to elaborate?" I asked, frowning. The Entity was clearly talking about the shard weapon.

[-]The shard you discovered is the foci of mana in an area. It is, for lack of a definition your flesh minds could comprehend, an *Attuned* Crystal. They are the monoarcane versions to our omniarcane purging. It is also due to them that an Entity can naturally shift into these Aberrant Entities you have encountered. [-]

"Woah," Arnold whispered to Rommel behind me. "I was not expecting this level of discussion when we tagged along…"

Gec continued unimpeded even as the black cracks continued to spread. I could tell they weren't doing it on purpose anymore, but it was an unfortunate side effect of hosting the stronger Entity.

[-] You have now *also* managed to bind the shard to your soul, making it as much a part of you as the arm you used as an example. [-]

They can eavesdrop. Good to know. "What does that mean for me then? I don't know what this shard weapon does, or why it is causing Tec problems. It seems they got it under control fairly easily."

[-]Weakens them![-] The cracks flared and Tec once again resumed their frantic patch job. [-]It cannot be difficult for you to comprehend that everything in this world stems from energy and will. The only reason things with such condensed potential energy as those beyond the Corporeal Limit retain a steady form is because of their *will* to do so![-]

That last bit of information was *not* new to my understanding of science, but was much more chilling in a world where real magic existed. I'd long hypothesized that there was an interplay between Pith, Dreg, infusions, infusion materials, as well as mana. Why could you power something with mana but also gain Dregs if you overdrew it? How could an infusion hold a portion of a creature's Pith, and why was it attuned instead of pure? What exactly were the Entities doing while they drew mana from the air, and what did the spell chains have to do with it all? Too many questions floated unanswered and, in all honesty, I didn't feel equipped to really pursue even half of them to a reasonable conclusion.

[-] So you are capable of contemplation after all. [-]

"For something without a tongue, you sure know how to run your mouth," I snapped, my train of thought derailed. "If you aren't going to be useful, I'm going to go test things out for myself. Surely that will mess with your 'ultimate goal' much more."

Gec remained silent for several seconds and I could practically hear the gears turning in its crystalline mind. With a garbled echo of tinkling chimes that I could only interpret as a sigh, the Entity started to explain.

[-] Shards either form *from* high mana density areas, or they *form* high mana areas. Mana of other attunements is taken and filtered to increase density of the shard's attunement in the air. It is a self-propagating cycle of purification. As you might

expect, this benefits creatures of said attunement in the area. [-]

"We gathered as much. What does it mean for the Entities and my weapon?"

[-]Entities strive to balance the mana in the atmosphere while evenly increasing the density. The range of that is determined by our domains and diffusion based on the environment of the planet. It takes a sufficiently strong Entity to contend with a naturally formed shard when said shard attempts to breach them directly.[-]

"The Aberrant and Galloway," I whisper, drawing the connection. I wasn't sure what Category the Aberrant was, but it certainly looked to be doing a number on Gec. Galloway's pretense couldn't have been a coincidence.

[-] Correct. While your shard has not corrupted an Entity, it very well could. As it is, it has become an extension of your soul and given you a slapstick way of purging mana at will.[-]

"Is that what the Arcane Sink does?"

[-] That is its main function, yes. However, it is entirely possible for that to change as the shard becomes more interwoven with your soul.[-]

"Is it...dangerous?" I asked, remembering the urgent need not to let go of the weapon.

[-]No. However, you will need to make sure it does not encroach in the domain of an Entity without you having a firm grasp on its power. Tec showed an undue amount of trust letting you store it so you could enter this place. [-]

At the mention of its name, the Entity turned from its work toward me, bobbed in the air, and then returned to keeping itself together to survive Gec *talking*.

"So it should be fine to experiment with it?" I asked, unsure.

[-]Yes. I urge you to remember that it is now a manifestation of your soul and *should not ever* be the other way around. As you grow in strength, so will it. Your wills must be in alignment. [-]

"It's alive!?" I asked, eyes bulging out of my face.

[-] It is as alive as any Entity can be, now that it has bound

itself to you. Its thoughts and actions, however, will be more aligned with its attunement rather than any sapient form of life you might be familiar with. Perhaps even more simplistic than that elemental abomination that lurks around you. [-]

"I'm going to need some time to process this," I mumbled, the second part of the Entity's proclamation barely registering.

[-]I suggest you do. Process, if my words weren't clear enough for your soft neurons. Natural formations should be considered before being plucked for use as weapons. We seek balance and strive for power to defend it, not the other way around. [-]

Apparently done talking, the three of us were *violently* ejected from the whitespace and Tec's crystal. We landed with a splash a hundred feet into Lake Sumter. Immediately, a flash of distress flowed through me. It took me a second to realize it hadn't come from me, but from the axe hammer which had been ejected along with us and was sinking.

Bubbles escaped my mouth in a shout as <Earth Shell> formed around me subconsciously. The mana-turned-stone added a surprising amount of weight to my body I never realized was added and I sank...like a stone.

The muck at the bottom of the lake was sucking, and I could feel the water pressing down on me. The waves of distress guided me to the spot where the axe hammer had sunk halfway to the haft into the lake bottom. As soon as I plucked it out, <Earth Wall>'s spell chain formed under my feet and pushed me up out of the water. I barely paid attention to the trickle of mana that flowed from the hammer, into me, then my helm, and then into the amplified skill.

Like a submarine breaching, I exploded out of the water only to belly flop and begin to sink again. The added weight from the hammer's Ballast trait worked against me as I tried to tread water and failed miserably. *Screw birds and screw water!* I screamed in my head.

Before I could lose hold of the last bits of air in my lungs, a blur of dark blue sped through the water and collided with me.

For a moment, the world was a ripple of flawless auburn hair suspended in the rays of sunlight that cracked through the murky lake water. Then we were beached on the shore not too far from the Blessing of Magic.

I turned to thank the person for the assist only for a slap to knock the helm off my head.

CHAPTER TWENTY-SIX

Unobstructed Obstacle

That had to have been a skill. I blinked the stars out of my eyes to see a soaking wet mermaid leaning over me. The perfect nose and eyes of emerald green quickly came into focus. Jolene.

"You bastard! You've been in town for weeks and you refuse to even come say hello? You couldn't even deliver your own goods in person!?" As soon as she saw that I was breathing, the woman started up a tirade while slapping the ever-loving crap out of me with mana-empowered hands.

"Jol—"

"And then I hear you come back from that trial thing, and still nothing! What did I do to you, Ronan!? Huh? Answer me!"

The last word was punctuated by what felt more like a left straight than a slap. I wasn't able to muster a response before Rommel and Arnold washed up on the shore, sputtering. The dwarf leaned heavily on the orc, struggling even with the shallows.

"What in the ever-loving hell crap did it do that for!? We were just the peanut gallery! I didn't even know it could *do* that!" Arnold complained, shaking like a wet dog and wringing water out of his beard. Rommel, however, had spotted the two of us.

"Jolene? What are you—"

"Rommel, you stay out of this!"The beautiful mermaid snapped her fingers and pointed a scaly hand at the orc. "Both of you are complicit. You know I've been looking for him, and you couldn't even bother to tell me? We have old world phones in our heads now!"

Using the slight redirection of the woman's wrath, I slipped out. The muck from the lake bottom that clung to my lower body actually served a purpose, allowing me to extricate myself from her grip and jump to my feet. The most impressive thing was that the hammer was still firmly secured in my hand. *I need to get some way of hanging this thing on me.*

"Jolene, you haven't done anything wrong," I said, backing up slowly.

"Then why have you been avoiding me? I just plucked you from the lake and you are already backing away," she said, pointing at the muddy tracks I'd left while backing up. *Et tu, soil?*

With the situation climbing exponentially quickly into telenovela drama, and I'd unfortunately seen more than I'd ever wanted thanks to Daniela's father, I stopped in place. Honesty had served me well many times, and there was no reason not to embrace it again. In all *honesty*, Jolene hadn't done anything to me and had actually been really helpful; she was just… intense.

"I'm sorry, Jolene. I *have* been avoiding you, but not because of anything you did. I appreciate your trust with building that item, but I'm not very good at dealing with those kinds of social situations. Most of the time, if I'm not telling someone what to do, we end up in a fist fight. Daniela and Samuel are quite thoroughly included in that count," I said, hoping to diffuse the situation.

The woman stared me down. The other two people in our strange gathering were frozen stiff, throwing glances between me and the woman. If I hadn't been concerned for Jolene's stormy expression, I would have burst out laughing at their reactions; they looked like owls.

"Fine. We shall talk on the way to the gator dungeon," she huffed and turned. Her feet were sure as she strode into the lake and disappeared in a perfect dive splash.

I'm not sure how long we stood still on the shore, but it was long enough for Irwin to appear. The man looked very confused as he stared at our soaked bodies and the glowing hammer in my hand. He let out a deep sigh and called us over.

— + —

"And you told her to her face that you had been avoiding her?"the councilman asked, jaw reaching for the floor. Arnold and Rommel were seated close to the fire, both shaking their heads as if to agree with the ridiculous choice I'd made in my conversation with Jolene.

"Wasn't like I could avoid her then! My uncle always said honesty is the best policy," I argued. It looked like Irwin wanted to disagree, but eventually had to concede the point. *It's not like you want to say lying is good, huh?*

"Let's move on from that. You mean to tell me you have a mini Entity on you now?" Irwin confirmed, leaning back on the log seat and gesturing vaguely at my hammer. It was sitting in the flames and I could vaguely feel undertones of contentment coming from it.

After feeling that spike of dread in the lake and being made aware of its living nature, I'd been able to pick up on broad feelings from the hammer. Mostly indifference about being carried, but it had liked the fire when I set it next to it in order to dry it off. Little did I know that it would nudge at my consciousness with a flash of the word, 'Fire.' It kept repeating the word the closer I put it until the hammerhead was *in* the coals.

"Something like that," I said, rehashing what Gec had said again. "The Entity made it sound like it was more a localized Blessing of Magic when I activated it. I haven't done much testing on it; I'm just trying to get used to walking with it at the moment."

"Should try that obstacle course," Arnold said, working a thick comb through his beard. "I worked on that bad boy for Sarah, and it will put you through the paces."

"I had been meaning to check it out…" I said, drifting off as I looked in the direction of the training area. There were a handful of buildings between the bonfires near downtown and the Wild Guard's obstacle course, but I could almost imagine the shouts and grunts of the trainees getting worked over.

"Perhaps it will be best to keep this news more… under-wraps," Irwin said, drawing my attention back to the conversation.

"Secrets?" Rommel asked, frowning.

"No, that would be pointless, considering you forced Tec to talk out loud." Irwin raised his clawed hand to stave me off. "I know you didn't do it intentionally. Regardless of that, everyone with ears knows you visited the crystal. I also wouldn't be surprised if many people saw you plunge into the lake. Noon was the worst possible time you could have picked to speak with Tec."

"It's not like we knew what else to do," I grumbled, looking away.

"Anyhow, with the fight against the gators coming up in a few days, why don't you take the rest of the day and tomorrow to get familiar with your… unique weapon? If someone asks, just say it was a particularly difficult infusion, and deflect it from the shard discovery.

"Sarah told me about the meeting you want to have between everyone before the offensive, so it will help to have your brain screwed on right. I'll get with the Allied Council and figure out how to pass out *this* information. The revelation about the Corporeal Limit is still causing ripples."

"You don't want to keep making waves?" I guessed.

"Precisely. Clara is still doing some testing—*respectful testing*—near the Summerfield Memorial. With what she's reported back to Sarah and the Wildwood Council, plus what you just told me, I can only assume there is a death shard there."

I felt a slight headache as I considered what throwing more wrenches into people's lives would do. First, our arrival had blown Wildwood's understanding of magic out of the water. Then we unveiled a traitor to humanity that had been a trusted member of the town, and vaguely recognized in the others. With that, we'd set the towns on a warpath that had just started to recede. With that one track mind disappearing with the immediate threat of the Dreg, they'd then been told about the dangerous threshold that was Q6. Just as *that* concern was being disseminated, Gec twisted it into a positive.

It's more than enough to make your head spin, especially for those not at the forefront.

From what Irwin proceeded to tell us, people were already flocking out of the allied towns to cross the threshold. Even if the Category 4 Entity had opened itself to give access to as many skills and implants as the towns needed, there were still limits to how much their minds could take at one time. That was a warning that had been given to any and all who received the implant's skills, instead of forming a Gift naturally. Despite all of that, it was like everyone *had* to step onto the road to Q7.

Even the crafters were rabid at the possibilities that more magic presented them. I could hardly argue with that; the proof of those efforts was sitting in a smoldering fire. While our attempt at simultaneous <Infusion> hadn't been quite success-ful, it was only the first attempt of what I was sure would be many. If Arnold's <Stone Anvil> hadn't been the base material of the weapon, I didn't think we would have gotten the frac-tured item; it would have just blown up in our faces. Just thinking about it, I winced at the memory of plastic splinters peppering my body.

"—Ronan will go see Sarah. Rommel, can you help Arnold patch that wall? The fewer questions about what happened there or the mana bubble, the better," Irwin said.

"Mr. Bellwick, I don't know if I like this," the orc rumbled.

"None of us like to keep things from others, but not everyone is in the position to think about the good of the many," the councilman countered. His expression was as serious as it had gotten during the conversation. "I need you boys to trust that deflecting the importance of the shard, for a time, will be the best thing right now."

The three of us, Rommel the most reluctant, agreed. Arnold complained about being sent to deal with the crafter's hall, but considering that Irwin was technically the one responsible for the budget of the crafters, his bellyaching was kept to a mumble. He wanted to see my performance on the obstacle course. Promising that he'd get to see me fail it miserably the following day, I parted ways with the three men.

The axe hammer was thrown over my shoulder as I walked to the training area and I tried to think about how I would carry the weapon without looking utterly silly. The weapon itself gave me the answer; an application of one of my skills that I hadn't considered before. I was a little stunned by the intensity of the vision showcasing it, but the implication wasn't lost on me. My weapon gave me a tip on how to use my skills, and I was one hundred percent going to take advantage of that.

"<Earth Shell>!"

I held the axe hammer diagonally across my back with the axe blade pointing away from my body. The fluid stone generated by my skill practically leapt off my skin to enclose the weapon in three thick bands before I stopped channeling it. The result was a half cuirass of gray stone clinging to my back and just over my shoulders. The Ballast trait, which somehow continued to be active while the weapon was affixed to my back, made it feel perfectly balanced as I turned, bent, and twisted my body. It looked a tad ridiculous, but I had embraced that magic being out in the world would result in some ridiculous things.

From then on, the walk to the training area was much less awkward, sans the occasional stumble from my heavier-than-usual legs. The small cluster of spires that rose up into the air quickly became visible the further south I walked, and before long I was standing at the foot of the obstacle course. The hanging platforms stretching from spire to spire were the same as I recalled, but the course had been changed significantly.

When I'd come back from Base Arachne, the course looked like a series of swinging beams and precarious jumps to avoid falling into the manmade pond at the base of the spires. There was absolutely no way the people of Wildwood would have been able to concoct that first one without the help of magic. The one that had risen from the ashes of that one was an order of magnitude greater. The swinging beams and jumps were there, but the trainees were now adding their own mix of obstacles. A bonfire floated over a pond while a vine hung inconspicuously in the air. Three person-tall vines were being operated by two life-attuned in order to man a crank dropping logs of wood along the path one was meant to take. There was even a patch of ice with jutting icicles that had to be slid on to reach the very end. All the while, the trainees taking breaks were lobbing small rocks at the one passing the obstacles.

Why in the hell would you build this!?

Apparently, I stood there long enough for the trainees to notice me. Several waved, excited to see one of the great members of the 'Bunker Buster' squad. Some looked concerned and yet some looked indifferent. *Is this that teenager attitude thing that Ava and Uncle always complained about?* My idle thoughts were interrupted as an orc split off from the group. Her smile was full of mischief and I did not like it one bit.

"Hey Ronan. Heard you had quite an interesting morning," Sarah said, smirking.

From her face, I was pretty sure that Irwin had updated her on the mess the earth shard had caused. I wasn't sure when, since the man had kept his attention trained on us during the whole conversation, but he'd managed it somehow. Considering his position, it was entirely possible that he had some ungodly level of multitasking experience. Pushing past that errant thought, I agreed.

"Is our humble training area finally worthy of your time?"
Sarah said.

"I always planned to come by, I've just been pushed into a
position where I think I need some... expedited refreshers
before going head-to-head against some giant gators."

"You must be wondering why we renovated to this extent,"
Sarah said, having read my expression perfectly.

"You know, it occurred to me."

"Attributes," Sarah responded simply.

"Come again?"

"Attribute gains. Ava has been keeping track of your gains
and how each attunement developed. There seems to be some
inherent correlation between the environments or the innate
attunement of a person in the way that their attributes develop.
Swim a lot, gain mobility. Lift a lot, gain strength. Lift weights
while underwater? Gain mobility and strength."

"How does that make sense?" My mind immediately started
to spin. From that statement, the nonsense before me started to
make sense. I hadn't seen a single one of the trainees make it
through the course, but they got right back on it with smiles on
their faces. If the multifaceted training gave them straight
attribute gains, then it was 'free' power ups!

"Ava is still trying to correlate the data from her attribute
census with some of Alan's research, but it seems to line up with
the attribute trend for items when you infuse them," Sarah
answered.

"Fire and earth for strength, and water and air for mobility,"
I mumbled, having messed around with infusions more than the
common member of the Wild Guard. "Life and death give
refinement and containment, respectively."

"That's right. We have noticed a drawback with this type of
training in the *distribution* of the attributes. Concentrated
training gives concentrated gains, but our current approach has
less gains overall. The benefit comes in not having a skewed
effect."

"What do you mean?" I asked.

"If your strength isn't tempered with a certain level of mobility, then you are strong but unable to move like you want. If your mobility is too high above your strength, then you won't be able to properly correct your own motions and flail around. The hidden, secondary natures of the attributes are still eluding us. The toughness side of strength and the dexterity side of mobility is something Ava is endlessly fascinated by. I'm pretty sure she said she is going to do something called a 'longevity study' on those kids going to the Bunker School." She paused, considering what else to add before snapping her fingers. "For the record, it seems earth-attuned gain more on the toughness side, while us fire-attuned gain it more on the muscle power, but she keeps telling me that we have too small a sample size."

"Wow, that's a lot of information. Now I'm slightly scared to check out what Sam's been cooking up on the other side of town," I said, shaking my head. He'd been working on secret projects using infused plants and skill-boosted growths almost since we reached the surface.

"To say you lit a fire under the collective asses of this town would be an understatement," Sarah chuckled. We shared some conversation on lighter topics and I answered some questions about my new weapon, but she quickly got serious when the upcoming attack came up in conversation. "I can't promise the course will help, but I think you will definitely benefit. So, you gonna take a crack at it?"

A grin split my face as I cracked my neck side to side. Mobility was almost my lowest attribute and the idea of putting it through its paces kindled a fire in me. It wasn't the same as practicing my magic, innovating crafts, or punching above my weight class against the beasts of the wilderness, but it dumped a full dose of adrenaline into my body. A quiet, almost imperceptible, hum filled the air that I believed was my ichor kicking into gear.

"If you don't have a leaderboard, then you best get one started."

CHAPTER TWENTY-SEVEN

No Excuses

SPLASH. Again!

My surge of confidence had been quickly smothered by the well-constructed obstacle course. The sun was already falling by the time I had managed to make it past the platforming portions that had been designed before adding ones to more specifically target attributes using mana.

Most of my early failures had come from the balance beam one had to cross over water to get to some alternating, angled jump platforms. In this particular stretch of the run, the added weight of my legs was actually a *boon*. I felt like I could tip much further to either side without falling, thanks to the concentration of my weight being way below my center of gravity. The problem with that was when a small rock pelted me in the side. I would subconsciously adjust as if I wasn't fifty pounds heavier and the extra weight would pull me off balance before I could correct it.

After becoming fairly acquainted with the mud at the bottom of the pond, I was almost ready to stomp off in frustration. The Wild Guard trainees had been somewhat stunned that I had been attempting their training, since most thought that the 'graduates' of the program had no reason to come back. Sarah, channeling her inner Ava even if she didn't know it, had explained that it was always important to keep yourself honed. My lack of success was a clear example of how just gaining attributes from Quotients could come with detriments.

At least she threw a caveat in there. These kids look just about ready to spit at my feet with contempt. It wasn't entirely unfounded. All of the trainees had managed to make it through the initial segment of the course easily, even being Q2 teenagers and young adults. They breezed through the first portion and it was only in the part that incorporated magic that they struggled.

There was *one* kid that barely paid attention to my failures and drew concerned glances from Sarah on more than one occasion. Billy. The half elemental, now that I understood what the Dreg affliction had pushed his body toward, was working even more feverishly than me. He didn't train on the obstacle course, but instead on the various vine climbs and platform jumps that hung between the training spires. They had been designed for the more agile air-attuned, which had many move-ment-type skills. His legs went incorporeal with each jump and I watched him catch himself more than once with his hands when the limbs failed to solidify properly. The third time he threw, and caught, himself while his air limbs failed him, I slapped myself across the face.

The force and slight sound of grinding stone drew the eyes of several of the trainees. One of the trainees working on the first part of the course was actually so surprised by that devel-opment that they missed a handhold. The hit hardly hurt as my synergistical traits ate the blow with aplomb, but it struck some-thing deeper. It struck the fact that I had absolutely no reason to complain just because I wasn't very balanced. It was a little unfair to myself to think like this, I recognized, but people had died while I still lived.

With my determination steadied, I attacked the obstacle course. I had never been one to think too deeply on things, instead opting to feel my way through. The realization of how hard I had been trying just to keep my balance instead of *doing* the course rankled, but I pushed the frustration out of mind. With a jump, I landed on the six-inch platform. The trainees eyed each other, unsure of if they should throw like they had been.

"Hit 'im!" Sarah called out from her open-air office at the edge of the training area. Her smile reached all the way to her tusks, and the adrenaline of my first run pumped through me.

The rocks flew and I remained steady. So much so, I actually leaned *into* the blows from the rocks I didn't think I could dodge well enough. The force pushed me back upright and I crossed the thirty-foot log flawlessly. I was fairly bruised, but I could already feel my passive regeneration easing the threads of pain. Force didn't disperse quite the same when my feet were on wood as opposed to soil or stone.

"Hell yeah!" I roared, pumping my fists as the dopamine hit. I faced down the shot step jumps followed by the slanted jumps like a hungry predator and threw myself at it.

Balancing beam, jump platforms, slanted jumps, monkey bars with vines instead of hard bars, hurdle jumps and limbo bars, a frame with muddy bars and a net wall up and over one of the training spires. The failures were relentless. Sweat, mud, and pond water dripped off me in droves as I pushed my endurance to the maximum. The other trainees had to take turns lobbing stones at me since I ran the course more times than any of them in the day. The contemptuous whispers silenced; my focus zeroed in on the course. The rock blows hardly shook my concentration anyway.

When I first got to the bonfire swing and my arms failed me on the grip, the world plunged into the muddy water of the pond, I knew I was spent. With a flash of emotion that could only be discontent, I hauled myself and the axe hammer out of the water. With a sigh, I slumped at the edge of the pond, head barely out of the water.

"I thought we were testing you, but you were testing our training capabilities right back. I think I'll have to push the trainees a bit harder with you around!" Sarah said. I opened my eyes a crack to spot the orc woman looming over me with a grin on her face. With the oranges and purples of sunset, she struck quite the figure.

"Just trying to be ready. We both know dying is a stumble away," I managed, closing my eyes and using vibro to 'see' her walk closer.

"You are right. Which is why I'm glad you spent some time with the trainees and showed them that there was a reason I didn't need to validate your abilities."

"Considering my fight with Devon that one time, I would have figured they knew I wasn't a slacker. Even... Well, even when I wasn't in the best headspace."

"I know," Sarah said softly. "You shouldn't underestimate the power of vision or icons. My father always says that people don't follow people, but the ideas they personify. *He* wouldn't be trying so hard if you guys didn't cast such a big shadow."

Sarah didn't need to point out who she was talking about. Billy had passed out not long before I'd called it quits. Considering he was Q3, the fact that he'd lasted as long as he did was impressive by itself. The fact that he'd almost managed to do a full run of the acrobatic platforms was even more so.

"Why is he pushing himself like this?" I wondered aloud, not really expecting an answer. Sarah surprised me with one.

"He asked to join the Freelance squadless for the fight against the gators."

"He what!?" I bolted upright.

"He says he's not going to get better wallowing in the dark. Let me tell you, he hasn't told Eric about our talks and I think he isn't going to until it's too late."

A flash of memory of the youth fighting against the black-space as it tried to consume him was vivid in my mind. I couldn't help but feel suddenly protective, but I reined that in. The situations weren't even close to similar, but I could remember those dark feelings of being trapped down in the

Bunker. The spiraling pressure that my life would amount to nothing but a name in the Bunker's data stores.

Since Billy thought that fighting was what he needed, I vowed to just become a harder wall to shield him, and any others seeking to find their legs, from anything that might cut them from *their* own 'trip to the surface.' *Uncle would be proud to see how my time up here has caused me to start waxing poetic*, I thought with a laugh.

"I'll keep my eye on him," I said, closing that thread of conversation by standing up with a bit of help from my axe hammer. Sarah gave me a curious expression, but didn't pry.

"Well, Billy might not meet the criteria I set for him. What I don't know is if I can allow the Vanguard to partake in the mission if he can't keep his word," Sarah said lightly, gesturing to the obstacle course. Her voice was a taunt if I'd ever heard one. "I had one of the crafters start work on a leaderboard just like you suggested, after all, but you barely made it to the new course…"

"Needed to get my legs under me; don't worry, I've still got a day yet." I smirked. She met my expression and we parted ways, each lost in our thoughts.

— + —

"How did you even walk over here with sprained ankles?" Samuel complained as he ran both his magic and creepy nerve filaments over my legs.

"Blame it on the traits and my high pain tolerance?" I said, shrugging, still face down on the couch.

"Ronan, you should be happy Mama isn't here," Danny drawled from the chair across us. She was holding one of the two sconces Sarah had provided us like she'd promised. The other was installed in the kitchen-dining room of the dojo.

"If your mother was here, Danny, she'd have her foot so far up his ass, I'd be having to help her extract it," Samuel said, not missing a beat.

The woman chortled, propping her feet up on the table before addressing the giant magical weapon in the room. "You gonna talk about your new friend?"

"What's there to tell? I'm sure you two heard what happened, and I just told you the part people *might* not hear," I said, groaning in relief as Samuel worked his way up my shins. He mumbled something about 'hairline fractures' before doubling down on the poking and prodding. When I'd noticed that I had a persistent six percent of my health that didn't regenerate, Samuel had practically attacked me with healing. A side benefit of the abuse was that the final bit of the unrefined Dreg on my Limestone Skin had been refined by the pummeling I took at the hands of the other trainees.

"Can it hear us?" Daniela asked. "And when do I get one?"

I gave the woman a flat stare. "I would recommend a fire shard for you, or maybe a water one. Maybe you'll finally be able to *chill out!* We don't even know what Fievil does. As far as communicating or hearing us, I'm not sure. All I get are impressions from it."

"Wait, wait, wait," Daniela said, holding up her hands to stop me. "You named it!?"

"Yeah, why wouldn't I? I can't just keep calling it 'axe hammer' in my head. It didn't send an impression of dislike, so I just assumed it was indifferent about it."

"Why Fievil?" Sam asked, shaken from his concentration due to our resident Latina's propensity for outbursts.

"The name the Entities generated was 'Asymmetrical Field Anvil' so I just took the 'Field Anvil' and combined it. Not sure why they called it that, but I'm sure I'll figure it out eventually. Or Fievil will tell me, one of the two."

"Samuel, I need you to do that creepy animal talking thing but with the mushroom network in the forests. I need to find a fire shard as soon as possible," Daniela stated, nodding at the blonde very seriously.

"What? I can't use it on trees... I think? Also, how do you even know about the mycorrhizal network!?" he replied, seeming more perturbed by her knowledge than the fact that she'd asked him to talk to a plant like it was a search bar in our computer terminals.

"You two aren't the only ones that spent time studying outside subjects!" Daniela replied, suddenly defensive. "I'll have you know that mushrooms are a big part of the culinary scene. At least, they were before the Fall, anyhow."

"Never mind that," I said, sweeping my hands through the air as if it could banish the sidetracked conversation. "If we run across another wild shard, we will need to think about how we use it or if we should leave it. They aren't the sole cause of high mana areas, but they do raise the attuned mana in a certain location. More the higher Category of shard."

"You think we can manage *more* area for dungeon-type farms?" Daniela asked, skeptical. "Wildwood is having enough trouble as is with the spider and ant territories. Thankfully, the predator territory is more of a toss-up, but that causes problems in and of itself."

It served to remember that Daniela was an active part of the culling efforts around Wildwood when creatures ignored the repulsing signal of Tec's influence. Now that she wasn't being kept on scout-only duty or babysitting trainees, she'd plunged herself back into leveling. As far as I knew, it was the only reason she'd come back; she'd also needed a hand from our friendly neighborhood life-attuned. There seemed to be a soft cap of how much Q6 density Dreg could be accumulated and banked before it started to affect regular mana use.

"I don't know if we have the option not to," I said. The woman was ready to shoot back an argument, but I plowed forward. "We need better gear and the town needs to improve their amenities. The solution, without relying on figuring out some way of isolating the entire power grid from mana effects, is to continue developing infusion crafting.

"That sconce there," I said, pointing at the hunk of glowing rock in her hand, "is a huge step forward, even more so than our pendulum cannons now that the town isn't in imminent danger. It represents an application not meant just for combat but for quality of life. Imagine, stoves that didn't need anything but your mana. Or mana-powered cars, or any number of other things that would fill the lives of those who don't want to 'step into the breach,' so to speak. In order to do that, we need more materials and infusions. They aren't going to just fall in our laps; we need to go out and get them from wherever they are hiding. On top of *that*, we need them stronger and we need them reliably."

"This is going to make things difficult," Daniela conceded, leaning back in her chair. Her brow was creased in thought. "Maybe we can actually farm something attuned, chickens or something from the world before."

"That could be an option," I said, shrugging.

"I'll have to experiment with the herd back at the Bunker Camp…" Samuel mumbled, seemingly lost in thought about something.

With my point recognized, the conversation turned to ways we could best make use of the shards *without* turning them into semi-sentient weapons. For the first time in a long while, the three of us alone spent time talking and fantasizing. Most of what we'd done when we were kids had revolved around the world before the Fall; fantasy had remained a product of video games and fiction books in our terminals. With fantasy stepping into the realm of reality, we let ourselves go on wild tangents.

We laughed and poked fun at each other like we hadn't done since the MetierTech Implants had come into the picture. Our individual paths were as divergent as they could get, but the root of our dreams was rock solid. We were just three life-long friends thinking about the future and just what sort of crazy things we would need to achieve it.

CHAPTER TWENTY-EIGHT

Setting the Bar...

The next day, I was up at the crack of dawn. My body felt like a rag that had been confused for a mop after a few rounds with a meat tenderizer that thought it was a steak. However, as I went through my status during breakfast out of habit, something gave me pause and lifted my spirits for the day ahead.

Growth to my strength, mobility and even my refinement attributes!

Attributes:
Strength: 1.94 > 1.95
Mobility: 1.68 > 1.75
Perception: 2.20
Refinement: 1.54 > 1.57
Containment: 2.41

It was one of the largest increases since I'd attained Harmonic Sinew. I hadn't noticed the change the previous night, so it was with thoughts of time actualized attribute gains and training methods that I ambled to the training area.

Surprisingly, a few of the trainees had beaten me to the field and they stood around awkwardly as Sarah checked through the course to make sure it was prepared for the day. Considering the abuse the thing went through, I was sure it only stayed together thanks to magic.

After finishing her inspection, the orc woman spoke some brief words with the trainees, who lined up in pairs, before walking up to me. "We won't run the course until after the morning session. Considering the advance tomorrow, I've got them on light duty so we are only doing Gift Wrestling and conditioning today."

"You run a tight ship," I said, chuckling at her structured plan so early in the morning.

"You try to tell a bunch of teenagers what to do for any length of time. It doesn't help that I'm not much older than some of them. Thankfully, none of them argue too much when the fire hand comes into play," Sarah said, chuckling as I watched a few of the trainees flinch.

"Anything you want me to do? I can throw up a few buildings in the meantime if you need them. Q6 really did a number with my ability to build."

"Maybe before we finish for the day, if you make it. No, I was hoping you'd Gift Wrestle with *me*,"the woman said. "A few of the kids with Gifts can give me a run for my money, but not after I draw on my full mana."

"The old quality vs quantity, huh?" I remembered the wrestle between Rachael and I. If I hadn't had the reserves and Quotient to overwhelm her, then I was sure she would have beaten me. It didn't take much thought to identify that Sarah was in a similar situation with her charges and her own development. "You got it. It will be good practice for me to manipulate my spell chains, and it should make your Hemisphere Trial easier."

"I hope to hit Q6 early on this mission just for that," Sarah said, a smoldering flame kindling in her eyes.

She led us to one of a dozen cleared circles that had been established ever since our first trip to Stonecrest. There were similar facilities in the other towns now, but the biggest training areas were in Wildwood. Lake Weir tended to have the most contact with wild creatures and since they didn't need to hide their presence anymore thanks to Wec, their fighters' training had become more…practical.

The two of us walked to the furthest one from the other trainees in the hopes of avoiding any skill discharge mishaps. I was much tougher than Sarah, that wasn't a secret, but the orc was much tougher than most of the trainees. The life-attuned trainee that was overseeing the wrestling shot concerned looks in our direction that were summarily ignored by the New Earth councilwoman.

"On three, we meet in the middle. Any particular skill you'd like to work?" Sarah asked.

"What is that hand attack of yours?"

"Oh? Bold, are we? It's my offensive direct Gift. Did you know, the status differentiates between Gifts and skills?"

"I didn't actually, but I can't be too surprised. Based on what the Entities have explained to me, Gifts aren't written in the same 'language' as the skills. They are less intensive than skills, but more aligned with your own mana and abilities. I'll put myself against that, thank you very much."

The woman harrumphed at my words, taking a loose boxing stance before beckoning with her hand. For my part, I leaned forward and put my hands on my knees. We didn't plan to actually spar so I just braced myself, focusing on the spot that had been marked in the middle of the space by a wooden disk. I'd seen enough of their training while doing my own conditioning to know the basic ground rules.

With a sigh, I manifested <Stone Spike>'s spell chain around me and held the skill just short of releasing it. It was a slight drain on my mana, but it helped time the initial contact better. Sarah mimed my actions, her flickering red mana shaping itself into a curling disk of fire. It might have been my imagination, but I could almost feel like the flickering flames looked like fingers searching out something to clasp. Visual effects aside, the two of us locked eyes and started the count.

"Three!" we yelled. I willed <Stone Spike> forward, going straight for the technique I'd used against Gec's spell chain. My skill shrank, presenting a more pointed end as it collided with the fiery ring. Both attacks fought for dominance instantly, their direct nature almost pitting them in a contest of strength as opposed to making use of any further will we infused them with.

Just before we had time to adjust and further refine the contact of our skills, the world was awash with caramel light. An impression of indignation and affront flashed by my mind. The burnt umber of my mana swelled with power, turning from its light earthy tone into a brown, bordering on black as it lanced through Sarah's skill. <Stone Spike> manifested, taking the rest of its mana cost and raising the ten-foot cone of compressed soil right in between us. The caramel field sputtered, retracting quickly into its epicenter; considering the color, the source didn't take long to divine.

"Fievil!" I grumbled, taking the axe hammer off my back.

Before I flew right into an admonishing speech, I watched the light in the femur's grooves and hammerhead dim and sputter like a faulty lightbulb. I channeled my mana into the weapon on instinct, the glow remaining dim but stabilizing as a pitiful version of the mana bubble formed around the weapon. It was barely enough to encircle the haft and my forearm. With a sigh, I walked out to the edge of the ring and placed the hammer down.

When I turned around, Sarah was still holding her hand forward as if she were controlling her fire hand. She blinked when I returned to the ring, processing what had just happened. "What the hell was that?"

"I am thinking the weapon had some defensive function. It's the first time it's done that, but it's not dissimilar to what it did while infusing," I said, giving the axe hammer the side eye. The connection remained, like an itch at the back of my mind, that urged me to go back and keep it in my grasp. *For the course, I promise. But if you are going to interfere like this, I can't have you on me while training!*

I wasn't sure if my thoughts reached the weapon, but I focused back on our ring. With more than a little shame, I used <Mudpit> to sever the spike at an angle. The tall rock slid and tipped to the ground where I rolled it out of the ring. With another flash of my liquifying earth skill, the ground was perfectly level and a new wood plate laid equidistant between me and Sarah.

"When this whole fighting business is done, remind me to hire you to reset the training sands," Sarah said, shaking her head in defeat.

Grinning, I returned to my previous stance. Still shaking her head, the orc woman did too and our spell chains blossomed around us. Three breaths later, they met with a vengeance.

— + —

"I still think you cheated." Sarah pouted, pouring a whole canteen of water on her head. A small steam cloud immediately rose up before being swept away by the morning breeze.

"You might have had me if I hadn't done the Trial. The difficulty is a lot worse just using one spell chain, but I think you might manage it," I said, honestly.

The orc didn't look happy, but she had no reason to be disappointed. As much as I'd wanted it not to be a factor, the density of my mana had played a role in our engagement. I wasn't sure if having all my Pathways was the cause of the strength or just the density that came fromQuotient 6. Either way, my spell chains were just that bit sturdier to withstand Sarah's scorching attacks. Each of her skills, and even worse when it came to her Gifts, were extremely oppressive. Refinement and the flexibility of Gifts was something I still hadn't gotten a good grasp on, but wrestling was as safe a way of exploring that as could be managed.

"A few more minutes and we'll be opening up the course for business," Sarah said after we'd sat in exhausted, companionable silence for almost half an hour.

"Good deal," I mumbled, the warming sand of the training area having lulled me into a half sleep.

"Ma'am!"a voice interrupted and I cracked an eye to see Billy standing at attention not far from Sarah. The woman had a bemused expression as she watched the youth bob up and down gently thanks to his ephemeral legs.

"Billy, what are you doing here?" Sarah asked.

"The rope course opens shortly, ma'am," he replied sharply. "I was hoping to resume my training as soon as possible."

"You mean you want to maximize your chances of meeting the baseline I set," she said, pinning Billy with a knowing look. The silent squirm was answer enough. "Very well, it isn't like I'm not in charge of when we switch gears."

The orc jumped to her feet with practiced ease and clapped her large hands to draw the attention of the other trainees. A plethora of skills and Gifts simultaneously lost cohesion. Flaming brambles, muddy sprays, and an icy fog of poison scattered as the spell chains melded before manifesting, no clear winner between the spells.

The pairs of wrestling trainees sputtered for a second, awash with the side effects of their mana, before they formed up in two neat rows. Sarah walked slowly in front of them, stopping in front of a young elf who seemed to still be having some trouble breathing. The woman didn't address it, merely keeping an eye on the struggling trainee until she was able to get her bearings. As if she hadn't noticed at all, Sarah continued to the end of the rows and turned.

"The Vanguard has exclaimed his need to be first upon the leaderboard. My only instruction for today is that you do your darndest to prevent him from doing so. That is a position that should be held by the people of Wildwood, don't you all think?"

"Yes, trainer!"they all exclaimed at once.

"Good. Run through your warm ups and get ready to stone him. Three at a time, of course. Don't want to seem *too* unfair," the orc said, smirking as she looked at me. I could hardly contain the eye roll I wanted to give her. "As for the elves, please complete a sequence of the rope course before joining in on the standard obstacle course. The two best performing trainees will get the chance to join the mission against the gator dungeon."

With those words, Sarah retreated to her small, open-air office. The trainees murmured amidst themselves for a second before throwing themselves into action. Billy in particular seemed like someone had slapped him across the face, but the fire in his eyes looked no less dim than I recalled from the previous day. With a stride that resembled a fog bank more than legs, the youth scurried to the ladders at the base of the starting spire.

As for me, I cracked my neck and took my position in front of the balance beam. Fievil was secured across my back and I could feel a thin thread of mana feeding the weapon as opposed to whatever self-sustaining voodoo it had been managing before. I was more than a little curious to experiment with that spell overwhelming feature of my soulbound weapon, but it wasn't the time.

No one actually required me to complete the course in order to join the offensive, but it was a matter of principle. The improvement in my mobility was more than I could have hoped for, and my familiarity with the increased weight of my legs was at a level where I didn't think I would make a huge blunder in a fight. However, I'd said I would make it on the leaderboard that Sarah was getting built and I would be damned if that wasn't going to happen.

With a final deep breath to steady myself, I charged forward on the balance beam. A stone zipped forward and clocked me right in the forehead. Vibrosense warbled as the ripples of force radiated from my head and were trapped in my skull like a pinball. By the time I came back to my senses and shunted vibro to the furthest corner of my mind, I was already falling. Instead of fighting it, I embraced the fall and held my breath as I became the first to splash down in the training pond.

It's going to be a long day…

I slid down the rope on the other side of the training spires with a frantic energy, receiving another rock to the shoulder for my troubles. I landed at the base platform with a heavy *thud* as the wood strained under my considerable weight even if I'd slowed myself down considerably. I waited for the next throw I knew was coming and dodged before I glared at the bonfire swing.

Three quick breaths and I was off. I was tempted to push off the spire with a cheeky <Earthen Barrier>, but I resisted the urge. I only had a few more runs left in the day and ruining my non-magic streak would wound more than just my pride. As the day had gone on, me and an unassuming youth had acquired something of an audience. As if we were racing the same course, Billy and I continued to push our limits with wild abandon. The youth refused to take breaks until he was heaving like a bellows, and I didn't stop until my body started to lose ticks of health.

I pictured his ghastly silhouette somewhere above me as I leapt for the thick vine. With somewhat practiced motion, I braced for the scorch and leaned on my Limestone Skin to take the brunt of the heat. It was an almost subconscious thing, but the blows I'd received and the energy I'd diverted to the trait with <Corporeal Infusion> made me all the more aware of it. Sure of my body, I endured the long stretch of fire burning below me before I let go and crashed on the next part of the course. My momentum was such that I almost rolled off the next platform, but a cheeky bump stopped me from rolling forward. Just like it stopped the logs rolling toward me from rolling into the fire burning behind me.

As tricky as the timing of the fire jump was, it was just that: timing. The next part required timing, agility, and at least six eyeballs on the trainees grinning as they lobbed rocks at me. After the first toss of the day had knocked me in the noggin, the cheeky bastards had been fueled into rock throwing madness. There was almost always some mermaid or lizard in the pond below fetching rocks when a dwarf wasn't in the tossing rotation.

Doing the best that I could to put the rocks out of mind, only keeping an arm up to protect my face from the ones that would surely be coming the moment I moved, I eyed the rolling logs clattering down. It was very mana intensive to load up the log obstacle since it required two life-attuned to operate. For my runs, however, Sarah had spared no expense and logs were being dropped at the fastest rate the trainees with <Vine Whip>-adjacent skills could manage. There was a slight gap below the drop platform that marked the exit out of the logging hellhole.

Fievil flashed with indignation, sending a mental image of <Terrasheath> pulping the incoming logs while *sanding* a path through the rest. I shoved back on the axe hammer, which had come more and more awake through the day, and refocused on the fifty-foot stretch in front of me. The moment one of the logs bumped against the barrier and rolled down to where they were being hauled up to the drop platform, I was off.

My legs shook the platform almost as badly as the logs when they landed and bounced, but I paid it no mind. I almost wanted the course to fail just so I could rub it in Sarah's face, but that thought was quickly discarded as I hurdle jumped over the first log, paused, then did a stationary jump to dodge the follow up. The one that came in at the tail of that one clipped my foot, bringing me crashing down on my chest. The landing barely took my breath away, but put me in a less than favorable position.

Instead of folding like I'd done most other times, I dug my fingers in between the gaps of the log platform and flexed my

Q6 strength. Just for the sake of my skull, I bent my elbows up like a ramp just in time for a log to put my Quake Osseum to the test. The ten-foot logs threatened *not* to roll over me for a second, but the one that came next knocked both up and over even as they pushed Fievil into the small of my back. The flash of indignation from the weapon was the starting pistol I needed to jump up and dash forward.

With no more than a hair's gap, I avoided the trio of rocks that focus-fired on me right as I was walking under the drop platform. Unfortunately, the move to dodge let one of the rolling logs clip me on the back. I felt a femur shaped bruise forming on my back as I glared at the trainees. They at least had the decency to look slightly sheepish as I squeezed into the safe zone between obstacles.

Don't know if I can make this last one. The slight incline filled with icicles and rocks looked positively daunting even before one considered the ice-covered rungs at the bottom of the slide that one had to climb in order to complete the course. The five-foot gap might seem trivial, but there was such a thing as *too* much momentum when jumping. The first time I'd managed to make it to the third magical stretch of the course, I'd run head first into the rungs instead of even grabbing hold.

The impromptu deflection I'd managed had cost me more than I expected and my fingers already throbbed from the impacts. I could almost feel my Ichor shifting to harden the area and reduce the pain. A boon, but also a drawback, that I'd only discovered after getting beaten black and blue by the trainee's rocks. As I considered that I just might not have enough time to wait for my body to regen before trying to course again, a shout of exultation had to draw my eye.

Billy hung by one arm from the final platform of the course. His legs were almost entirely gone, only a drifting trail of gray wafting from his lower body indicated they'd been there in the first place. And yet, the look of triumph was visible for all to see. With another whoop of joy, he let go and plunged into the much deeper section of the pond around the training spires.

One of the mer trainees immediately rushed to check on him, but the half-elf half-elemental surfaced all by himself. A steady stream of bubbles marked his swim as his ephemeral legs struggled to form in the water, but his arms were unimpeded as he paddled to shore.

Sarah was already heading toward him, a conflicted look on her face. I turned away. With that kind of showing, it wasn't as if I could do any less. It was entirely possible I would just face plant right on the rungs again or slip off or crash into one of the jutting icicles, but it didn't matter. Devoting everything I had to the last run, and mentally preparing myself for the lambasting that would follow at the hands of Samuel, I jumped forward.

My worn boots landed on the ice, immediately losing their grip on the supernaturally smooth surface regardless of what the Florida heat had to say about it. The trainees were distracted by Billy's success, but they quickly got to it as I leaned my body to the left or right to hit as many icicles as possible. Grunting as I hit the first one, I clung to it for as long as my fingers were able to hold the slippery surface. The gaps between icicles were long and I had no intention of taking the path down the middle that built up maximum speed at the cost of control. I built up enough momentum as it was as the second icicle shattered on my chest, followed by the next I bounced my way to.

The mana-formed ice clung to my clothes and sent goosebumps down my skin, but they slowed me enough that I managed to watch the trainees pelt the next icicle to powder in quick order. Maneuvering my increased weight, I flopped to the ground like a fish. My ribs creaked as I impacted the stump of the icicle, my skin trait not having anywhere to discharge the force it absorbed. A handful of rocks pelted me as I laid there, trying to gather my thoughts. *You need to go, Ron. The longer you stay, the more the cold is going to sap you and you aren't going to be able to even hold on to the rungs!*

With a roar, I used the stump to rise to a crouch. I was only halfway down the obstacle, better than any of my previous runs, but I didn't feel confident. Almost three hundred pounds of muscle and magical density picked up speed quick. *Nothing to it.*

A visual of one particularly antsy MMO player that rushed a dungeon before his team was ready flashed through my head before I slid out to the main track. My speed rose quickly, and icicles passed me by just as the platform leveled off and the rungs hung in the air. Like a coiled spring, I exploded out of my crouch the moment I hit the flat platform. The slight tingle of disorientation that followed losing the feedback from vibro tickled the back of my head, but I focused on the four rungs of frosted-over metal before me.

With a herculean effort and what I was sure was a cracked rib, I managed to catch myself on the second to last. My breath came in spurts, misting in the air as I scrabbled to get my legs on the lowest rung.

"No. No!"

My own body heat betrayed me as the ice turned to slush under me and my already numb grip started to fail. Contempt flashed through me as Fievil stirred and sent a flash of images too quickly for me to really process them. The response from my body, however, was instant. The blood in my arms slowed to crawl and my Ichor hardened right around my palms. The surface only got more slick, but with my palm wrapped almost all the way around and my elbow locked in an L-shape, I *couldn't* fall.

The strange response from my trait to the shard's intervention was yet another mystery, but I didn't plan to look a gift horse in the mouth. Alternating between locking one arm and then the other, I used my trait to complete the climb. By the end of it, my arms were a bruised and bloody mess as my Slurry Ichor had actually seeped out of the pores when it locked my limbs in place. The rest of my body wasn't in much better shape, and my core muscles felt like they were on the edge of shredding. The enhanced weight of my body wasn't something it had much practice handling. *That's why you did this.*

That was when it hit. I'd done it. It was a piss poor attempt, and Fievil had to come in at the end to bail me out with its strange understanding of my body, but I'd done it. I managed a strangled cry, more of a howl of agony to Billy's own exuberant one, before the afternoon sun faded from sight and I passed out.

CHAPTER TWENTY-NINE

Setting Expectations

I was not surprised in the least when I woke up in the infirmary. The familiar rows of beds washed through vibrosense clear as day even as I kept my eyes closed. Two pairs of feet moved amidst the beds, highlighting them and their occupants with ripples as the vibrations reached them. Based on the size of the ripples, I judged them to be either elves or fae. Those two Fallen were the lightest on their feet and it matched the signature I analyzed.

I spent a few minutes 'watching' them through my vibrosense until one walked up to check on me. With a cheeky grin, I opened my eyes right in their face.

"Gah!" They stumbled back in surprise, barely catching themselves before tipping over the adjacent bed. *Thankfully it was empty*.

I chuckled as I raised myself up, only to immediately tense from the pain. It wasn't overwhelming, but my muscles were definitely screaming at me. My arms, in particular, were displeased with the abuse I'd put them through. "Sorry, couldn't help myself."

"Mr. Terrigan, you almost put me *in here!*" The poor rosy fae panted as she gestured to the infirmary building.

"How long have I been out?" I asked, trying to see through the window behind her.

"A few hours. The councilwoman brought you here before nightfall, along with a handful of other trainees that apparently had fallen into a state not too dissimilar to your own," the woman chided. Sure enough, as I looked at the others in the room, I recognized some of the older trainees slumped in their beds. One not too far from mine included a smug-looking Billy that was certainly dreaming about all the gators he was going to get to fight.

"I'll get out of your hair," I said, groaning as I swung my legs over the side.

"Master Fallon insisted that if you woke up, you stay here," the woman urged. *Master Fallon? What's that about?* "He left us here just in case you or any of the others tried to return home. We are to give you doses of healing, and he will do a final one in the morning before a meeting he mentioned you are scheduled to attend."

"It wouldn't be possible for me to sneak out now, would it?" I asked, giving the fae the most charming smile I could manage.

"No. I'd much rather not have Master Fallon angry for failing to follow his prescribed treatment. If I need to rouse the squad on call to restrain The Vanguard, I will do it," the fae said, face perfectly polite, while placing her hands gently on my shoulders and pushing me back down. She didn't hesitate in her threat for one breath.

For a brief second, I felt indignation at being treated like an invalid but I stamped it out. My time dealing with the repercussions of freeing the afflicted had taught me much and it had given me a huge amount of respect for the healers amidst the Allied Towns. I was fairly certain that the Q4 healer wouldn't be able to stop me if I charged out of the room, but there was no point in causing a scene of that magnitude.

Even as I shot her a pseudo-glare, which she returned with a raised eyebrow before going to talk to her colleague, I felt the indignation simmer within me. I didn't need to be restrained. I was powerful enough to go where I wanted and deal with whatever happened. That final thought guided me to the source of indignation which I crushed underfoot even harder than my own. *Fievil.* As soon as I thought about the axe hammer, I became distinctly aware that it was resting on the ground just below me, invisible to vibro even after I'd swept through the room. *Just like Blobby…*

Listen here, you little knock off whack-a-mole, I thought at the shard weapon. *You can have whatever nascent thoughts you want, and you'll even get gratitude from me for the tips and tricks, but mess with my emotions one more time, and I swear I will find the deepest, darkest ocean to drop you in even if it feels like I have a hole in my chest for the rest of my life. If you are adjacent to my mind, you know I'm serious.*

The thread connecting me to the weapon quivered under my barely restrained fury before returning to the steady flow that told me where the shard was. A brief, gentle, flash of a nodding head that looked vaguely like a mole later and the shard's presence was gone from my mind. I was still aware of it, but I could tell the weapon had retreated from the direct brush it'd had against my own soul.

The whole situation was entirely too uncomfortable, but I wasn't going to deny the benefits I'd *already* gotten from Fievil. The connection felt a bit like what <Memory Canal> did when I connected with someone else's mind, except without plunging me into the memory itself. The more flashes I received, the more I realized that Fievil was piecing them together from my *own* memories, like some scrapbook shred of knowledge I held but hadn't put together. I wasn't sure what that meant as far as the budding personality of the living weapon, or how it would interact with me, but it did make me distinctly aware of my need to better understand the mechanisms of our new world.

I was still lost in my wayward train of thought when the

rosy fae returned, accompanied by a sky-blue companion holding the other lamp in the room. "I'll administer the healing, and Javvy will put you to sleep. Please don't fight it, and the process will go much more smoothly."

I looked at the blue fae, presumably Javvy, with a strange look. I'd encountered something similar before, but I hadn't been much willing to succumb that time. With a hint of a grimace, I nodded and took a deep breath to settle my thoughts. A small cloud of spores flashed into being over the rosy fae's hands as she worked them over my limbs. A tingling warmth eased my muscles before I started to feel them knit back together much more thoroughly than my passive regeneration had managed.

Just as that pain started up, my body grew tense. That was when Javvy struck, a fragrant lavender suffusing the air and making my head spin. I didn't try to fight it, even if my instincts screamed at me. Fievil stirred, but with a mental 'look' in the weapon's direction, it slumped down. I stared into the silent, smiling face of the fae as she counted down from five with her fingers. By two, my consciousness was already down the drain.

— + —

"Hup!" I yelled, spinning and throwing a jab in the direction of the surge of ripples. If Samuel had been any slower, he would have ended up *in* the infirmary instead of doing his final examinations of the people heading out on the mission the following day.

Bending back more than a human had any right to, Samuel pulled a Neo on me before snapping back like one of his own vines with a glare. "You don't need any more reason for me to be cross with you, Ron."

"Oh, uh… Sorry. Instinct?" I said, shrugging. Painless. *Man, I guess I* did *need to get out to sleep*. There was a flash of amusement from Fievil, and I glared at the haft of the axe hammer sticking out from under the bed. It was met with a visual of a mole blowing raspberries at me.

"Ronan, I'm up here," Sam said, snapping his fingers in my face. There was a frown on his face as he held a small light up to my eye. With it taking up my entire field of vision, its information as an item showed up yet another form of object Rommel had managed to infuse with light. "You seem to be doing fine. They told me you got knocked on the head a number of times."

"One of my traits is sturdier bones. No need to worry," I said, rising to my feet.

"Having tougher bones does nothing for the fleshy bits, rock brain," Samuel said, tapping his own head. "Now stay still so I can check you. I've still got a room full of people to check because a certain orc got the smart idea to challenge a bunch of hot-blooded youths to a competition, and my childhood friend more than encouraged it."

Properly chastised, I sat back down on the bed as he used his nerve filaments to check my head, arms, and legs. He tsked when he passed over my arms, but moved on only to repeat the sound when he got to my legs. At that point, he also noticed Fievil lying under the bed. "This what you were looking at?"

"It found me getting surprised for nothing amusing," I told the blond, who looked at the weapon with a curious expression. He then gave me the side eye. "No, I'm not using it as an excuse. You try having people talking into your head."

"How do you think I communicate with these?" Samuel said, holding up his palms and unspooling his filaments.

"Huh… I guess I didn't think about it…"

"You are fine," Sam said, waving me off. "I'll give your arms another check after the meeting so I can get through the rest of this sorry lot. You need to watch your arms and legs, though. That extra weight is putting a strain on your body. It's adapting —Lord, is it adapting—but there is such a thing as too much. Got it?"

"Yes, Master Fallon," I said, bowing my head in mock respect.

"Oh, bloody hell, now you heard about that? Just get out of here," Sam said, helping me to my feet and practically shoving me out the door.

With an easy nudge of my leg, I hooked Fievil's haft and pulled the weapon from under the bed. The moment we made contact, Ballast took effect and the weapon's weight became trivial. I flipped it up with the toe of my boot and caught it before the trait deactivated. With a slight blip of my mana, <Earth Shell> bound the weapon to my back again.

The walk to the meeting was uncomfortable, but mercifully brief. Sam had been more than right about the strain I'd been putting on my own body, and I vowed to take it easy considering the deployment scheduled for the following day.

Before long, I found myself crossing the threshold of Tec's Blessing of Magic and joining a small crowd that had been apparently waiting for my presence. Daniela was talking quietly with Sarah while Irwin argued something or other with Dylan. Both conversations ended when I finally appeared.

"Glad to see you *are* as tough as they say," Irwin said, shooting me a knowing look. If the man wasn't alluding to my blunder with Jolene, then I wasn't an earth mage.

"I can take a fall—"

"Or a hundred," Sarah said, giving me a smirk and a head-shake. "I told you to inspire the trainees, not turn them suicidal with fervor!"

"What can I say?" I said, shrugging and pointing with my chin toward Tec. "Are we all good to go?"

"Messengers came in twenty minutes ago with the confirmation. The other representatives should be in the whitespace conference," Dylan said.

"No time to waste. Getting everyone on the same page cannot be understated."

"No truer words, Mr. Terrigan," Dylan said, leading the way into Tec.

The Entity reached toward the wooden bridge, bringing everyone but me to the whitespace. I set down Fievil with only a hint of hesitation. "You behave now, you hear me? Just because you have some mana stored doesn't mean you get to be using it against our friends, understood?"

The mole image flashed, rolling its eyes but resting its head on its oversized claws in a clear sign of submission. I watched the hammer for a second before releasing my hand and being welcomed into the whitespace.

The round table, ala Gec style, had made a return and everyone had come to party. Ian and Maurice from Lake Weir, Angel and Jasmine from Stonecrest, and a surprising trio from the Bunker Camp.

"Elias! Alan! I wasn't expecting you all here," I said, smiling despite how rude my words might have come across.

"Yes, well, none but one of our children come visit, so I figured we'd come to you instead," the old man replied with a smirk on his face. While he still looked old, there was a solidity to his frame that I couldn't help but respect. Despite our... rocky arrival on the surface, the Bunker's mayor had been nothing but a force for better. So, I had the decency to look somewhat abashed at his call out.

"Been a little busy," I mumbled.

"Bah! I used to tell my father that same thing when I was young. Glad to see the end of the world hasn't diminished youth impaired time management," Elias chuckled.

"Indeed. I am happy to see you again, sir. Our previous meetings have been nothing but productive," Dylan said, arriving at our little conversation after having plied his political trade on the rest of the gathered group—sans Alan, of course. He was actually having a strangely mute conversation with Tec's manifestation while the rest of the attendees were making small talk.

"He heard there was new information to share about Q6 and practically pounced on Bec," Ava provided as she embraced her daughter and spoke to us both.

"True that. We've spread the message, but with our plans to make a big attack, it felt prudent to get everyone together again," I said, returning Ava's hug as she rounded on me.

"Dale sends his best wishes," Ava said, sending a dozen admonishments my way with just a sentence and a look.

"I wasn't mismanaging like Elias said, I really *am* busy," I said, wilting slightly.

"Your uncle said you'd say that. He also told me to tell you to get your head out of your butt and look to the horizon. Paraphrased, of course. He'll be there when you are free, but hopefully not before something takes a chunk out of you." Ava didn't mince words, that was for sure. Before I had to formulate a response of adequate quality to deflect, Gec came to my rescue for once.

[-] Speak your business. I am not seeking to subsidize this connection while there is work to be done. [-]

Elias, unfamiliar with Gec, flinched as the whitespace fractured for a moment before the Entity retracted its presence. Alan, of course, was fascinated, while the rest of the group merely looked wary. Angel and Jasmine must have been warned by the Weirdians, since they were joining the meeting from Wec, as the two just looked mildly concerned.

"Mr. Terrigan, you requested this meeting," Dylan said, giving me the floor. "Care to start?"

"Right, please," I said, clearing my throat and gesturing to the large table. Once everyone was seated, and Alan at least partially engaged, I began. "While I didn't have a primary objective for this meeting, I felt that with the number of developments that have transpired, it would be a good idea to make sure we are moving forward together.

"The alligator in the room, so to speak, is our offensive on the gator dungeon. While it hasn't been confirmed, thanks to the revelations from Gec it is almost guaranteed there is something of its ilk in that direction at least. Sarah, could you elaborate on our plan so far?"

"Of course." The orc woman stood, gesturing to everyone

present. "As it stands, Wildwood will make its biggest mobilization, even considering the offensive on the death territory and Summerfield. The window of peace following the removal of the Dreg leadership has allowed most of our squads to become highly effective, and new trainees to be field-ready thanks to live training in our adjacent dungeons, plus the upgraded training field. Ron can probably tell you all about that, though."

There were a few polite laughs from the group before Dylan brought the conversation back. "What are the contingencies that we are working with here? If the bulk of our forces will be out on the attack, what does that mean for Wildwood and the other towns?"

"The Bunker Boarding School is now in motion," Ava said. "While the Bunker is not equipped to handle an excessive amount of people, our group has managed to secure the area even against the ant dungeon."

"Indeed. The Bunker was, and will always be, a good fallback point should anyone need it," Elias added, nodding the whole while Ava explained.

"There will also be rotations of at least three squads remaining within the town. I've already coordinated with Stonecrest to hunker down while we complete this operation," Sarah added, getting an affirmative from Angel.

"We hope Rachael will... break her seclusion soon. With her present, Stonecrest has no concerns regardless," Jasmine provided.

Dylan and Irwin seemed to let out an imperceptible sigh of relief as the discussion continued. Unfortunately for them, I had a bucket of cold harsh reality ready to dump on them.

"Considering how well established those contingencies are... I believe it would be prudent for us to discuss how we are going to act not just within our sphere of influence but strike out further into the wilds."

"Right now?" Dylan asked, outraged. While the other towns weren't quite so overt, I could see a wave of uncertainty spread through everyone but our Bunkerites.

"When else? Gec all but confirmed that there are people in need. If we can wipe the dungeon threat off the map, what were you planning to do after?" I asked, quirking an eyebrow and leaning forward in my seat.

"Well, I... The thing isn't that, it's..."

"What would this entail?" Ian asked, his wrinkled brow furrowed deeply.

"People going places that we haven't been to before," I answered with a shrug. "Speculative as of right now, but we *do* need to expand our reach."

"I don't know that we have the numbers to spare," Angel said, stroking his flame beard in consideration. "Plus, this is assuming that you will take our strongest members with you just to pursue the goals of the Metier Crystals?"

"First of all," I said, counting down on my finger and shooting an irritated glare toward the other town leaders. "That is exactly the reason why we should act and try to connect to anyone beyond our current reach. What future prospects do we have, if the world is poisoned and warped by the Dreg we can't see? It might be more work, more risk, but it's also a promise of more allies and stability.

"Trade between the towns has kicked into high gear. Imagine if we had access to entirely new markets," I said, glancing at Irwin as I spoke. "Imagine mutual support, so that people don't have to fear what's around the corner. And with magic in the mix, it's a damn big corner!"

"Is this the time to double down on that?" Irwin asked. Despite his hesitance, I could see it starting to crumble a bit. It did help that despite everything, Wildwood wouldn't be lacking in defenses with the Bunker as close as it was and it being the central point of infused products.

"Helping the people and Entities beyond the Allied Towns *will* happen, with or without you," I replied, evenly. "This is merely me, putting the immediate future into perspective for everyone."

"We need to make sure our homes are safe," Ian argued

softly. Angel and Dylan seemed to agree on the topic, even if Irwin shot his fellow councilman a scandalized look.

"Look, it's more like *imminent* future," Sarah said, standing once again to forestall the argument I could see brewing between the Wildwoodians. "Let's continue gathering information, then we can figure out a path forward. The last update from Devon and Dai revolved around some river they found, and they were going to explore further, but the pair hadn't stayed in range very long. If we don't have a direction, there's no point worrying about it right now."

I couldn't help but sigh at the response. Sarah had opted for the diplomatic option with an open thread of discussion, but even so, I could see the lack of enthusiasm from the other town leadership present. They supported the preemptive strike against the gators, but not against the very things that suppressed them for years?

Elias tapped his knuckles gently on the table to draw everyone's attention. The severe expression on his face reminded me when he'd strapped on his big boy pants and told us the truth about our Bunker and my family; I could only hope he would speak out in support of my efforts, since most of the Bunkerites had remained silent on the issue.

"I believe the path forward is clear, despite how... raw emotions are right now. Ronan is not gainsaying the offensive to support Lake Weir or everyone's desire to keep their families safe. He is, however, stating his goals as representative of the Entities and their mission—*our* mission since, unless someone here has a rocket ship I am not aware of, we are stuck on this planet.

"Isolationism would have led to a slow, crippling death in our Bunker if it wasn't for those brave enough to strike back against the unknown. That blunder needs to be avoided here, on the surface. Rally your efforts for the future, keep hold of the present, and learn from the past. Not to be cliche, but if you do not, you are doomed to repeat it." The man leaned back in his chair, fingers steepled, and said no more.

The room fell silent for several moments as people digested what he'd said. It was a clear reminder that there were plenty of eloquent people out in the world and I was *not* one of them. I feared how bad things would have been had my uncle not instilled caring about other's opinions before acting as deeply as he tried.

Of course, the contemplative silence couldn't last with one particular brunette in the room. "Damn, old man. I was already on board with Ron's crazy plan, but now I want to kill the gators *just* so I can go and save more people instead."

There were a few chuckles from those present, the tension having been broken. I might be a tad rock brained, but I wasn't fool enough to realize that Daniela had thrown in her chips with me. I sent the woman a sincere thank you via the comm-plant, to which she replied with a cheeky grin. Before she could say anything more, Ava jumped at the opportunity to lecture her about proper respect for her elders and her language choices.

That was the opening of the floodgates as various smaller discussions broke out between the Allied Town Council. Speculation on the impacts of reduced squad counts, allocations of shifts to maintain proper coverage for the towns, and how all that affected existing plans for consolidating the territory gained after bearing back the Dreg.

The Weirdians spent several minutes discussing the specifics of the plan with Sarah, while Danny and I spoke at length about the changes that came with Q6. While it had only been a few days since the Trials had been implemented, progress and adaptations were occurring left and right; <Corporeal Infusion> had been a game changer in many ways. Chief in asking questions was Alan, but only for a few minutes. Partly through my explanation of how I'd gained better control of Slurry Ichor, the man had clapped his hands animatedly and disappeared from the whitespace.

Ava and Elias shared a look with me before they too excused themselves. After that point, the rest of the council members dismissed themselves, having solidified the plan for the deployment but putting a pin on the exploration I was adamant would follow the raid. It wasn't how I hoped the meeting would go, but considering how many minds I was looking to change, I could settle for being the one to put their best foot forward.

CHAPTER THIRTY

Invite to the Party

With the bigwig meeting out of the way, there wasn't much for us to do. Daniela headed off to put in a light attempt at *demolishing* my leaderboard position on the obstacle course, while I took the long way back to our apartment.

I reflected on what the people of the Allied Towns had said, feeling it resonated with my own desires, even if applied differently. Nothing about what I wanted included the people of Wildwood, Stonecrest, or Lake Weir suffering, but it made me realize that growing pains were unavoidable. When we'd first arrived, the idea of fighting back against Galloway would have been ludicrous and yet… here we stood.

Thoughts of what we might encounter in the mysterious river to the north, and yet more questions about what laid beyond the natural barriers to the east, west, and south, flittered through my mind as I let it wander. Fievil occasionally interjected when it noticed some strange feature on a pre-Fall building, or when it sensed some small insect in the vicinity, taking the opportunity of me acting on autopilot to explore its own unique brand of sentience.

FRANK G. ALBELO

Unfortunately, all things come to an end and I found myself at the foot of the old dojo. I could have done some light exercising, probably churned through some of my mana in an effort to improve my familiarity with Fievil's Arcane Sink, or even tidied up considering we planned to be gone for several days. I could have even reached out to respond to the dozen or so message pings I'd received on the comm-plant from people in Wildwood.

Instead, I ate a fresh-ish slice of bread with some curiously sweet and spicy jam I found in the kitchen of the apartment spread overtop. Warmth fizzled in my chest as I plopped on the couch and demolished my meal before I so totally unwillingly fell asleep.

— + —

My unintentional, but most enjoyable, nap turned into a full-on overnight coma. By the time I woke up, the sun was already lasering through the wooden blinds on the second floor of the dojo and my friends were making a ruckus.

"Look who decided to join us!" Daniela called, eliciting a wince from me and a chuckle from Samuel.

"When I said take it easy, Ron, I didn't mean sleep the day away," the blond said.

"Must have been more tired than I realized. It's not like we haven't all hit magical puberty recently and are changing radically or anything," I shot back.

My friends shook their heads, amused, but continued to dig into their breakfast which smelled divine. Daniela had somehow gotten a whole quintet of eggs for us. The fiery brunette had cooked and seasoned them to perfection, accompanying them with a slab of mystery meat that might have been ant or spider. I didn't care about that, all I knew was that it was delicious and I wanted it all in my belly.

After a quiet breakfast that left everyone licking their lips, the three of us got to business. Sam needed to do a final check up on the dummies that had followed in my deluded training regimen right before deployment, and he'd tasked Daniela with making sure our supplies were squared away. When I asked if he needed any help, he merely told me to follow along. *Sometimes I wonder if they just keep me around because I have such a punchable face.*

Smirking at the amusing thought, I would have missed the sounds of the crowd had it not been for the pervasive thrum growing in my vibrosense.

Waiting not far outside the infirmary was a veritable army of people. A cursory glance told me that it was easily three quarters of all the squads in Wildwood that had been gathered, along with their families in the old crafting pavilion area. Once again, I was shaken by the sheer mass of humanity gathered. Close to two hundred people was a miniscule number to how many had lived in the area before the Fall, but it was over five times as many people as I'd seen before coming to the surface.

A tinge of that guilt I'd been pushing through resurfaced as I spotted some of the reformed squads, graduated trainees being slotted in with veterans. There were bemused looks on the older guards as the energetic trainees showed off their spell chains and discussed their abilities overall. The families engaged with each other easily, many having grown closer as more people joined the Wild Guard. The reality that the world was dangerous only seemed to deter some, while it emboldened others to fight back. *Well, I can't say anything about that; I'm firmly in that group.*

Through the whole gathering of attunements, there was something different to the last time the guard had been gathered; Wildwood had grown. It was a subtle undercurrent, and I was only keenly aware because of a quiver coming through Fievil, but the mana around so many high Quotient people was almost palpable. There were a handful of Q6s now, and a large fraction of the teams had Q5s. It was a density of mana I had no means of measuring, just sensing, but it was enough for me to notice. Even without the unifying intent that had been a part

FRANK G. ALBELO

of the mourning walk for those lost in Summerfield, the atmosphere was almost *literally* charged.

While I was lost in my thoughts, Sarah pushed her way through the crowd. She was flanked by Danny, Anthony the fire ant, Billy, and Jolene. The scene was curious enough that I snapped my focus on it. When it was obvious they were headed toward me and not around me, I felt a cold sweat form on my back.

"Good to see you up on your feet, Ronan," Sarah said by way of greeting. There was a twitch at the corner of her mouth that said all I needed to know about the woman's thoughts on my stay at the infirmary.

"Sometimes you gotta dig deep. Morning everyone," I said, waving to the others in the group. Unsurprisingly, Daniela rolled her eyes, Billy snapped a salute by slamming a fist to his chest, and Jolene nodded her head minutely. Anthony wagged his antenna in the air. "To what do I owe the crowd?"

"I'm assigning these two freelancers to the Bunker Busters," Sarah said, dismissively.

"Oh, sur—Wait, what?"

"You heard me. I'm putting them on your team."

"You know we run just fine with the three of us," I said, gesturing to Daniela, and behind me to where Samuel was checking people in the infirmary.

"True, but I think a broader range of options for engagement could benefit your group. Plus, these two need to power level, and what better group to put them with than one made up of Q6s?" the orc said, the other corner of her mouth twitching up.

She's doing this on purpose.

"Great! I'm glad you consulted me on this. We'll be happy to have them then," I said, smiling, when I saw Billy's expression fall. That very instant, the youth stood straighter. His ephemeral legs gained more substance by the second, raising him to his original height to stand almost as tall as Sarah. *He really wears his heart on his sleeve.*

274

"Great. As soon as Samuel is done, please line up and we will make the final announcement before you all head out. Clara will be in charge of the expedition, but I expect your two squads will collaborate quite closely once you arrive at Lake Weir." Having said her piece, the orc woman stomped off toward the person she'd put in charge.

"You really need to check your comm-plant more regularly, Ron," Daniela said.

"What? Why?"

"The Entities made a change along with the parties. You get notifications if someone is trying to contact you unless you are actively in their party, in which case they can force connection. Sarah and Irwin have been trying to reach you about expanding our squad for the last few days. When they instead reached out to me and Sam, we just said sure."

I spent the last few days with Sarah! She could have just told me in person! Then I remembered the smirk on her face and I realized that she'd omitted the information on purpose. The choice of personnel to add to my squad also couldn't be random, which meant Sarah knew about my... tense situation with Jolene. Hoping to clarify some of what I'd been ignoring, I snapped open my status.

Sure enough, when I checked the Communications section, there were failed calls from both councilmembers, several from Irwin to Sarah's singular one. There were also a few calls from Samuel, Danny, and Clara, as well as five from Jolene. I didn't comment on that as the woman's eyes bore a hole in my back. "I wish we had full patch notes to look over or something..."

"Tell them, or at least tell Tec. That giant pebble loved your map suggestion so much, it's been trying non-stop to add more map customizing features, but Gec vetoed it," Danny said, shrugging.

I shook my head as if to clear it of the sidetracked conversation. "That's not important right now. Welcome to the Bunker Busters, you two. I know it was a bit sudden, but we *are* glad to have you. Considering the walk north, I think we'll have some time to get better acquainted with our abilities before we arrive at the lake."

"Willing to serve, sir!" Billy snapped. Jolene just rolled her eyes.

This is going to be a long mission…

CHAPTER THIRTY-ONE

No Longer Acquaintances

As it turned out, I was the sort of leader that provided good general direction and support but was not much for the micromanagement of things. I did make a mental note to work on that for the sake of our future excursions. *Samuel* had taken it upon himself to load up a wagon with all the provisions our squad would need for the trip up to Lake Weir. *Our* stuff, however, only took up a third of the space, even including the extra stuff Billy and Jolene added to the pile.

The wagon had several crates that tinked suspiciously as Anthony pulled it towards the front of the gathered Wild Guard. I'd watched as Samuel and the healers assigned to the squads loaded all but one crate onto our wagon.

As the Wildwood Council formed up, Samuel split from our group to stand next to Sarah and that final crate. Daniela and I shared a look as the life-attuned fidgeted under the attention of Wildwood. The whispers in the crowd picked up quickly at the sight of the man. It wasn't hard to guess that his presence meant he and his team of food infusers had cooked up some new scheme. The rot taters had been a huge boon for the forces fighting in Summerfield, and for the New Hopers that covered our behind while we fought Galloway. Whatever The Druid had made would revolutionize things. Again.

"Attention, please!" Councilman Dylan called out, his flame hair flaring up to draw everyone's attention from their speculative mumbling. The man waited several seconds for the last bits of talking to die down before speaking up. "Thank you, everyone. I only wish to praise all of you assembled here before me. We came together to survive the end of our world and we are once more coming together to reclaim it. I will pass the stage to Sarah as the main organizer."

The orc woman stepped forward, undaunted by the collective gazes of the crowd. I knew Dylan was practically built for it, and Sarah was probably used to it, but the thought of it sent a shiver down my spine that not even the creatures of the surface had given me. Public speaking sucked.

"Thank you, Father. Your sentiment is echoed. I will be brief, but there are some very important things that need to be kept in mind with this offensive." Sarah gestured out to the crowd, her hand lingering with our group, Igor's, Clara's, and a pair of others. "Amongst you are those who have reached the Quotient 6 threshold. I have made sure that each and every one of them has passed the Hemisphere Trial. They should be able to aid you should you arrive at the threshold yourselves. I urge you to lean on them as we become used to these new realities.

"Along with those realities is the fact that many of you are probably going to cross said threshold while on this offensive. What does that mean? It means that you will be taken out of the field until you complete the Trial. While it is possible to fight through the absorption of Dreg, I do not want any of you taking risks while fighting. Understood? If your squad's healer drops, you meld with another group. If your squad's numbers fall below three, you meld. Clara of the New Hopers will be your commanding point in the field, and has been given a list of configurations that should spread the load on the remaining squads.

"I cannot emphasize this enough. There is a reason we are

sending a force this large even with the hunters already present in Lake Weir. There will be downed squad members. If you are caught avoiding this regulation, you will be confined to Tec or Wec for a duration of twenty-four hours. There are no second chances." Sarah practically glared at the assembled squads. "Do I make myself clear?"

"Crystal!" shouted the recent trainee graduates and the handful that had been given the opportunity to participate. Billy almost blew my eardrum out when he joined his voice to the call. The more veteran fighters all made sounds of agreement too, just toned down about fifteen degrees.

"The final thing for you to keep in mind will be presented by the one and only Druid. I recommend you keep what he says in mind; once this operation is over, we will need people to join and expand on his work. I don't need to remind you here what his boons mean for our future survival."

The crowd was dead silent as Sarah stepped back and a slightly shaky Samuel stepped up. He cleared his throat as he pried the top off his crate, retrieving a small glass jar filled with a maroon substance. My eyes opened wider when I noticed the slight glow to the contents.

"This is Q1 health jam," the blond started, pausing to take a deep breath before he unleashed a veritable fountain of information. "Through the efforts of Lake Weir and our healers here in Wildwood, we've been able to consolidate the products of infused vegetation. There are many concoctions and varieties that we are working through, most unsuccessfully, but I am happy to announce this one. Thanks to the octoploid nature of strawberries, the infusion of life-attuned energies was accomplished. This Q1 health jam has roughly the same healing potential as a Q1 healing spell chain that isn't targeted. I am also working on a drinkable alternative to this, but I hope life in a jar is worth a little mess when ingesting it.

"It should be noted that you should not take more than one of the two doses in this jar within a few hours of each other. There is still much testing to be done, since it seems like strength and refinement affect this time period. Should you take both, you will not only receive diminishing returns, but also suffer from the <Overhealed>affliction. For those who have acquired it and know what it feels like while trying to keep fighting, I have no doubt you will heed my advice."

There was a moment of pause as everyone processed what Sam was saying before cheers broke out. The man had been doing a fantastic job presenting his work until the crowd responded. Thankfully, Sarah stepped forward and extracted the blond before the shakes of nervousness could get too bad.

The cheering continued even as the man walked away from the slightly elevated platform the council stood on. Several squads slapped Sam on the back, one even causing him to stumble, before he rejoined our group. Almost subconsciously, we formed a loose circle around him.

"Wha—"

"We'll hound you for details ourselves, don't worry," Daniela said, glaring at the handful of fighters that split off in an attempt to congratulate Sam on the creation of the jelly equivalent of a healing potion. Sarah let the rising volume go for almost a minute before she cleared her throat to draw attention.

"We will go to our fellows in Lake Weir and we will stamp out the threat to their lives. Because the future—"

"We guard!" The response came in total unison and I even found myself whispering the motto of the Wild Guard.

The gathered squads cheered and started to form up before heading toward the bridge over Lake Sumter. I gestured our group out of the way, intending to take a position somewhere in the middle of the column. Before we could get in position, Dennis popped up on the other side of our wagon.

"Ron! Clara wants to talk to you. Sorry, got to go! I'm working the other animaaaaallssss…" The satyr trailed off as he skip-ran to the other cluster of wagons that carried the provisions for the other squads.

"How much money on her having called Ron and he

completely ignored it?" Daniela said.

"No bet," Sam replied, shaking his head as he placed the crate with the Q1 healing jam back in the wagon.

"I'm proof enough he doesn't check," Jolene added.

"I've never tried to contact Mr. Terrigan!" Billy shouted, giving me a slick thumbs up as if he were on my side of the argument. All I could do was hang my head and rub at my temple. I was almost sure that if Anthony and Blobby, wherever the slime was lurking, could talk, they would also throw me under the wagon. Fievil certainly seemed amused that I was getting ribbed after I'd shut it down as hard as I had.

"Let's just get going. I'll reach out to her as we walk and you two can tell us a bit about yourselves," I said, trying to channel my uncle's team building skills. *I already feel like I know too much personal stuff about them, what with peeking in the memories of one and the soul of the other...*

I hopped up on the back of the wagon, the wheels groaning a bit thanks to my concentrated weight being added to the considerable load of goods. The squad eyed me, but I refused to comment as I spaced out to look at my status. I quickly tabbed over to the Communications and then to Clara's contact. Less than a second later, the demoness' voice echoed in my head.

"I was wondering if there was something wrong with your implant," she said through the comm-plant, the amusement clear in her voice.

"Sorry. I have a tendency to tunnel vision... Pun intended."

"Dry humor, just why I called. Actually, no, that wasn't why. Sarah was dead serious about that block out for Q6s. I passed mine last night and she almost didn't let me come on this mission."

I couldn't see the woman to inspect her information, but I was moderately surprised. "Congrats. Hope it wasn't too rough."

"Not a big deal. Let's just say that we may need to start patrolling the memorial at night and leave it at that for now," she said. You could practically hear the shudder in her voice.

"Death things. Got it. I think I've had enough of those for one life."

"Right. Back to why I contacted you. The plan is to attack the dungeon in waves. We need to check the squads after each wave to make sure we don't have any fledgling Q6ers trying to bypass us. I don't think the Q4 gators will push many over the hump, as spread out as the Pith will be, but we can't be too careful. The second and third waves, however, will probably get some level ups. When we get to the elite gators, the ones Lake Weir hasn't been able to kill, things will get a bit touchier."

"Do we have a number? Sarah said she was waiting on scout reports."

"Since we cleared out the Dreg, the lake has been overrun by the gators and some death frogs. The frogs were all reported at Q3 or lower, but the elite gators were all confirmed Q5s."

I sucked my teeth. It took a second to remember it wasn't going to be just my squad on the offensive but a collective effort. Still, thinking of the attributes of a giant, Q5 gator left a sour taste in my mouth. "Any magic?"

"Some, as I know Sarah told you, but it should only be a concern with the elites and whatever monstrosity has the Entity," Clara said.

"Good, we'll reassess after the first wave. You are more familiar with Lake Weir's teams, but if you need a hand, just give me a shout."

"A physical one, right?" Clara said, laughing.

"Yeah, yeah, yeah, laugh it up. You know I'm tuned in when we are in a fight," I grumbled. The woman agreed easily, cutting off her teasing and the call in one swift parting. The conversation of my companions quickly left the background of my thoughts.

"…Through things!" Billy told Daniela.

"Does magic phase through it?" Daniela asked, poking the youth in the hip. Billy quivered and scooched-jumped away from the Latina.

"No… magical attacks affect me a lot more, and things with

more mana are harder for me to phase through," Billy said, crestfallen.

"Oy, kid, give and take. I wouldn't beat yourself up about being able to dodge damage while standing still," Daniela said, shoving the kid in the shoulder gently.

The young elf lit up as he looked up at her. Their conversation drifted on to lighter topics where Billy started to talk about the two skills and one Gift he had. He came across as so mature, if a tad overeager, I had forgotten he was still a teenager. I focused on him as he talked to pull up his information on the Implant.

<William (Human)>

<Attunement: Air>

<Refinement: Cloud>

<Perceived Metier Quotient: 3>

"Before I got the implant, I got my <Smog> Gift. It's a sort of fog I can shape to obscure certain things and it seems to weaken certain attacks that go through it." He sounded a bit dejected about what I could only qualify as an extremely useful skill, mainly because of the level of energy that he followed that up with. "But! When I *did* get the implant, Tec said I was ready to take two skills right away. <Polarize> electrifies things I hit, and they take more damage the more I hit them with it, and <Cloud Prison> is sort of like <Smog>, but tangible. Kinda spongy. I'm still working on that one. After the thing with my legs…"

"It's alright, William," I said, patting the youth on the shoulder when I got off the wagon. "We understand. I think you'll be good support for Sam here, since he usually has his head a bit in the clouds when he starts chopping with his vines."

"I have very good spatial awareness, thank you very much, Ronan," the blond shot back. "And with my last set of skills, I actually got a suite of melee range options. Just wait until I <Life Tap> you next time you get snide with me!"

I chuckled as the youth smiled and Samuel shot me a discreet wink. The information about his skills was new, which I realized was true for both him and Daniela, since we hadn't updated each other about the last few skills we'd acquired. Thinking back, I wasn't sure that I'd even shown them <Terrasheath>.

"Samuel has a slew of buffs and heals, while his <Vine Whip> acts as his staple for attack and utility," I said, adding some more information for Jolene and Billy's benefit. "Daniela is very much in the DPS camp, with some mobility thrown in."

"My <Flamebreak>materialize skill gives me some crowd control, which I severely needed. Despite what you might think about fire, it has turned out to be very single target. Lighting stuff *on* fire takes a surprising amount of effort when magic makes things more fire resistant," the Latina added.

"And, as my reputation precedes, I just exist to take as much of the damage meant for you guys on myself."

That got a chuckle out of the group, even a slight head shake from Jolene, which was the most amusement she'd shown since she joined our group. I was distinctly aware about my promise to talk to her, but I wasn't going to be the one to broach the topic. I just tried to keep myself available.

"Ms. Jolene, it's your turn then!" Billy said, turning to the mermaid with an eager expression. Somehow, I was sure that the youth was absorbing every tidbit of information about our group like a sponge. There was a burning passion to learn more that I had seen mirrored only in a few people, Alan with his research being the one at the top of that list.

"Nothing particularly dazzling," she said, dragging out the words. "However, the amplitude item Ronan created has let me explore a further range of strength with my skills and Gifts. Before the implant, I was able to control two Gifts, my <Water Jet> which some of you have seen and my <Slipstream>, which Ronan has experienced. There is more to speed swimming than having gills."

"That's for sure. *Mine* just spit out fire," Danny said, shaking her head. She got an eyeroll from me and Sam, but Billy was spinning in place trying to look at both the mermaid's gills and the fire gills on my friend. I thought he was going to go cross-eyed.

"On top of <Slipstream>, being a mermaid means I swim faster than the lizardfolk, which I will put to use on this mission," she said. "The skills I acquired after the implant, <Cavitation>, <Turbulent Flow>, and <Depth Charge> all play on using water for physical impacts. I've been working to use <Turbulent Flow> in conjunction with <Slipstream> to be able to dodge better outside of water too."

Her voice was soft as she spoke, but it was unwavering in its confidence. Despite how much I didn't want to have 'a talk' with the fiery redhead, I couldn't help but to hang on each word she said. The lingering smile on her face as she talked a little bit about how she'd been training the currents of water she was able to manifest helped to highlight her almost preternatural beauty. More than once, I was caught looking by simmering emerald eyes, but all I could do was look away and try to play it cool. Fievil didn't think I was successful, if the visual of one dastardly cartoon dog villain snickering that flashed in my mind was any indication.

I shook my head of my drifting thoughts when I heard a call go up from the head of the column. Between Clara's coordinating call and the discussion with our new squad members, we'd reached Stonecrest. The speed of our trip and the safety we enjoyed was yet another example of how much things had changed with the potential of the towns unlocked.

By the time we passed Stonecrest proper, the head of the column was already headed toward Lake Weir. I was mildly surprised we hadn't stopped, but when I contacted Clara, she explained the rolling stop. Stonecrest didn't commit fighters, but instead two full teams of Stoneshapers that would help even the odds on the lake terrain for those less used to fighting in water conditions. After more than a second of cursory thought, I realized it made more than perfect sense. *I* didn't have much experience fighting in water, if my dip in Lake Sumter was anything to go by. *Man, now I'm* really *glad they didn't leave the macro plans of this mission to me.*

Unsurprisingly, on the short stretch from Stonecrest to Lake Weir, we were once again not attacked by anything. The number of people, plus the density of Pith they carried, must have been the biggest red flag the creatures of the wilderness had encountered since their own Darwinist climbs to power. It was a combined power that would have drowned Galloway and the death crow had it been in our grasp when we fought them.

When the verdant walls of the town came into view, the reception was much more intense than I anticipated. Adults, many of which looked to be water-attuned, clapped as they saw the column of fighters enter their town and walk directly towards Wec. The rest of the town looked to be in high spirits as they cheered when we passed the recently constructed buildings amidst the hanging gardens. Thanks to the comm-plants, the leaders of the town had known we were arriving and were waiting for us.

Maurice stepped forward, greeting some of the fighters he'd met before, or being introduced to others newer to the guard. A buzz filled the courtyard at Wec's foot even as I kept my team far to the sides. More than one of the plant tenders stopped by to talk to Samuel, while the rest of us were mostly ignored. Slinking in the shadow of what had once been the school's gym would do that.

Samuel was just starting to explain some of the minutiae of concocting his healing jam to Billy when Ian shambled into view. Clara, like a lithe shadow, trailed a step behind him.

"We're glad to have you," the skeletal limbed man said. "Even if I can tell you are avoiding our hospitality."

"You've put up with us plenty, Ian, we just want to stomp this before more people are in danger," I said, cutting right to the chase.

"Quite so. As I've informed Councilwoman Sage, the gators are most active between dusk and dawn. Clara has been kind enough to fill me in on your plan to send multiple waves deeper and deeper, yes?"

"That's right, Elder Ian. With that consideration, we were hoping to launch the first attack today, regroup, then launch the larger second wave at noon tomorrow," Clara said.

"Hmmm, a bit fast, but no one wants these overgrown lizards gone more than us. I shall reach out to Dundee and he can give you the latest on the way to the lake." Ian also grumbled under his breath as he walked away, "If he isn't plastered."

I was curious about the Dundee person, but didn't get much chance to ask as the squads started to form up again. Clara was looking off into space and I could tell it wasn't a coincidence as I saw a ping through my implant.

"Squad leaders, please start heading toward the eastern gate. Once we are joined by the Lake Weir forces, the Stoneshaper teams will begin work on our fortifications at the edge of the town. As soon as the first stage is complete, all non-emergency response squads will move into the dungeon territory and engage. Please be reminded of the level up constraints. The New Hopers and Bunker Buster squads will be enforcing this regulation. Thank you."

The woman repeated herself twice more before cutting the connection and meeting my eyes. When I raised an eyebrow in question, she shrugged. "We'll be going to the north side of the lake while your squad heads to the south shore. We are the linchpins of both of those fronts. What better way to get people to listen than by using our popularity against them."

"Hell yeah, let's get some gators!" Daniela cried, thumping her fist into her palm.

There were more muted responses from the rest of our squad, except for a giddy Billy, but I could feel my blood starting to pump. I became distinctly aware of Fievil's presence on my back and the shard responded with a visual of ripped and torn lizards. I didn't think moles were that vicious, but I wasn't going to complain. I had yet to test my new weapon in combat!

CHAPTER THIRTY-TWO

Rally at the Lake

"Crickey! You lot sure brought a whole party to my doorstep," Dundee said in the worst facsimile of an Australian accent I'd ever heard. He swayed as he raised the cowboy hat off his head in greeting. The lizardman held a bottle of rot gut that I could smell even twenty feet away. Considering it was barely afternoon, the man must have been day drinking quite hard.

"Mr. Dundee, these are the lead teams of the Wild Guard. They are going to start attacking the gators today. Like I told you," Maurice said, smile strained.

We'd almost made it to the lake, its murky presence visible through the trees, when we'd stumbled on Dundee's shack. Ian had attempted, and failed surely due to the lizard's inebriation, to contact their Q6 fighter to no avail. He had then sent Maurice with two of the town's four squads to lead our column towards the lake. It was only when we were practically knocking on his door that the man extracted himself from his house. I couldn't help but wonder how he'd managed to get booze *and* survive beyond the watch of the town. I didn't ask, because I felt my hairs curl just from being in proximity to him, but it told me there was more to the scaly man than met the eye.

"Ho! So you lot lent my chaps some help while I tussled with the gators. Much obliged!" Dundee tried to bow, but instead almost fell on his face. I did notice the way his tail swayed to keep him balanced, which was another way he stood out amidst the water-attuned Fallen. Not all lizardpeople had the tail, but the ones that did had supreme mobility in and out of water.

"It was no trouble. We need to do what we can to support each other," I said, extending an olive branch.

"Right you are, Mr. Guard Rock person!" Dundee slurred, a forked tongue tasting the air before retreating back into his mouth. The lizardman's face scales tightened and the sway to his body settled in a second. He spun to look towards the lake. "Best we get the party started, it seems."

"Hunters, lake formations!" Maurice said, his thorn hair uncoiling to form whips on either side of him.

Seeing the response from the men, Clara and I shared a look before zeroing in on our tasks. I was idly aware of her contacting the squad leaders to get them ready for a fight, while I reached out to my own. The party invites were quickly accepted and their range of awareness was added to my own as I let vibrosense loose.

The house and all of its messy features bloomed in my mind, but I didn't miss the collection of gator skulls that twitched with mana tucked away on a shelf. Beyond that, the smattering of trees were double highlighted by my vision and vibro, but what I was most interested in was the steady thrum that came from the distance. It was a slight thing, but after coming to grips with my Harmonic Sinews, I'd realized that *everything* vibrated to a certain extent. When the natural vibrations of things were being watered down from a particular direction, something was coming. That something was large, or many, if I trusted my senses.

"Billy, get cozy with Samuel," I said through a party-focused comm-plant message. I unhooked my shield from my back and plucked my helm from the wagon. Daniela was hustling to unstrap Anthony as the fire ant bucked. *I wouldn't be happy about being strapped to a wagon with enemies nearby. I feel your pain, buddy.* "Jolene, I want you in the middle ready to bail out anyone in our immediate vicinity. If I'm not here, push them back with your water until I'm back or they are dead."

"I can do that," the mermaid replied easily. She pulled out the gator-head item I'd made for her and her emerald eyes danced with a deep blue light as she looked out toward the water.

"Shapers! Wave break! Tanks, I want a wall to stop a charge. This is a faster engagement than we planned, but if they want to die so badly, how about we give them some!" Clara roared through the comm-plant.

"WE GUARD!"came the roared response of the Wild Guard, met with shouts of approval from the members of the other towns. The Stoneshapers—wearing strange, unassuming brown robes, considering the mismatched mess of armor and weapons on display—rushed out to the front of the group. Dwarves one and all, they stomped on the ground and reached out to each other. The non-dwarves in their two groups stood a step behind, brandishing a wide spread of long weapons and ready to intervene on their behalf.

Pitching my efforts into the roiling soil in front of the fighters, I dumped half my mana into <Earthen Barrier> with an almost casual wave of my hand. It wasn't amplified by my antler helm and it wasn't particularly empowered, but being one of the few Q6ers had its benefits. The efforts of one of the teams formed a twenty-foot-long, three-foot-high barrier of smooth stone. My <Earthen Barrier> stretched out almost thirty feet at the same height, sans the compression. I met the eyes of one of the shapers; their jaw wanted to scrape the ground. After throwing them a wink, I trundled my way up my barrier to stand on the opposite side.

Unsurprisingly, Igor and the Wild Fists were the next group to throw themselves on the least safe side of the fight.

"This is gonna be a good one! I can tell!" The one-armed

orc huffed, smoke curling from the corners of his mouth like an enraged bull.

"You just want to punch something!" I called.

"That's why it'll be good!" He thumped his hand against his chest, which was quickly picked up by the others on his squad. Even Fowler, the healer, joined in the primal display from up on the wall ridge.

As I shook my head at their antics, I watched more of the frontline fighters join us. The ranged support and healers stood upon our fortifications, which the Stoneshapers continued forming into a rough U-shape before raising the whole thing up, as the rogue types slunk about their business. The sight of a few tamed oxen from the Lake Weir hunters was a surprise, and drew some of the attention from the chest-high ant that approached my side.

I got a flash of indignation from Fievil when I patted the creature on the carapace. *Oh, be quiet. I've known Anthony longer than you, and you'll get to get your wimpy paws dirty in a minute.* My axe hammer was still not pleased, but seemed mollified at the least. I could see the slow pulse of caramel light speed to match my heartbeat. True to my thoughts, we did not need to wait long.

A fireball and two ice shards flew over our heads to impact against the crown of one of the trees. With an indignant croak, a horse-sized frog thumped out of camouflage. It was easily two hundred feet away, and those attacks had barely hurt it, but its potential ambush was foiled. In a fit of rage, the creature kicked the oak tree where it had been hiding and splintered part of the trunk. A good indicator that it wasn't a low Quotient creature if I'd ever seen one.

Similar engagements happened up and down the line as the more perceptive casters tore into the first line of attack. More frogs, lizards, and what looked like water striders flitted through the woods as they were shaken from the trees. A trio of spoon-bills actually tried to come in from above, just for two of the elves on our side to summon a miniature tornado that sucked them to the ground. The bodies splattering loudly against the ground seemed to be the starting pistol for our engagement and the beasts of the lake charged.

I wasn't sure what had caused the counterattack; snippets of conversation I caught suggested it was *because* of our massive show of force that the beasts had been stirred up, but that all faded to the background. <Earth Shell> bloomed as my legs, arms, and chest were encased in the magic stone. Since it was the closest target to me, I zeroed in on the frog as its information flashed in the corner of my vision once I was in range.

<Tree Frog>

<Attunement: Water>

<Refinement: Secretion>

<Perceived Metier Quotient: 4>

At least it's not a Tendril, but Secretion? Really? The refinement was as much of a clue about what the creature's ability would be as anything. Wanting to keep as much mana at my disposal as possible, I met the creature halfway through one of its jumps. It wasn't like hitting a brick wall, but it was a close thing. My tower shield warbled as I braced for the impact, a wave of heat leaving me slick with sweat. The frog had a much more unpleasant response to the heat.

The amphibian let out a warbling croak as its slimy skin flash-fried. Not wanting the creature to get enough time to react, I swung Fievil in an upward arc axe first. The response from the weapon was instant. Ballast, which had been redirecting the weapon's weight to my legs, reversed. The additional weight moved up through my body and returned to the hammer. It was yet another example of magic shenanigans, because the light, testing swing I'd done with the weapon turned into an unstoppable cleave for the squishy creature.

The sharpened chitin blade parted rubbery flesh in a vertical gash that burst the frog's eye. The croak quickly turned guttural as blood spilled all around me. I didn't get to do a follow-up attack before a blur of fire appeared atop of the creature. A wolf fang plunged wrist deep into the creature's head and I watched as the already fried skin started to flake like sunbaked mud.

"Running fight, rock brain. The frontliners are struggling," Daniela informed me before she backflipped off the frog.

In the fiery trail of her flip, her <Ember Wisp> swirled into existence and started to blast at things like a stationary turret. I followed the blasts to see three other frogs and a towering water strider heading toward my part of the defensive wall. Our squad was positively calm compared to the chaotic explosion of magic further to my left as anoles scurried into vision through the trees like revved up lowriders.

"Spend some mana, no kills. We want as many crippled as Danny and I mop up. Billy, I need you to keep Sam safe. Samuel, give me some leafy eldritch horrors, if you would?" I shot rapidly through the comm-plant.

Daniela sent back a throaty chuckle as she continued her fiery dance. Her <Heat Touch> and <Flare Cloak> were a constant drain, but I could see her practically *rocketing* from beast to beast as lower Quotient creatures tried to flank their much larger compatriots. Anthony scurried behind her, locking his mandibles on anything that tried to slow her down before drowning it in a gout of fire.

Just as I was ready to cast <Earthen Barrier> again, Samuel and Jolene burst into action. Each creature in my line of sight had a vine inconveniently appear around their limbs, snagging them and halting their charge. The large frogs that bound toward me fell flat on their stomachs, only to have a bubble burst right over their heads. The <Cavitation> left my ears ringing, and I noted the impact ripple through the ground with vibrosense even as it stunned the first, then second frog. One of the smaller, lower Quotient ones burst in a wave of gore I was happy to have avoided.

A grin split my face as I saw the two cooperate smoothly and threw myself forward. Fievil quivered in my hand, and I itched to sow some true discord amidst the creatures.

"<Terrasheath>!"

My mana dropped by a third from where it had recovered, but the halo of sand spun up behind me. With a sound like a crumbling building, Fievil flared as some of its energy infused the skill. The caramel glow of the weapon dimmed significantly, but I knew it would recover. I charged and swung, using the strange shift in momentum from Ballast to take me past one, two, and then the third frog. It wasn't perfect, or graceful, but as my mind overlaid the motion with the angled jump platforms of the obstacle course, it was possible for me to just complete the pseudo-acrobatic move.

The axe blade once again tore them open, but that wasn't all. Concentrated torrents of sand crammed themselves into the wounds, tearing them open, flaying their skin and mucus before the amphibians were practically sheared in half.

They aren't a problem anymore. My grin stretched wider as I eyed the last creature in the group and the halo of sand that, while diminished, still hovered behind me. *I think you and I are going to get along real well, Fievil.*

The hammer sent a weak flash of an eye roll before going silent. The water strider shot out a jet of water not too dissimilar to Jolene's, but it was no match for my tower shield. Using my extra weight and a slight flash of my mana to compress the muddy ground, I pushed against the creature's attack. It towered over me and I was almost holding my shield horizontal by the time I reached one of its legs, but its wrist-thick legs were no match for my shard weapon. The chitin added a burst of explosive heat that smacked the lower half of the leg away.

I didn't need as high a perception as I did to notice the slow collapse of the water strider the moment it lost its leg. In response, I reversed my grip on my hammer and used the rounded tortoise shell to hit the creature right in its thorax. Ballast didn't disappoint and neither did the jagged hunks of crustal that sprouted where the hammer head made contact. The stream of water that had been threatening to cut into me sputtered as it was replaced by the visceral contents of the creature's insides.

Like a very disgusting tree with beady, faceted eyes, the creature toppled to the ground. It twitched as I stepped over its legs and glared at the next denizen of the lake that had the gall to keep attacking. I wasn't sure from where, but there were definitely a handful of people cackling like madmen around me. *It's definitely not my voice. No chance.*

CHAPTER THIRTY-THREE

Sweeping Knockouts

"Incomin'!" I turned just in time to dodge a falling lizardman. The man then proceeded to wrestle-splatter the Q3 strider I'd been fighting with gusto. When he extracted himself from the corpse, I recognized him as Dundee. Somehow, he'd retained his hat through his water-powered jump and landing.

"You alright?" I called, parrying a smaller jumping frog with my shield. The force of the creature's jump and the swing of my arm caused enough heat for the poor Q2 creature to crisp itself out of the fight.

"Never better, chap! Considering you are the deepest in this mess, I felt it my duty to warn you that them gators will be poking out their ugly snouts soon if you get much closer to the water," Dundee said. A whip at his waist cracked so fast, all I saw was another water strider fall in two.

"Did you pass this to Clara?" I said, turning in a slow circle as I used both my eyes and vibro to reassess the impromptu battle field.

The most active patches of the fight, those around the Q4 creatures, had mostly died down as our enemies expired. Dozens of the reptiles, amphibians, and insects were spread up and down the portion of the lake we'd pushed towards. There were easily three times that number of their lower-level relatives dead at the feet of the combined forces of the Allied Towns. The corpses weren't the only things I noticed, however, as the guard moved with practice to cordon off sections to dissociate the bodies as soon as the call had been made. There were the occasional slips—there were just too many bodies for that not to happen—but the higher Quotients were the ones that had the most potential to push a breakthrough.

The Wild Guard weren't the only ones that got their hands dirty. Stoneshapers had worked the original wall an additional two feet higher before they took to the field. Their efforts stabilized the ground the water-attuned beasts had tried to muddy by creating long, thin platforms of stone where most of the melee fighters had engaged. Not only that, they had then pushed further and provided a smattering of five-foot square towers that the ranged fighters utilized to deadly efficiency.

One of the towers had an eye-catching display around it. Several arrows pincushioned the bodies where the Beast Tamers of Lake Weir had posted up. It was clear to see they had taken their own path with fighting and infusion crafting; regular arrows would not have punched through even Q2 carapace. Not only that, their oxen were chowing down on some of the insects, which was quite a sight in and of itself. There had been a spotty bit of success with archery in Wildwood proper, but Marie and the group of crafters she worked with were still the best at woodshaping. Their bowyer, wagonwright, furnishing workload had exploded even before the Dreg influence had been knocked down.

There were several more things going on in the battlefield, but Dundee yanked my attention with his boisterous personage.

"Why, of course I shared the tidbit! No one seems quite able to reach you or that punchy orc fellow though," he said, drawing back his whip and using a rag tucked in his belt to clean the length. I grimaced as I peeked at the corner of my vision where I could see 'missed calls'. It didn't look like my squad itself had bothered to contact me though. "She wanted to make sure you were out of the pan before the fire came on."

"Thanks," I huffed, extracting Fievil from the corpse of a particularly nasty death anole. Its debilitating aura had corroded every bit of clothes I had on not covered by <Earth Shell>. As I dismissed the skill, letting it crumble off of me, it looked like I was wearing a very badly made crop top. My tactical vest didn't help me look any less silly even if my now-much-defined-thanks-to-Quotients abs were exposed.

The axe hammer couldn't have possibly been experienced with crop tops outside of my own mind, but it sent me that snickering mole visual. In response, I activated its mana bubble. The trickle of energy it had been able to recover seeped out and the bubble winked out after a handful of seconds. I did notice that some of the lower Quotient creatures around me started to dissociate the moment the bubble appeared, glimmering clouds of Pith trickling to the hammer head. *More questions.*

"That there is an impressive piece of carnage, chap," Dundee said, eyebrows raised way higher than I thought was possible on a reptilian face. "You wouldn't happen to have a spare, now would you?"

"Trust me, it's more of a pain than you want to deal with," I said as I turned towards the defensive wall. Dundee followed a second later, but I didn't miss him eyeing Fievil. The weapon actually wasted *more* energy sending me a flash of a mole wiggling their eyebrows suggestively before the caramel light went almost completely inert. *Perhaps it and I have more in common than I want to admit.*

The fight hadn't gone further than three hundred feet beyond the wall, but the somewhat tranquil lake bank wasn't recognizable. We went over smoldering craters, melting ice spikes, a sea's worth of vines and grass and flowers that had no business growing where they did, and pits of acid that hissed as they evaporated. It took almost two minutes to make it back to the tower Clara was using as the command point. It was obvious, as the only tower that rose fifteen feet up, was much wider, and had a slanted ramp that spiraled up to the top.

Dundee peeled off towards a muck-covered Maurice as soon as I was at the foot of the tower. Both surprisingly and unsurprisingly, I found my squad waiting there.

"Finally deigned to join us?" Daniela shot.

"I may have…ehm… gotten carried away with Fievil," I said, scratching the back of my head in embarrassment. It'd been true. The weapon was so many leagues over and above any weapon I'd wielded, and Ballast melded perfectly with my bruiser fighting style, that I'd just killed and pushed and killed and pushed. Before I'd realized it, I was alone in a sea of creatures and yet felt perfectly safe with my shield and axe hammer.

"Perhaps some warning the next time you flake?" Jolene said, raising an immaculate eyebrow at me. The hidden reproach in those words came through loud and clear. Guilt scratched at my mind as I realized I'd just assumed the others would be safer with me drawing the creature aggro. Based on their disheveled state, they'd likely seen just as much fighting as everyone else up and down the line. *No bloodlust for you, Ron. Make sure they* are *set, then you can bash your head against the problem.*

"Noted," I coughed out, searching for something to redirect the conversation. A look around confirmed that Samuel was missing. "Where's Goldilocks?"

Daniela still kept her glare leveled at me but pointed with her shoulder toward the ramp. I spent a few more minutes getting updated on their status, especially how Billy held up around so much combat, before I headed towards the ramp and up the command tower. The young elf was practically vibrating thanks to Danny's glowing endorsement.

It was barely controlled chaos. Clara was flanked by her team as they made note of a hundred different things. Every few seconds, one of them would space out as they focused entirely on their comm-plant connections before resuming their note taking and passing. Samuel was also nowhere to be seen.

The demoness orchestrating the whole thing strode forward

the moment she saw me, flicked me on the forehead, gazed off when she got a message and then focused back on me. "Am I going to have to worry about the second strongest person in this group going AWOL again?"

"Second?"

"Daniela, of course," Clara said, waving her hand in the air. "She also told me what AWOL meant, and it fit you and your squad perfectly. If the people hadn't called you Bunker Busters, I would have put that forward in the vote."

"There was a vote?" I asked, thoroughly thrown by the conversation shifts.

"Not the problem right now. Are you going to go off alone again?"

"No, that was my bad. Fievil is a bit more effective than I was expecting, and I got carried away," I said, shaking my head.

"You got that in hand?" she asked, raising her eyebrow in question as her eyes locked on the haft sticking up over my shoulder.

"Far as I can tell, but you'll be the first to know if there's an issue, ma'am." I hadn't tried to come across as sarcastic, but apparently my tone of voice just couldn't help it. That, or my poor reputation with authority was rearing its ugly head. Just watching her orchestrate the aftermath of the first fight raised my opinion of Clara higher; it had been near the top of my list already.

"Hilarious. I'll just make sure to talk to Samuel if I need something. I wanted to talk to you because we are getting ready to get the call in for harvesting. The Q6ers will be doing over-watch in case we get any levels up or overbanked traits. My team is ready to haul people away if they are identified as Q6."

"I'll keep an eye out. This was way more resistance than we expected. Hopefully Billy doesn't cross all the way. I don't think he'll be ready for full Pathways, but maybe he could pass with only one of each Hemisphere?"

"That would be a first, even if having multiple Gifts makes the Trial easier. No one, not even those with Gifts originally, have been able to break the spell chains with just one of their own. But he did get Sarah to green light him coming here, so maybe between him and Rachael, they'll crack that Trial."

"Well, if that was all, couldn't you have told the others to tell me to be on the lookout?" I asked, confused that she'd singled me out.

"I needed you to be visible, Ronan. The people out in the fields already saw you fighting and then coming up here. *That* was purpose enough. When you are absorbing your Dregs, I need you center stage. You and Daniela were the first to pass the Trial, and these people need to be reminded that they have futures at this Quotient. The realities of what the Entities told us about the Corporeal Limit haven't even been fully announced. As much as everything is unknown beyond our walls, people hate the unknown within themselves ten times more. My father told me many, many stories about the struggles people had dealing with traits. Normalization came around more due to necessity than an actual impetus to accept the differences between the attunements." Clara looked out over the casters and recent recruits to the guard that were, even then, being instructed by the veterans.

"It hasn't been an issue because most are still coming to terms with it, but a lot of people just jumped onto the whole implant situation without considering what it meant. Dylan has received a handful of requests to *remove* them, but the Entities warned him that would be bad. Severe mental trauma being the best-case scenario.

"I need the *Vanguard* to watch, not Ronan," she said, holding my eyes before they flicked to the side. It was clear she was listening to some message. "I'm sorry. They are in position. Keep an eye on your comm-plant in case we need you for more than just show. I know the fight is where you prefer to be; there isn't going to be a shortage of that."

Without another word, Clara turned toward the edge of the tower facing the battlefield. A few quick messages were exchanged between the squad leaders and runners were sent out to initiate the dissociation on the furthest corpses. They passed me by as I headed back to my squad.

My thoughts rattled in my head as I considered her words. It was true that I was more than a fighter, but the idea of being a symbol still made my insides feel like jelly. It also, *again*, made me feel like I was being silly or even selfish for how I'd dealt with the deaths in Summerfield. *Is it wrong to give the dead so much meaning? Am I being disrespectful to their sacrifice by not doing my best to let everyone else live or are the survivors of the surface* too *callous?*

Danny and Sam met my eyes and some joke they must have been ready to lob at me died in their throats.

"You alright, Ron?" Sam asked, face scrunched up in concern.

"Yeah, I'll be fine. You guys should get ready. Are you topped up, Sam?"

"Yeah, I should be good," Sam said, his drawn out words telling me how unconvinced he was that I was actually fine.

"Try to keep an eye on anyone that might pass out, or any that flare too strongly. Danny, keep up with Billy please. If he gets too much Dreg, he may crest over one of his traits. He's already got one afflicted trait, we don't want him to get more. Jolene, how close to level are you?"

Daniela was nodding even as she put her arm on the youth's shoulder; Billy looked like a deer in headlights the moment I mentioned being re-afflicted was a possibility. Maybe even a tad green around the gills. Wec wasn't far, and a solid retreat path had been one of the first things built, but it paid to be prepared.

Samuel had half an eye on the procession of scouts and speedier fighters tasked with the dissociation. Jolene made a non-committal hand wave and said that she had halfway to go but had no clue how much Pith the fight would give. I was curious myself. I then did my best to use that train of thought to zero my mind away from the dark spiral of guilt and doubt that had taken residence in the back of my head.

With my group sorted, I turned my gaze to the battlefield before channeling <Corporeal Infusion>. The usual burnt umber of my mana coalesced into a soft bubble around me, but now it was shot through with fractures of caramel. The contribution of my new weapon in my Dreg absorption was a little concerning, but considering everything I'd done up to that point had been intruded on by the axe hammer, I wasn't surprised. Daniela and Samuel matched my display with maroon and gold-green spheres of their own.

The call to start went out and the scouts scurried about like ants, tapping any and all bodies they could. The dissociations stirred up the battlefield with the attunements of the scouts before a veritable fogbank of Pith and Dreg took to the air.

I braced along with my friends as the glimmering cloud swept past us to sink into their corresponding fighters. The actual distribution of Pith was still ambiguous, but it was entirely out of anyone's hands. It seemed to be fair most of the time, so there was hardly any griping about 'kill stealing' amidst those who farmed the ant or spider dungeons. However, even compared to Summerfield and the death territory, the first wave of fighting at the lake was the largest concentration of energy that had formed.

Almost instantly, the handful of lower Quotient people in the group started twitching, but the deluge of Pith and Dreg continued. I felt a slight hum filter through the air as the energy flowed into the fighters before what I assumed was my portion of the energy arrived. Like a ship's bow, iridescent Pith parted around <Corporeal Infusion>. Wisps of Dreg flowed into the space around me before being trapped. My body curled as my mana strained to keep the Dreg from plunging me into my side effects. I was thankful we'd practiced the process and I remained steadfast through it. My friends—and Igor and the New Hopers, from what it looked like—were also able to retain their faculties.

The rest of the Wild Guard, the Stoneshapers, and the Weirdian hunters were a different story. Like dominos, they toppled to the ground. A blanket of humanity that twitched, burned, smoked, or blossomed as the combined energy of our enemies fed their growth. It was more than we'd anticipated.

"S-Sam! You n-need to start d-dragging people!" I managed. My jaw was locked as the energy pulled my muscles tight. The scouts had already stopped tapping, but the damage was done. With a hint of desperation, I focused on the comm-plant and sent as wide a message as I could manage. "Full retreat! While you are able-bodied, return to Wec's influence!"

I didn't technically have the authority for that command, but most people recognized who I was and they didn't need to be told twice when their bodies were betraying them already. Most of the high Quotient fighters struggled to their knees and began to hobble, dragging those close to them along. I blinked as the golden glimmer of energy finally swept through us. I slumped to my knees as the pressure on my body eased, but I didn't let myself rest.

"D-Danny! How's Billy?" I asked, getting my jaw back under control.

"He's okay, but he said he was climbing into overbank terri-tory. Now he's hyperventilating," the woman said. Her voice quaked, not totally calm, but more composed than I expected when I saw she had steam rising off her body.

"Get him back! Jolene?"

"I… I'm alright. I can make it back," the woman clattered. Frost clung to her hair and her hands shook violently, but her legs were steady.

"Blobby! I need you to split and start dragging as many people as you can towards the town!" I called.

I wasn't sure that the slime was actually close by, but if I knew it like I thought I did, then the gelatinous creature was close. Sure enough, a cloud of dust and mud wheeled itself into range. I repeated the command to the chest high blob, who'd been consuming half of one of the giant water striders. Without an ounce of hesitation, Blobby spat out the half-dissolved corpse before splitting into three smaller copies. The closest unconscious people had their shoulders embraced by the lime goop and Blobby once again manipulated its body to make small leg-like appendages. Like a facsimile of a centipede, the slime shuffled away from the wall and towers. His charges were some of the fastest out of the battlefield.

Not bothering to see what my friends were doing, I rushed forward to the front of the wall. I slapped Fievil to my back, as well as my shield, before I threw an unconscious fae and a merman over my shoulders. My mana-strained body protested the move, but I ignored it. Muscles creaked as I picked up speed away from the battle. Before I got too far, Fievil flashed an image of him lending a clawed hand. Caramel energy started to flow from the axe hammer snug against my back to the shield buckled on my back. Four Quotients worth of strength coursed through me and my steps surged even as my bones creaked under my magic-enhanced muscles.

Within minutes, I was back at the edge of the wall where Blobby had deposited his charges before returning. Some of the Weirdians had seen the spectacle from the watchtowers and were rushing out of the town. I sent Ian a quick message about what had happened before I charged back to the battlefield. The other groups with Q6ers passed me by, a handful slumping with relief as soon as they felt Wec's influence purging the Dreg in their bodies.

Three trips. Between me and the other able-bodied fighters, we were able to retrieve all the lower Quotient people. When I returned for the fourth run, I spotted Clara and Rommel resting heavily against the command tower. The orc let out steam with each breath while the demoness looked more than a few shades of gray lighter. They spotted my approach and waved me over.

"The battlefield is cleared," she huffed.

I didn't reply. Instead, I slumped to the ground. A groan left my throat as I laid in the mud. Fievil poked at my back uncomfortably, but my body had hit the limit. I hadn't even realized that the trickle of mana my hammer had been feeding my shield had died out at some point during the trips.

"Next time... we need a portable Entity," Clara said as she and Rommel joined me on the ground.

I wasn't sure who started laughing first, but giggles overtook us. Even Rommel, whose voice sounded like a rumbling car engine, chuckled along with us. The fight hadn't gone at all like we'd expected, and the aftermath hadn't either, but I had a sneaking suspicion that things were going to be just fine. The camaraderie of the guard and the other towns swelled my spirit and banished a lot of my doubts once again. I'd vowed to fight for everyone that deserved their freedom, and I knew there would be bumps on the road, but it served me well to see I wasn't the only one unified in that purpose.

Perhaps... Perhaps that is why they are able to move forward with such confidence, buoyed by those around them.

CHAPTER THIRTY-FOUR

The Boss Posse

It took the rest of the day for some semblance of order to fall over Lake Weir after our sudden return. The results of the battle were leagues over what we'd expected. All but a handful of people hit Quotient 6, and they'd been Q2 or Q3 before the battle.

Most notably to our group was Jolene reaching Q6 and Billy crashing all the way to Q5. The elf had been overbarked and then some. Thankfully, Daniela had been able to cross into Wec's influence faster even than Blobby and the surplus energy had gone towards forming a new trait. That story was repeated with variable success throughout the fighters since most were already beyond forming new traits at Q6. *As far as I know.*

A patrol, formed from two of the conscious Q6ers and the squads that had remained in Lake Weir, was watching the lake like a hawk for any reaction from the denizens we'd *actually* intended to fight. It was for that reason that early in the morning, I'd been retrieved from the corner of the gymnasium that had been assigned to my squad.

"So, that's the status then?" I said, rubbing the sleep out of my eyes. My body still twinged if I moved too much, but it was leaps and bounds beyond how it had been.

"Yes. The patrol has posted up at the forward wall. Other than Dundee complaining about the fighters being on his property, there haven't been any disturbances," Ian said.

"And fighters?" I asked, turning to the leaders of the fighter groups. Clara, Maurice, and one of the Stoneshapers, a skinny dwarf named Josh, moved to reply.

"We've got three squads we can put together, without counting your squad or mine," Clara said.

"My people can tack on. We didn't get as much Pith since our direct contribution was limited, but most still jumped a Quotient at least," Josh said.

"We might be able to sub in the squads that didn't go, but most of our people ran up against that Q6 barrier you imposed," Maurice said. When Clara turned a baleful glare in his direction, he was quick to add, "I'm not mad about the baseline security, but I don't know if we can mount the attack like we wanted to."

"Dundee, what do you think?" Ian said before he turned to the cowboy hat wearing lizard who'd been quiet the whole time.

"I think this was botched from the start, chaps, if I'm honest with y'all," he drawled.

"Care to elaborate?" Clara said. I could just barely see her eyebrow twitch. *Thankfully, they didn't send Sarah out here. I think dollar store Aussie man would have been a smoldering pancake already.*

"It was the numbers. The dungeons, even before we knew they were what they were, always attacked with small groups. We all feel it, deep in our guts. When there are more of us, the air changes. It's like the wind before a thunderstorm. The creatures in our backyard puddle would have to be lethargic not to notice. It's the only thing that makes sense after that head-on collision we just had with half the lake's non-gator population!" The lizardman threw his hands up in frustration as if what he was suggesting was clear as day.

"I don't necessarily disagree," I said, cutting in and forestalling an explosion from Clara and some snide remark from Daniela. Dundee looked surprised.

"I thought this one was all brawn, no brains?" he asked Maurice 'quietly.' The thorn-headed man pressed his palms against his temples, surely staving off a headache.

I could hardly tell if it was an insult or the man was just that ridiculous. *Considering how Ian and Maurice feel about it, probably a bit of both.*

"To clarify," I said, loudly, as I pinned the lizard with my eyes. When the man had the decency to squirm a bit, I panned to the others. "I think it's possible he's right. Gec knows about locations with high concentration of pure mana, AKA Entities. Who's to say that ability can't be used the other way around?"

"So, we what? Give up? Set up a farming patrol like with the spiders and fire ants?" Clara asked, still somewhat aggravated, but already easing off that throttle. There was a reason she had been the only one diplomatic enough to travel to the other towns. Flexible, but she knew when to press. A stark contrast to my ass-over-teakettle approach. "I suppose it isn't like this mission wasn't already a resounding success."

Ian's wrinkled face scrunched up even more. His skeletal hands combed back his hair in a slow, deliberate part. "Personally, children, I don't know that I can handle this stress. Surviving has been tough, even before we had the Dreg, and now having to account for these creature-spewing locales has me way past my limit. These decisions I was hoping would be out of my hands. If Maurice thinks that Lake Weir can support that kind of persistent action, then I support it. Leave me to my accounting and progress reports. Please."

"Dad, it's okay. I've got it," Maurice said, standing and placing a firm hand over his father's shoulder. "I think we could handle it, but we would need assistance from Wildwood until some of our Gifted return from your training program."

"That's… doable. I would need to check with Sarah, but assigning a permanent squad here wouldn't be impossible.

Doing it so far from town would… complicate the schedule," Clara said after some deliberation.

"Hold on, guys," I said, raising my hands to draw the group's attention. "I think there might be a middle ground before we backpedal on the whole operation."

"What harebrained idea did you cook up now?" Daniela said, rolling her eyes as the rest of the group looked at me expectantly.

"It's not harebrained," I argued.

"Oh, can I take a crack, mate?" Dundee asked, jumping back in the conversation.

"You want to guess my idea?"

"Actually, I think I was ready to suggest the very same thing! An in-fil-tra-tion, eh? What do you all think?"

"Uhhh, well, yes. A select few, maybe two or three high level squads, aim to go deep into the territory to take out the creature with the Metier Crystal."

"Huh, sounds reasonable," Daniela said with a shrug.

"Wait, so because he said it first, it isn't harebrained!?" I said, blinking in confusion.

"Maybe it's because Dundee said it more eloquently?" Sam provided, unhelpfully.

"Whatever. Yes, that's my idea. Two squads to engage and a third on standby for when the attack inevitably goes sideways," I said. I crossed my arms and gave all the smirking people in the meeting a dirty look. Ian looked a tad less like a skeleton, so I let the poke at my expense go.

"Look at that! I suppose there is a reason we haven't died yet with him on the prow," Daniela said. "I almost feel confident!"

The room broke out into soft laughs. I joined along, seeing the easier smiles on everyone present. The situation was far from optimal, no one would deny, so I embraced it. Being a tank wasn't just a physical job; if I could ease the tension just a bit, then I knew everyone's mind was safer. I'd been neglecting that facet of my efforts for too long.

Even with my growing commitment, I was thankful Clara had mercy on me and turned the conversation more serious. The demoness started to talk strategy with the other town commanders and the discussions of who to select for the infiltration started in earnest.

It was a joint effort... except when it came to me and my two friends. I wasn't bothered by it, but I did notice that all the squad compositions included the Bunker Busters at the fore. It spoke something of what the towns thought about our abilities, even with my—false—reputation for being a musclebound idiot.

The discussions went on for most of the morning and the group finally agreed on a trio of squads. We checked in on Billy, who was in the infirmary, frustrated but doing just fine, and tried to check on Jolene until we realized she'd jumped into Wec for the Hemisphere Trial. After that, lunch was a hurried affair as we were practically booted out of town. The comm-plant had facilitated getting everyone to the right place at the right time without having to send runners out.

As we approached the command tower out toward the lake, I couldn't help but feel my blood start to pump. Fievil hummed in response, mostly recharged after the night of rest. The fight against the lower Quotient creatures had been intense, but I could immediately tell large scale battles was not where I excelled. Dundee had said it himself; almost without realizing it, I'd waded the deepest into the wave of creatures out of anyone. They would have overwhelmed me without the support of the other squads, but each fight had been a breeze. Something within me wanted conflict, and I didn't think it was Fievil.

— + —

The shore of the lake looked much like Lake Sumter back in Wildwood. The difference was the scale. Dark, muddy water reached out almost as far as I could see, blocked only by a place to the east that Dundee called Bird Island. It was from there that he believed most of the creatures we'd fought en masse came from, due to the time of day when we'd attacked. He himself had never dared to go into the depths of the lake, merely staying in the overgrown territory between the town, Bird Island, and some place called Lake Ranch along the southern shore of Lake Weir proper.

Surprisingly, Bird Island *wasn't* exactly the place where our group was headed. A rough overlay of the locations Gec had given us with old maps indicated that the Metier Crystal was a ways into the lake north of town, close to a 'Carney Island Rec Area.' Dundee was familiar with the terrain, so he took the lead of the second squad. The lizardman had his bottle of rot gut slung on his hip like a pistol, but his movements were steady as he used a blade of water to clear cut a path through the vegetation. Thick gatherings of knotweed and an ever-present carpet of maidencane grasses impeded our progress, but the lizard seemed an old hand at wading through the muck and brush.

My eyes moved over the selection of fighters the team leaders had decided on at the end. One of the groups was the New Hopers, sans Devon, which had been selected as our extraction team. They trailed at the back, spread out as Dennis jumped from tree to tree, listening for any threats the plants might warn us away from. In the group ahead, Dundee rattled off incessantly about the wonders and dangers of the western shore of the lake. For most of the group, who'd been present in the fight against the insectile-reptilian-amphibians, it was old news. The pair of Stoneshapers and Weirdian additions, however, listened with rapt attention. The man's accent dipped even further into offensive drawls as he ate up the attention.

For our part, our humble three squad had been jumped to six. Eight, if you considered the slime slinking nearby and the fire ant acting as a mount for Daniela. Thankfully, all the additions were people I was familiar with. Igor and his rocky, chipped-toothed squadmate Hilda, as well as Diana the satyr healer had all managed to hit Q6 *and* pass the Hemisphere Trial before the dungeon clear mission. I wasn't as impressed by Igor and Diana, since they'd been members of the guard for longer, but Hilda must have pushed hard with her Gifts and skills for the Entities to let her select them so close back to back.

Our squad was definitely frontloaded, but considering what we were planning to fight, it was the best that could be put together on short notice. I'd argued that some elves would have been a better option, but unfortunately that wasn't the people we had available.

Vibrosense rippled as Dundee cut another thick vine hanging in our way. Reacting faster than I could think, my shield bashed away an anole that dropped from above. Daniela and Dennis were already in the process of jumping out a warning, but my extrasensory abilities had given me the head start. The heat was mostly generated by *my* shield's momentum getting eaten up on impact, but when the creature landed ten feet beyond the area Dundee had cleared, it was a charbroiled mess.

"Uh…" Dennis said, looking uncertainly between Dundee, me, and Clara.

"Lock it down. If it attracts something, we will deal with it. Honestly, I am surprised we haven't encountered anything else yet," Clara said, addressing the situation in moments. The satyr still gave me an odd look, but moved to comply as the group tightened its formation. Around me and Dennis, I realized after a cursory look.

"We are crossing into the edge of the Weir Canal," Dundee said a few minutes later. "There is a short bridge not far that was built before stuff started getting too deadly, and that's what we'll use to get to the Carney Island Restoration area. I fully expect to run into gators there."

"Should we be worried about stuff from deep in the lake?" Clara asked. I knew for a fact that she'd already gotten the intel from the man, but most everyone had gotten a trickle of information in comparison. She didn't have to try hard to get the cowboy to speak up.

"Nah. Lake Weir is a fairly large lake, and that was before

the Fall. Most of the gators that harass the town come from Little Lake Weir. They like the shallower waters, and they take the little canal we are going to cross to get there. It is on those trips up and down from the main lake that they drift into the town's land. Unfortunately for Ian and his folks that set up shop at the old school, they didn't know the big lizards were going to develop behavior like that. Their growing strength has only caused them to drift further from the shores."

It was an interesting take I hadn't considered. While magic had been thrown into the mix when it came to creatures on the surface, their general behaviors hadn't drifted much from how they were before the Fall. Predators hunted, ants mounded, and spiders set up traps. Even the more passive creatures, like the skunks and deer, didn't attack unless provoked or tainted by Dreg. Since no one had assumed that the school would be anywhere in range of gators, they hadn't expected supersized versions of them to range further.

I was sure their sudden rise in numbers had something to do with the Aberrant Entities, but I couldn't be sure if it was due to their presence or their *absence*.

A wide ripple flowed through the ground. It wasn't sharp like the dislodged creature in the trees, and it wasn't steady like the vegetation. It was like our steps were sending waves out only to crash prematurely against something that swallowed them, only letting a trickle return back for my Harmonic Sinews. I held up a fist as Dundee started to ramble on about his pa and the food truck he'd run all up and down Lake Weir before the Fall.

Almost all of our group halted, sending out a thicker, challenging ripple towards the thing in our path. It got eaten up just the same, but I was able to determine the thing was just at the edge of my sensory range some five hundred feet away. It was large.

"Dundee," I called to the man at the lead. He finally stopped short and saw that the whole group had pulled back. He frowned, but backed up just the same.

"Talk to me, chap."

"How far is this canal?" I asked.

"Uh... shouldn't be too far. In fact, we could probably hear it if we are quiet enough," Dundee said. The question hung unasked on his lips.

"We need to sneak forward. Something is up there," I said, gesturing just slightly to the left of the path Dundee was carving.

"Defensive formation. Dennis, I want you to smooch these plants if you need to for more information. Rommel, stay and cover our backs. The rest of you, stay here with Rommel and focus on the sides. Dundee, Daniela, Ronan, you are with me," Clara shot out all in one breath.

The lizardman hesitated for a second before grumbling and following after Clara. The four of us crouched low as the woman produced a concentrated cloud of her caustic fog. I noticed the staff in her hand glow a gentle red, and realized that she'd augmented her Gift at the same time. It was impressive and reminded me that while I'd been focusing on getting a hang of my traits, weapon bound or otherwise, so they wouldn't bite me in the ass, others had focused on their magic. The vegetation in front of us withered at the same time as it desiccated.

Whatever comment Dundee had had against Clara's lead died in a second. I couldn't help but smirk as Danny followed after the demoness with predatorial grace. I pressed my hands to the ground, feeling the clarity of the ripples around me improve as I felt the feedback from more than my feet. The move didn't improve my range really, but everything within my sense range was much clearer. The shadow eating up the vibrations took on a distinctly reptilian shape as I crept forward with the others.

A few minutes of turtle speed later, the vegetation petered off to muddy grass. The void in my vibrosense had grown proportionally the closer I got. The long, scaly shadow was hard to see even with my sixth sense telling me it was right there. When my eyes and vibro finally got a clear enough picture of the beast, its information bloomed at the edge of my vision. Since all the leaders of the dungeon clearing group were in a party, our perceptions overlapped and we all received the information.

<Mature Alligator>

<Attunement: Water>

<Refinement: Mud>

<Perceived Metier Quotient: 5>

"Crickey, that's one of the biggens," Dundee cursed. A pair of aquamarine orbs flicked open and the ground all around us quivered like I'd activated my crowd control skill. "Oh bugger."

CHAPTER THIRTY-FIVE

A Boss' Posse

"Contact! Contact!" Clara yelled as she flared her caustic fog in a wide blanket forward.

A low groan rippled through the mud, loud and baritone enough that vibrosense responded to the feedback. With a frantic mental slap, I vanished the sense to the back of my mind as I flared <Mudpit>. I didn't trigger the skill, but instead took hold of the terrain the mud gator was trying to use against us. I brushed against a budding resistance, almost like a primal spell chain, as the creature tried to push for control of the mud we were ankle deep in. My mana started to fall precipitously.

"It's trying to bury us!" I called out. "Hit it!"

The words were barely out of my mouth when water, fire, and a glob of acid crashed against the alligator's flank. The creature hissed loud enough to make my ears ring. When I tried to cast <Stone Spike>, the mana side effects nearly caused me to lose control of <Mudpit>'s spell chain. I couldn't multicast while I kept the ponderous beast engaged, so I jumped to the fore with my shield in hand. That was when the tail whipped and tossed me back against a tree.

My teeth rattled in my mouth, but my traits were able to handle the halfhearted turn. The mud gator's hiss was much louder as fire dried the creature out and I saw that a thin covering of mud had been baked right off its already-tough scales.

"Hit it again!" I shouted as I extracted myself from the mud almost twenty feet from the fight. "It's got mud—!"

My next words were cut off as vibrosense pushed through my own mental restraints, coupled with an alarmed mole, to warn me of a ripple behind me. I had just enough time to put my shield between me and another, smaller, gator before the creature chomped down on my whole upper body. Frost flashed around me as the jaws clamped shut on the other side of my tower shield. Not even the Force Dispersal trait was enough to melt the ice that started to coat my surroundings.

The mud started to swirl under me, as if it was being slurped up through a straw, and I realized I'd lost my hold on my skill. With a groan, both pushing against the alligator that had blindsided me and the will of the Q5 mud lizard, I took my feet. The swirl stopped in its tracks and I heard the crackle of magic behind me as I shoved the gator off of me.

<Juvenile Alligator>

<Attunement: Water>

<Refinement: N/A >

<Perceived Metier Quotient: 4>

That's a juvenile! The creature was nowhere as small as the creatures I'd seen in the death territory. Dundee had mentioned most of the water-attuned gators were somewhere in the twenty-foot range in length. The one in front of me certainly matched that size, but it took a while for my brain to process the sheer bulk of the creature. *It has to weigh a ton!* I *almost* looked back over my shoulder at the ambulant island that was the mud gator, but I resisted the urge as the juvenile charged me down.

For a thing three times my size, it was *fast*. I deflected *me* with the help of my shield. The gator plowed into and over a nearby tree like it was almost not there before it noticed that I wasn't the only thing harassing its larger buddy. *Fievil!*

My mental scream was answered as the shard weapon fed energy into my shield and I extracted myself from the mud with a sucking squelch. My chitin axe crashed against the creature's tail, easily parting the scales to the bone. Its blood sizzled as the Force Dispersal of the blade exploded on impact. That was when I was introduced to the turning radius of the gator's maw.

Had I not pulled Fievil back from the creature's tail after my attack, the jaws would have locked around my entire arm. Instead, they got a mouthful of axe hammer. The force of the bite was enough to trigger the crystal spikes out of the hammer-head, two of which punched right out of the top of the gator while the axe blade sliced through the tongue and out the creature's gullet. It thrashed for a handful of seconds before dropping to the ground.

Its death had been so sudden, I almost froze up. Thankfully, I had my mana to remind me that the fight wasn't over. Muscles coiled in protest as my mana fell down below the fifty percent mark. My eyes zeroed in on the Q5 gator and I gasped in surprise. It had somehow managed to lift itself out of the canal and turned to the rest of the group. The nearly thirty-foot monstrosity was snapping at a pirouetting Dundee while Clara's eyes blazed purple with her <Fear> Gift. I wasn't sure what that did if it didn't take, but it seemed to provide the agile cowboy enough leeway to cut into the mud gator's flanks. A simmering cloud of black fog clung to the wounds on the creature as if it was emanating from within them.

Like a crashing rocket, Daniela landed at the base of the creature's neck, daggers first. The Q5 bellowed, doubling the drain on my mana and dropping me to a knee as I kept its magic locked down. When a ripple of fire exploded out across its skin, I knew the fight was over. Gouts of necrotic blood spurted from the dozens of cuts Dundee had made even as the scales dried and cracked. Danny had used her <Scorched Earth>skill, and it did a number on the mud-refined alligator.

With a thunderous splash, it dropped its head to the ground, less than a foot away from Dundee. The lizardman didn't hesitate, and coiled his whip tight around the gator's snout, jumping on and clasping the other end of his weapon to keep the thing sealed. He also braced the jaws with his legs, but they barely made it around the massive gator's jaws. The mud gator thrashed for a good minute longer, doing its best to buck and roll off the humanoid lizard and fiery Latina on its back, before it deflated like a balloon. The four of us stood there, panting for several seconds just to make sure the creature was truly dead.

Dundee released his whip, splatting onto the mud in a messy lump. "Crickey."

— + —

It didn't take long for the rest of the group to arrive, all of them staring somewhat stunned at the trashed forest. It wasn't even comparable to the almost idyllic sight that was upstream of our fight. Mud had exploded in a radius all the way up to the canopy, while several trees had just been straight uprooted during the scrap. Diana, Samuel, and Dennis fussed over us for any injuries, but other than three broken fingers on Daniela, and a sprained ankle on me, we'd come out peachy.

We finally turned to look at the beasts we'd killed, and unsurprisingly, Dundee was there with commentary.

"This one you killed, mate, is the bulk of their number. About twice as many of the smaller 'youth' ones lurk around, but those are more liable to leave you alone," Dundee said, gesturing to the Q4 gator I'd soloed. Then he turned to point a clawed finger into the dead mud gator. "This guy is our second concern after the momma lizard."

"How many of these things are out there?" I asked, worried about the disparity in strength between the Q4 and Q5. Galloway and the death crow weren't good representative samples of the capabilities of wild beasts. The presence of a spell chain instead of just wild magic effects was what had me the most concerned.

"I've only ever seen three of these big bastards. I knew this one, the mud one, and another was a frost one, but the third I've not seen since the implant. Not sure what tickles the fancies of *that* chap."

"And you haven't seen the boss, either," Sam added unhelpfully.

"No, no I haven't." The lizardman shook his head, serious for once since the time I'd known him. "I can only guess it's a female if it's able to chuck out more babies than I can smite."

"Do we abort?" Diana asked weakly. The other late additions to the dungeon infiltration seemed to quietly agree with the question.

"This is the minimal level of danger we expected," Clara said, shaking her head. Diana looked like she'd been punched in the gut, but she didn't waver. Despite her desire to flee, she'd faced unknowns before and I was not worried about her flaking. The others... not as much. "Our baseline expectations were to, at the very least, get eyes on the creature holding the Metier Crystal. If we need to run, then we run and rethink the plan. Probably the extra patrol we'd been discussing."

"We should take five then, and brace to gather the Pith while we rest," I said, eyeing the Q5 creature. The energy the creatures would provide was still barely a dent in all the Dreg I had to collect for my traits, but I'd managed to solo the juvenile and contribute in the fight against the elite reptile; the distribution should be weighed in my favor.

If I didn't keep working on my level and traits, then I would lag behind the monsters that were surely lurking out in the world. As much as the human herding the Aberrant did over the years hurt the Allied Towns, it had kept them safe from the bigger responsibilities holding a territory on an Attuned Earth entailed. If I wanted to make a difference, I had to collect the power to do that.

"I'll do the honors," Daniela said, sauntering over to the two corpses.

I watched with fascination as the entire creature immolated. The fire was so intense, the Latina actually had to intervene with a flex of her magic lest we burn the forest. The dissociation followed a second later, turning the two bodies to ash and letting the torrent of energy flow into us. I tracked the Q4 gator's Pith and saw most of that cloud of glimmering energy head to me, but some still split off to join the significant cloud forming over the Mud Gator.

<Corporeal Infusion> snapped on around me as the energy was filtered by the spell chain bubble. I noted that the ferns and grass around us quickly grew verdant and straighter as the Pith brushed through them, perfectly separated from Dreg. Then the pain hit and the world was agony for a minute.

My eyes locked on to a flashing set of words that appeared in my vision.

<Dreg Accumulation: 1%>

I saw the counter flash and tick up every few seconds until it stopped at 6%. It was more than I'd expected, but I wasn't going to complain, especially when I'd paid for the gains by writhing on the ground like a worm. I briefly considered asking for us to extend our break in order to assign the Dreg to a trait, but I opted against it. Engaging the alligators when they were most likely to be resting had already worked in our favor.

"How's everyone?" I asked, doing my best to stretch out my body. It creaked in protest, but I knew the muscle soreness would pass quickly. *No pain, no gain,* or so Ava would say when I didn't meet the health goals she set. I was immensely thankful for that mentality now that my body was being put through its paces.

"B-b-bit chilly, mate," Dundee clattered. He tried to move his tail, but it moved with a jerky twitch instead of the graceful coils I'd seen it do. "G-give'er a minute."

"Good to know bigger doses still suck," Clara said from

where she was leaning against a tree. For a gray-colored demoness, she looked quite green.

"Is this what we have to look forward to?"one of the Q5 Stoneshapers asked as he looked at us with concern. He'd been part of the deluge of Pith the battlefield had provided but he hadn't seen how it had affected the existing Q6ers.

"It's not as pronounced if it's from smaller creatures," I answered. "The alternative without <Corporeal Infusion> is much less appealing."

"You know that's right," Daniela agreed as she swatted dried mud off her still steaming skin.

The whole group spent a few minutes working through the side effects before straightening. I glanced at my status to refresh myself and was stunned at the changes to my attributes. I quickly realized I hadn't looked at it since before my jaunt through the final portion of the obstacle course and my efforts had been more than rewarded.

Subject: Ronan Terrigan
Health: 87% (Unafflicted)
Mana: 32%
Metier Quotient: 6 (19.25%)
Dreg Accumulation: 6%
LPS: Wildwood Bunker, FL
Communications
Party
Skills - *(1) Selections Available*
Traits - *(14% Banked)*
Attributes - *Growth Quantified*
Skills:
Offensive
- <Stone Spike> / <Terrasheath>/ <Mineral Strike>
- <Freeform>
Defensive
- <Mudpit> / <Earth Shell> / <Earthen Barrier>

- \<Freeform>
Misc
- \<Pith Mana Lock>
- \<Infusion>
- \<Memory Canal>
- \<Corporeal Infusion>
Traits:
Limestone Skin (14%)
Quake Osseum (24%)
Slurry Ichor (8%)
Harmonic Sinew (31%)
Attributes:
Strength: 1.95 > 2.09
Mobility: 1.75 > 1.73
Perception: 2.20 > 2.23
Refinement: 1.57 > 1.59
Containment: 2.41 > 2.43

I just leaned against the tree and let the changes wash over me. It was hard to conceptualize the growth of my traits and skills and attributes, but at the same time it was also inherent. I'd noticed how I'd been just that bit stronger or just that bit more perceptive. It wouldn't have been possible to get as early a warning for the mud gator—even if Dundee squandered most of it— without the growth to my Harmonic Sinews trait and Perception.

Rommel came by and nudged me with his foot while I was lost in thought. He didn't say anything, but he used his head to point to where the rest of the group was gathering around Samuel. I tuned in to the conversation as I walked over to the gathering.

"…Only have a handful that I felt comfortable carrying, so we'll leave them with the fast members of our group for deployment. Remember, these are very breakable, and remember *not* to take two doses back to back," the blond said, handing over five of his healing jams. One went to Clara and her team, while my team and Dundee's received another two.

I was distinctly aware of how fragile the containers were. They were scavenged, glorified mason jars that had Fowler the light mage *not* sanitized with burning light—according to Sam —they would have been more of a health concern than not. *Maybe we can use one of those bamboo materials as carriers...*

"Alright, let's head out," Clara said. "We'll hold on to the drops, but they are minor priorities if we get in a fight. I want full alertness on our scouts. Ronan should be the *last* person warning us of danger."

"Hey, I'll take that as a compliment!" I said, smirking as the demoness strode away after Dundee. Samuel just hit me with an eye roll when I looked in his direction, and Daniela was chuckling silently as she took to the canopy. I didn't get the chance to rib her about the tank being more perceptive than the scout before she was out of sight in a hazy blur of heat.

Our group slunk through the trees with renewed purpose. While the cobbled-together group was still somewhat hesitant, they plowed through the foliage just the same. Dundee looked not at all diminished as he made his water blade wider to clear a bigger view. Before long, the vegetation started to recede from untamed wilds to something our group was more familiar with; overgrown structures.

Some cracked asphalt there, a shed that was more plants than building, and the distinct gaps in the trees that even three decades of magical overgrowth hadn't been able to erase. A few minutes of wading through, instead of chopping through, these obstructions led us to a mostly intact but overgrown building I barely spotted the restroom signs thanks to my growing perception, but what the building was didn't matter. What it let us *see*, did.

"Crickey," Dundee said. I almost slapped the man across the face for saying the very thing that had broken our stealthy approach, but I realized he'd said it via the comm-plant. I took a steadying breath before turning back to the 'rec' area.

The evidence of the world before the Fall was actually clear before us. The thin coating of ice over the walls and concrete boat ramp seemed to do the buildings justice even under the Florida heat. They glistened like a painting of the world before, trapped in time. The things *above, around, and within* some of the ice were what was concerning.

Two of the massive thirty-foot gators loitered at the base of the ramp into Lake Weir proper. Around the two monstrosities were a half-dozen of the Q4 gators and a smattering of lower Quotient ones. Despite the reptilian soup of death sunning before us, the thing that my eyes locked on was the jagged *glacier* floating almost casually out in the lake.

Thanks to the bend in Lake Weir's western shore, the thing wasn't visible unless you went out near the old rec area. A thick mist hung over the lake, obscuring the majority of the glacier even as the wind whipped wisps of it away, revealing the jagged spires of ice floating around the main hunk of ice.

"We need to go," I whispered.

It was through the comm-plant, but the tension that hung in the air made my heart clench even through the mental call. I wasn't sure what about the situation didn't sit right with me, but I felt very familiar levels of uncomfortable whenever I gazed at the glacier out in the lake. The hammer on my back quaked with anticipation, but thankfully I was able to stamp down any magical response from it before we were given away.

"Agreed. Slow retreat. Dundee, take the lead. Bunker Busters at the back, Dennis will take midpoint to cover our tracks," Clara said.

Me and my friends extricated ourselves from our viewing location with ease, but a whimper drew my attention louder than a gunshot would have at that moment. One of the Stone-shapers was trying to yank his arms free from the ledge of the building and failing. Frost started to crawl over his fingers and up his arm at a visible rate. The panic screamed out of his eyes.

"Daniela!" I called, but she and Rommel were already there. The orc was pulling away at the poor dwarf while the woman produced a flame that blazed up her arm but retracted to just her palm after a moment of concentration.

"Oh no," Dennis whispered, hand wrapped around one of the vines on the building. "It's a trap!"

That was when the hail started to fall.

CHAPTER THIRTY-SIX

Appetizers

Thumb-sized chunks of ice fell down from a cloud that had distinctly *not* been in the sky before. The hail started slow, but within seconds, it was pelting into the group. A low hiss filled the air, and I knew we'd been had.

"Get him out of that ice!" I called, reaching forward and swinging Fievil at the small half wall. The stone buckled like cheap wood under the infused weapon, freeing the man along with a group of bricks still attached.

Hail battered against my helm as I cast <Rock Cocoon> and gave the least armored of our group protection against the elemental attack. As Daniela continued to melt the ice that had crept up the man's arm, I turned to look at the gators. A shard of ice the size of my hand exploded from below, clipping my armor and pushing me back on my ass.

I felt my Ichor drip where the attack had penetrated my <Earth Shell>, but I paid it no mind. I stayed hunkered down and slowly backed away from the broken half-wall toward the rest of the team. Blind as I was, I focused on my vibrosense as much as I could and the picture arrayed around us wasn't great.

"Got a half-dozen small boys coming in!" I called out. "Daniela, I want a bombardment!"

"Wisp away!" The brunette kept a hand on the thawing Stoneshaper and lifted the other to the sky. Steam hissed for a second, louder than the reptiles approaching our building, as her <Ember Wisp> took to the air. Just the presence of the Q6 density summon alleviated the strain against the pelting hail, and when it hovered twenty feet above us, it started to rain fiery hell on the lizards. When <Flame Blasts> collided with the hail a lingering fog remained.

"He's good!" Sam said, placing his palm on the man's body. The Stoneshaper immediately jerked to his feet and I knew Samuel had hit him with his <Adrenal Surge>.

"Let's get out of here!" Clara yelled, not bothering with the comm-plant and releasing a veritable wall of caustic fog over the half-wall and towards the ground.

That was when the Q5s joined the mix. Like a train's rumble, I felt the creature's approach. A blinding ripple of mass was all it showed as in my vibrosense, but the source was undeniable.

"Brace!" I yelled. "Shapers, compress the roof!"

The warning had been just in time for the half-healed Stoneshaper, his leader, and myself to channel our passive mana into the roof. We did a bad imitation of surfing as the building below us crumbled under the elite gator's loping charge. The building only cut the gator's momentum by half, so we rode it the rest of the way into the treeline.

"Hit it with everything!" Clara called, releasing a smoldering ball of acid right into the gator as it realized we were somehow still on its back. A slew of attacks struck the creature in the hide. However, unlike the previous large gator we'd fought, we hadn't been able to interrupt its innate magic. Thick plates of ice hung off its body like hovering walls on the enormous creature. It laughed in our face.

The gator bucked its head, tossing us all into the air with contempt, regardless of how much we tried to cling to the estranged hunk of roof. Magic still flew at the beast even as we fell, but it seemed just as ineffective. I flared my magic, covering *everyone* with a thin, locking <Rock Cocoon> even as my mana tanked below a third and my muscles creaked their protest as I funneled magic into my amplified skill. We hit the treeline like a torn sack of potatoes.

A chorus of groans sounded out behind me, but all I could feel was the giant gator turning towards us. I scrambled to come to my feet. The visage of death was less than two hundred feet away, forcing its way through the trees towards where our group had fallen. It would be seconds before the bus-sized monstrosity steamrolled us. *It's not even going to need to bite us.* My mind blanked for a precious second, but a flare of energy brought me back. *Fight.*

Fievil, I got nothing! A flashing image of me crafting my first amplitude item was the only response I got. As if vibrosense had been perfectly attuned to the item's signature, its position just to my left *quivered* in my senses. It wasn't the only weapon discarded around me thanks to our fall, but I knew what to do with the stinger staff.

My armor cracked as I willed it to release its hold on my body. A stream of mana flowed from Fievil into my body as I grasped the staff with both hands. I didn't need my eyes; the frost gator was lit up clear as day by vibro. I dumped the rest of my mana, and then Fievil's, into the item as I yanked the mental lever for <Stone Spike>.

Several things happened in quick succession after that. The first, very distinct one, was the feeling of every muscle and bone in me lighting on fire while simultaneously being turned into hand-crafted pretzel displays. I could vaguely see my Slurry Ichor blood vessels highlighted by an internal orange light that had no business being in my body.

The second thing that I was only vaguely aware of was the monstrosity of a spell chain that bloomed out of my chest. The normal disk of <Stone Spike> was there, but it was quickly followed by the amplified skill I'd only used a handful of times. I hadn't even intended to cast that. Said amplified skill was further augmented by fire. The whole spell chain took on a sinister red glow, overlaying the original glyphs with the foreign attunement. After seeing that transformation, I was almost sure of the reason why my body was fighting not to tear itself apart.

The last thing that happened was that the world got terraformed before my very eyes. Where there had once been an idyllic, if utterly trashed, forest that featured a massive murder-intent alligator, there was now a miniature volcano.

A series of notifications flashed in the corner of my vision, briefly distracting me from the mind-numbing pain threatening to pull me into unconsciousness.

\<Stone Spike\>
\<Infusion Amplification\>
\<Tectonic Rise\>
\<Infusion Augmentation: Fire\>
\<Eruption\>

Just as I was processing what I'd done, another wrench was thrown into my thoughts. Namely the corpse of the Q5 frost gator with a sizzling hole in its abdomen. The remnants of its armor were sublimating even as they crashed all around us. I barely heard someone call out for cover. A thick, green-skinned arm hauled me back just in time to prevent one of the ice armor hunks from pulping my leg.

"As much as I appreciate the limb-for-a-life comedy of the situation," a voice grunted. "I think you need all of yours to be a good sparring partner."

"Igor…" I mumbled.

"Quiet, smart guy," the orc huffed as he propped me against a tree that had yet to be decimated.

From my poor vantage, I saw our group recovering and forming a loose semi-circle with me at the center. Blobby peeled out of the shadows. The slime split into three smaller bodies, with two attaching themselves to me and the third moving to join the group of fighters. Clara wobbled over to where I'd apparently stabbed her staff into the ground, wincing as if the item had been hot but gripping it nonetheless. "Shapers! I want a V wall. Hilda! Give me some thorns. New Hopers, I want eyes and triggers at the ready! Dundee, keep an eye on that last elite!"

"Oy, you don't need to tell *me* twice, missy." The lizardman clambered up a nearby tree and started letting loose with compressed blades of water.

I could hear the staccato of Daniela's <Flame Blast> still firing in the distance, but the woman was nowhere in sight. I tried to turn my head to look, but a spasm wracked my body. Had my slime companion not been literally glued to my chest and legs, I would have fallen on my face. Instead, I was treated to a concentrated emplacement of forces as the three squads scrapped any semblance of individuality and started to attack the small wave of lower Quotient gators rounding the new geological feature I'd created.

The smaller lizards quickly showed themselves the culprits of the hail as the lingering cloud disappeared along with their numbers. That wasn't to say we were out of the woods, literally or figuratively, since the elite still hadn't shown. Not to mention the actual target of the mission.

Vibro was like a sputtering engine any time I tried to focus on it, and I quickly realized what the problem was: I'd over-drawn my mana. What I'd associated as the steady pool dispersed across my body for my mana was like a raging storm of ripples and numbness. Just trying to perceive the energy using my Harmonic Sinews sent a renewed wave of pain through my body, but I had taken a peek at what went on under the hood of my body. *More questions, not enough time!*

I yanked my derailed mind back on track and focused on the fight. After having come to terms with vibro, I almost felt blind with it on the fritz. However, I barely needed my eyeballs to see the battle was really joined. The last elite had over a dozen of its smaller kin hanging from its mouth as it charged forward towards the defenses the other had set up. Small whirlpools of fog, water, and snow orbited the creature and each flew forward towards our group, aiming to throw us into disarray.

Thankfully, Clara was an old hand at coordinating teams on the fly. With Igor at the head and the two other Weirdian orcs for support, they bodily forced their way through the whirlpools. The Stoneshapers continued to work the ground, creating drainage paths for the water to move away from where we'd hunkered down. Lilly, who I'd barely seen in a long while, was waving her arms in the air in something short of an interpretive dance just to keep the remains of the hail off our heads.

The rest of the team was working in concert to cut down the smaller creatures and keep the elite gator busy. The third bus-size creature we'd encountered in as many hours seemed to be done with our attacks, because it inhaled only to exhale the mouthful of alligators it'd been holding along with a chest thick stream of water. Some part of me vaguely associated the whirl-wind of scales, tails, and maws with a poor idea about sharks that had way too many movies made, but that was all the warning I got before it started raining gator.

Blobby was a deadly pincushion as the slime shifted me out of harm's way and impaled the gator that flew on a perfect trajectory, mouth agape, towards my immobile form. Beyond me, Rommel put himself to work.

Whirling disks of fire left afterimages in my eyes as the orc spun in circles. What didn't cleave the lower Quotient gators, or dispel the whirlpool attacks from the elite gator, struck the crea-ture directly in the side. Slinking amidst the deadly choreog-raphy of offense and defense, Sam and the Weirdian satyr dished out heals almost as fast as our group accumulated damage. A bush would grow out of nowhere and it would be followed by a touch-range heal from one of them.

Godfrey suddenly blocked off my view just as Daniela rock-eted into the elite gator's side. "We need you mobile, Ron."

The dwarf didn't say anything else as he pinched my nose and jammed half the contents of one of the jam jars down my gullet. I sputtered for a second as the thick substance made its way down my throat, but I could almost instantly feel it jumping into action.

It tasted like rainbows and candies had been drowned in a sea of cavities. It also tasted like eating a live battery and waves of energy flowed through my torn muscles. Blobby released its tight grip on me, allowing me to stand against the tree with help from Godfrey. I was vaguely aware of buffeting gusts of biting winds and scalding gales, but the overall temperature was dropping.

"What…what's going on?" I asked weakly as the energy of the potion petered out to a mild buzz.

"Dundee and Daniela have the whirlpool gator in hand, but the mom is waking up," Godfrey said, casually slapping a tree out of my way with his shovel hammer.

"The…mom?"

"Yep. We wanted eyes and boy did we get them. All we had to do was kill her biggest kids," the dwarf said, voice dripping with sarcasm. "Easy peasy."

"But wait, then—"

"Focus on walking, Ron. The squads are dealing with the little ones and Clara is burning our trail. Well, Daniela is, but Clara is the one keeping the thing <Feared>."

"You…need to make sure…they loot the elites," I managed. My implant was just as out of whack as my vibrosense, and it made me realize how much I'd come to rely on it. "Deny them food."

"Oh crap, you're right," Godfrey said, pausing. His eyes glazed over in the familiar looking-at-my-status face. "Clara wants to know why you had me tell her instead of you."

"Overdrawn mana," I mumbled, flagging along with the potion's effect.

"Crap! I'm losing him. Kill the elite and get them out of there, Clara!" Godfrey yelled at nothing. The shout actually attracted the attention of an anole that had been hiding away in a tree. Godfrey almost casually pancaked its head with a swing of his weapon before bearing down on me. "They warned us about this, but I don't think I have much choice. If your muscles ache like mine do, then this is going to double suck."

Godfrey proceeded to shove the rest of the jam into my mouth while also encasing me in sand. Blobby looked alarmed for a second, but when the sand started to shape itself around me and my body started to move like I was being puppeted, I realized the man had cast an <Earth Shell>-adjacent skill on me. What I also realized was how much it hurt.

If drinking the first dose of the healing jam tasted like eating a lightning bolt, then the second was the whole storm. At the same time, however, my body protested any kind of movement. That was where the strange sand suit came into play as it nudged me to take step after step away from the conflict. It took all I had not to shriek nonsensical curses.

Even through this, I could feel a chill crawling lower down my spine. Godfrey's and my breath were crystal clear in the air. The boss gator was moving.

A bellow that was equal parts agony and deflating air mattress shook the air behind us. The temperature dropped noticeably and Godfrey paused. With a jerk, he course-corrected towards the same path we'd taken to get to the rec area, but several hundred feet to the west. A few seconds after, a haze of iridescent Pith blindsided me through the trees.

The combination of Dreg-filtered-Pith, healing potion, and overdrawn mana was too much for my mind. The world swirled down the drain of consciousness. I was vaguely aware of screams, a flash of a concerned mole, and Godfrey reaching for my collar.

CHAPTER THIRTY-SEVEN

An Unexpected Report

"The boss!" I screamed, reaching forward, and clasping the arm that had been moving closer. Instead of grabbing the vision in my dream, I whiffed. I fell off balance and smashed my face against the ground before my protesting muscles could react.

"Oy, he's awake. I'm going to go meet them." Daniela's voice reached my ears as I attempted to untangle myself from the nefarious comforter that had been draped over me.

"You could wait to talk to him like a normal friend, you know," Samuel added from somewhere behind me.

"He's a grown pebble, he can sieve his own tears if I hurt his marbles by leaving," Daniela said. Her words were underscored by a door slam and her slowly disappearing ripples.

Vibro is back, I realized. I was still fighting with the cloth and my muscles for freedom when I heard a resigned sigh. Vines uncoiled from the posts of the bed, plucking me up and extracting me from my self-made straightjacket.

"Good morning, Ron," the blond said, walking and sitting at the bed opposite where I'd been.

"Sam, what happened? I... When the Pith reached out, all—"

"You blacked out, yeah. It's been two days." He shook his head. "I need to give better training on administering those healing smoothie-jelly-goop things. I don't know what possessed Godfrey to give you a *second dose* with how juiced up on energy you were. Overhealing was the least of your concerns."

"What? What do you mean?" My brain flailed for something to grasp.

"The potion, it sort of put you in a coma when it went past Overhealed. First time we encountered it, but then again, you aren't most people, and you took a double dose. I may need to tone those down, even if the healing is less impressive," Sam said. The last part was more to himself than me.

"What happened with the boss? Did everyone make it?"

The blond made a sour face when I mentioned the mother gator I hadn't even seen, but had felt stir in the distance. "We all made it, yes, but that boss did a number on us. That shaper you helped lost his hand and most of us life-attuned are working through the frostbite on the others."

Samuel pulled up his shirt to show a purple-blue gash in his side that was actively being poked and prodded by his nerve filaments, all while weeping the slightest bit of black blood. It almost looked like the wound was alive, and I felt the contents of my stomach surge up. Only practice from suffering from my mana side effects kept whatever they'd fed me while I was unconscious from splashing out onto the floor.

"Are you okay?" I asked once I swallowed down my bile.

"Mostly thanks to my filaments—they are numbing the area —but the others are struggling. Putting them through the trial has delayed some of the pain, but Wec can't house all the new Q6ers in town anymore, even with how much it's grown with each purging pass." Sam sighed, dropping back to lay on the bed.

"What the hell are we doing, Sam? How are we supposed to fight things like that?" I whispered, my mind having latched to the unfortunate memory of the glacier out in the lake.

"Honestly, Ron? I have no idea. Hell, I'm glad I made those

potions and took them out relatively untested. Without them, a missing hand would have been the least of our problems."

"The spider boss… it wasn't like this. What's different?" I mumbled, trying to piece together the differences. It was true that no one had gone deep enough into the spider territory to lay eyes on the boss since Danny had been kidnapped, even if the elites were spotted on occasion.

"Oh, yeah. Clara got a *goooood* look at her before we made a break for it. Said when it moved, it split the damn glacial thing in half. She memorized the information and wrote it down, so at least we know what's out there." Sam pulled a crumpled piece of paper from his cargos and passed it over to me. I absently opened it, the words washing through me. It was just out of the norm to bring confusion, but clearly it was more information than when we'd seen the gray jumper monarch.

<American Alligator Monarch (Soulbonded)>

<Attunement: Water / Pure>

<Refinement: Cluster Bonded (Turbulent)>

<Perceived Metier Quotient: 7 (Category 2)>

A flash appeared in my mind. It was weak, but I saw a mole with oversized hands patting a slime in my head. My eyes immediately went toward the corner of the room. Blobby was slumped over in a shallow puddle, its gelatinous body almost thin enough that its two cores were visible. *It lost one of its bodies.* I stood on shaky feet and shuffled over. When my legs almost gave out, Samuel had to drag himself forward and help me to where I was going. The blond was very confused until he noticed Blobby and the axe hammer nestled between both Metier Crystals.

"Blobby helped with the monarch's hailstorm. He did this thing where he turned into a net and he…Never mind. When we got back, he checked on you before rushing back out. He came back with your hammer and your shield. It hasn't left since."

I dropped to my knees and pet the jiggly mass. "Thanks,

friend. Friends. You both dragged our collective asses out of the fire there."

Blobby formed a pitiful appendage, and wrapped it around my fingers before slumping back down. It was the most pathetic I'd ever seen the energetic ball of mystery ooze, and it hurt deep in my chest. Its humanoid mockery of flexing muscles flashed in my mind, and I felt angry and lost all at the same time. *If only I could have killed that first one faster! It was so cold... If the ice plates hadn't been so powerf—*

"Holy hydroponics," I said, the pieces clicking into place. The picture they showed did not make me feel better at all.

"That's not good. You haven't used that expression since we left the Bunker," Sam said, shuffling to meet my eyes.

"The gator boss. It has a shard somehow. That's what it means by soulbonded; it's got a Fievil all of its own or something. That shard was squeezing things in their favor from the start. I don't even know if that hail was even theirs, or if the frost that grabbed that man's arm was a trap. Their whole area is to their benefit."

"Holy hydroponics, indeed," Sam said, eyes widening with the realization. He also started to absently pet the slime, which seemed to give the poor creature some of its energy back.

"We need to stay well enough away from the gator boss for now," I said, thoughts coming faster and faster by the second. "We need to make sure it doesn't get the chance to nurture any more elites. And...And we need to talk to Sarah. She needs to run teams deep into the known dungeons to get eyes on the boss, or at the least the elites. If not all bosses have shards, then things will be leagues easier. But that's a paradox, because if the creatures around the boss grow stronger, then more shards are liable to form, which will in turn make more of these soul-bonded boss abominations. Or not? What does it take for a boss to bind with a Shard? Shit, it seems the Dreg were doing a whole lot more than just keeping the creatures at bay."

"Wait, if the Dreg were fighting things this big, then why

were Galloway and the death crow the only Appendages we saw?" Samuel asked, hand pausing in his stroking to shake. "The death crow was a deadly piece of garbage that deserved never to have been on the surface of this planet, but it was Q7 and nowhere near as strong as the gator monarch. I've sort of fought both, I might be the definitive expert. I suppose Igor could pitch in and—"

"Questions, Samuel. More and more of them for each minute we spend up here. Being isolated has left us on the back foot," I said. With my mind somewhat clear, Daniela's words came back to me. Wait…'Meet them'?

"What?" Sam asked, confused by my non sequitur.

"Daniela. Before she left, she said she was going to 'meet them.' If my brain is finally firing right, that has to be Devon and Dai. She wouldn't actively seek out anyone else that shouldn't still be in Wildwood," I said.

"Oh, right, I didn't get to talk about that before you slapped me across the face with more problems," Sam replied.

"More?"

"Let's get you a shirt. It'll probably be best if we make this a conference call," Sam said, wincing as he stood. It was clear that despite however much of a handle he had on his injury, it still affected him. He offered me a hand to stand, but I waved it away. I grasped Fievil tight as I stood and felt the familiar weight shift of Ballast activating. It sucked, big time. However, as the caramel glow of the weapon dimmed to its passive hue, I immediately felt leagues better.

I still felt like I'd done leg day fifty times in a row, plus another thirty for each muscle group I had and the ones my traits possibly added, but now that I was awake, my body was already working to repair itself. The healers had long ago discovered that concentrating on an injury caused your passive regeneration to 'focus' there. It wasn't usually noticeable, but considering the extent of my body's injuries…

"Earth to Ronan?" Sam asked from the doorway. The blond had already crossed the room in a few lanky steps.

I gave Blobby another pitying look, which the faceless slime somehow returned with a wave from its appendage. I couldn't help myself and chuckled at the absurdity of the situation. The slime got one more gentle pat before the two of us walked and hobbled, respectively, towards the school building and Wec.

— + —

"Damn, you guys look like crap," Devon said by way of greeting.

"Thanks," I said, flatly. My eyebrow twitched and it had nothing to do with my twitching muscles.

"Ronan, is everyone okay? I've tried to reach out to the New Hopers, but Clara just says we'll talk in person," Dai asked, arms crossed, as the large lizardman hovered uncertainly. Our trio of Bunker Busters, plus the two scouts, just stood by Wec while we waited. I'd already talked to Clara myself, and the demoness had said they'd sent a squad of runners out to get the 'conference call' going at mid-day.

"We had a close encounter of the reptilian kind, and not with lizardpeople," Daniela provided. The Latina was edging closer and closer to Devon, but I did my best not to let my eyebrow twitch. It was her decision, and I needed to stop sticking my nose where it was liable to get seared off.

Instead of dwelling on whatever was going on between the elf and my childhood friend, I gave the scouts an abbreviated sequence of events. I also gave them the gist of what I hypothesized had happened to the boss, access to both an Entity and a shard, which I had to showcase with a little help from Fievil. The axe hammer was still mostly drained, but it was able to release a small earth mana bubble for the others to encounter. Dai looked like he'd eaten a sour candy when I was done, and for the first time since I'd met an elf, I saw frown wrinkles form on Devon's face. The concern for our now-freed community was clear as day, and it eased some of the dislike I had for Devon's blatant advances. It helped that he was actually a decent guy, but just liked to clash against anything I said.

"So, spreading information. That's why you called a conference?" Dai asked after several minutes of silent consideration.

"That, and we want to know what you found. If my math is right, you two are at least a day over expected," I said.

"Tell that to the wilds," Devon huffed. After a second, he and his ego seemed to deflate. "We just had to travel farther, though. We encountered a problem."

"So I've heard. Care to elaborate?"

"Since we are going to do this conference thing, might as well do it only one time. Wec, can we just wait inside?" Devon asked, facing directly at the Metier Crystal. In response, an articulated shard of the Entity reached out to encapsulate Devon before dragging him in like a hooked fish. The elf didn't struggle.

"He just doesn't want to talk to me, does he?"

"If I had to warrant a guess, Ronan, I would say no," Dai said, patting me on the back gently as he strode into Wec and disappeared.

"Come on, Ron. Don't get bent out of shape," Danny said. The Latina took an almost casual half-step into Wec. Her voice lingered as she disappeared. "We all know how much of a fan of suspense you are."

"She is getting way too used to this magic stuff," Samuel said, shaking his head and following.

"Because screw Ron. That it?" I said, spinning around in a half circle to look at Dai. "No one else has a better butt for their jokes?"

"Apologies, Ronan, but my guess would be because they can get a reaction out of you easier. Perhaps you need to work on that?" Dai said, shrugging and stepping into Wec also.

"That was a joke, wasn't it?" I called after the lizardman. I marched forward, fueled by my indignation. "You were kidding, right? I am the epitome of stoicism!"

Thankfully, I remembered at the last second to channel a

tiny bit of mana into Fievil and the caramel bubble of energy formed as I transitioned into the Entity. Once the shard weapon was put in holding, I appeared in the whitespace to the uproarious laughter of the others. *So it's going to be one of those days… No rest for the wicked.*

CHAPTER THIRTY-EIGHT

Concrete Options

"I know we were late," Devon started, almost an hour after we'd entered Wec's whitespace. "But it was for good reason. It also sounds like you all were very busy while we were gone, but we can talk about that in a minute."

"Yes, we can and will, so now I want to know why I almost had to send out a search party for you two," Sarah huffed from across the table.

Once again, the complementary round table made its appearance. Thanks to Gec's capabilities in subsidizing these 'long range' calls within the Entities domains, most of the leadership was present, including the squad leaders for those that had participated. It was almost like a conference call, but more three dimensional. Gec itself wasn't present, for the sake of Wec's health, but I could almost feel its presence lurking at the edges of the whitespace. It was at least listening.

"We went where we planned to," Devon started. "We took the old Highway 484 east to Gec, then cut north when we got to the interstate. That went well for about two days, until we encountered the problem."

"A river," Dai said matter-of-factly.

"A big goddamn river," Devon 'clarified.'

"You mentioned that in your last report. So there's a river between us and whatever Metier Crystals to the north. Why did you take so long to get back or contact us?" Sarah insisted.

"I think that when I say 'big' you hear 'big deal,'" the elf said, gesturing with his hands in nonsensical ways. "What I meant to say was I almost didn't make it to the other side and I sure as shit wasn't going to tell Dai to swim across that thing."

"You tapped out?" I said, leaning forward in my seat. Whatever I might say about Devon, he wasn't one to do things half-way. He'd been involved in building the pendulum cannons, helping defenders in the Allied Towns without Gifts or skills of real relevance. Even so, he'd figured out ways to contribute that helped change the game.

"Yeah, just getting to the other side took my entire mana pool and I'm not stupid enough to scout beyond solo."

"Arguable…" I mumbled.

"You got something to say, pebble boy?" The elf jumped to his feet, sparks manifesting in his hair.

"Enough," Sarah said, chopping her hand through the air. "You two can throw rocks at each other later. Okay, we get it's a big river. Why did you stay away for so long?"

"I found signs of people," Devon said, drawing the attention of everyone present. "Nothing crazy, but the ruins had been neatly cleaned out. *And*, unless some critter has taken up wood-working as a hobby, the new fences I ran into spoke for themselves."

"So Gec wasn't lying to us," Dylan said, crossing his arms with a frown as his fiery hair simmered low on his head.

[-] I speak only truth, you insignificant sack of protein! [-] Gec's voice ground out, once more joining the conversation as more than an observer and forcing Wec to patch up their outburst.

"For a *superior* crystalline being, you sure feel the need to give out petty responses," I mumbled, enough that only the eaves-dropping Entities could hear. The black cracks twitched like someone's poor attempt at controlling a rising blood pressure before Wec could banish the majority into obscurity.

"My apologies," Dylan coughed out. "The scope of the situation was simply…"

"Large," Angel provided, the Stonecrest leader rolling his eyes at the Wildwoodian's need to pick his words after having already put his foot in his mouth. "What else did you find out?"

"When Devon crossed back over, we walked the shore to see if there might be a thinner stretch. Good news and bad news on that. Good news is that it *is* thinner in some spots, but the bad news is that it turns into churning rapids. I'm not sure when this river formed, because it's not on old maps or anything, but it is extremely aggressive. The volume might give some of those big rivers from up north in the old country a run for their chips. When it gets narrow, it *erased* the terrain," Dai explained.

"There has to be something supplementing the water supply," I said. "There are springs in Florida, but there shouldn't be enough water pressure below ground to cause that, though…"

"Magic," Daniela provided.

"Right. Who knows what the topography of the area looks like if there are shards or Lord knows what creatures living in the area," I said, working my fingers through my beard as I thought.

"So we are stuck?" Daniela asked, throwing her hands up in the air. "The south is underwater, the east has giant gators, and the north has an uncrossable river? Can we go around to the west?"

Sarah was shaking her head even as I responded. "We could, but then we'd be crossing marshes and swamps for who knows how many miles. Not to mention, Gec indicated our enemies are northbound."

"None of this sounds like good news," Ian said, speaking up for the first time. "I don't want to be the one to bring it up again, Mr. Terrigan, but if no direction is viable, then we would have to wait until it becomes manageable."

"Manageable," I mumbled, a crazy idea forming in my mind.

"Oh no," Clara, Sam, Daniela, and almost all the other people gathered immediately intoned.

I was offended, but when no one added anything else after a full five seconds, I pushed through with my idea. "You said the water erased the existing roads?" I asked Dai.

"That's right. The erosion at the thinner sections was quite aggressive, but it was still present on the wider stretches. The interstate bridge was collapsed, but I'm not so sure it was just because of the water."

"Hmmm."

"Can you go ahead and spit it out, Ron?" Daniela said, rolling her eyes and making a 'go on' gesture with her hand.

I almost opted to remain quiet longer just to mess with her, but I could feel myself getting excited about my idea the more I thought about it. "Well, maybe it doesn't have to be a problem. Quite easy actually. It should be entirely possible for *us* to build a bridge, which should let more than air-and maybe water-attuned cross the river."

"Oh yeah, let's just build a bridge all willy nilly," Daniela said, rolling her eyes so hard I thought they were going to fall out of her face.

"Actually," Dylan said, speaking up in what I could only assume was an attempt to salvage some pride. "We've had to do a number of repairs to the bridge over Lake Sumter thanks to the creatures in the lake, so we do have a team of crafters with some experience. If the Stoneshapers were to join in——"

"Are you kidding me?" Patrick Patrick, the leader of the Stoneshapers in Rachael's sudden seclusion, shouted as he stood from the edge of the whitespace. He'd been amidst the squads building the defensive towers, but apparently he couldn't contain himself like the rest of the squad leaders acting as the audience for our meeting. "There is *no way* we are going to *miss out* on building the first bridge we've recorded since the Fall."

"Are we in favor of trying to build a bridge over this river?" I asked, looking around.

"The Wild Guard will need to reevaluate our patrol distribution due to the gator territory, but I think it will be possible to assign a squad to that area. If we don't have to build in a certain location, then we could build it in the closest convenient spot for the current path of AE-1," Sarah said.

"This project will take the Stoneshapers out of some of their current scheduled construction, but nothing critical was slated," Patrick Patrick added. "It will be a handful of days before I can get a bulk of the Shapers together to go on this expedition."

"Are we going to talk about the debacle that was this raid?" Maurice asked, his frown accentuated by his vine-like hair. "How can we talk about stretching even more without having our borders be secured?"

"It didn't go well," Clara replied evenly. "But we eliminated the mud, frost, and whirlpool elites from their ranks even if we couldn't retrieve the materials or the third gator. Not to mention the more than a dozen smaller ones that we wiped out. If anything other than the mother gator is of concern in the territory for a long while then things have gone terribly off course."

"It *is* the most significant blow our town has managed against the scaly turds," Maurice conceded. His father smacked him on the back of the head for his word choice before nodding in agreement.

"I think this raid is a perfect example of why we need to reach out," I said, meeting the man's eyes before moving to everyone else that had been present in the fighting. "We didn't even know about the implications of squad sizes on ambient natural responses. The dungeon boss is leagues stronger than even the elites; I believe it might be possible to send a mob of people after it, but then we deal with another beast wave like that. We wouldn't be able to guarantee *anyone's* safety.

"Even with dungeon farming, we need access to higher level creatures for levels and materials if we have any hope of truly subjugating the gators, or any other dungeon for that matter. If we can help those also suffering from the Aberrants, we would gain more allies; a clear counter to the limitations the population of the Allied Towns are running face first into."

Patrick Patrick sat back down, but I could see Igor twitching in his seat not far behind Sarah. I didn't need to guess the talk of stronger creatures had him riled up.

"A deficit now, for a leap forward in the future?" Irwin rephrased.

"If the more politician wording works better for you then, sure," I said, rolling my eyes. Dylan, Irwin, Ian, and Angel all grumbled in their own unique ways. It was understandable, since they would be the ones needing to pass this along to the population, but it didn't mean I liked sugarcoating our efforts; it was more 'risk strife now or get trampled in the future.'

"That sounds like agreement to me," Sarah said. "All in favor of the first joint construction project of the Allied Towns?"

Hands went up from Maurice and Ian, who had successfully managed to secure further aid for the Weirdians. Even if the Weirdians didn't seem totally convinced, I just knew our efforts would bear fruit. If not with us, with the connections we left in our wake just like Clara had done the other smaller towns.

Similarly, Patrick and Angel from Stonecrest and Dylan, Clara, and Sarah representing Wildwood voiced their agreement with the caveat to discuss the specifics of the logistics soon. Daniela added her vote into the mix, even if technically I was the one with the vote in our group as the Dreg Warrior Leader.

I rolled my eyes at her, but couldn't hide my grin. Despite getting our collective asses handed to us by the matriarch gator, I felt like our response was the best I could have hoped for. Not only would we be committing to an explorative effort, but also a large-scale build. *This is exactly the avenue of constructive energy redirection that my uncle would tell me to focus on.*

I thought about the Bunker and how they might be

handling the sudden influx of kids. Elias had already gotten a second lease on life with Quotients, and I knew how much the man loved to teach; he'd looked almost young in the meeting before the raid. Ben was probably complaining the whole time while also coming up with funky experiments for the kids to do. Without being in the closed system of the Bunker, the kids might even get to *do* more, not just watch videos and create simulated projects. It was a slew of possibilities that I felt like I wanted to be a part of, while also far away from.

I wanted to be part of the Bunker Camp's development, but I felt a distinct pull to reach out beyond what we knew. The trip to the gators, the assimilating Dreg with <Corporeal Infusion>, and every other cutting-edge development happened when we clashed against the unknown. When I'd hardened my conviction to help and keep pushing, I felt like I couldn't stop. Even sitting within Wec, I felt itchy to integrate the energy into my traits before gathering resources for the bridge.

As the others discussed some of the logistics, I jumped up and left the whitespace. All in all, the Stoneshapers were the only ones I hoped to hear discuss the project and the trip to the site would give plenty of time for that. I didn't think any of them noticed me blend through the ground, retrieve Fievil, and appear back at the school. There was testing to be done.

— + —

It was almost a week and one, thankfully half-hearted, raid by the Lake Weir population of gators later that we gathered at the Weirdian gate to AE-1. The Bunker Busters were together, all of us standing around silently as the others in the expedition did final checks of their provisions. Billy was practically vibrating with excitement, specifically because the goal of the expedition wasn't actually combat; he was going to get to adventure without the guarantee of danger. Neither Jolene, who'd known the youth longer, nor Daniela, who seemed to have a soft spot for the spry elf, had had the heart to tell him that it was unlikely an expedition would go 'smoothly'.

A familiar set of faces in Igor's Wild Fists squad had been assigned to our group in conjunction with our Bunker Busters for defense and utility. Somehow, Sarah had staved off Arnold from coming, even if the dwarf had sent one of his <Stone Anvils> for the sake of being included in the project. He'd sent a very strongly worded letter that I was sure Sarah hadn't read attached to said hunk of rock. Joining us were the Stoneshapers and two Wildwoodians who'd worked on Lake Sumter before and after the Fall. They'd been tasked with assisting me and Patrick while we worked on the basic bridge design as conditions dictated.

Everyone had made it to town the day before, but putting together the resources to establish a temporary base, possibly a permanent one, wasn't an insignificant effort. Of the four wagons lined up, two were loaded with food supplies and healing *smoothies*. I wasn't sure if Sam had had enough time to make modifications to his recipe yet, but the things were imperative regardless. The others were weighed down with various construction staples ranging from nails to bits of half assembled furniture for those that would be stationed at the bridge for any length of time. The four satyr that had acted as beast tamers during the raid on the lake had volunteered to act as the supply chain as well as helping to clear the road and work area of obstructions.

The final crossing spot had been suggested by Devon and Dai, who were also a part of the expedition, and would be attempting to scout *beyond* as soon as the bridge was halfway completed. There was a brief discussion around setting up *another* base on the other side of the bridge, but that particular avenue had been left up in the air. We didn't quite yet know what was going on on the other side of the river, and building the bridge was as much a boon to us as it could be a doorway for unpleasantries to cross over.

Despite all that the more experienced members in the expedition *expected* to happen, and as much as the Shapers and I were the ones most excited by the project, there was a buzz in the air when Clara arrived. It was time.

"Good morning, everyone," the demoness started, drawing everyone's attention with a brief flash of her <Fear>. It didn't actually trigger whatever physiological response the skill resonated with, but it still drew the attention of those present. It was a type of side use that hadn't been tested much, especially on the more esoteric based skills and Gifts that life-and death-attuned acquired versus the more... traditional elements. Clara had mastered the subtlety of its use extremely quickly. "As you all well know, you've been selected for this second foray into building infrastructure for our new world. The Allied Council offers support, but asks that you maintain realistic plans. We just need a bridge, not a spider building or moveable walls at this time."

There was a round of laughter at my and the Shapers' expense, but I didn't mind. I'd rather have a reputation for awesome, over-the-top buildings than just layman brick cubes like Arnold.

"The final consideration is for your own safeties. While the ultimate goal of our scouting is important, it is secondary to your lives. Resources and effort can be recovered or rebuilt, your lives cannot," Clara said, meeting the eyes of everyone present. The mood sobered at her words, but thankfully she turned it right around. "That is why we will seize every opportunity that comes, so that we'll be stronger and lives will no longer be a price we need to pay."

"For the future!" Igor roared.

"We guard!"the group, even the Weirdians and Shapers, called back. With our grins back in place, the crowd that had been watching our expedition members cheered at the top of their lungs.

The injection of energy was just the thing our group needed to kick it into gear. The Beast Tamers kept a clear line of sight with their oxen but moved to the front. They each tapped out a rhythmic step on the hardened soil of AE-1. The grass and bushes all around us quivered as the satyrs connected with the plants. Even the trees felt the pull and low-hanging branches folded back into the canopy. A thin spell chain circled the quartet as they marched forward at the head of the group, wagons trailing behind.

The Weirdians took up the dance, couples forming as they matched their movements to the beat. I even spotted a handful of the guards up on the wall swaying at the display, but recent days kept them attentive in their spots even with the strength of our expedition close by. Vibro tickled at the back of my mind and I watched, mesmerized, as the ripples of the steps were intertwined with magic. Each turn of the square dance the Beast Tamers did sent a gentle pulse through the ground that lit up smaller living things in the ground I assumed to be plants or root systems. That, however, wasn't what had me entranced. The subtlest of pulses, more like an inaudible ping in the cacophony that was life with the ability to sense vibrations.

That ping was immediately drowned out when the Shapers got involved in our progress as they grabbed a firm hold of the soil all around us with mana and molded it to their will. Only Patrick had made it to the Corporeal Limit and through the Hemisphere Trial, but his control was qualitatively different. The earth kowtowed to the magic of the Shapers.

Even as I used my amplified <Mudpit> to ease the burden of massaging the extension of AE-1, my mind kept floating over to the memory of that ping. It had been natural magic, unbound by a spell chain, controlled by a shared effort. It wasn't the first time I'd seen a multi-member skill or Gift being used, but it was the first time I'd seen it augmented or mirrored. There had even been pre-Fall humans in the group!

My mind was awash with thoughts, ideas, and questions. There was a hidden power in humanity's ability to rally together, and it was knocking at the door of the knowledge we'd been discovering. My hand absently went to the shard weapon on my back as I thought about the spider and gator bosses.

My Slurry sped up just slightly as I remembered that I'd come to the surface for freedom and found that I wanted more than just that. I wanted to protect, and I wanted to learn. Each hidden secret fed that fire like coals in a steam engine, and I finally realized why the losses in Summerfield had hit me so hard. I'd failed them, true, but I had also failed myself. I felt a pang of guilt for making their loss about me, but if I wanted to deal with the realities of the surface, I needed to be honest with myself. In losing momentum, I'd let that steam engine wallow, and for the sake of myself and those around me, I couldn't let that happen.

For the rest of the day, I alternated between casting <Landslide> and refining my use of my Harmonic Sinews to sense the magic of things around me. If I had a sixth, magically sponsored sense, why not use it for the arcane on top of seismology?

CHAPTER THIRTY-NINE

Nature's Flow

Four days. Double the time that even Devon and Dai being cautious took to get to the first river site. It wasn't a surprise, not really, considering our group was reclaiming a piece of the wilderness a foot at a time via the Beast Tamers and the Stoneshapers. What it *was* was a drag. One curious thing I noted the Stoneshapers did was add markers every so often on the road. They were simple pillars with a circular bulb at the top. When I asked them about it, they explained it was a comm indicator. Someone standing at one of the markers could contact another at the following or previous one and be guaranteed to be within comm-plant range. It was a genius idea I couldn't believe we hadn't thought of on the first run from Wildwood to Lake Weir.

Despite the wonder that was watching the Stoneshapers work in concert and the Beast Tamers feeding their energy into the forest around us, I was more than a little relieved to encounter the change in vista. It was subtle at first. When we passed Gec's crystal, the trees had been tropical before returning to the more mundane oaks and pines of the area. Less than a mile beyond, it was like the world opened up to a whole new region.

The further north we traveled on what was once known as Highway 475, the shorter and the more sparse the plants grew. Monstrous live oaks that I was sure had to be attuned in their own right dotted clear open plains. A ruined house here, or a worn-down gate from the old world there, attempted to denote who had once lived in the area. The more I explored the world, the happier I was that we hadn't needed to find more titanium to use in the printer down in the Bunker. We wouldn't have been able to provide implants and make the difference that we had. *You go, Tec! You awkward, recklessly handsy magic rock.*

A sense of wonder I hadn't felt since we'd first discovered Wildwood lightened my steps the further we got from the Allied Towns. I hadn't realized that even with how massively expanded our horizons were compared to the Bunker, I'd been feeling suffocated. Exploring, clearing paths, and building connections beyond our home resonated louder than I'd argued for it; any bit of hesitation that I held about the expedition vanished along with my view of 'safety.'

We spotted herds of wild cattle and a handful of horses running wild at speeds that would have put their thoroughbred pre-Fall cousins to shame. Neither of those approached our group, but I did spot a few of the horses pause to stare at our odd grouping. Samuel and the Beast Tamers, on the other hand, had to be physically restrained from pursuing the creatures.

"You have a whole herd and a Raymond waiting for you. Why the eagerness to make contact?" I asked Sam on the second day. He didn't have a good answer, but grumbled something about 'animals are nicer than people' under his breath before he returned to the back of the wagon holding our infused jelly. He'd been 'talking' with the oxen and with Anthony the fire ant for the majority of the trip; based on the gesticulation towards the wagon, I was fairly sure he was using them as sounding boards for whatever mad scientist stuff he did to create the healing goop.

For the others, sans Billy, the novelty of the area wore off quickly and they each kept to themselves while watching for any potential threats. Daniela ranged far and Jolene left to go with her on more than one occasion. The Wild Fists kept up their training even while we traveled. The whole squad would rush forward ahead of the expedition, blasting out a quarter of their mana pools on various attacks mixed with martial art-looking movements while we caught up. Then they would repeat, but spar with each other until their mana was regenerated. Their energetic 'tsks' and 'ha!' and 'one-twos' had become background noise by the end of the first day.

Supper was a muted affair since we only spent a token amount of time building camp. A two-person watch rotation was established and the group called it a day.

The following two days were almost carbon copies of the first. It was on the fourth that the open areas around us turned…mushy. The usually dry expanses of grass that had flanked our expansion of AE-1 manifested ponds and small creeks that drifted away into the distance. Devon and Dai had shared their maps ahead of time and a glance at the LPS showed we were less than a mile out from the river. The oaks that had pushed through the nothing were quickly replaced by a nubby expanse of roots I quickly recognized as cypress trees. The scope of the trees was extreme compared to what I'd seen of the ones near Lake Weir, but the answer made itself known when the first trunks came into view.

<Cypress Tree>
<Attunement: Life>
<Refinement: Absorption>
<Perceived Metier Quotient: 3>

They were neck and neck with the oaks for size, but instead of reaching up and out, they did so below ground. The further north we went, the more I sensed them through vibro and I realized that we would have been walking through muck if the tree roots weren't stabilizing the ground to an extent. When a handful of death-attuned cedar trees and air-attuned birch trees, in addition to their mundane counterparts, started to mingle with the cypress ones, we arrived at the end of the road. Literally.

The asphalt had been torn off and the base materials were eroded away to a slow, swirling pool of mud. Beyond the muddy water was the river.

"That's big," I whispered.

"I told you it was," Devon air whispered to me from where the agile elf had perched himself on a nearby birch.

Slow waves painted a deceptive picture of how much water something with the cross-section of the river would be moving. The manifestation of nature dwarfed anything I'd expected. I'd seen out towards Lake Weir and been amazed, but there was something about tons of water flowing by you each minute that just hit different. The banks of the river brushed up against the forest around us, watermarks telling of how high the water got during the rainy periods. Beyond that was what had to be a half mile of water.

"Does it have a name?" Daniela asked. The brunette had been sitting at the edge of the water when the main group arrived. Her expression was soft, none of her usual snark or tongue-in-cheekiness in sight.

"This didn't exist in the world before," Robert, the only non-Fallen in the group, said. "There were a few nature parks to the east, but nothing that would have led to this. Well, not before the Fall."

"What was that place called?" I asked, turning to Robert.

"Ocklawaha Prairie, if I recall." Robert took several minutes to try to recall, but no one in the group begrudged him the effort. *It must be weird to come back to something you once knew to see it changed in its entirety.It's almost the opposite of what Daniela, Sam, and I are experiencing...*

"The Ock River, huh?" Daniela said, quietly.

"We did not name it," Dai said. "I don't see why we can't call it that."

"The Ock River it is," Robert finished, smiling softly.

I had a sneaking suspicion that I would get some river-related memories if I touched the man. It had been a while since <Memory Canal> had triggered, and I hoped to keep it that way unless absolutely necessary. Guilt over the dead and the flashes of memory I'd already taken were enough nightmare fuel.

I waited a beat before being the spoilsport of the sober moment. As the one with the 'crazy' idea to build over the hydrological monster that was the newly christened river, I'd been assigned as the expedition leader. Just for major decisions, thankfully. Sam had still been placed in charge of our supply chain. "Now, let's dig in. If we work quickly, maybe we can sleep on some properly secured hammocks tonight."

That statement was met with both groans and cheers in equal measures. The more punchy members of our group made up the bulk of the cheers, since they got to just punch more stuff. The Stoneshapers and the Beast Tamers were the ones with the terra and biomancing skills to construct our temporary domicile. *More like barracks...* I thought as the comment about my over-the-top buildings flashed through my mind.

Just you watch, I am going to make the most ridiculous bridge you've ever seen. The crenelations are going to have crenelations. How about a fountain? I'm sure we could manage to form a siphon to move the water from the river up high enough if I take into account the velocity of the river moving into a stone pipe and—

"Ronan?" Sam's voice broke me out of my reverie.

"Leave him. He's got the nerd face again. If we don't leave him alone, he's going to be all butt hurt for the whole time we are here," Daniela said.

I glared at the brunette as she smirked. Instead of rising to the bait, I thanked Sam for pulling me back from my thoughts. I didn't tend to drift so far into my mind... except when it went to creating. The simulation programs in the Bunker had been great—amazing, even—but they didn't compare to reality. Now that we were on the surface, I needed to remind myself that I had the ability to turn my thoughts to reality. *It's all just some mana away.*

Grinning widely, I closed my eyes before slapping both of my hands down on the ground as hard as I could. Limestone Skin redirected the force through my body, strumming my Harmonic Sinews as it reverberated off of my Quake Osseum. A detailed picture of the soil around me lit up ripple after ripple. "Time to build again."

— + —

It took less than ten minutes to find the optimal location to build. Some two hundred feet from AE-1 were the remains of a building from before the Fall. Hilda from the Wild Fists found a mostly rotted sign that read 'caloloclu.' Robert was once again kind enough to provide his knowledge of the world before to point out it probably said it was the Ocala Polo Club. Despite a sudden bout of interest to ask about the sport I'd only learned about adjacently, I focused on doing another in-depth vibro scan of the area. A thick footing around the old walls complemented a thin slab of concrete that made up the floor of the old building. After probing around while the other arcane shapers recovered their mana, I had a good picture of what we had to work with. Even if part of the old footprint was partially broken into the banks of the Ock River, the material's reinforcement would save a lot of work.

"Alright. We'll want to raise the structure to at least the water mark," I said, pointing out the closest tree. Before I got too carried away, I turned to where the Beast Tamers and Sam were discussing something quietly. "I think we'll want clear line of sight to the road and to the bridge. Can you guys work on that? Maybe that's where we can set up the local garden?"

"I think that might be manageable. Everett might be able to coax these attuned plants out of the way," Veronica, the leader of the Tamers, said.

"If not, I've got the solution right here," Igor said, grinning wide to show off his prominent tusks. Fire flickered around his fingers, sparking in concert with the man's eagerness as he flexed his impressive bicep.

"I don't know if gaining the animosity of the trees is the first step we want to take in the area," Fowler said, patting the orc on the shoulder.

"Not you too," Igor lamented, head drooping as his own squad's healer reeled back his enthusiasm. The red fae continued to comfort his squad leader as he led him away towards the water where Dai and Daniela were talking animatedly.

"Right. Elevation," Patrick Patrick said, bringing my focus back.

"Yeah, I'm thinking ten feet would be good. Maybe reinforce the existing concrete with some passive mana effects before raising it on stilts."

"Hmmm, I think I can work some cross bracing into the structure once we get it up in the air, but that sounds reasonable. We can start on that if you want to flatten the area. Francis can help you reinforce a path from the road and make an area where we can keep the oxen at ground level."

"Let's do it," I said, clapping my hands together.

Three Shapers split off to clear away debris from the husk of the structure while channeling mana to their feet. Gentle, swooping beige spell chains wrapped around their ankles without actually triggering. *I didn't know you could do that...*

I shook my head to focus back on my task. After seeing that little bit of control, I felt ambitious for my side of the task. Primarily, getting the path from the road to the building restored in one shot. A brief discussion with Francis set him to work on mounds to be compressed into a fence for the beasts of burden of the Tamers while I focused on the path.

I focused on the area I wanted to affect as I took hold of the lever for <Mudpit> in my mind. With the training I'd been doing, the mana cost of the skill got brought down to the single-digit percents but was maintained consistently. It was a twofold drain of power that often ended up draining more mana as I tried to liquify material. For the pathway, I fed the base power into the skill, but I ground my will against it to reshape the *intent* from a circle into a four-foot-wide path. I tried to visualize the 'shortcut' that <Landslide> presented by focusing its liquidation force forward. The spell chain snapped into being around me. It twitched like a worm as I strangled my Foundational Hemisphere for all the control it was willing to yield.

Several of the glyph-like formations on the chain turned into puffs of umber light that flowed to different areas of the skill. This went on for a handful of seconds before the skill finished adjusting to my desires. Then I folded like a house of cards. Half my mana was gone in a second and I could practically feel it being wrenched from my muscles, bones, and tendons thanks to the ripples they sent through my traits. The trigger had been faster than any I'd done before where the skill just *happened* before I even had time to register it.

By the time Samuel had made it to me and worked the kinks out of my body, the modified skill had run its course. There was a swath of *over* two hundred feet cleared and hardened before me. The modified <Mudpit> had actually bisected the road the Shapers had made, leaving a clear-cut dip in the packed soil before it pushed beyond. There was a tree toppled over where my skill had weakened the hold its roots had on the earth.

"What the hell was that, Ron!?" Sam asked, slapping my face gently to get me to focus on him. I tried not to say anything about the dozens of nerve filaments poking and prodding my cheek out of respect for the healer. Plus, if I'd acknowledged it, I would have been squirming with discomfort that would have set my muscles burning again.

"Tweaked a skill. Just a tad," I managed, already feeling the easing of my mana side effects being further soothed by Sam's <Health Bump>.

"Can we maybe not try new techniques out in the middle of nowhere? Yeah? Stick to tried and true, please?" the blond said, sighing in exasperation as he let my head drop to the ground. The gentleness of his concern was all but gone. He walked away from me, mumbling and shaking his head. "Crazy bastard. He really *does* have rocks for a brain."

Francis looked distinctly uncomfortable as he approached where I just laid on the ground, unmoving. "Sir?"

"Just give me a minute. You can go ahead and work on the beast pen," I replied.

Francis hesitated for a moment before nodding and walking away. I closed my eyes and felt for the man's ripples as he headed for the spot where we'd discussed putting the pen. His, and the mana of the other Shapers, sent pulses of energy barely perceptible by my vibrosense. If I hadn't been practicing since we left Lake Weir, I wouldn't have been able to spot them through the natural frequency of everything around me. I focused on that sense as a meditation of sorts, waiting for my body to set itself back together.

Eventually, I actually managed to doze off but it didn't last. A slimy appendage tugged at my beard and I cracked my eyes to see Blobby looming over me. Even if the creature had shrunk, it was still too large for it to rest right next to one's head. I'd seen the creature suffocate more than its fair share of enemies to know how deadly the bulk of my silent companion was, size notwithstanding.

Obviously, the slime didn't say anything. Its appendages, however, spoke volumes as it pointed in the direction of the construction. The construction that was well on its way to complete without much input of mine other than the pathway. I got a flash of that snickering mole that seemed to be Fievil's desired mental visage as I groaned my way to my feet.

"I'm gonna hear about this," I said, shaking off some of the loose dirt that had accumulated on my hair and clothes from my dirt nap.

CHAPTER FORTY

Terrafirma

Sure enough, I kept hearing about my dirt nap for the next two days. The jokes about how I was a stiff breeze away from knocking myself unconscious grew old quickly, but that didn't seem to deter Devon and Danny. The two were inseparable as they explored up and down the shore of the Ock River while the rest of us worked on the river base. When they were at the construction area, they fed off each other to rib on me. I put their childish insults aside as I refocused on our work, which quickly forced *them* to resume theirs lest they come across as actually rude. *Success! Something, something, sticks and stones.*

The river base had been mostly secured on the first day, but we'd all silently agreed to spend some extra time on the second day to really dig in before we started work on the bridge.

As it stood, the river base was hoisted almost twenty feet in the air. A dozen stone stilts held up the foundation with Xs made of stone and vines to reinforce the structure. A ramp, as well as a ladder, led up to the building proper. It was a simple T-shaped box, but we'd made great use of the space thanks to our plethora of crafters.

The Tamers, when they weren't feeding and tending to their

oxen, worked with Samuel to woodshape the basic furniture pieces that had been crafted in Wildwood. They were leagues behind Marie and even Sam's vine weaves, but their efforts allowed the expedition to sleep in semi-comfortable hammocks and bunk beds.

At the juncture of the T, we'd added a stairwell that led up to the roof of the river base. It was a simple triangle design, with the opening to the stairwell leading to a small, downward-angled observation platform. A stretch of the road back towards the Allied Towns was visible to the south and most of the area we'd selected to build on the bank of the river were visible. The other side was a stretch for most, but Robert and Devon were able to use their Focused Eye traits to get a clear visual on the opposing shore.

Their scouting prowess, even with Robert being a simple worker in town, went to show how different senses and terrains could affect the use of abilities. It also raised a subconscious fear I had for airborne enemies. Despite everything, <Mineral Strike> remained my only true weapon against flying creatures. If my human companions could spot me from over half a mile away easily, then what did that say about creatures that special-ized in dive bombing their prey?

I had to suppress a shiver as I followed the other Shapers to the end of the road we'd constructed.

"I'll be honest, I didn't expect the river to be quite so…" Patrick said, trailing off as he searched for the right word.

"Big?" Francis added.

"Not exactly what I was looking for, but sure. This thing is massive. How are we supposed to build anything that doesn't get swept away?"

"Step one is we reinforce the heck out of this platform area," I said, gesturing at the bank of the river. "I didn't get much of a chance to go back to the Bunker and research what-ever they might have on bridge design, but as the only locations we can reinforce *easily*, it stands to reason we want to bulk it up as much as we could."

"We should excavate deeper before we start to compress things. I can throw down some of my <Crystal Brace> to act as reinforcement," Patrick said, running his hand through his magnificent dwarven beard.

"I'll try to survey as much of the river as I can as we go. Water tends to mess with my vibration sense, but maybe I can get a good picture of what we are working with."

"I'll get Jolene. She should be able to help keep the water out of our work area," Sue, the only female Stoneshaper that didn't also happen to be a city leader, added.

It was still weird to see female dwarves, since most I'd interacted with were men. Hilda and then Rachael had been the first I'd interacted with. Instead of the waist long beards, female dwarves got exorbitant amounts of thick hair. Considering they were as short as their male counterparts, it took many, many braids to keep them off the ground.

"Good idea. We are probably going to hit water as soon as we dig with the river so close," Patrick said, patting Sue on the shoulder before turning to the area the life-attuned in our group had cleared. I didn't need to turn.

My hands slapped down on the surface of our packed earth road before a thick ripple flowed out to give me a subterranean three-dimensional depiction of the area. The ripples were clear, especially where we'd formed the road, but quickly petered out toward the treeline. When it reached the bank of the river and further, it was muffled into uselessness. Nevertheless, I could feel the thirty-foot area we'd cleared and even feel the Shapers starting to work on their excavation. The soil wasn't great, likely on account of the amount of organic scraps that had accumulated since the Fall, but it wouldn't be a problem since the Shapers were already clearing away that layer.

I moved closer to the bank and repeated my sounding ripple. While my sensory range expanded much further into the river, it was still much less than what I sensed in the opposite direction. Thankfully, the response I did get from the soil was fairly uniform. I didn't feel confident or even familiar enough with my Harmonic Sinews to make a call on what material composition the soil had, but I could, at the very least, tell it wasn't far off from what the bank was made of. That was to say, some kind of clay with a decent amount of sand mixed in. I wished Ben was here. *My geological knowledge was always based around cool things rather than practical uses. He could have told me the best way to approach this.*

Despite my distinct lack of Teach, I did remember something he taught me. His voice rang clear in my mind.

"If you aren't confident, look for more data. If you can't find more data, gather it. If you gathered it, but don't know what to do with the damn things, compare them. Not the most scientific of methods, but it's served me well."

"Comparison, huh?" I said, running my fingers through my beard as I thought. I looked at the bank and then I looked at the road. Shrugging, I cast <Stone Spike> at both locations.

The sudden bit of offensive magic caused poor Francis to jump out of the hole he was using his Gift to dig. He panted and held his chest as he turned from my skill to me and then shook his head before he returned to the hole.

Not much of a combat person, eh? It made sense the more I thought about it. Especially something like the Shaper path, since it directed your efforts to act as a support, not to be on the front lines. As much as I enjoyed building, fighting made all my efforts come together. That didn't mean it was the only way forward. Even without my contribution, the Stoneshapers whipped up a perfectly constructed base and the wall around Stonecrest was as impressive a construction as any of the ones the others had built.

Snapping out of my drifting thoughts, I focused on the two spikes. I wondered what would be the best way of testing their relative strength when I got a flash from Fievil. It showed the mana bubble and me placing my hand directly against the material.

When I tried to prod the shard weapon for more, I got silence in return.

"Fine. Be that way," I shot back. I was being sarcastic, but of course the shard didn't agree and I got flipped off by a mole. *First time for everything I suppose.*

Pushing the cantankerous weapon out of mind, I pressed my hand to one of the spikes and channeled mana into Fievil to activate the Arcane Sink. The now-familiar bubble of caramel energy formed a radius of five feet around me. However, where I'd placed my hand, the stone started to give. Sand bled between my fingers as the center portion of the spike where I had my hand crumpled. A minute later, a crack like a gunshot came from the spike before the top slumped to the side, thankfully away from me. Francis started, but at least he stayed in his hole this time. The Shapers collectively seemed to realize I'd been doing something with my weapon and approached as I retracted my mana bubble.

"Ronan, what are you doing?" Patrick asked.

"I'm trying to figure out what we are working with here or at least have a baseline."

"Is that why there is a ten-foot spike sticking out of the water?" Francis asked, pointing to the other skill trigger.

"That's right. My sensory trait has let me peek further out into the river and it's fairly homogeneous, so if we can account for the weight each support can hold, then our bridge design should hold," I said.

"I'm not sure what 'homogeneous' means," Patrick said, "but I think I get it. We can try that with our own reinforcement skills if you think that would be helpful."

"That would be, actually. The more data the better!" *Maybe I should have brought Alan along.* One grimace-inducing memory about how he was doing after the fight with the Aberrant dissipated that thought. Plus, as difficult as he could be, if the spunky researcher wanted to do something, it was damn hard to deflect his attention. If he'd wanted to come on the expedition, it would have been entirely possible I would have just turned around to find him there, scratching out some notes on his tablet on the back of one of the wagons.

Just in case, I checked the wagons from a distance before wading out into the water. It was cold, but the day was warm enough that it actually felt quite refreshing. Letting the steady current splash water against the knees of my cargo pants, I placed my palm against the middle of the <Stone Spike> again. When I fed Fievil energy to form the mana bubble, it was much smaller than before. The drain on me was greater as I watched my mana ticking down, whereas before it had only done that when I compressed the spike. What I quickly noticed, however, was that the water that filtered through my bubble came out darker and muddy. A snaking stain trailed out into the river the longer I stood as I counted the seconds it took for my test spike to break. It was only a handful of seconds less.

The Stoneshapers immediately jumped into discussions for how they could use the technique to establish different areas of strength and basing it on their relative skills to optimize build times and scale for projects. It sounded ambitious and like way too much work when they were talking about using magic to build things, but then again, it had been that engineering approach that had allowed Alan to build his MetierTech Purger for the Aberrant. *I don't entirely dislike the idea. I already spend so much time trying to figure out how to manipulate my skills to get them to do what I want, research isn't that big of a—*

"LUNCH!" Devon air whispered to everyone in the vicinity. Unlike his usual subtle whispers to reach people, the man went for maximum volume. I wasn't the only one to cringe and hold my head. A bit louder and I felt like my Limestone Skin would have come into play to help me dissipate the force.

I rolled my eyes as the elf chuckled from his perch at the top of the river base. I didn't need my enhanced perception to see his smug grin all the way down the steps to the small kitchen that had been set up in the base. Then it hit me. Daniela was cooking and the Wild Fists had hunted down one of the numerous cows in the plains to our south.

With all the force my twice-above human average strength could manage, I bolted for the base. I felt the Shapers pause for a moment before charging after me. They'd all had the pleasure of witnessing the true magic that Daniela managed in the cooking department. With some actual meat and fresh grown veggies from Sam's new garden, it was liable to be a feast and I was determined to be first in line. Devon could eat last for all the favoritism my Latina friend showed the smug elf.

I couldn't help the chuckle that escaped me as a quartet of short-legged dwarves tried to keep pace with my over-six-foot frame. Building, magic research, and delicious food. *What more could I ask for?*

— + —

"Are you sure this is how you want to do it?" Patrick asked across the table from me.

"I don't think you all have many options. Before the Fall, there were all sorts of machines and equipment to tell you what was below the ground. Now?" Robert shrugged, holding his hands palm up. "I'm honestly amazed you have figured out as much as you have already."

After what could only be described as a free-for-all, scavenging hunt for lunch, we'd gone back to the river to test the various earth manipulation techniques and their relative strengths with the materials at hand. It was eye-opening as far as my attunement was concerned, since I saw the same general concept of how my <Earthen Barrier> and <Stone Spike> were applied in a number of ways. The most notable were Patrick's crystal filaments, which seemed to be almost *stretchy,* for lack of a better word to describe flexible rock, and Sue's <Ore Deposit>skill, which produced a nugget of unrefined iron after compressing a variable amount of earth. The rest of the shapers had variations of compressing, exploding, and shifting earth. The neatest was a hexagonal version of my <Stone Spike> that reminded me of the rock formations that existed in Northern Ireland before the Fall.

By observing how long it took for the Arcane Sink to fail the material, we determined that the strongest skills were Sue's deposits, my <Stone Spike>, Francis' hexagonal <Lava Rocks>, and Patrick's filaments. Unfortunately, working with Sue's ore products was time prohibitive. It was possible that if we found a way of combining her skill with the scrap that was littered around the world after the Fall, the skill would gain a new significance. When I brought that point up, the female dwarf *vanished* and the rest of us were left to figure out how to make a bridge across the river with the abilities we had on hand.

That was when Robert came into the picture. He served as the even keel to the overactive imagination of the Shapers and I. The preliminary design for the bridge was simplified further and Robert repeated KISS many times. None of us knew what he was talking about, but the gist came through. In the end, we decided to go with a combination of our skills that seemed the most likely to work. Thanks to my access to <Earth Wall>, I would be responsible for the slabs that took up the bulk of the bridge. Francis would make the pillars with his <Lava Rocks>, and then Patrick and the other Shapers would use his filaments and compression abilities to merge the two bigger structures.

"Do we have any idea how deep it is?" Francis asked, absently braiding his beard as he looked at the scratched together sketch for the bridge. "I've never tried to make my <Lava Rocks> longer than ten feet."

"Well, better get to testing. From what I can tell, the river is fairly flat close to the bank—after the first initial drop, of course —but beyond it drops lower than twenty feet. At the middle of the river? No idea," I said. I gestured from the sketch we had for the bridge to the rough profile I'd put together.

"Sounds like you all have a plan," Robert said, smiling and brushing himself off. "No sense in delaying if there is going to be some trial and error. I'll work on getting everything offloaded from the wagons and cutting down some more of the attuned wood of that birch the Wild Fists took out so the Tamers can haul it back. Leave the base to me!"

Our group discussed the information we had for a few minutes, but the older human had hit the colloquial nail on the head. There was only so much speculation they could do. With that, our group got to work. The Shapers had finished reinforcing the portion of the bank that connected with the road, so we jumped straight into the bridge construction. Since Francis felt comfortable with raising ten-foot pillars, the first section of the bridge was easy to start. Everyone had a job to do.

Francis scrunched up his face as he glared at the soil where we'd marked the first set of pillars. The slew of test formations rose out of the water to the east like a small monument to what we were hoping to accomplish. With little warning, the two hexagonal pillars rose out of the ground. They rose quickly at first, but slowed the further they went. The muted gray stone was shaded with tan and hints of red when the mana-created stone pulled on the local materials. The moment the pillars were raised, Francis gave me a shaky thumbs up before he sat down to recover. It was honestly impressive, considering the man hadn't been but Q2 not long ago.

Shaking the distractions from my mind, I pulled Fievil from my back as I stared at the space between the reinforced bank and the two pillars. Five feet separated the two pillars, with an additional two if I took into account the diameter of the hexagons. The plan was to use those additional feet to create a railing that would help prevent people from just ending up in the drink. It wasn't a complex flexing of my power, not compared to some of the other changes I'd forced into existence, but I was determined not to use more mana than I needed while being consistent.

"Any tips?" I asked the shard weapon. A vision of a pulse of mana that rippled up from where I rested the axe hammer on the ground, through the femur haft and into me before working its way to my helm to be amplified into <Earth Wall> was what I got in response. There were no details, no explanations. Yet, I was beginning to understand how the shard was able to help me as much as it was. It had an area of influence like the Entities, and it was using said area to my benefit. The trick was leveraging that *more*, not saving it like a neat consumable in an RPG.

Shrugging, I visualized the spell chain for <Earthen Barrier>. I focused on having the skill concentrate around the head of my weapon before I channeled it up through the weapon like Fievil had shown me. The difference was immediate. The casting was slow, torturously so if I intended to do it in combat, but the draw on my mana was almost half of the original. Instead of the forty percent of my mana pool amplifying the skill took, it was a meager twenty-three percent. As I watched the spell chain bend, gaining the additional band that marked the amplified form, I focused on my intent for the skill. Then the ground at my feet exploded.

A perfect, six-inch slab of stone sent all the loose dirt of the reinforced slope raining down before stretching at just shy of the perfect angle. The mana of the skill ran out as the slab went three feet past the pillars before dropping down with a heavy thump. The Stoneshapers that had been holding their breath behind me let out raucous cheers as the first segment of the bridge was in place. Patrick, Lucius, and Sue clapped me on the back as they went forward to secure the slab to the pillars with the crystal filaments.

A scattered clapping reached me as I noticed a small crowd had gathered up on the river base's observation platform to watch the first bit of building. Robert had done more than just take care of the base, it seemed. He was grinning as he waved when the other Shapers noticed. They waved back awkwardly, unsure of how to deal with the praise before returning to their tasks. I shook my head, leaning on Fievil to hide the strain the spell had put me through. It wasn't the worst I'd experienced, but manipulating the skill to flow through my hammer had been a new exercise in control.

It was an exercise in control I would get to practice over, and over. We were planning to cross one chonky river.

CHAPTER FORTY-ONE

Splashdown

As straining as the process of building the bridge was, it quickly became repetitive. The true shifts in pacing were when the *river* fought back our efforts. As threatening as our expedition group was, with its impressive number of Q6ers, the moment we spread out to take care of tasks was when nature moved back in. Frogs, water striders, a handful of smaller gators, and just a silly number of fish of many types tried to prevent our advance. The scouts and the Wild Fists were eventually forced to set up a rotation to watch over our bridge crew to prevent the creatures from the river from affecting the work we were attempting to do.

There was more than one occasion where I was forced to intervene, mana deficit be damned, when fish would jump clear out of the river to try to attack us on the bridge. Amidst those there was even a growing number of sturgeons that seemed intent on knocking us *off* the bridge instead of fighting us directly. Due to that, our progress was slowed further as we opted to form the side barriers as we progressed, instead of closer to the end of construction as we'd planned. This slowed our progress even more, as the lower Quotient denizens of the Ock River tried to take their due for our construction.

When we were able to hide from sight of the river, the attacks became more concentrated on the shore instead. It was as if the creatures realized that they could get to me and the Shapers up on the bridge if they took the banks. That was where the catfish excelled. The creatures would flop onto shore, gasping for breath, before spitting mud or shards of ice. There was even one that formed a miniature tornado to try to swallow Daniela from one of her usual spots at the edge of the river. Suffice it to say, we had a good meal that night.

There was even a handful of times where we were forced to repair the newly constructed bridge thanks to the magic the river creatures used. It was a fight of attrition. Catfish, panfish, bass, and even a particularly dangerous Q4 Florida gar that collapsed a fresh section of bridge, crashed like waves against our bridge.

When the animals started to attack the structure directly, we were forced to refine our construction efforts even more to Francis' chagrin. With our original plan for the bridge, we'd slanted it up over the water to be some three feet above it. In the hopes of avoiding the river creatures, we pushed that to a full ten. The dwarf had been pushing himself to extend the length of his <Lava Rock> pillars when the depth reached twenty feet. When we asked if he could turn that into thirty, he practically collapsed on his feet but pulled through. With the level, things got easier until we reached closer to the center of the river where the water dropped almost thirty feet. Even with his increased density, it took most of his mana pool to create *one* of the pillars by the time we reached the center of the river.

On top of that, each pillar was upped to a grouping of two. The outer pillar would help support the weight of the slabs I put down, but mainly it served as redundancy against the creatures of the river damaging the structure. Not to mention, it also helped as a wave breaker. The current in the middle of the lake, where it dropped low, sped up considerably. The rush of the river, which was a gentle babble on the banks, was a constant grind when you stood right near the middle.

Nevertheless, me and the Shapers were in our element. For all that fighting challenged my mind's control of my body, I felt each new bit of construction challenged my mind as a whole. How to compensate for an issue, how to get a better mana-created product when the base materials were subpar. Sue's ore ability was a key example of what our magic did. It took existing matter, duplicated it, and augmented it with mana. It was energy to matter conversion that Einstein would have been salivating to see. It was during the building process that I felt some of what Alan must feel when he observed *anything* new in the world. It was exhilarating and utterly daunting at the same time.

The bridge project wasn't all bad, however. The most distinct benefit of this was the slew of food variety we were able to acquire. Thanks to the fish *throwing* themselves at our expedition, they became a common part of our meals. The low Quotient of most of the creatures that attacked also incentivized the effort of mana locking them as opposed to dissociating them, since they provided an almost marginal benefit to our traits and levels.

After the efforts of applying my skills to construction during the day, at night I saw yet another whole world that magic had unlocked for humanity. The culinary arcane arts. Daniela and Devon were a whole kitchen staff crammed into two people. The elf had managed to Freeform his gust Gift to juggle items around in the small kitchen of the river base. A handful of vegetables, fish filets, and small containers with spices danced around while the rest of the expedition crammed the open spaces.

While the others were content socializing, and just being a rambunctious crowd in general, Billy and I took up posts in the kitchen. The youth was determined to master his new condition; at some point he'd started using his gaseous limbs to form *extra* arms that he used to serve the rest of the expedition. It was going moderately well. As for me, I tried to endure the mushy faces and hip nudges that my childhood friend and the lanky pointed ear waste of space shared in the hopes of furthering my grasp of magic.

There was definitely something rigid about the approach dwarves had to magic, mainly because it was about oomph and pow, rather than finesse. The gentle flame of Danny's wisp that she used to boil and cook was a very precise use of her magic. Devon's way of searing vegetables and filets alike with the help of his lightning was refined. The whole thing was an example of control as they Freeformed to their heart's content. Even more, I only caught sight of their spell chains a handful of times, which told me their Freeforming was almost reflexive instead of the gradual change that I did for my spell chains.

It was an inspiring display of the potential magic had outside of combat.

In that fashion, troubleshooting the bridge construction and exploring some of the finer things our new life on the surface provided, time passed faster than I could recall. The slow grind of the creatures had some further benefits for those that weren't frontline fighters. The lower leveled Stoneshapers, as well as Robert and his helper Jillian, started to climb in power over the first week of building. By the end of the second week, our little construction crew had managed to make it to the halfway mark on the river before we were forced to take a break. PatPat, as the quirky Patrick Patrick had been nicknamed for all the time he spent tamping down his crystal filaments, had hit Quotient 6. He'd been fairly close thanks to the battle in the gator territory, but the gar that had nearly dropped us all in the river had given him that last chunk of progress he needed. Francis and Sue, having climbed up to Q5, were on the precipice of unlocking traits. Pushing those into being would require the safety of an Entity's purge, at the least, and no one felt rushed enough about the construction not to take a break.

Patrick hoped to be able to pass his Hemisphere Trial before returning, which meant there would be at least half a week before the group could make the hike back. The travel time would be significantly reduced thanks to the now-established road, but that didn't mean that the group could be negligent of the wilderness. For that reason, the Wild Fists volunteered to escort them back along with two of the Beast Tamers. The leader, Veronica, had been itching to get the attuned wood in the hands of the crafters and the Trial was the perfect excuse to make a safe trip back.

Since we'd also reached the halfway mark, Devon and Dai also decided to take the opportunity to begin their scouting of the far side of the river. For the lizardman's benefit, Samuel created a long, woven rope out of his <Vine Whip> that was secured to the bridge. He used it to lower himself to the water before starting a sinuous swim to the opposite side. Whenever the current threatened to overwhelm him, a flash of mana would appear around him and he would shoot forward. A few seconds later, a mini-iceberg floated to the surface further downriver.

As for the elf, he simply did a front flip off the open end of our bridge before releasing a terrifying gust of wind against the structure that propelled him several feet forward. Once in the air, he reached out wide with his arms as gusts of wind whipped at his body to keep him afloat. Two minutes later, he landed in a plume of sand on the other side of the river.

Everyone bid the scouts farewell off the bridge and the pair quickly disappeared from sight. Sam had stocked each of them with two healing smoothies for emergencies and they had proven themselves more than capable of leveraging their full suite of abilities to escape. Nevertheless, when the two had left and the bulk of the Shapers had left with the Wild Fists, I found Daniela with her feet dangling from the end of our bridge. She looked lost in thought, but her gaze was locked on that opposite shore.

"We'll be at the other side in three weeks if those shorties can hoof it," I said by way of greeting as I plopped beside her.

"You might as well throw the schedule out the window

then," the brunette said, not taking her eyes off the opposite bank.

"True. At the very least, we get to eat some fresh Vega Eatery productions."

"Ha! I will say, these wild fish taste a lot better than the ones Papa got from the hydroponics floor." Daniela shook her head. Her voice quieted down. "I hope he's made the trip to the surface."

"I doubt it."

"Hey! This is where you agree with me and tell me some hopeful thing like 'I'll bet you'll see him waiting when we get back to Wildwood,' or some other nonsense like that! It's been over a month since we've been to the Bunker!" She whipped to look at me, squinting the moment she spotted my cheeky grin.

"Listen, we both know Mr. Vega is knee deep in the kitchen, cooking up the things coming out of Sam's first garden to feed the small army of children the Allied Towns sent over."

Danny chuckled, propping herself back on her elbows. A soft smile played on her face as she finally tore her eyes away from the shore to, at least, watch a piece of driftwood making its way downstream. "Yeah, you are right. There's no chance he isn't cooking like his life depends on it if there are hungry people to feed. I bet he's laughing right now while Mama berates him for poking a hole in her 'dietary plan.'"

"He does like to push her buttons," I said, smiling as I remembered one of the few couples we'd been exposed to in our lives. That number had since skyrocketed by comparison, but it was nice to remember where we'd come from.

"You know, it might be childish since this is my first foray into love, but that's what I hope Devon and I can have," she whispered. It was as if admitting in clear words that the two of them were dating would cause the pressure between us to finally explode.

I held quiet for several seconds before letting out a sigh. "I know, Danny. I would have to blind not to see it, even if I can't claim to be a master in the field of romance."

"Jolene would agree with you," Daniela said, nodding and reacquiring her cheeky smile when she saw my mortified expression. "You are going to have a proper talk with the poor girl, Ron."

"There has just been so much—"

"Nope. Not an excuse. If there is something I've learned after the blasted mess we discovered here on the surface it's that you gotta value the time at hand. You *make* the time and it means all the more. Do you think I wanted to burn so many poor filets teaching Devon to cook? That man is all thumbs. I swear, Igor was going to break his nose if he wasted one more bit of the fish he killed." Daniela laughed as she stared wistfully at the water.

"I... I didn't know," I whispered.

"That's okay too. As much as you still aggravate me, and as much as you and Dev butt heads like those bulls in the plains, I've noticed your effort. You probably waxed poetic about something to do with magic or cooking when you rooked Billy into helping in the kitchen, but I know you were just trying to connect with us. Hell, for Sam being the introvert, I think he has more friends than you! Your closest friends were stuck underground with you for two decades while the other two are a living glob of Jell-O and an inanimate object that sometimes talks back."

Fievil sent a flash of a mole mimicking a courtly bow while flicking her off behind his back. That was when I lost it. Laughter bubbled up and I just let it rise to the surface. I actually had to squirm my way away from the edge so as not to fall in the water as I fought to breathe. Daniela let out a handful of polite chuckles, but she didn't say anything for the whole minute it took me to pull myself together.

"Sorry, sorry. Let's just say that Fievil doesn't appreciate being called an inanimate object and leave it at that," I said, coughing to clear my throat.

"Good. You tell that anime-proportioned facsimile of a weapon that if it's got something to say, it can say it to my face,"

Daniela replied evenly, twirling her hand as if dismissing it all together. The axe hammer vibrated on my back in response.

"I think you two would get along gre—"

Vibrosense blared as something struck the bridge. It wasn't unusual. Fish and debris passed it by at all hours of the day. There were hardly any times when it *wasn't* lit up along the entire length of it. However, the impact had to have been significant enough for my senses to pick it up even after I'd pushed them into the back of my mind. I waited, tense, for a second to see if there was anything ready to jump at us. When nothing happened for a full minute, I got to my feet, frowning at the water.

"What hap— Look out!" Daniela cut herself off as she pulled me out of the way in an instant. A gray streak flopped past, arcing over the bridge before it returned to the water. Its description almost burned through my retinas as it sailed by us.

<Atlantic Sturgeon Fry>

<Attunement: Water>

<Refinement: School>

<Perceived Metier Quotient: 2>

"What kind of refinement is 'School'?" I asked out loud before the information had a chance to click. A shiver ran down my spine. That was when Daniela yanked me back out of the way of another flying sturgeon and the bridge started to light up with ripples as things brushed against the supports.

"Sam! We need an assist on the bridge!" Danny called through the comm-plant. I watched the river as a trio of sturgeon surged out of the water like scaly bullets. The water let out a barely audible *pop* as they broke the surface, indicating something else was going on beneath the surface. Two flew wide while I smacked the third out of the air and onto the bridge. It flopped, practically glaring at me with its beady little eyes, before Daniela planted a dagger in the creature's brain.

"I'm coming! Lucius was working on the road so he should be—" Sam was cut off.

"OhGodOhGodOhGod—" The voice of the dwarf in

question joined the conversation as he broadcasted to everyone within range. "They are squirming onto shore!"

Something thumped against the bridge, causing me to wobble even as Daniela remained stable. I shared a look with her before pointing back towards shore. "Go! I'll catch up!"

The brunette hesitated for a second before nodding and blasting her way south. Her <Heat Touch> and <Flare Cloak> sprung up around her to leave her steps as light as a leaf on the wind. By comparison, I was a bull in a china shop, but I leveraged my strength for big strides instead. Or I would have, if I hadn't been thrown up in the air when the bridge beneath my feet bucked.

The water beneath the bridge roiled angrily and my implant highlighted at least a dozen sturgeons before my mind realized I was out over the water. *Nope! That's a big nope! <Stone Spike>!*

A whole section of the bridge molded like plasticine, reaching out over the water to catch me. One of my ribs creaked in protest, but my traits held me together.Before the spike had a chance to react to my weight, I clambered back over the low wall and to semi-firm ground. A pair of sturgeon sailed over me as I tried to catch my breath. An arch of river water had punched a gaping hole through the bridge deck before breaking apart in the wind.

The attack slowly drizzled its contents over the smoothed stone as I cast <Earth Shell> to armor me completely. My shield was back at the base, and I felt its absence sharply as I punched and cleaved Sturgeons that surged out of the river to attack me. They were inconsequential in low numbers, but their refinement gave me a clue as to just what was going on below the surface of the river and possibly at the shore. Even with that worry nagging at the back of my mind, whatever had broken the bridge was the true threat, and I was already down a third of my mana.

"Come on!" I yelled at the river, stomping my foot down as hard as I could. I'd never taunted nature before, but I was hoping that whatever creature was lurking out there would stop probing me and get the attack on its way.

It was all too happy to comply.

A massive gray form streaked with cobalt blue rose out of the water to my left on a column of frothing foam. Along with its super-sized flat head, a half-dozen whiskers waved in the air as they seemed to manipulate the tendrils of water that curled around the creature. The blue boney plates along its back and sides pulsed with an inner light that was dim compared to the fog lights that were its eyes. The whole creature was easily the size of a bus. It was glaring at me.

<Mature Atlantic Sturgeon>

<Attunement: Water>

<Refinement: Spawn>

<Perceived Metier Quotient: 6>

"Oh mother—" One of the tendrils of water swelled in size before coming straight for where I stood on the bridge.

CHAPTER FORTY-TWO

Water Under the Bridge

I rolled to the side while flaring <Earth Shell> to add a helmet to my stony armor ensemble just in time to hit the lip of the bridge. The water tendril sent spiderweb cracks through the bridge deck before delivering a metric ton of murky river water to the bridge deck. I slipped and slid another five feet along the barrier wall before the attack ran out of juice. *Boy, am I glad we installed these, but we should add some drainage options.* I slapped my mind into focus enough to cast <Mineral Strike>. A hunk of olivine coalesced.

Before it had a chance to fully form, I peeked over the edge of the railing to see that the humongo sturgeon was dead set on dropping another ton of water in the hopes of crushing me. The shimmering emerald mineral flew through the air and struck near the creature's snout. The hunk fragmented, embedding itself on the creature's face and severing one of the four whiskers. The creature let out a series of weird gasps as it thrashed back below the water, taking its magic water tentacles with it. A dark bloodstain in the water was quickly diluted by the smaller sturgeon thrashing below me.

"I've got a Q6er here! I could use some range attacks," I called through the comm-plant.

"Busy! There must be hundreds on the shore!" Daniela yelled back.

"Blobby is on his way to you, Ron!" Sam added. "Back up, future sushi!"

"I don't know how to cook that, Samuel!"

"Focus!" Robert yelled over the call; the hint of desperation was clear in his voice. I was concerned that Lucius hadn't said anything since he encountered the creatures on the shore.

While the others talked, I kept an eye on the water and a mental hand on <Mineral Strike> just in case the creature reappeared. I knew for a fact that it would take more than a lucky <Mineral Strike> to kill the creature, and I had no idea what a natural beast at the Corporeal threshold would be capable of. As if seeking to answer my question, a whole slew of those bubble pops filled the air and a barrage of spinning sturgeon shot towards me.

I ducked behind the barrier wall to dodge the first few fish, only to have the follow up ones drill through the thin barriers. It sounded like a grenade going off as I put my arms in front of my face to protect my eyes from the stone spray. They were already stinging from the water and blood the first wave of sturgeons had thrown my way. Somehow the pair of sturgeons that had managed to break the barrier were still alive after their impact. Their information bloomed in my vision, mildly explaining the extra oomph behind the new fish.

<Atlantic Sturgeon Fry>
<Attunement: Water>
<Refinement: Torpedo>
<Perceived Metier Quotient: 3>

Not waiting for the creatures to pull some other nonsense, I released Fievil off my back and dove while swinging. The shift in weight of Ballast proved essential as my awkward swing had barely any power behind it. As it was, the weight of the weapon was enough to tenderize one of the torpedo sturgeons with the crystal spikes and send the other careening off the bridge. A handful more of the creatures collided against the bridge, but none were able to time their collisions enough to break through the stone. Their damage, however, started to build up quickly.

The new creatures weren't the only problem, however. Vibro lit up beneath me as something collided against the pillars below me. One and then the second crumbled. The bridge deck dipped, the already cracked portions straining as they lost their support. The very pillars that were secured to it added weight the deck could barely hold alone. *That's the momma!*

Without much thought, and taking a torpedoing sturgeon to the shoulder for my efforts, I lobbed another <Mineral Strike> into the water. A plume of water sprayed up as the skill dropped out of view. Bubbles fizzled below the surface and I saw another cloud of blood rise to the surface, accompanied by the bodies of two of the smaller sturgeons. No other pillars fell, but I was even less convinced that the mineral fragments had done enough damage below water.

I shuffled away from the cracked portion of the bridge and further towards land, even as I bobbed and weaved under the regular sturgeons and the torpedo ones. My Slurry Ichor patched up my armor where the torpedo fish had cut all the way to the skin, but the limb was tender. I glanced at my mana and grimaced.

Mana: 56%

I cursed my low refinement attribute as I felt the bridge shake under me. Ripples of force traveled through it as the mother sturgeon destroyed another of the pillars, causing that whole section of bridge to sink into the river. Had I not moved away, I would have been plopping into the water along with it. I watched as a handful of sturgeon ate what had to be almost a thousand pounds of compressed earth. Even if they weren't crushed by the stone, the impact would have rocked their little fishy brains in the water. A crazy plan started to crystallize in my head. Of course, as I tried to move forward, that was when yet *another* subspecies of the sturgeon made its appearance in my way.

Waving limbs of water pulled the creatures up the broken section of the bridge. They were like miniature versions of the mother, but that didn't inspire much confidence. I was almost sure that they were the ones coordinating the assault on the shore. The thought that fish were coordinating anything was scary enough.

<Atlantic Sturgeon Fry>

<Attunement: Water>

<Refinement: Spawn>

<Perceived Metier Quotient: 3>

A quintet of spawners pushed forward as more of the wannabe flying fish tried to catch me off guard from the river. Then the whips of water joined the fight. Like boneless grasping hands, each of the sturgeons used their extra-long whiskers and mana tentacles to try to pin me down enough for their torpedo relatives to punch my ticket. Other than backing up, I didn't have an immediate response to the increasingly bleak odds, plan or no plan.

Fievil triggered his mana bubble and the whips of water turned a shade darker, slowing down in the process. The spawners did *not* like that. They formed shorter, stubbier tentacles of mana and shuffled forward like scaly centipedes. The sudden boost in speed left me on the defensive as I batted the attacks with Fievil and dodged the whips of mana as best I could. A torpedo sturgeon clipped my helm, dropping me back. Ripples emanating from my head sent waves of nausea as my Harmonic Sinews were overwhelmed, but I shut the sensory input down as much as I could.

A growl mixed with bile escaped my throat. *Fine! I'll figure out some other way to kill your parent!*

No longer holding back on my skills, I let the spell chain for <Mineral Strike> form in my hand. A very situationally appropriate hunk of unrefined beryl coalesced. I rolled the crystal forward while dragging myself back. Trusting my balance while I had my bell rung was a sketchy proposition.

One of the spawners tried to grab hold of the magic attack as if it was familiar, but thankfully the beryl fragmented the moment the foreign, mana-forged limb came in contact with it. Sky blue shards of rock downed the two closest creatures and peppered the other three. Their tentacles lost most of their cohesion, causing the sturgeon to flop to the ground like the fish out of water they were. I didn't squander the opening. Fievil tenderized one of the injured ones and I lopped the tail off a second with the backswing. Before I could get to the final one, my feet slipped on the slimy gore of the four dead creatures.

I locked eyes to beady orbs with the last creature as I got a <Stone Spike> ready to fire. It would eradicate any chances of the plan I was forming from coming to fruition even after the <Mineral Strike>, but the fish's glare told me it was out for blood. Before I could yank on the lever for my skill, a lime green blur rolled past me. Fragments of stone formed a cleat around an appendage that pancaked the spawner to the ground.

"Blobby!" I grunted, grimacing as I lost my feet again. "You glorious slimy bastard!"

The slime rolled back towards me, leaving a trail of clean stone as he passed. I didn't miss the addition of the blood to his gelatinous bulk, but I didn't question it. The slime had come at the perfect time.

"I'm going to need you to cover me from the fish while I draw the Q6er," I said, voice picking up speed as I slapped a school sturgeon out of the air. The concussed fish landed right on Blobby, but the slime was unperturbed as it immediately started to digest the creature. Neither did Blobby react to my request, but I knew it had heard me.

I suppressed a shudder as I tried to calm the thump of my heart; it wouldn't do to tunnel vision when I needed to be aware of everything that was going on. A trickle of short orders and directions finally reached me through the comm-plant, but they were focused on whatever was happening on the banks. There wouldn't be back-up.

"How do I get the mother to surface aga—" I ducked as another sturgeon flipped out of the water. It was pointless; Blobby was on the task. The slime formed that strange cleat appendage and punted the fish back in the water. I did notice a part of its lower body formed some ridged stone that seemed to grip the bridge deck, but otherwise the gelatinous creature was undisturbed. "Right, I've got a second to think."

Every few seconds, a sturgeon would try to leap over the bridge to attack, but Blobby halted their attempts. The torpedo sturgeons were able to avoid getting punted, but my slime companion instead opted to deflect them up and over. I shook my head as I looked at what I had available. Obviously my magic, but I would need that to do the finishing touches on my plan. There was rubble from where the barrier had broken and some rock chunks from when the mother sturgeon had blown a hole in the deck.

Stop thinking of rocks! If you throw one in the water to try to draw her out, she's liable to move away because she thinks it might explode like <Mineral Strike>. My eyes flitted from mud to rocks to Blobby until they finally locked on the final resource. A resource that the Q6er had provided itself.

"Never made sashimi before, but I think I can manage some chum," I mumbled to myself as I hefted Fievil's axe head.

The shard sent me a flash of irritation and holding his nose against the stench, but the weapon didn't have much choice in the matter. I turned the spawners into convenient filets before pulping them closer to the edge. Blobby snuck a little snack, but considering how helpful he was being, he could have taken a whole 'nother of the sturgeons if he wanted.

Turning to the side away from the smell, I took a deep breath before I started to lob fish bits into the water. I had been on the edge of my metaphorical seat for the plan to work, but the response was immediate. A roiling mass of sturgeon surged up out of the water. The fish lost their collective minds to get at a piece of their fellows, and I quickly realized that the handful of fish I'd killed earlier had been disposed of as quickly as the chum was being gobbled up. Whatever direction the mother and the other spawners provided had folded under their base instincts.

A dark shadow beneath the surface told me I'd gotten the attention of my target.

"Yeah. Come get some, you freak of nature. You know you want some," I whispered as I pushed more and more of the guts out. The sturgeon started to frenzy and a massive fin broke the surface. <*Mineral Strike*>.

The skill broke against the large creature's back, drawing its attention back above the surface. Its beady eyes glared as foam rose up to bring the creature to eye level less than twenty feet away from me.

"You got something to say!" I taunted the fish, ducking as Blobby swatted another sturgeon from the air. "Send more and I'll return them in pieces!"

It was almost guaranteed that the mother sturgeon had no idea what I was saying, but there was a chilling amount of intelligence in its eyes. The massive clubs of water started to form out of the river water even as she dove beneath the surface. *Didn't know it could do that without looking...*

"Dodge, Blobby!" I yelled as one of the limbs smashed down on the bridge again faster than I could have expected. Slick with gore, it was even harder to keep a grip on the deck. My handy slime companion was also countered completely as he was easily washed away.

I hadn't expected the mother sturgeon to separate us with its attack, but I had to focus on capitalizing. Mainly because the oversized fish started to follow my plan to the T before I had a chance to get in position. A thump reverberated through the floor as the sturgeon slammed against one of the pillars.

"Give me a damn second!" I complained, slapping a palm against the bridge deck to get a better picture of the structure. One of the four pillars of the section I was on was cracked at the base, but the others still held the structure in place. A breath later, a huge ripple flowed through the structure. My vibrosense would have rattled me almost as much as a blow to the head if I hadn't been bracing for it, but as it was, I let the ripple of seismic information flow to me before confirming that the sturgeon had collapsed another one. *It's time.*

Pulling on every bit of control I could, I cast <Mudpit> around the pillars. The softened joint between the columns and the deck yielded the moment the sturgeon's attack followed up. The ground gave way, pitching me to the side as it fell towards the first set of broken pillars. *No! Not that way!* I had to think quickly or the mother sturgeon would just swim away.

"<Terrasheath>!" It wasn't my original plan, but if it didn't work, I was going to end up in the drink with a bus-sized creature perfectly capable of drowning me with a thought. Desperation more than will drove the skill to trigger not on me or on Fievil but on the hunk of bridge deck I was riding down to the water. The ten-foot drop to the water rattled me. The halo of sand manifested in the air around me before surging downward the moment the deck slapped down on the water.

I couldn't see what happened, but the sand entered the river with a hiss. That was all the warning I got before I got put on a level playing field with the sturgeon I'd been batting away. A torpedo subspecies punched straight into my gut, sending spiderweb cracks through my armor. Another of the school subspecies swam right up to me to sucker onto my leg. Its whiskers formed a death grip around my calf as the deck started to sink below the water. I was barely able to put Fievil between me and the next torpedo fish that struck, pushing me back against the far barrier.

Out of instinct, I slapped at the creature weighing me down to try to pry it off. <Terrasheath> took that personally. The second swill of sand blasted the creature at point blank range. All I was left with was a fish head attached to my leg and a bunch of muddy chum around my feet. It was said muddy chum that saved me from the second wave of fish that zeroed in on *it* rather than *me*.

The water was up to my waist and I risked releasing my <Earth Shell> from my arms and legs as I felt the river's current starting to press me against the barrier wall. That was when the mother sturgeon had had enough. The bus-sized creature breached the water like a whale, tipping the broken section of the bridge back. A handful of smaller sturgeon flopped past me as I held onto Fievil and the barrier wall with all I had.

The last thing I saw before plunging below the water was the mother sturgeon looking mighty displeased. Several of the large bone plates along its back oozed blood as if they'd been ripped clean off, and there was a stretch of skin running from its mouth to its gills across an eye that had been descaled by what I could only assume was <Terrasheath>.

It's not enough. That thought echoed in my head over and over as I saw the broken bridge deck start to drift toward me. *All or nothing, Ronan.*Mana swirled around me as I focused on the broken bridge deck and where I'd last seen the mother sturgeon. It had been only a few seconds since I'd been holding my breath beneath the surface but I prayed that the creature had continued rampaging in the same spot.

<Stone Spike>!

The center of the bridge deck dipped as stone was drawn away from it. *More!* I sent Fievil a mental yank and the shard opened up the gates on its caramel mana. The entire fragmented section of the bridge turned into a lance of stone. I watched with morbid fascination as my spike *widened* where it had impaled the sturgeon. Blood gushed from the wound, muddying any further sight of the battle as the river started to pull on me. *That fish better be dead.*

Before I could think many more coherent thoughts, my body shook as the skill finally sent mana side effects wracking through my body. The weak kicking I was using to keep myself from sinking turned into spasms as my muscles lost any semblance of coordination. I nearly took a breath as my chest compressed around the numerous wounds I'd taken during the fight. A blinking notification drew my attention as I tried to wrest back control of my body.

Health: 43% (Asphyxia)

I watched in horror as my health ticked down another percent and the edges of my vision started to grow dark. Silhouettes blurred past me as I sunk deeper. One of them collided with me and the light of the afternoon sun trickling in from above spun out of view. Panic rose, my health dropped, and the dark crept closer.

As the stray thought crossed my mind, the urge to inhale continued to claw its way up my throat. Copying the trick I'd learned at the obstacle course, I willed my Slurry Ichor to clench tight around my throat. The sludge I had for blood complied, essentially choking me for the sake of not drowning. I wasn't sure which alternative was worse as the black took over all but a speck of my sight. An eerie green glow from some strange plant or another trickled through my eyes as I reached what had to be the bottom of the river.

Stay safe, guys... Frantic flashes of an anthropomorphized mole shaking me awake were the last thing I saw before I fell unconscious. The corner of my mouth quirked up before the world faded.

CHAPTER FORTY-THREE

The Other Shore

A glowing green goop popped off my face like a suction cup. A small torrent of water erupted from my throat as the suction force broke the seal I'd used my blood to make. The surge of bloody water I'd inhaled while unconscious was followed by a raspy cough that set every muscle in my body tingling. The green goop approached my face like a looming cloud of acid but I managed to swat it away.

The goop quivered with excitement and I realized my body was quivering too. It was only then that the peculiar lime green color of the goop triggered my oxygen deprived brain. *Blobby*!?

Even while coughing out a lung, I forced my eyes open wider. The answers came quick after that. Somehow my gelatinous companion had turned itself into an inner tube. Blobby was easily twice its usual size but almost looked washed out. Beyond that, a tiny slime appendage had been working to resuscitate me and get me some air as the bulk of the creature held my shoulders out of the water by the armpits.

As for where we were, I had no idea. I opened my status and cringed when I saw my health in the twenties. Pushing past that, I focused on the LPS and pulled up the map with my location.

Another grimace twisted my face. I'd drifted almost two miles downriver in the process of Blobby rescuing me.

"How did you rescue me, Blobby?" I asked the slime. My voice was two jagged stones grinding against each other in an attempt to make sound. My Slurry Ichor had definitely done a number on me, but I didn't want to think of the alternative.

The slime actually seemed excited to showcase its prowess. Some of the swollen bulk of my companion deflated and I sank lower in the water. The appendage that had saved my life dipped into the water before it split in two, flattened then compressed into stone. To my utter astonishment, the slime then proceeded to turn its body into a trolling motor.

"You magnificent bastard." I chuckled, which prompted a new slew of hacking and coughing. The slime didn't form a new appendage, apparently needing its full body to operate in pseudo-boat mode, but it clenched gently around me before focusing on moving against the current.

Progress was torturously slow, but I felt much better about the whole situation with access to oxygen. No creatures even bothered us. I could deal with a sunburn and a little waiting in exchange for being rescued.

Regardless, I didn't have to wait long before the sounds of a Latina blasting her way through the forest reached my ears. I'd been so out of it, I hadn't even been thinking to check my comm-plant, but with her appearance I focused on her name in the communication section of my status. Not having to use my throat definitely helped speak more coherently.

"I'm safe. I'm in the water close to you. Just heard you explode something."

"Ronan! Oh my God, are you okay!?" Daniela's breathless voice followed through the communication.

"I've been better, but I'll make it," I replied, sighing.

"I'm coming, stay right there!"

"Can't really go anywhere. Pretty sure I tore at least all my muscles, and Blobby is keeping me afloat."

"Blobby? Never mind. I'm coming!"

I chuckled at her surprise, closing my eyes, and dipping into a half sleep to the light slapping sound of Blobby's river propulsion.

— + —

To say the break week was much of a break was a total lie. The part of the fight I'd missed had been just as pitched as my own, with the entire area around the bridge landing reshaped thanks to magic. Lucius had been able to get Sam and the two Beast Tamers that had stayed back up in the air thanks to an ability similar to my <Earthen Barrier>. The dwarf, with the help of the two oxen, Robert, Jillian, as well as Jolene and Billy, had then kept the tide of land squirming sturgeon that tried to get at the humans at bay until The Torch arrived.

Daniela had then proceeded to flash fry the bulk of the school sturgeon while Sam and the Tamers kept her healed up. From what I understood, Jolene had tried to assist a number of times but had been relegated to support; her attunement and spread of skills was more in line with single-target combat than a crowd. Regardless, their efforts gave Lucius enough time to form some makeshift ditches to slow the approach of the creatures enough that they dispersed the moment I offed their Q6 support. And thankfully, I *had* succeeded.

As soon as I was back to some decent health and capable of casting <Corporeal Infusion>, Jolene dove into the water, along with a rope courtesy of Samuel, to retrieve our first set of Corporeal-level infusion and material. The glowing bead of blue Pith was a sight to behold, but the boney scale left my crafting hands itching to work.

Apart from the physical gains, the Pith that surged through me was also enough to attune two of the nearby trees as I stripped it of all Dreg. I'd stared at my status for a long time, realizing I really needed to start applying the energy to my traits. I didn't know if a new trait would form at the 100%

mark, but I didn't want to risk pulling further away from my goal of leveling up.

Beyond that, we also discovered that there was a point at which a creature could be too badly damaged in death to trigger the dissociation process. The dozens of sturgeon the group at the base had defeated were in various states of char-broiled black, half-eaten, or pulped; the Pith gain from those creatures had been disappointingly negligible.

Nonetheless, I was determined to make the best of the situation. No one in the expedition, including myself, had died in the attack, and the waves of leaping fish that had been plaguing our construction work had all but vanished along with the mother sturgeon. Clearly there had been a connection there.

So, I was on utterly light duty while Sam helped to purge the clots my own blood had made around my neck along with a dozen other smaller injuries that seemed to take a surprising amount of time to heal. The blond had some theories as to why that was, but he merely mumbled to himself as he returned to his vegetable garden to think.

Even on light duty, me and Lucius were able to repair most of the damage to the structure of the bridge that remained. Instead of trying to make further progress, we doubled down even more on the segments where the water grew deeper. Lucius added a tar-like resin he was able to produce to the deck in the hopes of helping it maintain structural integrity while under attack. It also helped that it made the ground grippy when he mixed it with a sand Gift he'd already possessed. As for me, I raised the barrier wall over three feet higher on each side. For the sake of ventilation and drainage, I added small holes along the barrier walls at chest level and at foot level; getting swept away because the water had nowhere to go was an experience I hoped not to replicate. The overall effort was pretty rough with just the two of us, but after the fight with the sturgeons, we were tapped out on dealing with jumping fish crashing into our bridge.

And so, it was eight days after they left that the rest of the expedition returned. Unsurprisingly, the first day was spent explaining just what the heck happened as well as unloading a new set of supplies for the river base. After that, the group that had missed out on the action was more than raring to go.

The Wild Fists hunted the small patch of forest on the south side of the river to near extinction before they recruited Sue to build them training dummies that could withstand attacks from their full Q6 squad. Two of them were posted at the bridge at all times while we worked, and one of them was always on watch even during the day. It felt a bit like overkill, but it wasn't hard to see how upset leaving the quarter-strength expedition to endure had made them.

The Shapers and I turned the bridge building process into a science. On top of our familiarity with the construction process, the newly unlocked skills Patrick, Francis, and Sue had worked wonders at speeding up our compression process. I wanted to halt everything and really dig in to the various ways in which earth mana worked while I had the spread of abilities of the Stoneshapers close at hand, but the closer we got to the opposite bank, the more we wanted to finish.

Days got longer and rest margins tighter, but even with the additions and further bits of reinforcement, the north shore was one last deck section away at the end of the fifth week of the project.

"Normally, when you build something, maybe you deal with some overhead hazards, or maybe traffic concerns. Possibly some supply issues. But nooo~. In the apocalypse, you've got to account for the giant bugs, and the monster fishy. I suppose those could be considered overhead hazards... Those smaller sturgeons really jumped high," I grumbled to myself. Fievil, for once, seemed to agree and sent a flash of a mole strangling a cartoony sturgeon.

"True. What I'm more concerned about is where Devon and Dai are," Daniela said. I could practically hear her grinding her teeth in frustration from her perch on the barrier wall.

Danny had picked herself as the 'guard' of the construction

crew over the last week when there had been neither hide nor hair from either of the scouts. It had taken an act of God— Samuel and the Beast Tamers binding her physically on more than one occasion—after I was forced to stop her the first time. Eventually she'd agreed to follow after the two once we'd arrived on the other side of the river and hunkered down. She was the only scout-abled person out of our very much bull-dozing expedition.

Technically, Billy fit the bill to join her as a scouting partner, but Daniela was adamant the youth wasn't ready to head out on his own. I also agreed with her, but she was the most vocal about it and the first to point out he was still working on getting his Djinn Limb trait, as it had come to be called—and then subsequently edited by the Entities on his status—under control.

"We just need to finish the bridge and the landing, then we'll head out, Ms. Vega," Patrick said, seamlessly joining the conversation. "I'm as worried about their safety as you. Devon has pulled my beard out of the oven more than once."

"No time like the present then," I said, turning to PatPat. "Francis ready yet?"

Patrick nodded, hooking his thumb over his shoulder at the shore behind him. "Yes. The landing will take some more effort, but you should be more than able to start the defensive wall while we work on the rest."

"Let's do it."

With practiced ease, and especially without needing to accommodate for creating four thirty-foot pillars per new section of bridge, Francis glared at the ground in front of us. He simultaneously cast his skill four times, dumping his entire mana pool, for the sake of being flashy and raising all of the supports at the same time. I approved. With just as much flair, even going so far as to circumvent the efficiency of casting through Fievil, I pushed forward with both hands. Mana flowed through me and into my helm. The piece of armor, and my shield, were going to be permanent staples on my person so long as I could help it. Even if it was to amble over to my friend for emotional support and a heart-to-heart.

"<Earth Wall>!"

The spell chain took its due to form and adjust to the requirements. It bloomed from the existing deck, drawing on the material blueprint for form, before speeding forward. It cleared Francis' pillars by inches before plowing into the sandy shore with as much force as I could muster. The sound of my skill touching down on solid ground was a melody to my ears; the others seemed to agree. A cheer went up, and even though the rest of the expedition wasn't present, they sent their congratulations via the comm-plant group conversation.

As happy as we were to be done with the building process, there were still many, many things to work on and the celebration was short. PatPat and the Shapers got to work connecting the last set of pillars and reinforcing the landing. Daniela disappeared, after getting a contingent of my trusty slime friend to make sure she didn't run off, to clear any beastie bold enough to try to attack us at the new bridge landing. I didn't waste time and hefted Fievil to start a long session of casting <Earth Wall> in a full circle around the landing area. With Daniela roaming the woods, I focused on the river side; there wouldn't be any easy beach landings on either side of our bridge.

By the second day, I'd finished a primary wall and we'd set up a small observation tower with an animal pen identical to the one at the river base. The Beast Tamers had come across the bridge to mark the first official wagon crossing to some additional cheering from the whole expedition that had accompanied them. She didn't interfere with the joyous reaction, but I didn't miss the Torch burning up on the observation tower.

— + —

"—est... Test...Test..." a message droned through the comm-plant, blasting as wide as it would reach.

I frowned, noticing that I was the furthest from the others.

Daniela was perched on the observation tower and the Shapers were making some minor detailing on the bridge, neither the wiser. I was working on raising the walls of the north landing higher when the strange message pinged on my status. The moment my eyes identified the source, I immediately opened my comm-plant.

"Devon! Are you all okay? Where's Dai?"

"Ronan? Just my luck. We hit a bit of a complication," the man panted through the connection. "I could use some help though."

Without him needing to say anything else, I sent a message to Daniela. The woman's reaction was instantaneous. A <Flame Blast> that had to be massively empowered *demolished* the small barrier around the top of the tower before she flew in the direction I'd pointed. I knew for a fact she couldn't keep her flight powered long, but the acceleration she was capable of left me speechless. The red-orange blur that was my friend quickly shot out of sight, leaving a smoldering hole in the canopy.

The first layer of help dispatched, I found Sam's contact and updated him as well as Igor. Before I had time to finish, the Wild Fists, the other half of the Bunker Busters, and two of the Beast Tamers were on their way to the north landing. Surprisingly, the Tamers, sans wagons, were the first to arrive. Their oxen put the bridge to the test as they thundered down the deck with their satyr riders bound on their backs. They were closely followed by Igor and one of the Wild Fists called Elva. The lizardwoman had turned into a superhero character from a kids movie I'd seen long ago as she spread ice in front of her before skating on it with her scaled feet.

Behind them was most of the expedition rushing forward in the closest thing to an excited mob that I'd ever seen. Billy led the group, but I wasn't sure if the youth was speedy or if he just feared for his life. It certainly looked like the short-legged Hilda wanted to run him down.

Regardless of the order of their arrival, they were all at the north landing before Daniela and Devon were anywhere close.

Despite the severity of the situation, I couldn't help but let out a chuckle as Daniela burst into the walled space with her elf boy toy carried like a princess. When he got close enough that I could see the extent of his injuries, the smile was wiped from my face and I dropped down from the wall.

"Here, set him down inside the tower," Sam said, still a little winded from his dash across the bridge. Samuel and the Tamers had already crafted more beds for the north landing tower and Daniela set him down with ease.

A burning line had seared a line down the side of Devon's irritatingly long hair. The parts of his hair that had survived curled in on themselves. *A fire attack.* One of his arms was still shivering, and I could see a slight mist of steam rising from his clothes where Daniela's passive heat must have melted some water. *A water attack.* Beyond those two magic remnants, there was a quartet of cuts along his back that had to have come from a bladed weapon or an edged attack. The lack of injuries on the front of his body spoke volumes of how he'd acquired them, but the variety left a bitter taste in my mouth. *He was running away from a very determined group of somethings.*

"Igor, leave Fowler and get the rest of the Fists watching beyond the walls. Patrick, get the walls built up and reinforced. Yesterday, if you would. Veronica, get your Tamers and clear two hundred feet out from them. I don't care if you need to fight an attuned tree or demolish a ruin. Get Igor to help," I said, turning away from where Sam was gently feeding healing into Devon while prodding him with his nerve filaments. Daniela hadn't reacted to my words; the elf's hand was held firmly in hers.

"What's going on?" Patrick asked. His eyes flicked between Veronica, who looked equally as confused, and Igor who'd rushed out of the small building and up on the wall before I could reply.

"*Something* was chasing Devon and I don't want that something sneaking up on us. I've got vibro running as loud as I can, but that only serves us if something lands in the base. I'll go up on the tower and keep watch; my perception should be one of the highest."

The two still looked somewhat confused at the sudden orders, but when I strode out of the tower and up the three-story vine ladder hanging from the side, they jumped to it. I frowned as I overlooked the Beast Tamers and the Wild Fist patrolling the area just outside the wall.

Three hours ticked by before Sam called me down. Veronica and her team were still working in tandem with their beasts, but the Stoneshapers were slumped on the ground recovering their mana. When I entered the room, Devon was still laid out on his chest, but his shirt had been trashed. Four vivid scabs lined his back and a purple-shaded bruise was visibly healing on the arm where I'd spotted the traces of water magic. The hair on the side of his head had been cut back and laid in the same pile as the ruined clothes.

"Is he gonna be alright?" I asked, frowning from my position at the door.

"Scars are inevitable, but he shouldn't have any problems," Sam said. Fowler nodded in agreement, passing the blond a rag soaked in some red substance. The red fae turned behind him to screw the lid back on a mason jar filled with Sam's healing concoction. "He might have bled out if he hadn't smeared some of the healing paste on himself."

"Those bastards hit me so fast I couldn't even down it," Devon said, his voice muffled as he spoke into the woven bed.

"'Bastards'?" I asked, picking up the word choice and hoping it wasn't what I expected.

"Yes. Bastards. They were holding us hostage. Things in Ocala are a lot pricklier than we expected."

EPILOGUE

Sweat poured down Ponzio's back as he weaved his way through the forest to the south of the city. As hot as the day was, it wasn't because of the frantic pace he set for himself. His mind kept drifting back to the sight of the human comet plummeting into the canopy. That level of power screamed of danger. If he had his measure right, and he always had his measure right, then the group he'd discovered at the Ocala Torrent meant business. Out of all the Zebelos, him and Grandfather were the ones with the best senses for magic, even if neither had a lick of talent for trades work.

Pushing the stray thoughts from his mind, he focused as the tree cover started to dwindle. The elf activated his Lightning Blip ability just as he exited the woods into cultivated land. The terrain blurred past him as he turned into a living bolt of lightning flashing from cover to cover. He stopped each time to check for a tail, tuning his ears as widely as he could in search of any hidden observers. The Breakers didn't know he'd been the one to help the other pompous elf out of their clutches, and he wasn't about to be caught on the way back.

Farmland passed him by until he entered the trading block.

Buildings cobbled together from the old and the new rose up like stubborn pillars of humanity. The workers and hagglers of the Nash Family were going at it as usual, with the Zebelos crafters peddling their wares, totally unaware of the crap storm brewing. *Someone had built a bridge across the Torrent.* Just the implications that someone had put in the effort left him shaking his head.

He slowed his jog and tried to catch his breath after funneling most of his mana on escaping undetected. There was no sense in drawing undue attention with a brisk pace. He nodded at the handful of business owners closing up shop around the edges of the trading block. No one batted an eye at Ponzio. As a matter of fact, many of the owners affiliated with the Family tried to give him small gifts or sent regards to the Padre. They were always hoping to open up a more prestigious location closer to the Crystal, instead of having to risk it at the edge of its relative protection.

Excusing himself at every opportunity, Ponzio eventually made it into Zebelos territory proper. With practiced motions, he blended into the shadows and resumed his zipping, using the remaining power lines in the city to hide the flash of his power. He knew Grandfather had argued against their removal for parts in the hope of one day restoring the grid. It wasn't entirely altruistic, since it allowed him and the few other flash runners in his employ to move almost unimpeded through the city. With the path mostly clear, Ponzio dumped the rest of his mana and zipped straight to the warehouse that served as the main home of the Family.

A preprepared mattress awaited him as he ran out of mana and was ejected from the powerline. He laid there gasping for air until the slight creaking of a rocking chair overpowered the thrum of the blood in his veins.

"It has been some time since you arrived in this fashion, Ponziolino," a gravelly voice filled the air of the musty room.

"Grandfather!" Ponzio flipped with only the agility an elf

could muster and bowed toward the head of the Family. He did his best to master the bellows in his chest.

"Bah, no one's here but us. Tell me, what troubles you that I sensed your approach on the wire?"

"The strangers you sent me to watch. I… may have interceded on their behalf," Ponzio said, eyes still firmly planted on the ground.

"Oh? No offense, my boy, but I don't recall you ever having this level of initiative before."

"I believe I found their companions after tracing their steps and…Well, I don't think being on the receiving end will be a smart idea, Grandfather. When they found their friend after I assisted, their response was… overwhelming."

Radolfo Zebelos frowned at his grandson. There was a reason the boy was his favorite and it was simply because he had his head firmly placed on his shoulders. Filomena was reliable, but also liable to fly off the handle, and Otello… well, he was a boy after his own name. That Ponzio had rushed back said one thing, that he'd intervened showed another, and his choice of words put the nail on the coffin. Radolfo sat forward in his chair, light kindling within his eyes to stoke the fires of his mind. "Tell me what you know of the strangers and their companions."

ABOUT FRANK G. ALBELO

Frank is a Civil Engineer graduate who rediscovered his passion for writing. The twenty-something year old is happily married and has a toddler who is a cute, but huge, troublemaker. Originally born in Cuba, Frank moved to Costa Rica at a young age and then to Miami, Florida giving him a wonderfully diverse view of the world to draw on for the worlds he creates.

He has been writing stories since he was young and reading them way before that. He hopes to continue to write tales and create wondrous systems to share them with readers. Some of Frank's other hobbies include Magic the Gathering, video gaming, and bugging his wife about buying new bookshelves to accommodate the books that seem to magically appear in their home.

Connect with Frank G. Albelo:
Patreon.com/Falbelo
Facebook.com/FAlbeloWriter
Discord.gg/A6srSxk

ABOUT MOUNTAINDALE PRESS

Dakota and Danielle Krout, a husband and wife team, strive to create as well as publish excellent fantasy and science fiction novels. Self-publishing *The Divine Dungeon: Dungeon Born* in 2016 transformed their careers from Dakota's military and programming background and Danielle's Ph.D. in pharmacology to President and CEO, respectively, of a small press. Their goal is to share their success with other authors and provide captivating fiction to readers with the purpose of solidifying Mountaindale Press as the place 'Where Fantasy Transforms Reality.'

Connect with Mountaindale Press:
MountaindalePress.com
Facebook.com/MountaindalePress
Twitter.com/_Mountaindale
Instagram.com/MountaindalePress

MOUNTAINDALE PRESS TITLES
GameLit and LitRPG

The Completionist Chronicles,
The Divine Dungeon,
Full Murderhobo, and
Year of the Sword by Dakota Krout

Metier Apocalypse by Frank G. Albelo

Arcana Unlocked by Gregory Blackburn

A Touch of Power by Jay Boyce

Red Mage and
Farming Livia by Xander Boyce

Ether Collapse and
Ether Flows by Ryan DeBruyn

Dr. Druid by Maxwell Farmer

Bloodgames by Christian J. Gilliland

Unbound by Nicoli Gonnella

Threads of Fate by Michael Head

Lion's Lineage by Rohan Hublikar and Dakota Krout

Wolfman Warlock by James Hunter and Dakota Krout

Axe Druid,
Mephisto's Magic Online, and
High Table Hijinks by Christopher Johns

Skeleton in Space by Andries Louws

Dragon Core Chronicles by Lars Machmüller

Chronicles of Ethan by John L. Monk

Pixel Dust and
Necrotic Apocalypse by David Petrie

Viceroy's Pride by Cale Plamann

Henchman by Carl Stubblefield

Artorian's Archives by Dennis Vanderkerken and Dakota Krout

Vaudevillain by Alex Wolf

www.ingramcontent.com/pod-product-compliance
Lightning Source LLC
Chambersburg PA
CBHW030246270626
47156CB00020B/116

BIBLIOTHÈQUE
CHRÉTIENNE ET MORALE

APPROUVÉE

PAR MONSEIGNEUR L'ÉVÊQUE DE LIMOGES.

—

Tout exemplaire qui ne sera pas revêtu de notre griffe sera réputé contrefait, et poursuivi conformément aux lois.

Barbier frères

CAROLINE

CAROLINE

OU

LE MODÈLE DES JEUNES PERSONNES

LIMOGES.

BARBOU FRÈRES, IMPRIMEURS-LIBRAIRES.

CAROLINE.

I

Caroline Poulain du Bois-Anger, fille de M. Parc-Poulain, aussi recommandable par les qualités de son cœur que par ses talents, jurisconsulte célèbre, auteur d'ouvrages estimés sur la coutume de Bretagne, et de madame .Guillette-Françoise de la Mothe-Fablet, naquit à Rennes, le 19 février 1756, et fut baptisé le lendemain , dans l'église de Toussaint , paroisse de cette ville. Dès son berceau , deux maladies la conduisaient aux portes de la mort; mais Dieu veillait sur des jours qui devaient être consacrés à sa gloire. Elle trouva dans ses parents les principes et les exemples de toutes les vertus. Son enfance s'écoula sous les yeux d'une mère pieuse, qui prit le plus grand soin d'écarter loin d'elle tout ce qui était capable de blesser son innocence ; elle eut la consolation d'éprouver dès-lors combien son zèle était agréable au Seigneur. Les caresses naïves, l'air aimable, le cœur tendre et compatissant de la petite Caroline , firent espérer qu'un jour elle ferait

les délices de sa famille, et qu'on la corrige-
rait aisément des légers défauts qu'on avait
à lui reprocher. Ceux auxquels son penchant
l'entraînait davantage étaient des moments
d'humeur assez fréquents, quelquefois de l'in -
docilité. Dès ses premières années, ou jugea
qu'elle serait une jeune personne accomplie:
avec tous les agréments que la nature peut
donner du côté de la figure, elle avait une
très-jolie voix, une manière agréable et naïve
d'exprimer sa pensée, les plus heureuses dispositions du côté de l'esprit et du cœur. La
vanité pouvait sans doute lui rendre ces présents dangereux ; mais la grâce les sanctifia,
en lui inspirant de généreux sacrifices.

Cependant elle laissait échapper des fautes qui semblaient être l'effet de sa vivacité ;

elle la portait assez souvent à des impatien-
ces : mais l'instant qui la voyait coupable la
voyait ordinairement touchée de ses torts,
et volant, pour les réparer, dans les bras de
ceux qui se trouvaient chargés de sa conduite, elle les priait, par les plus vives caresses et d'un air de candeur admirable, de la
corriger : « Grondez-moi, leur disait-elle avec
un courage au-dessus de son âge, reprenez-
moi, car je sens que je le mérite. » Puis
avec ce sourire ingénu qui savait si bien demander grâce, elle ajoutait : « Mais que ce
soit avec douceur. » Lorsqu'elle avait eu quelque accès d'humeur un peu considérable,
on la punissait en lui disant : « Allez, mademoiselle, je ne veux plus me mêler de
vous : je vous abandonne à vos défauts. —Ah!

répondait-elle aussitôt en versant des larmes, vous êtes obligés de veiller sur ma conduite; non , je ne crains pas que vous exécutiez cette menace ; la religion vous fait un devoir de me corriger. Les marques de tendresse qu'on lui refusait, lorsqu'elle avait donné des sujets de mécontentement, étaient pour son cœur les mortifications les plus pénibles. Elle eût mille fois préféré de dures péniten·ces à l'air de froideur et d'indifférence qu'on affectait de lui montrer: néanmoins l'humeur était sa passion dominante, et elle ne la réprimait toujours pas sur-le-champ. Un soir qu'elle avait commis une désobéissance, on lui fit grâce de la punition, pourvu qu'elle promît d'avouer que sa conduite était répréhensible : elle refusa ; mais bientôt le silence de la nuit fait naître en elle des réflexions salutaires ; elle se lève, court à sa gouvernante qui parut effrayée de la trouver en ce moment auprès d'elle, et elle lui dit avec empressement : « Conduisez-moi , je vous prie, à ma sœur ; je veux lui demander pardon. — Vous le ferez demain, lui répondit-on, retournez-vous coucher. » Cette réponse calme Caroline, elle se recouche, mais le souvenir d'avoir pu désobliger la tourmente encore, elle se lève une seconde fois de son lit, en disant d'un ton attendri : « Je ne puis dormir, ma sœur est fâchée contre moi. » D'aussi heureuses dispositions confirmèrent les espérances qu'on avait conçues : sa vivacité même annonçait le zèle ardent qui l'animerait dans le service de Dieu, dès qu'elle aurait acquis une solide vertu : L'obstination qu'elle faisait quelquefois paraître était presque toujours occasionée par le désir de soutenir ce qui lui paraissait juste ou vrai, mais elle se défendait avec un peu d'impatience, lorsqu'on n'adoptait pas sa façon de penser, surtout quand on ne l'en croyait pas sur sa parole. Dans ces occasions, et dans celles où l'on tenait à quelque opinion qui lui semblait fausse, elle disait avec autant de vivacité que de franchise : « Je n'aime point que l'on croie ce qui n'est pas vrai.

Cependant Caroline sut bientôt posséder sou âme en paix; lors même qu'elle éprouvait des combats intérieurs elle annonçait un calme parfait; peu démonstrative à l'é-

gard de ceux qu'elle ne connaissait qu'im-
parfaitement, elle avait un sourire simple et
ingénu qui la rendait aimable, toutes les
personnes qui l'approchaient ne pouvaient se
défendre de concevoir pour elle un tendre
attachement.

Avec un fond de générosité naturelle, elle
aimait à faire à ses amis de petits présents,
pour gagner de plus en plus leur bienveil-
lance, et savait user d'innocents artifices qui
lui réussissaient toujours. Ses sœurs étaient-
elles absentes, elle se livrait à mille légères
occupations qu'elle savait être de leur goût,
et jouissait d'avance de la satisfaction de les
surprendre agréablement à leur retour. Pénétrée de reconnaissance pour les services qu'on
lui rendait, et caressant les personnes aux-

quelles elle croyait avoir obligation : « Que je serais ingrate, disait-elle, si je ne vous aimais pas après tout ce que vous faites pour moi ! »

Son bon cœur ne s'épanchait jamais davantage qu'à l'égard de son père, pour qui nous retracerions difficilement la vivacité de ses sentiments et ses prévenances continuelles. Non-seulement elle ne lui désobéissait pas une seule fois, mais, cherchant en tout à lui plaire, étudiant ses goûts, saisissant les plus légères occasions de le contenter, elle sacrifiait volontiers, ou du moins remettait à un autre temps ses occupations, et même, par la suite, ses exercices de piété ou ses bonnes œuvres, quand elle croyait convenable de rester auprès de lui ou de l'accompagner à la promenade. Caroline se comporta ainsi toute sa vie, mais, dès sa première jeunesse, son amour filial éclata dans mille circonstances : un jour entre autres que son père badinait avec elle en se mettant à table, il se blessa la main ; à l'instant sa fille fondit en larmes, et ses pleurs coulèrent avec tant d'abondance, que M. du Parc-Poulain, vivement touché de cette marque de tendresse, ne put s'empêcher d'en verser aussi.

A peu près dans ces mêmes temps, la Providence lui procura pour confesseur un homme bien propre à lui inspirer l'amour de ses devoirs. Elle entra au premier monastère de Sainte-Marie de Rennes, pour assister aux instructions que les dames de cette communauté faisaient aux jeunes personnes sur les premières vérités de la religion, et particulièrement sur l'action importante à laquelle elle se disposait. Profondément émue de ce qu'elle voyait d'édifiant autour d'elle, elle ne fut pas longtemps sans donner des marques d'une piété tendre , et sans gagner par sa bonne conduite le cœur de ses compagnes et celui des religieuses qui veillaient à son éducation. Dans tout le temps qu'elle reçut leurs leçons, elle les reçut avec un esprit docile et soumis, un caractère prévenant et caressant. Le seul reproche qu'on pouvait lui faire était une sensibilité extrême qui, à la plus légère réprimande la faisait fondre en pleurs.

Après d'aussi favorables dispotions , l'ai ·

mable enfant tira les plus grands fruits des exemples et des conseils qu'on lui donnait. Plus elle approcha du jour de sa première communion, plus elle était pénétrée d'amour et de reconnaissance pour un Dieu qui consentait à l'honorer de sa présence ; chaque instant diminuait l'illusion qui l'avait séduite à son entrée dans le monde ; quoique si jeune encore, elle entrevoyait déjà le vide et l'ennui qui suivent ces amusements, elle s'affermissait dans cette façon de penser, et par assuidité aux exercices qui devaient la disposer au bonheur qu'on lui promettait, et par ses confessions fréquentes.

Ses fautes étaient assez légères pour la rassurer ; cependant elle ne s'en accusait qu'en versant un torrent de larmes. Après de si grandes marques de contrition, quelle dut être la vivacité de ses sentiments à la table sainte! la manière dont elle commença dès-lors, et continua depuis à se comporter, nous fait assez connaître de quelle abondance de grâces Dieu l'enrichit en se donnant à elle. Il descendait dans un cœur qui désirait, avec l'amour de l'Epouse des Cantiques, de s'unir à lui : il prenait possession d'une âme qui avait soupiré apres cette union, comme le cerf altéré soupire après les sources d'eau vive où il pourra étancher sa soif.

Dès qu'elle eut participé aux saints mystères, elle revint dans le sein de sa famille, très-différente de ce qu'elle était autrefois. Elle regretta beaucoup un séjour où elle avait commencé à éprouver combien le Sei-

gneur est doux , et ne quitta point ses compagnes sans que son cœur souffrît de cette
séparation. De retour au milieu du monde,
elle y observa à la lettre les règles de piété
auxquels elle s'était assujettie avant et après
l'action sainte qu'elle venait de faire · chaque jour elle augmenta sa ferveur par une
méditation d'un quart-d'heure sur les vérités
du christianisme, par une lecture de piété,
par le chapelet en l'honneur de celle qu'elle
aimait à nommer sa bonne mère, par le saint
sacrifice de la Messe auquel elle assistait
avec une dévotion exemplaire ; et l'après-
midi, par une visite au très-saint Sacrement,
exercices qui formaient un règlement con-
forme à son âge.

II

Les premières années de Caroline com-
blaient de joie ses parents : ils se flattaient
qu'après avoir si bien commencé, elle termi-
nerait avec une sainte ardeur l'ouvrage de
son salut. Cependant la vertu, dans les en-

fants, est comme une tendre fleur que le moindre souffle ternit. L'âge de douze ans auquel elle était à peine arrivée, la grande sensibilité de son caractère, auraient pu faire douter de sa persévérance, surtout si elle venait à éprouver ces dégoûts qui suivent quelquefois une ferveur naissante. La sienne fut véritablement attaquée par de violentes tentations, qui ne l'empêchèrent point de continuer ses exercices avec exactitude depuis sa première communion. Elle tira même de ces combats un avantage réel, adressant à Dieu, dans ses épreuves, des prières plus animées, où elle redoublait d'attention.

Dans le désir ardent et continuel de la félicité des saints, elle crut que la vie religieuse était pour elle le plus sûr moyen d'y parvenir, et elle souhaita beaucoup de l'embrasser. Son âge mettant pour le moment à ses vœux un obstacle invincible, elle s'en consola, en formant une société d'enfants remplis comme elle de piété. Il était juste que cette petite réunion d'enfants vertueux eût des constitutions particulières : l'obéissance à leurs parents, la charité, l'assiduité au travail, des prières conformes à leur situation, de légères pratiques de mortifications et d'humilité : voilà les points principaux des règles qu'elle établit. Dans ce temps, sa charité pour les pauvres s'étendit à tout ce que cette vertu inspire de plus généreux. Elle montra d'abord pour les domestiques beaucoup de compassion : attentive à prévenir leurs désirs, à excuser leurs fautes, elle se chargeait pour eux d'occupations difficiles, ennuyeuses ; et lorsqu'ils s'y opposaient : « J'aurais, disait-elle, beaucoup plus de peine à vous voir vous en occuper qu'à m'y livrer moi-même, et je vous assure que j'y trouve un plaisir très-sensible. » Loin de se montrer exigeante à leur égard, elle les servait de ses propres mains ; et, les aidant à tout ce qui n'était point au-dessus de ses forces, elle allait jusqu'à leur éviter les peines les plus légères.

C'était, sans doute, par cette tendresse de cœur qui se manifesta en elle dès sa première enfance, qu'elle était comme naturellement portée à désirer de faire toujours du bien : elle s'aperçut que cette sensibilité, pour devenir véritablement utile à son salut, devait être fondée sur un grand amour de Dieu, et exigeait, par conséqueut la réforme de ses moindres imperfections. Quoi qu'il pût lui coûter pour dompter le secret amour-propre qui, dans ses plus jeunes années, voulait qu'elle n'eût jamais tort, Caroline, par un effet de la grâce et de son courage, montra tout à coup une docilité parfaite ; toujours prête à soumettre sa façon de penser à celle des autres, elle savait deviner ce que ses parents pouvaient désirer d'elle ; les simples avertissements que son père lui donnait pour sa santé, étaient à ses yeux des ordres dont elle se serait fait un crime de s'écarter ; les conseils qu'elle recevait de sa famille, elle les observait avec la plus exacte fidélité.

Ce ne fut pas seulement à ses supérieurs, mais encore à ses égaux, mais à ses inférieurs même, lorsque par là elle ne risquait point de troubler l'ordre et de se compromettre, que, sans affectation, elle témoigna depuis une sorte d'obéissance dont on voit peu d'exemples. Cette vertu atteignit en elle un si haut degré, qu'on craignait de lui donner des avis , tant elle était prompte à les exécuter, pour peu qu'elle les crût raisonnables. Une demoiselle qui passa quelque temps avec elle, étonnée de voir qu'elle était soumise en tout, ne put s'empêcher de lui dire : « Mais Caroline, vous obéissez donc à tout le monde. — Autant que cela est juste, et qu'il est en moi, répondit-elle avec simplicité ; je suis la dernière de toutes. »

Elle approchait de sa quatorzième année, lorsque. pour s'affermir dans l'amour de ses devoirs, elle ajouta au règlement de vie qu'elle s'était tracé à sa première communion, de nouvelles résolutions; nous les proposons aux jeunes personnes, comme un plan de conduite dans lequel elles ne trouveront rien qui soit au-dessus de leurs forces; la promesse d'une prompte obéissance, de légères pratiques d'humilité, de mortification, le zèle pour secourir les pauvres, l'engagement d'aimer toujours le Seigneur, celui de ne se regarder dans un miroir que lorsqu'il est nécessaire, cet ensemble d'obligations n'est pas sans doute assez pénible pour qu'un enfant de douze ans ne puisse le pratiquer; et le dernier article, en particulier, n'est point un objet à négliger, puisqu'il suffit pour faire éviter une foule de fautes où l'on tombe souvent dans la jeunesse.

« Dès ses premières années, elle avait beaucoup d'aversion pour l'oisiveté; et ce qui contribuait à lui donner pour le travail une ardeur inexprimable , c'est qu'elle consacrait tous ses ouvrages au soulagement des pauvres, ou à l'ornement des autels, Un jour où elle s'était trouvée longtemps seule, on lui demanda si elle n'avait point éprouvé d'ennui : « Non, je vous assure, répondit-elle; je pensais que le bon Dieu me regardait travailler, et j'allais bien vite, bien vite, pour lui plaire davantage. »

Instruite de l'affection que la Mère de Dieu a pour tous les hommes, et surtout pour les enfants, elle l'honorait par une confiance sans bornes, et ce qui nous reste écrit de sa main nous en fournira la preuve. Saint Joseph, sainte Caroline, son ange gardien, avaient des droits particuliers à ses hommages ; cet ange tutélaire était à ses yeux un ami précieux qu'on ne saurait trop ménager, quoique cependant bien des chrétiens l'oublient souvent. Chaque jour Caroline le saluait en esprit, et lui rendait mille actions de grâces, ainsi qu'aux anges gardiens de tous ceux qui l'approchaient ; et dans les compagnies où la bienséance la conduisait, elle priait quelquefois ces esprits bienheureux d'agréer ses bénédictions et ses louanges.

En se déclarant spécialement la servante

de Marie, en consacrant ses hommages particuliers à quelques saints, elle mettait un
grand zèle à les imiter. Comme elle pensait
que l'exemple est ce qu'il y a de plus per-
suasif, elle lisait souvent les vies édifiantes,
et prenait de chaque saint sa vertu favorite,
lorsqu'elle convenait à sa situation, afin
d'acquérir, à quelque prix que ce fût, tout
ce qui lui manquait ; elle avait choisi cette
pratique, d'après un solitaire qui réunis-
sant en lui toutes les vertus, était parvenu
à les faire aimer à ses compagnons et travailler par là à leur sanctification. Dans ses lettres à ses amis, non-seulement elle les ani-
mait, par des conseils pleins d'une vive tendresse, à la pratique des bonnes œuvres,
mais encore elle leur proposait avec beau-

coup d'intérèt des modèles qu'elle s'engageait toujours la première à imiter.

Cependant sa vertu était fortement combattue : souvent le démon lui présentait le monde avec ses charmes trompeurs, cher-chant à lui insinuer l'idée qu'un jour peut-ètre elle se repentirait d'avoir sacrifié des plaisirs qui ne seraient plus alors de saison ; au-dehors, on lui tendait les mêmes piéges, on lui disait souvent qu'à son âge il fallait nécessairement s'amuser ; qu'il était étonnant qu'elle renonçàt à des délassements que toutes les jeunes personnes recherchent, et qu'enfin, si elle voulait mépriser le monde, il fallait du moins le connaître auparavant. Mais comment se fait-il, ajoutait-on, que vous n'aimiez pas les plaisirs? « S'ils m'étaient indifférents, répondait Caroline, âgée au plus de quatorze ans, le sacrifice ne serait pas d'un grand prix aux yeux du Seigneur. Le monde est si aveugle, qu'il juge que l'on doit prendre ses penchants pour guides ; il ne s'imagine pas qu'on puisse sacrifier à Dieu d'autres plaisirs que ceux dont on ne se soucie que faiblement ; quel extravagant conseil de voir le monde afin de le mépriser ! C'est donc à dire qu'il faut offenser Dieu, afin de s'en repentir. » Malgré cette généreuse façon de penser, elle résistait avec peine quelquefois à de violentes tentations qu'elle éprouva jusqu'à l'âge de dix-sept ans, et qui la portaient à se rapprocher du monde. Lorsqu'elles étaient pressantes, elle disait à ses sœurs : « J'espère que si je voulais succomber, vous y mettriez obstacle, et je vous en prie très-instamment. »

Autant le monde, par l'empire qu'elle avait obtenu sur ses inclinations, lui devint indifférent, autant ses applaudissements lui étaient-ils à charge. Elle ne témoignait que du mépris pour les éloges qu'on faisait de sa figure, dans les promenades et dans les assemblées où elle était absolument forcée de se trouver quelquefois. Pour n'être aimable qu'aux yeux de son Sauveur, elle cachait, autant qu'elle pouvait, ses agréments, en choisissant les coiffures les moins propres à faire ressortir ses traits ; et, si l'on ne s'en fiait pas à son goût, elle priait confidemment la personne qui la coiffait de se conformer à ses désirs.

Afin d'éloigner des autres le danger de déplaire au Seigneur, elle recourait à mille artifices ingénieux : voyait-elle une personne occupée d'une chose qui pouvait lui devenir l'occasion d'une chute prochaine, aussitôt elle lui en mettait une autre sous les yeux, et celle qu'elle croyait la plus capable de la distraire de la première. Ayant un jour écrit sa confession, elle la perdit, et, en apprenant son chagrin à ses meilleures amies, elle leur dit : « Que je suis fâchée ! ceux qui liront ma confession offenseront Dieu. » Elle s'imagina que la permission qu'elle donnerait de la lire remédierait à tout; ainsi elle déclara à ceux qui l'approchaient, et dont un avait montré beaucoup de curiosité, qu'elle donnait sur cette matière une entière liberté.

Si l'aimable enfant ne pouvait absolument empêcher que Dieu fût offensé, alors sa ressource était de gémir sur le pécheur, et de demander au ciel la grâce qu'il fût épargné. Un matin qu'on l'entendit pleurer dans son lit, on l'interrogea pour savoir la cause de ses larmes, elle répondit : « Ignorez-vous les péchés qui se sont commis cette nuit, si près de nous ? » Son appartement était voisin de la salle du spectacle ; et tandis qu'il durait, elle passait, autant qu'elle le pouvait, un temps considérable à prier pour ceux qui se livraient à ces plaisirs dangereux.

Ce zèle, qui s'étendait à tous ceux qu'elle

pouvait gagner à Dieu, devenait plus vif encore auprès de ses amies. Elle savait choisir celles auxquelles elle donnait sa confiance, et ses amies de cœur étaient très-pieuses. Elle n'avait besoin que de les exciter à une perfection plus grande; mais elle le faisait avec des caresses si naïves, et leur peignait avec **des** sentiments si tendres les charmes de son bien-aimé, qu'en sortant d'auprès d'elle, elles éprouvaient, ainsi qu'elles l'ont depuis rapporté, un courage tout nouveau. Dans la persuasion que le souvenir de la présence de Dieu peut nous empêcher à chaque instant de commettre des fautes, elle engageait ses compagnes à conserver en elles ce souvenir salutaire: elle leur rappelait si souvent cette douce obligation, qu'une d'en-

tre-elles racontait un jour que les recomman-
dations de Caroline lui étaient devenues en
quelque sorte superflues, parce qu'il suffi-
sait de la voir pour penser intérieurement à
Dieu.

Il n'est point étonnant qu'on produise sur
les autres un si heureux effet, quand on
parle de la piété avec cette effusion de cœur
que mademoiselle de Bois-Auger mettait dans
tout ce qu'elle en disait, ou de vive voix, ou
par écrit.

Chaque jour, en allant à la messe, et en
revenant à la maison, elle trouvait sur son
passage, pour recevoir ses aumônes et ses
instructions, beaucoup de pauvres. Autant
qu'il lui était possible, elle ménageait quel-

3,

ques bonnes œuvres pour sanctifier ses promenades en ville. La complaisance l'engageait assez souvent à se trouver dans les endroits publics ; quand elle y était avec des amies intimes, elle se plaçait auprès d'une personne du peuple, et lui adressait la parole avec un air affable et poli, mais sans affectation ; ensuite la conversation étant engagée, elle la tournait adroitement vers un objet qui pouvait rappeler les devoirs du chrétien. Si la promenade était fixée au jardin de son père, elle rassemblait beaucoup d'enfants du faubourg, pour les y instruire avec plus de facilité ; prévoyant, dans les belles soirées d'été, que sa famille, pour prendre l'air, irait dans les lieux où les écoliers ont coutume de se rendre, elle écrivait à la maison les pensées les plus propres à inspirer le goût de la vertu, et semait ensuite ces papiers dans les champs, se flattant que la curiosité engagerait des jeunes gens à les lire. Elle préparait ces innocents artifices, qu'elle avait imaginés pour exciter à l'amour de Dieu, avec une joie qui donnait à son action un nouveau prix, surtout quand elle avait plus d'espoir que le succès répondrait à ses vœux.

III

Quoique la charité de Caroline fût partout
également vive, elle l'exerçait encore d'une
manière plus parfaite à la terre de son père.
Tout concourait à lui rendre cette retraite
aimable : il est si doux pour un cœur qui

aime de n'être point distrait dans son amour!
et le séjonr de la ville n'est que trop capable
d'inspirer la dissipation. C'était pour elle la
plus flatteuse nouvelle que celle du départ
pour la campagne. Sans être sauvage et sans
vouloir paraître singulière, elle aurait désiré
y être souvent seule. S'enfonçant dans un
bocage, ou s'échappant le long d'une avenue,
il lui arrivait, en pensant aux attraits de son
bien-aimé, de tomber dans une sorte de
ravissement, où on l'a surprise plus d'une
fois ; mais bientôt elle s'arrachait à cette
chère solitude, parce que, durant les vacan-
ces, les objets de son zèle lui enlevait pres-
·que tous ses moments. Quelquefois elle était
occupée depuis dix heures du matin jusqu'à
huit heures du soir, voulant prendre le temps

qui convenait le mieux aux enfants, qui se succédaient les uns aux autres. Lorsqu'ils l'avaient quittée, elle se rendait dans les métairies voisines de la maison, pour entretenir des vérités du salut les ouvriers rassemblés au retour de leurs travaux. Elle les instruisait avec tant de douceur, de patience et de bonté, qu'en pleurant sa mort, ils se rappelaient longtemps après les discours qu'elle leur avait tenus. Afin de les attacher davantage, elle faisait renaître souvent, dans ces entretiens familiers, l'idée des récompenses éternelles promises à la vertu; et alors elle faisait du paradis un tableau si touchant, que ces hommes simples se figuraient qu'elle voyait déjà Dieu, comme le voient les esprits bienheureux,

A cette attention continuelle à remplir ses devoirs, ou s'acquitter des bonnes œuvres qu'elle s'était imposées, elle n'eut rien de cette piété sauvage, plus faite pour dégoûter du bien que pour y porter. La sienne, toujours aimable, montrait combien le joug du Seigneur est doux. Après avoir marqué dans son règlement l'heure de ses exercices, suivant l'esprit d'une sage condescendance, elle dérangeait quelquefois cet ordre, guidée par la vue d'un plus grand bien, et d'ailleurs persuadée que le Seigneur la verrait avec plaisir céder aux volontés des personnes avec lesquelles elle vivait. Quoiqu'elle soupirât sans cesse après le paradis, et que l'absence d'un Dieu qu'elle aimait tant lui fît souvent répandre des larmes; comme ces pleurs, qui coulaient en secret, venaient d'un cœur aussi soumis qu'il était tendre, elle ne perdait rien, à l'extérieur, de sa gaîté; et, par un effet de sa résignation, elle conserva, jusqu'au dernier soupir, un air content et serein; de même aussi son extrême horreur pour le péché ne produisait en elle ni l'accablement ni la pusillanimité. Son éloignement pour tout ce qui offense Dieu n'était point excité par la seule crainte de ses jugements. Sa confiance était grande, puisqu'elle prenait sa source dans un grand amour ; elle trem-blait sans doute à l'ombre de la faute la plus légère ; mais c'est qu'envisageant son divin Maître comme le meilleur des pères, elle pensait que plus il chérit les hommes, plus on doit être affligé de lui avoir déplu, et plus

on doit appréhendre de lui déplaire encore.
Elle ne concevait aucune frayeur des tourments de l'enfer; le purgatoire faisait sur
son âme une impression aussi profonde que
les tourments éternels en font sur celle des
autres : elle se trouvait accablée de l'idée
seule de la séparation de Dieu, au point
qu'elle était convaincue que la peine qu'elle
ressentait de ne pas le voir ici-bas pourrait
lui servir de purgatoire. Ces sentiments lui
donnaient une vive compassion pour les
fidèles qui y sont détenus ; et les lui ren-
daient extrêmement chers, les jugeant bien
à plaindre, puisqu'ils ne jouissaient pas du
seul objet qu'ils aimaient. Aussi ne faisait-
elle des bonnes œuvres que dans l'espoir de
les soulager ou de mettre fin à leur exil.

Les vœux qu'elle adressait pour eux au Seigneur plaisaient chaque jour davantage au divin Maître ; parce qu'il voyait chaque jour, ou ses vertus se perfectionner, ou une nouvelle vertu naître en elle. La pureté, qu'elle aima dès ses plus tendres années, lui devint plus aimable avec l'âge, et lui inspira pour la virginité le respect que mérite une vertu si rare et si précieuse.

Cet amour de la virginité la détermina pour l'état religieux, sur le choix duquel elle avait soigneusement consulté le Seigneur, en lui disant avec le Roi prophète : « Seigneur, montrez-moi vos voies, et découvrez-moi les sentiers par lesquels vous voulez me conduire. » Elle mit tout en œuvre, prières, caresses et larmes, pour obtenir de son père son entrée dans le cloître : cependant il fixa pour ce bonheur tant désiré une époque fort éloi- gnée, et il se flattait même qu'il réussirait à faire changer la façon de penser de Caro- line; mais, ayant refusé plusieurs partis avantageux, elle s'affermissait chaque jour dans la résolution de se consacrer à Dieu par des vœux indissolubles.

La piété de mademoiselle du Bois–Auger paraissait trop solidement établie pour ne pas atteindre à la perfection. Un des plus sûrs moyens pour y parvenir est l'amour des souffrances, et depuis longtemps elle en faisait l'objet de ses désirs, mettant tout son bonheur à se voir victimes de la croix. Comme elle trouvait que les peines d'esprit surpas- sent les peines du corps en mérite, elle chérissait celles-là davantage, et ne pouvait assez s'étonner des gémissements et des plaintes que l'affliction arrachait à des personnes vertueuses. Pour les consoler, elle s'empressait de leur dire : « Mais c'est une croix. »

Depuis l'âge de treize ans, elle avait considéré la vie comme un exil, et cette façon de penser lui semblait si naturelle au véritable chrétien, qu'elle ne doutait pas que toutes les personnes pieuses ne soupirassent après leur céleste patrie, comme elle y aspirait elle-même. Avant d'avoir atteint l'âge de dix-huit ans, elle crut que son Sauveur allait combler ses vœux : attaquée d'une fièvre maligne, elle ne s'occupa, dans un contentement inexprimable, que de sa mort, qu'elle appelait à tout moment sa meilleure amie,

Sa famille et les habitants de la maison frémissaient du danger auquel souriait Caroline : sa sainteté les avait fait trembler sur la brièveté de ses jours, pendant sa bonne santé, et alors ils disaient : C'est un fruit mûr pour le Ciel, Dieu se rendra à l'ardent désir qu'elle a de le voir.

Chaque jour augmentait leur crainte et les transports de joie de la malade. Ses sentiments excitaient l'admiration de tous ceux qui pouvaient l'approcher. Frappés des actes d'amour qu'elle adressait sans cesse au Seigneur, ils ne pouvaient s'empêcher de répandre des larmes, et croyaient voir en elle un ange. Les ecclésiastiques qui l'administrèrent, étonnés à la vue d'une vertu si épurée, convenaient n'avoir jamais rencontré de spectacle aussi touchant dans l'exercice de leur ministère. La veille du jour où on lui apporta le saint Viatique, on lui annonça que, le lendemain, elle recevrait la sainte Eucharistie : Pourvu, s'écria-t-elle aussitôt, pourvu que je sois encore dans le même état, car je serais privée d'un aussi grand bien, si ma santé devenait meilleure. » La vue de son Sauveur lui inspira la joie la plus vive ; et le curé qui la communia, enchanté de la piété qu'elle lui témoignait, ne put s'empêcher de dire : Oui, je voudrais que beaucoup de jeunes personnes eussent été présentes au spectacle édifiant dont j'ai été témoin.

Malgré ses désirs d'être réunie à Dieu, dans cette maladie, comme dans toutes celles qu'elle a éprouvées, elle ne refusait jamais aucun remède, et allait, au contraire, jusqu'à faire ses délices de la potion la plus amère ; elle l'avalait lentement : on voyait sa main trembler des répugnances qu'elle éprouvait.

Elle joignait à ce courage une patience bien digne d'être proposée pour modèle aux personnes souffrantes. Quoiqu'elle eût des maux de tête considérables, elle ne se plaignait point ; et, lorsqu'on l'interrogeait sur son état, elle avouait que, toutes les fois qu'on lui soulevait la tête pour lui donner quelque tisane, elle ressentait des battements bien douloureux : cependant à chaque quart-d'heure on lui présentait quelque chose à boire, et jamais elle ne donnait à entendre que par là on renouvelait ses maux.

Cette rigueur, qu'elle exerçait envers elle, ne lui ôtait rien de ses soins et de ses attentions pour les autres ; elle ne semblait s'oublier que pour s'occuper des malheureux ; et parce que les oranges étaient la seule chose qui la flattât, elle priait instamment qu'on les envoyât à des pauvres malades, afin, disait-elle, de régaler ses chers pauvres.

Ses vœux pour une mort prochaine n'ayant point été alors exaucés, elle ne put cacher la peine qu'elle ressentait de revenir à la vie ; dès que le danger eut disparu, une personne qui ne connaissait point ses sentiments se hâta de lui apprendre qu'on ne craignait plus pour ses jours : « Eh bien ! répondit-elle aussitôt d'un air très-affligé, mais qui marquait sa résignation, eh bien ! ce sera pour une autre fois. » A peine la personne se fût-elle retirée, qu'elle fondit en larmes, ne pouvant, disait-elle, regretter assez de n'être pas allée jouir du Ciel. Elle ajouta ensuite qu'elle pensait bien qu'il serait beaucoup plus parfait de ne désirer que la volonté de Dieu, mais qu'elle n'était pas maîtresse de sa sensibilité.

IV

La tendresse de Caroline pour le Seigneur
était si ardente, que le souvenir de la félicité
des saints, un seul mot quelquefois, un
cantique sur les joies du paradis, lui faisaient répandre des larmes. Les cantiques
qu'elle aimait particulièrement, et qu'elle

chantait sans cesse, rappelaient ou à la mort, ou à la céleste Sion. D'une voix qui, par ses doux accents, peignait si bien la langue de son âme, dans l'absence de son bien-aimé, elle répétait : « Ce bas séjour n'est qu'un pèlerinage; cherchons, mon âme, un séjour permanent. » Souvent elle chantait ainsi : « Qu'heureux est l'homme à la fin de sa vie ! » Souvent encore ces mots d'un cantique si touchant et si beau : « Quand vous contemplerai-je, ô céleste séjour ? etc. » Mais plus souvent celui qui commençait ainsi : « O digne objet de mes chants ! » Il renferme un couplet dont elle était enchantée, et qu'elle ne se lassait point de dire, parce qu'il exprime l'affection qu'elle éprouvait loin de sa vraie patrie : Mon exil est prolongé, etc.

Ne cessant de penser à l'instant qui la réunirait à son céleste époux, elle comptait les mois, les jours qui abrégeaient son exil; souvent elle disait le soir, avec une joie peinte dans tous ses traits : « Voilà encore un jour de passé; je suis plus près de l'éternité. »

Par l'espérance d'y parvenir bientôt, elle ne trouvait plus rien de difficile dans les voies du salut. Les peines et les maux de cette vie, tous les genres de souffrances, elle ne les endurait pas seulement avec la plus grande patience, elle les désirait ardemment, et la devise de sainte Thérèse, « ou souffrir ou mourir, » était aussi la sienne. On ne s'apercevait des douleurs violentes qu'elle éprouvait dans certains temps, parce qu'on lui voyait plus de gaieté qu'auparavant, et plus d'envie de chanter des cantiques. Elle conservait toujours un air aimable et content, mais le redoublement de sa gaieté donnait à soupçonner aux personnes qui connaissaient le mieux ses sentiments, qu'elle avait quelque douleur qu'elle voulait dissimuler : alors on l'interrogeait, et sa bonne foi confirmait ce soupçon.

Par une suite de l'infirmité humaine, le plus juste n'est pas exempt de fautes : celles dont elle se trouvait coupable n'étaient que de légères imperfections, qui, chez tout autre, peut être, eussent passé pour des vertus. Empressement un peu trop vif pour une bonne œuvre ; regrets suivis de quelques larmes, lorsqu'une circonstance imprévue la

privait de la communion ; trop grande attache à certains ouvrages ; sourire toujours
modeste, mais qui quelquefois semblait à
ses yeux immodéré : voilà ses plus grands
crimes, ceux que les personnes qui l'ont
connue regardent comme l'unique matière
de ses confessions, parce qu'on la voyait se
les reprocher avec rigueur, et que depuis
longtemps on n'aurait pu l'accuser d'autres
fautes. Convaincue, comme elle l'était, que,
selon la parole de Jésus-Christ même, ce
n'est qu'autant qu'on est fidèle dans les petites choses qu'on l'est aussi dans les grandes, souvent on la voyait fondre en larmes
quand elle sortait du tribunal de la pénitence.
Un jour qu'après sa confession elle pleurait
amèrement, une personne, dans laquelle

4

mademoiselle de Bois-Augers avait confiance, lui dit pour la consoler : « Caroline, il est bon de s'humilier de ses fautes ; mais les vôtres ne sont pas de nature à vous inquiéter. » « Je sais, lui répondit-elle avec cette simplicité qui fait le caractère des âmes saintes, je sais que, par la grâce de Dieu, ce ne sont pas des péchés mortels ; mais tout ce qui peut déplaire le moins du monde à Dieu est infiniment digne de nos larmes. »

Des sentiments aussi généreux nous apprennent assez jusqu'à quel point elle savait s'armer contre elle-même, pour se vaincre et pour se réformer en tout. Souvent les plus heureux caractères ne sont point à l'abri de ces antipathies qui, dès qu'elles sont volontaires, détruisent la charité chrétienne :

lorsqu'elle éprouvait, à l'égard de quelqu'un un éloignement secret, c'était alors qu'elle lui témoignait un attachement plus tendre et les prévenances les plus remarquées. Une de ses amis, instruite de cette façon de penser et d'agir, disait un jour : « Je n'aime point à être regardée avec trop de complaisance par Caroline, je crains toujours que ce ne soit uniquement par un motif surnaturel. Dans une de ses maladies, elle eut auprès d'elle une garde maladroite, et dont les manières étaient insupportables. On se douta du dégoût que la malade avait pour elle, par les témoignages excessifs d'amitié qu'elle ne cessait de lui donner : on lui proposa de la placer ailleurs : « Non, non, je vous en prie, répliqua-t-elle avec vivacité; j'aime cette fille. » Mais sa franchise ne lui permit pas de contredire ouvertement un soupçon trop bien fondé.

Fidèle à remplir ses engagements envers le Seigneur, elle n'oubliait jamais les trois vœux que nous l'avons vu former ; elle en avait gardé le secret à l'égard des personnes avec lesquelles elle vivait, sa conduite seule la trahit à leurs yeux. Frappée de l'exemple d'un Dieu pauvre dans sa vie mortelle, mademoiselle du Bois-Auger ne voulut, afin de l'imiter, posséder rien en propre ; elle pria ses sœurs de disposer de sa possession pour le soulagement des pauvres, et lorsqu'on jugeait à propos, ce qui arrivait souvent, qu'elle fît elle-même la distribution de ses aumônes, elle demandait son argent comme s'il ne lui eût point appartenu, et faisait en sorte, quoique sans affectation, que l'on fixât ce qu'elle devait donner. Tout, dans ses actions, annonçait qu'elle ne connaissait plus aucun droit aux biens de la terre ; sans aller contre les bienséances nécessaires, elle recherchait, dans ses habillements, et dans tous ses petits meubles de dévotion, ce qui pouvait être le plus analogue à la pauvreté : nous n'exagérons point en disant qu'elle éprouvait, pour cette pauvreté volontaire, autant d'attachement qu'un avare en a pour ses richesses.

Son amour envers le Seigneur, son détachement des biens de la terre et son humilité, la défendaient trop bien des attaques du démon, pour qu'il se flattât désormais de la vaincre. A l'âge de dix-huit ans, elle vit disparaître absolument les tentations qu'elle avait éprouvées pour le monde. « Il me serait impossible, disait-elle avec joie, de trouver du plaisir dans les bals et les autres divertissements dangereux. » Des récréations innocentes étaient pour elle une source d'ennui, dès qu'elle ne lui retraçaient pas le souvenir de celui qu'elle aimait au-dessus de tout, ou bien encore, dès qu'on ne lui laissait la liberté d'en faire le sacrifice à Dieu ; elle avait étudié avec soin la musique dans sa grande jeunesse, et s'était même servie de cette occupation pour se faire une image des concerts céleste; elle était enchantée toutes les fois qu'elle entendait une symphonie ou une xoix agréable : cependant elle résolut, par esprit de mortification, de se priver, autant qu'elle le pourrait, de cet amusement.

V

Les sacrifices de la jeune vierge étonne-
ront sans doute, et scandaliseront peut-être
les gens du monde; mais quiconque aime
avec ardeur un objet infiniment aimable n'a
plus rien qui l'attache ici-bas; moins il tient

à la terre, plus il goûte la joie dans son amour, et plus, pour le soulager lui-même, il cherche à les répandre. Telle était Caroline, dont les discours, les actions, les gestes mêmes, invitaient à aimer et à servir Jésus-Christ : les égards et les politesses dont elle usait envers tout le monde, les petits services qu'elle avait le pouvoir de rendre, avaient pour but de gagner les âmes à Dieu : et pour procurer des conquêtes à ce divin Maître, elle était inépuisable en ressource. Si l'absence d'une amie ne lui permettait plus de parler de vive voix des charmes de son bien-aimé, elle se dédommageait en confiant au papier ses tendres et généreux sentiments.

Nous offrons ici quelques-unes de ses lettres à de jeunes demoiselles, ses amies.

Malgré nos soins, ce recueil est court ; mais il est édifiant, et bien propre à prouver le zèle dont elle était pénétrée pour le salut des âmes.

Dans la lettre suivante, elle félicite une amie sur ses peines, et l'encourage, par l'exemple des saints et par tous les motifs que lui suggère une amitié chrétienne, à reconnaître le mérite des souffrances.

« Vive le sacré Cœur de Jésus et celui de Marie ! Que votre sort est heureux et digne d'envie, ma bien bonne amie ! vous êtes sur la croix : chérissez-la, cette croix, c'est elle qui vous conduira au ciel. Plus vous souffrirez étant résignée, plus vous serez agréable à l'époux céleste. Qu'il se plaît dans votre âme, ma bonne amie, quand elle est sur la croix! Ne savez-vous pas qu'heureux est celui qui souffre ? plus heureux est celui qui souffre davantage, qui n'a de consolation, en quelque sorte, ni de Dieu ni des hommes, pouvant presque dire, avec Jésus-Christ mourant : Mon Père, pourquoi m'avez-vous abandonné ! Dieu vous aime bien, puisqu'il vous crucifie ; c'est qu'il a de grands desseins sur vous : vous ne pouvez mieux lui marquer que vous l'aimez, qu'en souffrant. Si les saints qui sont dans le ciel revenaient sur la terre, comme ils chériraient l'aimable croix ! O bonne croix ! qui nous mériterez les plus grands biens ; disons comme sainte Thérèse : ou souffrir, ou mourir ; c'est la croix qui nous conduit à cette aimable demeure où le Roi des rois est assis sur un trône parsemé d'étoiles... Les peines de l'esprit son ordinairement plus dures à supporter que les pénitences qu'on impose. Quand on ne sent point qu'on mérite, c'est là qu'on acquiert de plus grands mérites. Oui, ma bonne amie, c'est la plus grande faveur que Dieu puisse faire; c'est le partage des âmes privilégiées. Bienheureux ceux qui ne vivent que de croix, et qui meurent enfin avec Jésus sur la croix! Je suis, ma chère amie, dans le saint amour de Jésus, qui brûlait du désir de souffrir pour nous.

» Caroline du Bois-Auger. »

Dans une autre lettre, pour faire connaître à son amie l'avantage des souffrances,

Caroline. 5

elle lui représente qu'elles seules nous conduisent au ciel, et que le temps de l'épreuve
ici-bas ne dure qu'un moment : elle parle
avec le plus vif intérêt des délices de la sainte
Sion.

« Vive Jésus! Aimons, ma tendre amie,
ce qui nous crucifie davantage ; regardons
la souffrance comme le plus grand don que
notre cher époux puisse nous faire dans cette
terre étrangère. L'heureux moment, le trop
heureux moment que celui qui sépare notre
âme de notre corps! mais il faut mourir bien
des fois avant d'arriver à la dernière mort ;
aimables souffrances, qui nous procurez les
délices des cieux ! Sion, ô sainte Sion, quand
te verrons-nous ? Il ne tardera pas, ce bonheur : car qu'est-ce que la vie ? nous l'aime-

rons dans l'autre ; nous jouirons de lui pendant toute l'éternité, nous le contemplerons dans toute la suite des siècles. Son amour le porte à se cacher dans son admirable Sacrement ; son même amour le portera à se dévoiler tout entier à nos yeux : alors nous le verrons tel qu'il est.

» Je vous quitte bien vite, je suis dans le saint amour de Jésus, avec le plus parfait attachement.

» Caroline du Bois-Auger. »

« Dieu soit béni dans le temps et dans l'éternité ! »

Ailleurs elle découvre les agréments de la solitude, et raconte toutes les douceurs qu'on

y goûte avec Dieu, dans le sein de son amour;
elle parle encore de ce divin amour.

« Gloire au trois personnes de la très-sainte
Trinité ! Que vous êtes heureuse, ma bien
bonne amie, d'avoir fait une retraite ! C'est
dans cette solitude que Dieu se fait entendre
à l'âme fidèle ; il dit, ce cher époux : Je mè-
nerai l'âme dans la solitude, et là je lui par-
lerai au cœur. Quelles pures délices ne vous
y a-t-il point fait goûter, celui que vous aimez
seul ! c'est là qu'il fait éprouver un avant-
goût des délices du ciel. Aimable lieu où,
seul à seul avec Dieu, on s'entretient comme
un ami avec son ami ! O âmes solitaires ! que
vous êtes heureuses ! Dieu vous en a tirée,
ma bonne ami, de ce charmant séjour ; vous
l'avez aimé dans la retraite, vous l'aimerez

au milieu des villes. Que j'aime ce qui est rapporté dans la Vie de sainte Gertrude, qu'elle se fit une retraite au milieu de son cœur! Dieu révéla, en faveur de sainte Meltide, qu'elle était l'âme dans laquelle il se plaisait le plus. Que nous serions heureuses d'être comme cette grande sainte! Je suis avec tout l'attachement possible, en notre Seigneur. « *Caroline de Bois-Auger.* » Dieu soit béni, la très-sainte Vierge, Saint-Joseph et tous les saints du paradis! Unissons-nous à eux pour aimer Dieu sans mesure. Eh! comment n'aimerions-nous pas celui qui est seul aimable? Je me recommande aux fervents actes d'amour de mademoiselle votre sœur; car je ne doute pas qu'elle n'ait bien fait des progrès en dévotion et en amour depuis sa retraite : priez Jésus qu'il m'enflamme de son très-pur amour.

» Portons notre croix tous les jours de notre vie : c'est ce qu'il y a de plus précieux pour nous aux yeux de la foi. Je vous souhaite l'amour de toutes sortes de croix; je crois que vous en êtes déjà très-bien partagée. Disons, comme saint André, en voyant la croix sur laquelle il allait avoir le bonheur d'être attaché : O bonne croix, si longtemps désirée! Disons-le à chaque croix qui nous arrive; ô aimable martyre ! aimons celui qui nous crucifie, et qui nous fera la grâce de mourir en croix avec lui. »

Dans une autre lettre, après avoir parlé de la nécessité d'aimer Jésus et Marie, elle dépeint de la manière la plus affectueuse la beauté du ciel, et prouve, par l'exemple de la mère de Dieu et par celui de tous les martyrs, que les souffrances seules nous y conduisent ; elle termine sa lettre en présentant le divin amour comme le plus doux remèdes à nos peines.

« Vive Jésus et Marie ! Je désire, ma bonne amie, que nous ne respirions plus que pour notre cher époux ; priez-le sans cesse qu'il m'enflamme du feu si doux de son amour ; il nous demande nos cœurs ; il n'est pas possible de les lui refuser. Jésus, l'aimable Jésus doit les posséder tous, nous ne sommes créées que pour l'aimer. Aimons aussi l'admirable Marie ; c'est une bonne

Mère, mettons-nous sous sa sainte protection; dans quelque état que nous soyons,
elle ne nous abandonnera pas. Tout ce qui
est sur la terre ne mérite pas qu'on y pense;
il n'y a que Jésus qui doive remplir nos pensées : vous le savez bien, ma bonne amie,
il a toujours régné dans votre cœur. Ne sou-
pirons plus qu'après le ciel, notre chère patrie, où nous règnerons à jamais avec lui.
Que je suis contente de pouvoir m'entretenir
avec vous de ce charmant séjour, où nous
verrons Dieu sans ombre et sans nuage!
Qu'il fera beau là, ma bonne amie! C'est
par la souffrance que nous y parviendrons :
voilà le seul chemin qui y conduit. Les martyrs, après avoir répandu leur sang, croyaient
n'avoir rien fait, en considérant l'incompré-

hensible récompense qui leur était préparée.
Que cela doit bien nous encourager ! C'est
la béatitude de cette vie que la souffrance :
celui qui aime, la chérit de tout son cœur.
La sainte Vierge a souffert plus que tous les
autres saints, parce qu'elle était plus chérie
de Dieu. Nous ne voyons pas, dans cette
vie, l'extrême faveur que Dieu nous fait de
nous donner des croix ; plus elles sont pe-
santes, plus Dieu nous aime ; n'est-on pas
trop heureux d'avoir de la ressemblance
avec Jésus crucifié? Nous n'en sommes pas
même dignes. La croix est nécessaire; heureuse nécessité de souffrir pour l'objet qu'on
aime ! On doit ménager les plus petites souffrances, c'est le plus grand présent que
Dieu puisse nous faire; prier n'est rien en

5..

comparaison : ce sera dans la Jérusalem céleste que nous connaîtrons le grand avantage de la souffrance. Là, occupées de Dieu seul, nous serons ravies de sa beauté, nous en serons extasiées. Perdons-nous en Dieu dans cette vie, pour y être perdues à jamais dans le sein de la Divinité. Qui est comme Dieu, ma bonne amie, qui est semblable à Dieu ? Il n'y a que lui qui soit à estimer, lui seul saint, seul aimable, seul adorable, seul digne d'être aimé. Perdons-nous dans cette fournaise d'amour. Là, nous n'aurons point à craindre les ennemis de notre salut ; ô l'aimable demeure ! Quand, dans la sainte communion, les âmes pures et innocentes s'unissent à leur bien-aimé, c'est là que le sacré Cœur prend en elle ses délices ; il les inonde d'un torrent de douceurs. Le Cœur de Jésus s'unit avec le cœur de sa chaste épouse, il l'embrasse des doux feux de son amour ; si quelquefois il la prive de ses consolations, ce n'est que pour qu'elle ait plus de mérites et qu'elle l'aime plus purement. C'est ce sacré Cœur qui a tant souffert sur le Calvaire, par amour pour nous ; ne sommes-nous pas trop heureux de partager ses tristesses ? Que ne pouvons-nous être embrasées d'amour comme tous les anges, comme tous les archanges !

» Je désire, ma bonne amie, que nous amassions de grands mérites pour le Ciel, d'ici à ce que nous nous revoyons ; aimons toujours de plus en plus ; que nos cœurs ne se fondent-ils d'amour ! La belle chose que

l'amour de Dieu! Aimable amour! c'est
dans le renoncement à soi-même que s'é-
prouve l'amour, comme vous le savez par
expérience. Quand viendra donc l'heureux
temps où nous serons consumées d'amour
dans la Jérusalem céleste? Heureux moment
qui séparera notre âme de ce corps de péché,
pour la réunir à la Divinité! Que les saints
sont heureux! ils n'offensent plus l'aimable
Jésus. Imitons-les; ils ne sont pas arrivés
là sans peine; il leur en a bien coûté : nous
pouvons devenir ce qu'ils sont. C'est par la
croix qu'ils sont parvenus à la récompense.
On n'arrive au repos que par le travail; tra-
vaillons sans cesse à embellir notre cou-
ronne, et nous jouirons bientôt du bonheur
de voir Dieu comme eux.

» Je vous prie de faire une communion pour quelque chose qui regarde la gloire de Dieu. Je vous fais mille excuses des fautes qui sont dans ma lettre ; mais j'espère que nous ne serons point sur le ton de cérémonie : priez le bon Dieu qu'il m'embrase du feu de son amour, quand vous l'aurez dans votre cœur par la sainte communion. Je ferai la même chose pour vous, c'est le moment favorable. »

Dans une autre lettre, elle retrace les consolations et les délices qu'on éprouve dans la sainte communion. Elle raconte ensuite avec beaucoup de zèle la gloire et les vertus de Marie, et nous confirme, par son exemple, que la vraie dévotion pour la Mère de Dieu fut constamment une marque de prédestination du divin amour.

VI

Parvenue depuis peu à l'âge de dix-neuf ans, elle avait fait dans la vertu des progrès si rapides, que tout en elle, jusqu'aux actions les plus indifférentes, était sanctifié par des intentions pures, et devenait l'occa-

sion de nouveaux mérites ; on l'obligeait
d'aller à cheval pour sa santé, et elle choi-
sissait ce temps pour faire des cantiques. Le
Seigneur voulut récompenser ses vertus :
une maladie de langueur répandit l'effroi
dans sa famille, qui avait longtemps ignoré
son état. On consulta les médecins ; ils pa-
rurent craindre pour ses jours. On ne négli-
gea rien pour l'attacher à la vie, cherchant
tous les plaisirs propres à la récréer. Un
jour qu'on lui faisait de nouvelles instances
pour qu'elle déclarât ce qui pourrait l'amuser : « Ah ! comment est-il possible, répondit-elle, de trouver du plaisir sur la terre,
où l'on est éloigné de Dieu ? Dans les transports qui animaient le saint Roi d'Israël,
lorsqu'il allait jouir de son Dieu, souvent

elle avait à la bouche ces plaintes si tou-
chantes par lesquelles il lui demande de ne
pas prolonger plus longtemps son exil.
Cependant on cherchait à découvrir tout ce
qui était de nature à la flatter. On l'engageait
à s'occuper, à la promenade, des objets
capables de la distraire, et qui étaient si
souvent pour elle une occasion de renoncement et de sacrifice : « Je le ferais très-volon-
tiers, disait-elle ; mais rien de ce qui est sur
la terre ne peut me causer de vrais plaisirs. »
Ses sœurs s'empressant de prévenir ses
moindres désirs, elle était touchée de leur
tendresse, et, leur prenant la main, leur
prodiguait mille caresses : Vous ne pouvez,
mes bonnes amies, leur disait-elle, me
donner la seule chose que je désire, c'est

Dieu ; nulle autre ne peut me plaire. »
Déjà bien affaiblie par l'état de langueur
où ses maux la réduisaient, elle se traînait
encore chaque jour à l'église ; là elle trouvait
le paradis de la terre, disait-elle, en se ser-
vant des mêmes expressions que nous l'avons
déjà vue employer pour la sainte communion : afin de n'être distraite par aucun objet
extérieur, elle était dans l'usage de fermer
les yeux en entrant dans le lieu saint, et de
ne les rouvrir qu'en sortant. On craignit que
cette contrainte ne lui devînt trop fatigante
dans son état d'infirmité : elle obéit, et tint
les yeux ouverts pendant sa prière, mais
uniquement pour regarder le très-saint Sacrement, qui était exposé. Elle dit ensuite à
la personne dont elle avait suivi le conseil :

« Ah !. que j'ai senti de douceur à attacher
mes regards sur l'adorable Sacrement de
nos autels ! je me suis rappelé une sainte
qui eût voulu pouvoir ne contempler jamais
d'autre objet que celui-là, tant son cœur en
était touché, tant sa foi y découvrait de mer-
veille ! »

Sa maladie la défigura bientôt au point
qu'elle était absolument méconnaissable.
On n'eût jamais su qu'elle eût la moindre
connaissance de sa beauté, si l'on n'avait
été témoin de la joie qu'elle témoigna quand
son extrême maigreur l'eut fait disparaître ;
le monde jugeait encore sa figure intéressante, lorsque déjà elle disait ; « Que je suis
aise d'être devenue laide ! » Puis, en riant à
la vue de cette maigreur qui augmentait tous

les jours, elle ajoutait d'un air de satisfaction : « Mes amies, la muraille tombe. »

Sa patience augmentait avec ses souffrances. Pendant les huit mois que dura sa maladie, et dont les quatre derniers surtout
furent accompagnés des plus cuisantes douleurs, jamais il ne lui échappa la plainte la
plus légère. Toujours contente, elle bénis-
sait sans cesse le divin Sauveur ; l'augmentation seule de la joie put faire juger qu'elles devenaient plus vives encore. Les domestiques connaissaient si bien son courage,
que lorsqu'on allait savoir de ses nouvelles,
ils répondaient souvent : « Mademoiselle est
certainement plus malade, car elle est plus
gaie. « Obligée de déclarer les maux qu'elle
ressentait : « Que le bon Dieu est bon, disait-

elle, de m'avoir envoyé cette maladie ! cela vaut mieux qu'un royaume. » Cependant un jour, et c'est la seule fois qu'elle ait paru céder à la vivacité de ses souffrances, elles lui arrachèrent quelques larmes ; mais aussitôt elle s'écria : « Je n'envie plus le sort des martyrs, puisque j'ai le bonheur de souffrir pour mon Dieu. Si je ne devais désirer ma chère patrie, je souhaiterais de rester mille ans sur la terre, s'il était possible, puisque Dieu m'accorde ce que je n'aurais osé lui demander. »

Quelque amour qu'elle eût pour les croix, elle n'osait les solliciter ni presque les souhaiter, ne s'en croyant pas digne ; mais qu'elle embrassait avec joie celles que la Providence lui envoyait ! Elle eut, dans ces temps, occasion de montrer, à cet égard, sa façon de penser; elle avait alors extrêmement à cœur le succès d'une affaire dont l'événement fut absolument contraire à ses désirs. A la nouvelle qu'elle en reçut, et qui devait lui causer la plus grande peine, Caroline, au lieu de s'affliger ou de laisser paraître la moindre altération dans ses traits, chanta le *Te Deum.*

Un jour qu'on cherchait à lui procurer les mets les plus propres à flatter son appétit, la crainte d'incommoder ceux qui l'entouraient lui fit trahir son secret : « Ne vous gênez point, de grâce; les recherches sont inutiles, tous les mets me sont égaux; depuis longtemps j'ai perdu absolument le goût. » Une de ses amies lui disant, lorsqu'elle était presque mourante : Je crains que vous n'ayez de la répugnance pour ce que vous mangez actuellement : « Des répugnances, reprit-elle en souriant, je n'en ai que pour le péché. »

Cette réponse fait sentir qu'elle ne perdait point de vue, et moins alors que jamais le souvenir de son bien-aimé ; s'occupant toujours de lui seul, son zèle pour sa gloire ne fit qu'augmenter jusqu'à son dernier moment : ce zèle la rendait inconsolable, lorsque quelqu'un de sa connaissance s'était un peu écarté des routes de la vertu, pour tourner ses regards vers le monde. Une jeune personne avec laquelle les circonstances, la conformité de l'âge et celle des sentiments, l'avaient liée autrefois très-étroitement,

n'ayant pas eu le courage de l'imiter, cessait
depuis quelque temps de la fréquenter. Caroline, songeant que le spectacle de la jeunesse aux prises avec la mort pourrait lui
être salutaire, l'envoya prier de venir la voir ;
l'ancienne amie se rendit auprès de la malade, qui, lui faisant l'accueil le plus gracieux.
entama une conversation intéressante, et lui
dit, comme pour ouvrir son cœur : « Que je
suis heureuse de ne pas m'être laissée en-
traîner au goût naturel que j'avais pour le
monde ! il m'en a bien coûté pour résister à
ce penchant : où en serais-je si je m'y étais
livrée ? » Ces paroles firent beaucoup d'impression sur celle qui l'écoutait. Quand elle
se fut retirée, la pieuse vierge consacra une
partie de ses derniers moments à prier le

Seigneur de toucher son cœur par l'onction de sa grâce, et ses vœux furent exaucés. Sa bonne amie, encouragée par l'exemple de ses vertus, toujours occupée de cet adieu attendrissant qu'elle lui avait fait, se détermina, peu de mois après, au genre de vie le plus parfait. Les circonstances qui accompagnaient cet événement se réunirent si bien pour prouver qu'il était l'ouvrage de mademoiselle du Bois-Auzer, que l'épouse de Jésus-Christ a dit mille fois, depuis le moment où elle se donna tout à Dieu : Oui, c'est à ma chère Caroline que je dois mon bonheur.

Quoiqu'elle ne fût alitée que les derniers jours de sa maladie, sa situation devenait à chaque instant plus critique, et cependant sa famille ne cessait point encore de se flatter

6

de sa guérison. Une de ses amies, persuadée que cette espérance était une illusion, sentit qu'elle était d'autant plus cruelle, qu'une perte à laquelle nous ne nous attendons que faiblement est beaucoup plus difficile à supporter. Elle connaissait d'ailleurs le désir extrême que la sainte mourante avait de quitter son exil : elle s'adressa directement à elle pour l'engager à préparer son père et ses sœurs au sacrifice que leur tendresse pour elle devait faire à la religion. A peine se fut-elle expliquée suffisamment, que Caroline lui dit aussitôt. » Ah ! ma bonne amie, que je vous ai d'obligation ! je n'aurais jamais cru que vous fussiez venue m'annoncer une nouvelle aussi agréable. » A ces mots, elle lui tendit la main, l'embrassa, et ses larmes

commencèrent à couler. Son amie, décon-
certée par ses pleurs, les prit pour l'effet de
ces sortes d'appréhensions ou de regrets que
l'image d'une fin prochaine arrache quelquefois aux âmes les plus vertueuses : « Quoi!
reprit-elle à l'instant, vous aurais-je causé
de la peine? — Non, non, répondit vivement
mademoiselle du Bois-Auger; c'est de joie
que je pleure. » Dans le même instant elle
ajouta : « Il serait bien plus parfait de ne rien
désirer; mais, mon Dieu, vous le savez, ma
joie est bien légitime. » D'après la connaissance qu'elle venait d'acquérir sur son état,
elle voulut préparer peu à peu ses sœurs à
sa séparation, désirant qu'elles pussent ensuite plus aisément adoucir la peine d'un
père qu'elle était désolée de voir affligé. En

leur annonçant qu'il fallait se quitter, elle employa tous les moyens capables de diminuer l'amertume que leur causait cette nouvelle : « Mes bonnes amies, de quoi vous chagrinez-vous? leur disait-elle, nous nous reverrons. Quand nous partons pour la campagne, les uns vont dans une voiture la veille, les autres dans celle du lendemain. Est-ce que ceux qui partent dans la seconde voiture s'avisent de pleurer ceux qui s'en vont dans la première? La vie n'est qu'un jour. » Ne croyons pas que la joie de mourir étouffât dans son cœur les sentiments de la nature : elle aimait trop ses parents pour n'être pas vivement affectée de leur situation; et lorsqu'on lui répétait souvent : Mais vous désirez de mourir; votre père et vos sœurs, comment pourront-ils supporter cette perte?

« J'attends tout de Dieu, répondit-elle; il leur donnera sûrement la force dont ils ont besoin. » De son côté, elle s'efforçait de les distraire et de les consoler. Ses sœurs ne pouvant s'empêcher de verser des larmes en sa présence, elle leur faisait cet aveu : Ah! mes bonnes amies, vous empoisonnez ma joie par votre douleur; vous m'attristez dans l'instant où je trouve du plaisir à mourir. »

6.

VII

Sa famille, ayant perdu l'espoir de sa guérison, aurait du moins voulu prolonger ses jours, en lui procurant tout ce qu'elle jugeait propre à la satisfaire. Comme elle lui disait : Caroline, que ferait-on bien pour vous causer quelque plaisir? « Si quelque chose pouvait m'en causer, répondit-elle, ce serait d'avoir le bonheur d'aller dans une communauté. « On se rendit à ses vœux, et au commencement de février 1776, elle fut portée dans le couvent des Dames carmélites de Rennes. En quittant la maison paternelle, elle témoigna aux domestiques beaucoup de reconnaissance des soins qu'ils avaient pris d'elle, et leur fit des excuses du chagrin qu'elle croyait leur avoir causé; le seul qu'ils eussent jamais ressenti auprès d'elle, avait été celui de la voir tant souffrir. Elle craignait alors d'attendrir par ses remerciments une de ses sœurs qu'elle quittait : mais son bon cœur ne pouvait rester muet, il lui échappa de dire avec le ton le plus tendre : « Que tu m'as fait de bien ! »

Quelle joie vive, dès qu'elle se vit dans la maison du Seigneur ! et son contentement croissait encore par l'idée qu'elle épargnait à une partie de sa famille le chagrin de la voir mourir. Elle s'occupait avec le plus grand soin des moyens de cacher à son père, alors incommodé, le moment de sa mort, qui ne lui fut véritablement annoncée que plusieurs jours après qu'elle n'était plus. Le lendemain du jour auquel elle était arrivée dans la communauté, une maladie généralement répandue dans la ville se joignit à ses autres maux.

Toutes ces infirmités rendant sa situation de plus en plus douloureuse, inspiraient une vive compassion aux personnes qui l'entouraient ; elles s'empressaient à la distraire, à la récréer, mais elle leur disait en souriant :

« Je n'ai pas besoin d'autres récréations que celles que m'offre l'état où je suis, puisque j'ai tout lieu d'espérer que je jouirai bientôt du bonheur de voir mon Dieu ; mais, ajoutait-elle, les médecins ont-ils fixé un terme ? »

En attendant l'instant qui devait la mettre au comble de ses vœux, elle fut administrée dans son lit. Le religieux, directeur de la maison, qui lui donna le saint Viatique, crut qu'il était convenable de prendre, à l'égard d'une personne aussi jeune, quelque ménagement, avant de lui proposer de faire à Dieu le sacrifice de ses jours : mais il n'en eut pas besoin ; lorsqu'il lui eut demandé si elle consentait à mourir, elle répondit, avec une joie inexprimable : Ah! mon père, il y a longtemps que je n'aspire qu'à ce moment : quand on perd les biens de l'éternité, toutes les choses de la terre ne sont rien. » Cette réponse surprit autant qu'elle édifia le ministre de la religion, ainsi que tous les assistants, attendris jusqu'aux larmes. Un ecclésiastique l'ayant, à peu près dans le même temps, engagé à renouveler l'offrande de sa jeunesse au Seigneur : « Monsieur, lui dit-elle de ce ton qui laissait voir le peu de cas qu'elle faisait de la vie, le sacrifice est bien petit. »

Elle paraissait ne trouver la durée de ses jours dans un sentiment supportable que par la joie qu'elle ressentait à souffrir. Les religieuses, qui venaient souvent la visiter s'aperçurent avec le plus grand étonnement que, plus ses maux étaient aigus, plus elle paraissait satisfaite. Elle conserva ces sentiments jusqu'au dernier soupir. Son extrême maigreur lui ayant enlevé la peau dans différentes parties du corps, elle en témoigna beaucoup de contentement : on crut d'abord qu'elle ne s'en réjouissait que par l'idée d'une mort prochaine; mais ce qui lui causait alors de la joie était uniquement de se voir attachée à la croix de son divin Maître; elle disait : « C'est au moins quelque chose d'ajouté à mes autres maux. » De là cette préférence qu'elle semblait donner, dans son lit, à la position la moins commode, et l'on fut contraint d'exiger de sa docilité qu'elle en prît une moins pénible, de là encore cette réponse à l'une des femmes qui la soignaient, laquelle n'osait la toucher, dans la crainte de lui faire quelque meurtrissure. « Ah! je voudrais que cette chair fût meurtrie depuis la tête jusqu'aux pieds, afin d'avoir le bonheur de souffrir pour mon Dieu. »

Depuis, ses entretiens avec Dieu ne furent presque interrompus que par des questions fréquentes sur les rapprochements de sa dernière heure; elle demandait encore de la manière la plus affectueuse à toutes les personnes qu'elle voyait, et spécialement à l'une d'entre elles, si au moins elles aimaient bien le bon Dieu. Le jour suivant, elle eut une faiblesse si considérable, que l'on crut qu'elle allait expirer. Après cette crise, elle fit appeler son médecin, et lui demanda s'il croyait qu'elle vécût jusqu'au lendemain ; il parut embarrassé sur sa réponse : « Monsieur, lui dit-elle, c'est que, si je ne vis pas jusqu'à demain, je voudrais être communiée ce soir, parce que je désirerais sortir de cette vie en portant Jésus-Christ dans mon cœur. » Prévoyant qu'elle mourrait dans la nuit, le médecin, extrêmement édifié des sentiments de sa malade, fut lui-même prier les supérieurs ecclésiastiques de lui accorder encore le saint Viatique.

Quand elle eut reçu cette nouvelle grâce de son Sauveur, on récita les oraisons qui sont en usage pour les agonisants ; elle témoigna beaucoup de reconnaissance des prières qu'on faisait pour elle ; elle voulut aussi mourir dans l'acte d'obéissance, et dit à celle de ses sœurs qu'elle avait auprès d'elle : « Retenez bien, je vous prie, tous les ordres du médecin, pour les exécuter à la lettre. » Cependant elle devait se faire bien des violences pour boire les potions qu'on lui préparait. Le Seigneur, qui continuait de l'unir de plus en plus à sa croix, joignit à tous ces maux une fluxion à la gorge, qui, lorsqu'elle avalait quelque liqueur, lui causait les douleurs les plus cuisantes ! néanmoins, loin de refuser jamais ce qu'on lui présentait, elle était la première à demander les boissons que le médecin ordonnait ; et l'une de ses gardes, hésitant à lui faire prendre, au moment qu'elle était expirante, la potion indiquée dans la crainte que cela ne la suffoquât : « Il faut obéir, répondit

Caroline ; » et , par cette raison , elle la détermina. Un autre motif plus puissant , son
tendre amour pour Dieu, la conduisait à tous
ces sacrifices ; lorsque , pour la réveiller de
l'accablement où elle était, on lui disait :
C'est pour l'amour de Dieu qu'il faut boire ;
ayant presque perdu la parole, elle trouvait
des forces pour répéter avec une ardeur in-
concevable : « Oui, tout pour l'amour de
Dieu. »

On réussissait encore à la tirer de ce pro-
fond assoupissement toutes les fois qu'on lui
parlait du bonheur du Ciel. Une personne,
sachant que c'était vers ce séjour que se
portaient tous les élans de son cœur, se plaça
près de son lit, et lui rappela de petits vers
qu'elle disait très-souvent, parce qu'ils expri-

maient le désir de quitter la terre; ils finis-
saient par ces mots : « Ah ! puissé-je bientôt
contempler ma patrie, et m'écrier : Paradis !
paradis! » La malade les répéta, et d'une
manière si touchante et si expressive, qu'on
ne peut la rendre ici. Quelques moments
après, elle voulut les prononcer de nouveau,
mais elle ne put dire que ceux-ci : « Cher
paradis, paradis? et ce furent ses dernières
paroles. Un instant avant qu'elle rendît le
dernier soupir , les religieuses qui étaient
auprès d'elle lui ayant suggéré des actes
d'amour , d'abandon, elle remua les lèvres,
mais ne put faire davantage. Une de ces
dames l'engagea à prononcer, dans le fond
de son cœur, cette prière à Dieu : Je ne veux
que Jésus, je n'aime que Jésus ; si je n'ai

pas, ô mon Dieu, le bonheur de mourir comme les martyrs pour la foi, que j'aie celui de mourir par l'effort de la charité. A peine la sainte mourante eut-elle entendu cette formule, tiré du père Nouet, qu'elle fit paraître un mouvement extraordinaire, et la jeune religieuse qui lui avait suggéré cette inspiration, en demeura comme interdite par un saisissement de joie et de surprise. Dans le même moment, Caroline leva les yeux au ciel, et s'endormit dans le Seigneur, le lundi 19 février 1776, à deux heures du matin, âgée de vingt ans, et le jour même de l'anniversaire de sa naissance : sa mort et son triomphe rappelaient ainsi de bien près l'heureuse époque de son baptême.

SERAPION.

Sérapion, surnommé le *Sidonite*, touché du malheureux état d'un farceur païen, se servit, pour procurer sa conversion, d'un moyen qui supposait beaucoup de zèle et de charité : il se vendit à lui en qualité d'esclave pour la somme de vingt pièces d'argent, et saisit avec soin toutes les occasions qu'il avait de l'instruire et de l'édifier. Ses discours et ses exemples produisirent enfin l'effet qu'il en attendait : le farceur se convertit avec sa famille, et renonça au théâtre. Il ne voulut plus souffrir que Sérapion fût son esclave : il le mit en liberté par reconnaissance; mais il ne put le déterminer à garder pour son usage, ou du moins pour les pauvres les vingt pièces d'argent qu'il avait reçues en se vendant. Quelque temps après, le saint se vendit encore afin de se mettre en état de soulager une veuve affligée. Son nouveau maître fut si content de ses services, qu'il l'affranchit. Il lui fit encore présent d'un habit, d'une tunique et d'un livre d'Evangiles. A peine Sérapion fut-il sorti, qu'il rencontra un pauvre auquel il donna son habit. A quelque distance de là, un second pauvre, transi de froid, eut la tunique, et il ne restait plus au saint pour se couvrir qu'un simple linge. Quelqu'un lui ayant demandé ce qu'étaient devenus ses habits : « Voilà, dit-il en montrant le livre des Evangiles voilà ce qui m'en a dépouillé. » Ce livre ne fut pas longtemps en sa possession : il le vendit pour assister une personne réduite à la dernière misère ; et n'ayant plus rien que sa personne, il l'engagea encore plusieurs fois, afin de procurer au prochain des secours spirituels et temporels. On chercherait en vain dans les fastes de la philosophie des hommes aussi désintéressés et aussi généreux. Il n'y a que la religion qui puisse les former, parce qu'il n'y a qu'elle qui, en nous faisant envisager Dieu même dans la personne des pauvres, puisse nous porter efficacement à les secourir, à les aimer, et à nous sacrifier même pour eux.

L'APOTRE INTRÉPIDE.

Saint François d'Assise, étant allé en Egypte
pour y prêcher l'Evangile, apprit, dans le camp
des croisés, où il s'était rendu, qu'aucun fidèle ne
pouvait en sortir sans un danger funeste, parce
qu'il était cerné de tous côtés par les Sarrasins,

et que leur sultan Mélic-Camel avait promis une récompense à quiconque lui apporterait la tête d'un chrétien. Une situation aussi périlleuse tenait dans l'inaction le courage des plus vaillants guerriers ; mais rien ne put arrêter ou intimider celui de François, qui trouva moyen de se dérober, et marchant au camp des infidèles avec un seul compagnon. Ayant rencontré deux brebis, il dit au religieux qui l'accompagnait :

— Prenons courage, mon frère, sur les promesses de celui qui nous envoie comme des brebis au milieu des loups.

Bientôt ils virent accourir sur eux des Sarrasins, qui les garrotèrent en les chargeant de coups et d'injures. François leur dit avec assurance :

— Je suis chrétien ; j'ai affaire avec votre maître; ne tardez point à me conduire.

Lorsqu'on le présenta au sultan, il leur demanda qui les envoyait. François répondit :

— C'est le Seigneur Très-Haut qui m'envoie pour vous montrer le chemin du ciel, à vous et à votre peuple.

Le sultan, charmé de sa fermeté, lui donna plusieurs audiences dans l'espace de plusieurs jours, et l'invita à se fixer auprès de lui.

— Je demeurerai volontiers, répondit François, si vous voulez vous convertir avec votre peuple. Que si vous avez quelques doutes sur la nécessité d'abandonner la loi de Mahomet pour embrasser celle de Jésus-Christ, faites allumer un grand bûcher, et j'y entrerai avec les docteurs de votre religion, afin que le Dieu créateur des chrétiens vous fasse connaître quelle est la loi qu'il faut suivre.

— Je doute fort, reprit Meladin en souriant,

qu'aucun des imans veuille entrer dans le feu
pour sa religion.

En effet, un des plus anciens avait déjà disparu,
tremblant au premier défi du saint homme, qui
répartit au sultan :

— Eh bien ! j'y entrerai seul, si vous me pro-
mettez, pour vous et pour vos sujets, de vous faire
chrétiens, supposé que j'en sorte sain et sauf.

Meladin répondit alors sérieusement qu'il craignait une révolte s'il faisait cette convention. Il
offrit de riches présents au saint, qui, en les re-
fusant, se rendit encore vénérable à ses yeux.
Puis il le congédia, et lui dit en soupirant :

— Priez pour moi, mon père, afin que Dieu
me fasse connaître la religion qui lui est la plus
agréable.

TRAITS DÉTACHES.

Un jour que saint Dominique venait de prêcher, on lui demanda dans quel livre il avait étudié son sermon.

— Le livre dont je me suis servi, répondit-il, est la charité.

Tandis que Ferdinand, roi d'Aragon et de Castille, faisait la guerre aux Maures, un de ces prétendus politiques qui comptent pour rien la misère des peuples, s'avisa de lui proposer un moyen de lever un subside extraordinaire.

— A Dieu ne plaise, dit le prince avec indignation, que j'adopte votre projet ! La Providence saura m'assister par d'autres voies. Je crains plus les malédictions d'une pauvre femme que toute une armée de Maures.